I0675257

The Sunken

Garden

BY JUANITA TISCHENDORF

DEDICATION

This is dedicated to all the people I have met in life and who might wonder if I am writing about them. I write what I know and what I experience and in that way the words ring true, but the actual tale that I create is fiction.

I hope it brings joy and wonderment to those who I know and those who recognize the places I write about. Because this is what sparked an interest in my mind and ended in a book. It's fiction, based on life.

ACKNOWLEDGMENTS

I have to thank my awesome husband, Mark. From writing, to editing and publishing he has supported my need to read and to write. Thank you for letting me do my thing.

Chapter 1
2019

It happened suddenly. One minute they were together and the next he was gone. She noticed the change in him, but she was trying to handle it herself.

It had been a long time since anyone had invited people to a party. Since Covid-19 hit in 2019, everyone kept their distance. Life had changed from spending time with friends and eating out, to being sequestered in our own homes and seeing them on Zoom. If it hadn't been for the internet, the ability to buy what was needed would have been impossible. How many times did she find herself in Wegmans looking for some staples, like toilet paper, to find there was nothing on the shelf so even if someone had decided to have a get together, it would have been stressful getting what they needed.

Then came Omicron and now, four years later it was deemed safe to remove the mask and figure out a way to live our lives again. As far as she was concerned, the sooner the better because who knew when the next wave would come and put them back where they started. There was always the chance of a new variant.

Barbara laughed sarcastically. "Yes," she said

mournfully, it was safe all right. Safe for most, but not for her."

She frowned, thinking how wonderful it would have been if she had only acknowledged the truth of what was happening to him. "God, it is so unfair." She said aloud in the quiet house.

They had such plans, but it was all snatched away, and their future dreams all shattered that night. It just wasn't fair.

She had a plan, and it would have worked. It was like someone decided they had used up all their happy moments and stepped in and cancelled the life she loved that night, that night when he disappeared.

She should have known better than to let him out of her sight that night. She had been warned, but once she had a plan, she got reckless.

Proof of history repeating itself had come and gone throughout their time in Rochester, so why had she let her guard down.

She started crying and seeing no reason why she shouldn't, she allowed herself to sob uncontrollably until her tears dried up. Then she walked over to the dresser and grabbed a Kleenex to wipe her eyes, then another to wipe her nose.

Chapter 2
1918

New York City had changed. New immigrants arriving in the 1800s changed the theme of the 'American Dream' as they faced grim, cramped living conditions in tenement housing that had dominated the Lower East Side. More arrived every day causing New York City's population to keep doubling during the decade.

In an effort to keep up with the city's rapid growth, every inch of the impoverished areas was used to provide shrewd and economical housing options. Soon houses that were for single families were divided to accommodate as many people as possible by putting up walls to create extra rooms and adding on floors. Then when those options were exhausted, the housing spread into backyard areas.

Construction had to be done quickly and cheaply to meet the demand, so tenement buildings were constructed with shoddy materials, and some had little or no indoor plumbing. These cramped and often unsafe quarters led to a rapid spread of diseases, crime and constant fires.

They had seen it happening. By 1900, more than 80,000 tenements had been built and housed 2.3 million people. There were still 4.6 million more occupying space in the city.

The year was 1918 and William Bemish, a successful art dealer brought his bride Georgia, heir to the J.K. Post Drug Company, to a small suburb known as Irondequoit in Rochester, New York. William had heard wonderful things about Rochester's art culture and that, plus the need to have more space boosted his confidence in settling in the area.

William had done his homework and knew that in a brief period of time, Rochester grew from a city of 48,000 to a city of just slightly less than 200,000, and to him that spoke of progress worth risking. But what was more interesting was that during this period the city expanded dramatically in area on both sides of the Genesee River, which ran through the city. To do this they had annexed parts of the towns of Brighton, Gates, Greece and Irondequoit. It was a city that was growing not only in population, but in the area to accommodate them. That he could appreciate.

It hadn't been easy selling his wife on the idea since she had been born into a family of distinction and wealth. He had not. He had worked hard to be noticed by the social elite. For him, the transition was easy, but Georgia couldn't imagine herself fitting into the social atmosphere of farmers, or not having places to go shopping. But William quickly assured her that there were more than farmers in Rochester. He told her about John Jacob Bausch and Henry Lomb, George Eastman, Hiram Sibley and William Gleason, all of whom he had some dealings with before making the decision on this move. That seemed to satisfy her.

Chapter 3

There was more to his reason for wanting to leave New York City; reasons he thought best not to share with Georgia. William had heard rumors of a highly contagious flu virus and thought it best to go to a less populated area if indeed it was true.

The danger of contagion was said to be most serious in crowded places which also had him worried about traveling the 400-mile distance by train that would take three and a half days, but that distance was too far to drive. He also heard the railways would take every precaution for safety. They had added cars to eliminate overcrowding and put up signs everywhere encouraging passengers to open windows and wash their hands. In the end, they had a safe trip, which may be because they kept mostly to themselves.

He had help in making the arrangements that would take them to the area known as Irondequoit. He had chosen the area after talking with those distinguish gentlemen he had mentioned to Georgia.

After that long, tedious train ride, the last thing he wanted to face was being stranded since transportation at the time was hard enough in the city. He couldn't imagine it even being close to that in the small city of Rochester, and probably worse going to one of the suburbs.

So he was happy when they arrived in Rochester that there was only a short wait at the station before the City of Rochester pulled up at the port. They had two choices to reach their final destination and William was glad he had chosen the City of Rochester for the final leg of their trip.

Glad to be out in the fresh air, Willliam personally supervised the transfer of their luggage onto the boat and then helped Georgia climb aboard.

He was proud of how smoothly this entry into their new life was happening and he relaxed knowing that the boat would dock right at the Glen House where they would be staying until their house was completed.

He had considered taking the Windsor Ferry, that ran a stretch between Summerville and Charlotte. From his friend's description it would have been nice, but not as convenient as the City of Rochester, since it was taking them to the front door of their final destination.

Once enroute, the City of Rochester made a stop midway at the Spencer House located at the mouth of the Genesee River in an area called Charlotte, to discharge and pick up passengers. Since the start of the trip, the Bemishes had remained up top taking in the scenery, but William wanted to explore the rest of the boat, so he escorted Georgia inside.

As they stood waiting for their eyes to adjust, the first thing they saw was a man who had an uncanny resemblance to Lincoln. His resemblance wasn't lost to others on the boat as he struggled with his daughter in tow trying desperately to get away from the photographer who insisted on taking his picture.

William felt sorry for him and hoping to ease his tension, he made his way toward them and along with his wife they escorted him outside. The man thanked him, and William modestly replied he was glad to help. He then asked where he was headed, and the man told him the Sea Breeze Hotel. They chatted for a while. and William informed the man they were going to the Glen House. After shaking hands, the Bemishes moved on.

Back inside they heard a voice ask, "You're new to the area?" William turned and came face to face with a man who introduced himself as John Carroll Leake.

"Is it that obvious?"

"Yes, it is."

"So, what do you think of the area?"

The man paused and added, "You've arrived at the right time."

"How so?"

"Well, it was only a few years back, around 1912 I would say, that the town's first water main was laid along the Culver-Ridge-Hudson-Titus-Cooper-St. Paul Boulevard area." John paused and took a deep breath, making William laugh. "Yes, it's a mouthful, but a grateful one since me being a farmer can tell you how urgently it was needed." He grinned and said, "By the way, I own the Leake homestead at Lot 3073 on St. Paul Blvd."

William smiled. "My name is William Bemish." And turning to face her, added, "And this is my wife, Georgia. We are coming from New York City, so all of this is new, but extremely exciting." He paused and then added, "We are building a house on St. Paul Blvd."

"Well, William, seems we will be neighbors. I should introduce you to some of the people in the area."

John walked him over to Henry Miller who began a discussion of how profitable it was to grow vegetables in Irondequoit, stating the secret of this success was the sandy soil. "Long before anybody else's soil dried out our gardeners could get their planting done. Consequently Irondequoit produce got to market first and reaped a bonus price."

William smiled again and nodded his head. Henry went on to share that his father Charles and he worked the farm and would welcome them for a visit.

William couldn't help thinking this wouldn't have happened in New York City. They had yet to set foot on the ground and in a sense had already become a part of the community.

William glanced at Georgia and could tell she was enjoying herself. Henry asked if he had any children and he told them not yet. "Well, when you do you will be glad to know they have almost finished building the Sea Breeze Park. Rumor has it they will have four roller coasters there, one to be called the Jack Rabbit, another the Wildcat."

"That sounds like fun."

"Yes, everything in Irondequoit is fun. This is a fun place. They think of everything, and it will be easy to get to the new park since the streetcars run right in front of the entrance to the park."

Henry had a mischievous smile on his face before saying, "Not only that, but they also march elephants down Culver Road to Sea Breeze Park where they perform twice a day."

Getting the reaction he hoped he said, "When you have children you will enjoy the significance of that."

William started to say something when Henry started walking again. "Let me introduce you to George." William followed Henry across to another gentleman, a tidy sort wearing a white shirt, tie and a derby hat. "This is George Grabb. The mail is carried in rural Irondequoit by rigs, and this here is our mail carrier." William held out his hand and George shook it.

He was getting the picture. There were no stations in

Irondequoit. Everyone was treated as equals. He liked that.

As he met more people, he learned that the Town Board held their meetings at the Forest House; and that would be his check-in point on building his home. They also informed him that apart from the lake, there were ponds close by that they could canoe on. Three interconnected ponds: the Titus Pond, the Coy Pond and the Johnson Pond.

They talked for several minutes longer, and William shared with the men that he had already purchased land on St. Paul Blvd and was in the process of building a house there.

Two women standing nearby turned to William's wife. They could see her discomfort and said, "Don't worry my dear, it's not as isolated as you think. We are quite civilized and often take the streetcar into the city." That made Georgia smile. The women introduced themselves as Mrs. Leonard Strehle and Miss Amelia Strehle. Then smiling, Mrs. Strehle said, "You can call me Alfreda."

A conversation began and Georgia asked them about the snow. "I've heard rumors that the whole area shuts down during the winter." The women laughed, then apologized as they explained that it was true that the snowbanks were sometimes higher than their heads, but it didn't keep them from their shopping trip because they wouldn't have to wait exceptionally long before the snow was plowed, and the street cars ran again at frequent intervals.

"It's quite amazing, really. After every heavy snowfall, a trolley plow clears the trolley tracks which run along each side of St. Paul Boulevard. The northbound tracks are near Mr. Leake's farmhouse on the west side of St. Paul. He's the man talking to your husband."

Feeling quite at home with the woman she asked about places to eat. "I'm only recently married so I'm not the best cook and until our house is built, we will be staying at the Glen House."

"Oh, the food is good there, but if you want a change, there is the Glendale Restaurant, on Culver Road at the lake. It's operated by Mrs. Belmont and Mrs. Glawe. Lovely woman, just lovely and great cooks."

The woman assured Georgia that the Glen House was indeed a delightful place to stay, but if they tired of it, they should check out the Lake Shore Hotel. It stood on piles on the beach at the end of Culver Road in Sea Breeze. "It's where we stay all week long during the summer, while our husbands commute to their jobs in Rochester or oversee harvest."

"You can meet a lot of people there. Russell and Margaret Hallauer and Beatrice and Paul Graffrath go often to Sea Breeze for picnics."

The names were lost on Georgia. But that didn't faze them as they continued their light gossip. "They have a horse they named Princess and treat like a human. When they reach the beach they unharness Princess, and she will join the four youngsters going swimming!" Mrs. Strehle and Amelia were laughing now, and Georgia joined in.

Georgia was just getting comfortable with her new acquaintances when she was introduced to another woman who had been listening to their conversation and now joined them. She introduced herself as Mrs. Belmont then added, "Besides the only place you don't want to stay is Schooley's Hotel."

"Why's that," Georgia asked turning toward her. "Well, my dear, the trolley tends to speed north on Portland and twice, in the same spot as it turned east on Ridge Road, let's say, Schooley's Hotel entertained an uninvited guest. No one suffered in the first accident, but in the second accident, one death and over a hundred injuries resulted from the disaster."

"Oh my! I'll stay away from there."

"It only happened twice and since then they have corrected the problem," Alfreda added with a stern expression in Mrs. Belmont's direction. You should stick to what you know best my friend. Not wanting to be out done, Mrs. Belmont added, "Just because I cook doesn't mean I'm not up on things." Turning to Georgia her voiced softened, "Well, it did happen."

Taking the conversation in another direction, Georgia asked, "So what about other people to meet."

The women thought for a moment and said, "Besides us, the Heflers. There's Sarah Hefler, Grace Hefler, Susie Hefler, Alice Hefler, Charles Hefler and Susan Scott. They are quite a family. Early on Charles Hefler had his wagon converted to a horseless carriage, but after two trips he had the motor removed for some reason that he cares not to share with anyone. He went back to the horse and buggy."

William went over to join his wife and her newfound friends told Georgia and William about the Irondequoit Social Club, the upcoming sleigh ride party and dances at the Forest House on Tuesday evenings. They heard of a summer theater that puts on an impressive performance of 'Hiawatha' by the Tuscaroras in Sea Breeze Park. For its stage, the cast used the pond and one bank of the pond while the audience sat on bleachers on the other side.

Mrs. Belmont adds, "Ever since its first presentation, 'Hiawatha' proved so popular the Park continues to put on free shows!" She paused checking their faces, "Don't get me wrong, I like 'free' as much as the next person, but they could make a fortune if they charged."

"Come on, it's not all about money."

Mrs. Belmont frowned, "Isn't it?"

The other women gave Mrs. Belmont a stern look and turned toward Georgia and William. They told them about the social clubs all around the Bay. They were mostly cooperative summer vacation clubs; each member's family occupied the club house in turn, usually for one week. But all members and their guests were welcome on weekends.

"Well, Georgia said, there is a lot going on."

"That's what is nice about settling in Irondequoit." The man who spoke had turned toward the women. He paused and his expression changed as he added. "There are lots of secrets, a lot of unknowns yet to be discovered."

"What an interesting way of putting it," Georgia said smiling.

The men continued their conversation with William, informing him that most in the area made their living on their produce. "William Hefler along with all the other farmers go to market during the summer on Tuesday, Thursday and Saturday to sell their produce and the woman stay home.

The men couldn't see the women's faces, nor did they care as they turned to Georgia. "Being a newly married couple, you might want to check in with George and Laura Thompson over at No 1, Le Gran Road. They just recently married. Laura is the daughter of William Leake who was talking with your husband earlier."

"Oh yes, and if you like wine, The Vineyards Of The Irondequoit Wine Company are located on the shores of Irondequoit Bay, just south of the Newport House. The vines were planted by Joseph Vinton and later taken over by Asa McBride who then built a winery." With a sly smile on his face he added, "The wine company has been Irondequoit's most profitable single enterprise." First a grin and then the men broke out in laughter. One man added, "Cleverly put my friend, cleverly put."

They could feel the boat slowing and then docking. Everyone started heading toward the exit and William and Georgia followed. They said their goodbyes and were wished good luck. Then as they stepped on the pier one of the men he had met came over to William and said, "We'll be in touch." They shook hands and William turned his attention to supervising the unloading of their possessions.

Chapter 4

As Georgia prepared to disembark, her eyes were immediately drawn to the structure in front of her. She had been raised in a beautiful home all her life, but the Glen House had more than beauty. This four-story structure was halfway between being a log cabin and a royal resort home. As she stood taking in its beauty she studied every inch of it, from the lower entrance with stairs running on its left side, to the upper ramp on the opposite side that continued down to ground level. There were wood diamond peaks on the overhead at the lower level and the same pattern, but in an open 'v' on the upper level. It was all wood and brick with extra-long windows all around and on the third level, there were three dormers. She also counted three chimneys.

Georgia observed the grounds behind the hotel rose upward with an abundance of trees everywhere. This was not something she saw often in New York City. She visually surveyed further up the hill, and she noticed the stone tower on the left. There were six long windows running up the front and at the very top, a bump out with three windows.

Georgia leaned her head to the right and saw there was a fully covered overpass with many windows that ended in a structure similar to that at their end, but it went down below the hill so she couldn't be sure. In the center of all this was some kind of wooden trestle-like structure.

Someone behind her spoke, "It's breathtaking, isn't it." And all she could do was nod her head.

One of the gentlemen they had met moved up beside Georgia and William and told them, "In 1870 Ellwanger & Barry owned this spot along the west bank of the Genesee River gorge which is known as Maple Grove. They recognized its potential as the Lake Avenue streetcar line stretched all the way to this point. So with encouragement they built Rochester's first water-side resort and named it the Glen House."

"It's glorious," Georgia replied.

"It's in a scenic spot as it stands between the river gorge cliff and the riverbank, and once it opened it attracted many visitors and locals to its fine restaurant with scenic views of the Genesee River. It became the place to go for dining and dancing."

Standing on the lower deck Georgia pointed out the tower to William and they paused to let their eyes travel up its height. Seeing their interest, the same gentleman added, "That tower is attention-grabbing. When the Glen House was first built, patrons had to reach it on land by climbing down approximately 150 steps. That structure was built to house a hydraulic elevator that allows for easier access."

"Who built that?" William asked.

"A man called A.J. Warner I believe to be the building's architect. He had an eye for finding ways to create structures that fit in with nature and also how to tackle any structural or physical problems that arose. Wait until you see inside. There's another interesting feature that draws your eyes up. Inside the restaurant has long sloping roof lines."

Interesting, William thought his mind storing the name for later consideration. He would need a man with foresight to help design his museum. Georgia on the other hand thought it would be nice to have long sloping ceilings in their home.

"I heard that Seabreeze is quite popular here," Georgia said, turning slightly to face the man who seemed to be a wealth of information.

"Yes, it is. It helps that excursion steamers like the City of Rochester have a travel pattern that not only includes the Glen House but go further down Lake Ontario." He paused pointing with his arm as he added, "The steamer leaves here heading to the mouth of the river and sails out onto Lake Ontario which is about five miles north and travels as far as Seabreeze. There's the sidewheeler steamboat named the Sylvan Stream, that is owned by the Rochester and Lake Ontario Steamboat Company. It makes daily summer trips between the Glen House and Charlotte."

"Is it a big steamer?"

"It can carry 800 passengers."

Georgia interrupted asking. "I heard there is an electric trolley service that also carries passengers all the way north to Ontario Beach Park."

"Yes, that's true."

"Well, I'll let you good folks go. I see they have unloaded your luggage and I should be on my way."

"Well thank you for talking with us," William said as he extended his hand.

"Anytime. Welcome to Irondequoit."

They watched as he walked down the ramp and soon disappeared from view.

William and Georgia turned around in time to see a bellhop approaching them. "Are you folks staying at the hotel?"

"Yes, we are."

"Well, if these are your baggage I will bring them

inside. You needn't worry about them. Once you are given your room number I will know where to take your luggage for you."

"Well thank you sir."

"It's my job." The bell hop turned and over his shoulder said, "Please, follow me."

William and Georgia took one last look around and followed the bellhop. He paused in front of the registration desk, nodded and soon left with their luggage in tow.

"Have you stayed here before?"

"No, in fact this is our first time being in Rochester."

"Well, you will find it to be a pleasant place and we will make your stay as comfortable as possible." Leaning forward the receptionist added, "How long do you plan to stay?"

William chuckled, "As long as it takes to build our home."

The clerk's eyes rose. "So, you are moving here?"

"Yes, we purchased a lot on St. Paul Blvd in Irondequoit, and it should be completed soon. We decided to build as many houses already built do not have central heating, plumbing, and in some cases, electricity and I was told it would be expensive to add those, so we decided to build. It shouldn't be long now as the builders have completed the foundation and the basement."

"Well, that's wonderful. Welcome," She paused and asked their names. William smiled and said, Mr. and Mrs. William Bemish. The receptionist returned the smile as she reached under the desk and came up with a box where the room reservations were stored and placed it on the counter. She quickly went through the box and pulled out their reservation. "So, let's get you folks checked in. I am assuming that since you will have an extended stay with us you might want a suite?"

"Yes, definitely."

"One or two bedrooms?"

William turned to Georgia. "Two, please. And with a parlor."

The clerk next asked, "Do you want a river view or a room with a view of the grounds and beyond."

Again William turned to Georgia. "Let's have a river view, please."

In a few minutes she had them registered in the Jewel Suite that had two separate bedrooms, a large parlor and wall to wall windows overlooking the river. She heard the clerk give the bellhop instructions for taking their luggage to Room 410 and then showed them how to enter the elevator.

The Bemishes weren't strangers to elevators. The Haughwout Department Store in New York had the first one installed back in 1857. But like anything new, people balked at the idea and eventually it was shut down after only three years in use. But, it made a comeback after that, though William understood that most people just hated change. He did at one time too.

It had been a long day for the both of them and they were happy to be at the end of their travel. Once in the suite, they found their luggage had already been delivered and Georgia started unpacking. She found all their necessities and put them in place, then turned to William and said, "That's it for now. I'm going to take a bath and get ready for dinner. I'm starving."

William agreed.

They had learned a lot about this place called Rochester and it assured him they could have a good life here. The area was beautiful, the people friendly and the means of transportation would allow them to get around much easier than he had anticipated. He smiled. Here, no doubt, his business would flourish and in no time he would be able to give Georgia the life she was used to; one of privilege and acceptance.

These thoughts played in his head as he prepared for dinner and later, in the dining room that was now empty at this late hour, he had time to recap all he had learned about this place called Irondequoit.

When the waiter came to take their dinner order, William and Georgia had assumed it would be soup and sandwiches. They were pleasantly surprised that they could get a full meal this late in the evening. So with a quick review of the menu they placed their orders.

They sat sipping the complimentary wine brought to their table and William looked at the label, *Compliments of The Vineyards Of The Irondequoit Wine Company*. He smiled thinking of the man they had met on the boat. He pointed it out to Georgia who also smiled. "That's why they are so successful."

William nodded, grinning as he did.

Their food was placed on the table and William couldn't help hearing his mother's voice in his head as his stomach cried to be fed. *You must not lick your fingers, nibble at bones, wipe your mouth with your hand, scratch yourself, or slurp and sniff.* So, with less urgency than he felt, he lifted his fork.

Neither one talked much as they silently ate and when finished, they thanked the staff before going up to their room.

It was late. They were tired and soon had undressed and climbed into bed. In minutes they were fast asleep.

Chapter 5

William spent half of his days taking the trolley downtown in search of a space for his business and the rest of the time at the construction site. Eventually he found what he was looking for in the Neighborhood of the Arts. That was what Rochester's arts district was called and rightfully so.

Before settling on the location he had walked through many areas getting comfortable with the people, the architect and the general atmosphere. He was confident he had made the right choice.

While the building was being refurbished, he made his presence known as an art dealer and began finding and acquiring local pieces. When the art he had acquired in New York City arrived, he went about making sure it was displayed properly. It was a busy time, but he enjoyed every minute of it.

Each evening when Georgia and he shared their days, he could see Georgia was happy and that made him happier. She told him about the people she met, and he tried to make it interesting to share what he had been up to. When she asked about going to the property site, he paused a moment then said, "I think you should wait. Right now there's nothing of interest to see, but as soon as it's further along, I'll take you." He smiled and reached over to pull her to him. "I'm sure you are going to like it."

"Me too," Georgia said. She trusted him and let the matter drop. Instead she asked about his art gallery and William not only told her every minute detail but asked if she would like to see it. Georgia said she would, and they set up a date for her visit.

In the meantime Georgia's newfound friends invited her to go with them to a lecture given by the women's group and Georgia said, "Yes, she would love to go."

She was excited, never having gone to such a lecture before and was in the lecture hall before her friends arrived. They chatted as they made their way to their seats, but once seated, and the speaker took the stage, quiet, ascended.

"Good afternoon. My name is Edith Scott. Most of you already know me so are quite aware of what I am about to share with you now. I know you are interested. Otherwise you wouldn't be here."

Some of the guests giggled, and others smiled, but all oozed excitement as they waited for her to speak.

"We are in a period of great prosperity, and it has led to many bay resorts at our fingertips. Thousands of people are taking advantage of the round trip offers by which one can go by rail to Charlotte, or cross on the boat to Sea Breeze and then take either a steamboat or a gasoline launch to Glen Haven. Then they can take the trolley back to Rochester; or the trolley could be taken in reverse. Stopover privileges are granted at most of the Bay resorts. including Point Pleasant, Birds and Worms, Newport and Glen Edith."

There was a slight pause and one of Georgia's friends leaned over and whispered in her ear. "They call that trip *The Pink Ticket Trip*". Her friend started to explain, but Edith continued her lecture.

"Tickets for the trip are sold by Mr. J. D. Scott, owner of the Lake boat by the same name and my husband. Most of you already know him, but did you know his career actually began as a conductor on what became the J.D. Scott boats."

Many of the guests shook their heads.

"Anyway, he was the first, I believe to run boats from the Glen House at the Lower Falls on the Genesee River, down the river, across the Lake to Sea Breeze and later from Charlotte to Sea Breeze."

Barbara was listening and visualizing such a trip and made note to suggest it to William. She was sorry when the lecture ended, and they all said their goodbyes. It had indeed been a wonderful afternoon, but it was late, and dinners had to be made.

While Barbara spent her time learning as much as she could about the area, William worked diligently on setting up his museum. The complete process of translating an idea and opening the doors as a museum he knew firsthand can be a challenging and foreboding process.

Back in New York when he first had the idea of starting a museum, he had been advised to always keep in mind that climate changes; and as such his museum must change with it. That, he understood and had made sure to do his research around each collection so that he could include writings on each piece.

Once he made his mind up he had spent time talking with people in Rochester to make sure he was creating something meaningful and useful for the areas he wanted to serve. Luckily, his trip to Rochester afforded him a chance to meet people working as artists, community leaders, farmers, amongst others.

William knew the particulars of running a museum, but he had local input on the actual structure of the museum. Georgia had helped by reading everything she could find on museums in small towns and on several occasions she visited the George Eastman House for ideas to share with her husband.

William again took the advice of his newfound friends in hiring people to fill the positions instead of starting the business solo. With their advice he was able to find individuals with an artistic flair and others who could help in managing the museum.

In hiring his staff he lectured them. He needed to bring them to his understanding of museums being the most important institutions available to the public as they were responsible for preserving, sharing as well as culling together some of the most important exhibits, objects, and artifacts known to human history. He went over the positions he needed filled from curating and archiving to conservation and art handling, explaining there were a number of opportunities for individuals of varying backgrounds to work with and around the museum.

During his interviews he studied their reactions and those he felt comfortable with were further studied for the position he would place them in. In the end he was confident he had hired the right men for each job and knew they would be as dedicated as he was in making the museum a success.

He chose Mr. Warren to be the archivist. He seemed

well versed in maintaining the collection of artifacts, art, objects, documents, and historical or otherwise relevant items he had acquired for the museum. He had discussed choosing an archivist with his earlier clients, John Bausch and Henry Lomb and later with George Eastman, Hiram Sibley and William Gleason, all of whom he respected and who had knowledge of the importance of the archivist.

William never tired of his work. That made it easier to put in the long hours needed at the museum while keeping track of the property where their house was being built.

At night when he returned to The Glen House he was hyped and each evening when they finally turned in for the night, he had no trouble sleeping.

He now had more free time and was able to spend many a lunch with his new friends from the boat trip and found their input invaluable. When he told them he had hired Mr. Warren, they of course knew him and said, "Perfect choice." They thought him to be the most detail-oriented and scrupulous person they had the pleasure of meeting.

William's next job was to fill the position of curator. The curator would be responsible for managing and overseeing collections for a specific exhibit, gallery, or section of the museum. The recommendation came from George Eastman who suggested Elwood Blatt who had worked at planning and organizing exhibits with many local companies. He was also well known and would be good at seeking funds to promote ventures.

William had spent a lot of time interviewing and talking with friends to finally round out his staff of a museum conservator, exhibit designer and museum educator.

Finally he was done setting up the business and took

a final survey of what he had accomplished. It was time to bring Georgia for a visit.

That evening as they reviewed their day, William said, "Georgia, if you're free, I would like to take you to see the museum tomorrow."

"Oh, yes. Even if I had something planned, which I don't, that would be my first choice."

The next day Georgia and William were up early and caught the trolley into town. William could sense her anxiousness and hoped she would approve of what he had done. He had gained confidence in his ability, but Georgia was the one he wanted to impress the most.

When the trolley stopped and they got out, he walked beside her to the building, pausing so she could get a good look at the exterior before entering the museum itself.

Georgia was quiet, not commending as they stood outside and said not a word as he walked her through the interior. By the time she had viewed all the exhibits and the style he had chosen for the inside of the building, he was the one anxious as he waited for her to tell him what she thought. Finally she spoke and it wasn't until that moment had he noticed the tears falling from her eyes.

"This is perfect, William." She paused to catch her breath. "It is the perfect location, and the building is exquisite."

It wasn't until that moment that William knew he had been holding his breath and he pursed his lips and expelled the air. Then he walked proudly to the office to introduce her to the staff. When they left for lunch, he was so happy he could barely contain himself.

Chapter 6

William had no doubt that his wife would be an asset to the business, but he could never have phantom how helpful Georgia could be.

While William traveled downtown to establish his business, Georgia was with her friends being shown what Rochester had to offer in shopping. The first stop was Sibley's, but not before she was filled in on the company, firsthand. They had lunch with Mrs. Adelaide Hatch Lindsay, the wife of part owner Alexander Lindsay. Georgia found Adelaide to be the proud mother of seven children, Harriet, Marion, Alexander, Jesse Williams, Jean, Robert Bruce, and Adelaide.

Likewise at the luncheon was the wife of John Curr who was another partner in Sibley's, and of course, Mrs. Elizabeth Sibley, the wife of Rufus Sibley and a member of the Conkey family of Rochester. They had two children, John and Elizabeth, which to Georgia was a more appealing family size.

During the luncheon Georgia learned that the men had met in Boston as employees of the Hogg, Brown & Taylor dry goods store. They all three wanted to go into business for themselves so like Georgia's husband they investigated potential sites and settled on the growing city of Rochester. Their first storefront was called the Boston store by locals, but when they opened a new 12-story, 23-acre flagship store in the Granite Building, it was at that time among the five largest department stores in the country. It was from this group she was told that in order to grow a business it was necessary to have many social and charitable interests.

From there the conversation led to Elizabeth and her friends discussing the fire in 1904 that had gutted the Granite Building and much of Rochester's *dry goods* district. It was what forced the men to move the store to its final location, the Sibley Building at the corner of East Main Street and Clinton Avenue.

The women would later set up a luncheon with Benjamin Forman's wife, Dorah. At that luncheon, the conversation of course turned to a discussion on the B. Forman Company.

Dorah would share, mainly with Georgia that The B. Forman Company was a retail store in Rochester, specializing primarily in high-end women's clothing. Dorah openly shared that her husband was originally from Austria, and she met him when he worked at the Vienna Tailors, a tailoring establishment of women clothing.

But when the Vienna Tailors closed their doors, in 1903 her husband, Benjamin, opened the tailor shop on East Main Street with two partners, Mr. Max Lessen and Mr. I. Rocker. Dorah giggled; "they made a big deal out of a warning that I can still see. *Do not confuse us with the people who formerly ran a business here under our name. Don't be deceived, there is but one place of our name in the city, and that is conducted by the undersigned who guarantee satisfaction or no sale.*

The tone of her voice had everyone laughing and

when they stopped, Georgia asked, "Excuse me, but why didn't he just give the business a new name."

"You don't have to excuse yourself. If the shoe were on the other foot, I would ask the same thing. But to answer your question, he did, later. He gave his tailor shop the name B. Forman's Ladies' Tailor and advertised it as a lady's tailor store because that set him slightly apart from the competition. The store did well and I, not being from money, could appreciate success and what he brought with it."

Seeing the confused expressions around the table, Dorah added, "Connections and prestige my friends, connections and prestige."

Just as confused, Georgia ventured, "But you have that Dorah."

"Yes, I do, but if I were poor and my husband hadn't made a success of it, I know, I wouldn't be sitting here. I know because I wouldn't want a, shall we say, 'nobody' to be part of our group. You have to earn your way in."

Georgia thought for a moment. She was realizing that the friendly people on the boat were not the full representation of the atmosphere in Rochester. Just like in New York City, there were class distinctions. Finally she said, "But I was a nobody when I came here."

The group laughed and Elizabeth said, "I'll take this one." She turned toward Georgia. "My dear, you were never a nobody. You came here as the heir to the J.K. Post Drug company, so you were of the *elite*, shall I say, before your husband became part of the establishment."

Georgia wasn't sure how to take this but nodded her head and remained quiet. The conversation then went back to where it left off.

"So what happened next."

"Well a year later he moved his shop, B. Forman's, Ladies' Tailor, to the second floor on North Clinton Avenue, but by 1906 he outgrew the space and moved next to the new

Sibley, Lindsay & Curr department store.

There he opened a new ready-to-wear store like the competition but setting it apart from Sibley's by his slogan, *'Every Garment Will Be Properly Fitted By Mr. Forman Personally'*. The same supervision that is exercised in the made-to-measure department will also be exercised in the ready-to-wear department."

Dorah continued, "Business went well and later that year my husband expanded the store into a three-story retail store, He renamed the store, B. Forman Co. on my birthday, August 22, 1912."

Though several had heard the story before, they were still in awe. Each one around the table knew that trying and competing with Sibley's took guts and her husband had respectfully succeeded. Plus having chosen his daughter's birthday to rename the store added that extra inspirational touch.

What Dorah shared with her was not only the encouragement of starting new, but how to work around competition. This was something she thought would interest her husband, and Georgia made note of it. She also learned that Dorah's husband took another route in that he was a founding member of a trade association, the Retail Research Association. Other members included Abraham & Straus of Brooklyn, L. S. Ayers of Indianapolis, L. Bamberger of Newark; Filene's of Boston, Joseph Horne Co. of Pittsburgh, Hudson Company of Detroit, Hutzler Brothers of Baltimore, Rike-Kumler Company of Dayton, Strawbridge & Clothier of Philadelphia, and Wm. Taylor Sons of Cleveland. All of these names represented well known and successful men in business. Georgia could see the benefits of contacts in taking this route.

Her friends would next arrange a lunch with Mr. John C. McCurdy's wife, Maralynn and immediately Georgia could see the difference between her and the other women. She had not come from money so knew what it was like to struggle; something Georgia couldn't relate to, but respected. Maralynn's husband founded his company in 1901. He had been born in Ireland and was transplanted to Philadelphia before making his way to Rochester and starting the company. Their son, Gilbert, played a key role in the business. Gilbert was the one who had the ideal to expand the business and he knew how to attract notable people. Before she was told, Georgia had already figured out that McCurdy's was a medium to high priced establishment, in direct competition with Sibley, Lindsay and Curr. The location of McCurdy's was directly across the street from Sibley's and although McCurdy's was a bit more conservative in merchandising it was just as successful.

All of the wives were friends and not in competition with each other like their husbands had been but now also accepted and respected each other. It was this type of information that Georgia shared with her husband, and it was her information along with that of William's friends, that helped the museum grow rapidly. He was established and able to complete with his competition which was the Memorial Art Gallery on the University of Rochester's Prince Street Campus.

The fact that his wife had become friends with Emily Sibley Watson would also prove helpful to them.

Chapter 7

Now that the business was functioning successfully, William spent most of his time at the building site. It wasn't that he wasn't sure of J. Foster Warner or McKim, Mead and White, it was that he saw it as another type of sculpture like those he had in his museum. It fascinated him to see it molded into existence. From time to time he was called in to meet with the contractors and he enjoyed those meetings immensely. At the first meeting when they were just breaking ground, he was told that it usually took 3-4 months for a 1000 sq. ft. home so since his was over 3000 sq. ft., they were looking at a year to completion.

William had no problem with that, nor did his wife, whom he kept informed. He would share with her each stage of the building progress, making sure to ask questions at each visit to the site so he could explain it to her. And Georgia listened intently, careful not to show she wasn't as interested in it being built as he.

Georgia was most interested in the interior, while William was interested in the outside. He wanted it to be of brick and have clean lines, which J. Foster Warner was famous for, and Georgia had been on board, adding her own ideas to the outside structural design before she had gone on to consult with the interior decorator to get ideas on how the inside should be carved out and decorated.

She had already picked out every chandelier and light fixtures. She worked with the designer to choose walls decorated with beadboard, wallpaper, and wood trim, while the floors were tile in bathrooms and foyer, with hardwood everywhere else.

Rich and deep colors were planned for the walls, that would be painted or wallpapered. It would work well since there were a lot of large windows and glass doors that would flood the house with light.

As for the appliances she chooses a gas cook stove top with burners left of the baking oven and a broiler below. It was constructed of sheet metal and cast iron with a baked enamel finish.

She was happy to find that a new model of refrigerator had arrived on the market, and she immediately went to see it. It was the first home refrigerator with a self-contained compressor, but they were still considered a luxury item because of their price, so after discussing it with William he agreed she should have it.

Though she hadn't thought about it, she decided she wanted a dishwasher; especially when she was told a woman named Josephine Cochrane, had actually invented a dishwasher that was automatic. It seemed simple enough when Georgia went to see a model. It consisted of a wooden wheel lying flat against a copper boiler. It was hand operated, but quite an approvement and she ordered one. This kept Georgia busy during that long wait until the house would be completed.

William was elated when the digging was completed, and the concrete footings were going in. He enjoyed watching them install the heating system which was a stove placed in a brick chamber under the rooms. It was explained that the outside air was ducted into the chamber under the stove, and the heated air then flowed through openings into the rooms above.

Consulting with Georgia he had laid out the arrangement for the fireplaces installed in several locations of the house. They would help in keeping this size home warm and toasty through the winter months.

It was fascinating to watch it grow into a dwelling that would be their first home and having watched the progress he knew it was a sturdy built <u>home with no short cuts taken during its construction.</u>

The progress continued even through the cold of winter with most of the exterior done so that the workers were not out in the elements, though there was still work to be done on the heating unit.

Several times he took Georgia out to see the house walking her proudly through the areas. On one visit her parents joined them, followed by a visit from his parents. They marveled over the layout and the knowledge William had of the construction until he admitted to them that he had been in almost daily contact with the builders and had asked questions. He also gave them a tour of the business downtown and introduced them to his staff.

At one point during the visit of Georgia's parents his father-in-law pulled him aside and said, "William, we were against you taking our baby girl to some remote town, but we had faith in you. You seemed to know what you were doing and were confident where you had the best chance of being successful."

Well, I read up on this area. That's why I chose it."

"That's what makes me proud. You knew that in the city you would gain some success but building it here in a city that is going forward rapidly in so many areas was a brilliant decision on your part."

So far he felt as sure of himself as his in laws did, but there were things going on in the world that he couldn't have predicted.

Chapter 8

The First World War was brutal. Millions were sent to fight away from home for months, even years at a time, and underwent a series of terrible physical and emotional experiences. Luckily, the late entrance of the United States, saved the soldiers from experiencing years of physical and emotional trauma.

There were modern technologies available during the war, that made artillery and machine guns extraordinarily effective defensive weapons. Soldiers and laborers dug trenches and machine gun placements, which would protect from enemy shelling and allow them to fire back without exposing themselves to danger. The new weapons included poison gas and tanks which made combat more unpredictable.

Men were living outside for days or weeks on end, with limited shelter from the elements. The incredible noise of artillery and machine gun fire, both enemy and friendly, was often incessant and life in the trenches was '*grim and monotonous*' and at times the order to attack was welcomed.

When the order came the men had to climb out of their trenches, carrying their weapons and heavy equipment, and move through the enemy's 'field of fire' sometimes over complex networks of barbed wire, keeping low to the ground for safety. The objective was to reach the enemy's front line, where the defending troops would be sheltering in their own trenches, and use rifles or bayonets to attack them directly.

Once the defenders were eliminated, the attacking force seized the position.

Casualties were extremely high, with many men killed and wounded with the majority of those being the attackers. Those wounded men were carried or escorted back to field hospitals for treatment, while the dead could only be buried if there was a suitable break in the fighting.

At the time, the United States had a standing army of just over 100,000 but the passing of the Selective Service Act in 1917, authorized the President to increase, temporarily, the military. Therefore men had to register with the Selective Service within 30 days of turning eighteen.

During World War I there were three registrations. The first was for all men between the ages of 21 and 31. Second, those who attained age 21 after June 5, 1917. The third registration was for men aged 18 through 45.

William had been willing to serve his country in the war, but though he met the 5' 7-inch height and hadn't reached his 24th birthday, his weight was below 144 pounds. How he would have loved to brag to his future children that he had played a major part in the Great War. It would have been wonderful to see Europe and even go to the Middle East, places he never dreamed he would see in his lifetime.

Though disappointed he was not able to serve. secretly he was glad that President Woodrow Wilson who at first did not want to go to war, changed his mind because Germany kept attacking U.S. supply ships. That was reason enough to enter the war, but when the United States found out that Germany had promised to give Texas, New Mexico, and Arizona to Mexico in return for Mexico's help in the war, the United States had no choice but to declare war on Germany.

Under the command of General John J. Pershing, they began arriving in Europe by June of 1917 and because of the quick entry the majority of the new draftees still needed to be mobilized, transported and trained. Luckily, the fighting in France didn't happen until nearly a year later.

By the spring of 1918, Russia had withdrawn from the conflict and the Germans launched an aggressive new offensive on the Western Front.

The U.S. gave its allies help in the form of economic assistance by extending vast amounts of credit to Britain, France and Italy and they did this by raising income taxes to generate more revenue for the war effort; and selling what was called, liberty bonds to finance purchases of products and raw materials.

WWI ended in November 1918 with many Rochester families suffering losses. At home, many found ways to play a role, including William and Georgia.

The men and women who served came back with stories of what they endured, and each story was more horrific than the other. Millions were sent to fight away from home for months and underwent a series of terrible physical and emotional experiences they would never forget.

After the signing of the armistice of November 11, 1918, the activities of the Selective Service System were rapidly curtailed. In March 1919, all local, district, and medical advisory boards were closed, and in May 1919, the last state headquarters closed its operations.

But as hard as the war was on individuals and business, it was not to be the end of the suffering.

Chapter 9

As devastating as the War had been on the country, the Spanish flu pandemic of 1918 added more pain and suffering. This was the deadliest pandemic in world history, infecting close to five hundred million people across the globe, which at the time represented one-third of the population. In its toll there were fifty million deaths including nearly 675,000 deaths registered in the United States alone.

By the start of September 1918 only two cases of influenza had been reported to the Rochester Board of Health, and neither was confirmed since influenza was not yet a reportable disease in Rochester.

A week later, it was estimated there were nearly 1,000 cases in Rochester. Officials realized that the city was either in the midst of or about to experience a severe pandemic and began to prepare. Rochester General Hospital set up a separate influenza ward. Education officials discussed the possibility of closing schools.

On October 9, the Commissioner of Public Safety announced that all public, private, and parochial schools would close at noon, after students received instructions on influenza prevention and care. By 11:30 pm that evening, all theaters, movie houses, skating rinks, bowling alleys, and other places were also closed.

Retail stores were asked to stagger business hours and the Eastman Kodak Camera Company as well as other large industries were asked to stagger their shifts to prevent crowding on trolley cars.

Soon churches, lodges and civic associates were asked to close.

Rochester's pandemic grew in intensity over the course of the next several weeks and by early-October it became clear that the hospitals soon would be overrun with patients. With the help of the Red Cross and local institutions, Rochester opened and equipped several additional emergency hospitals:

The flu was a new variant of the influenza virus and was spread in part by troops returning from the war. With no vaccines or effective treatments, the pandemic caused massive disruption.

When bodies began to pile up in makeshift morgues as this '*killer*' marched it way from city to city and country to country leaving devastation in its wake, no one fought against the rulings that came down.

No one was immune and young children, people over age 65, pregnant women and people with certain medical conditions, such as asthma, diabetes or heart disease, faced a higher risk of flu-related complications, including pneumonia, ear and sinus infections and bronchitis.

Unfortunately, World War I had left parts of America with a shortage of physicians and other health workers and of the available medical personnel in the U.S., many came down with the flu themselves.

Additionally, hospitals in some areas were so overloaded with flu patients that schools, private homes and other buildings had to be converted into makeshift hospitals, some of which were staffed by medical students.

With no cure for the flu, many doctors prescribed medication that they felt would alleviate symptoms. One of the drugs prescribed was aspirin and it was recommended to take up to 30 grams per day.

Soon aspirin spearheaded it's on war. People who were using aspirin to alleviate the flu were now suffering from aspirin poisoning. There were reports of hyperventilation and pulmonary edema, and the buildup of fluid in the lungs. It was becoming a win, lose situation, with *lose* being the operative word.

Just as devastating as the war, the flu took a heavy human toll, wiping out entire families and leaving countless widows and orphans in its wake. Funeral parlors were overwhelmed, and bodies piled up. Many people had to dig graves for their own family members.

Everyday William along with his friends faced the devastation caused by the war and the pandemic. The effect on the crops of most of the farms in the area was disheartening and farm production was critical to not only American and Allied troops overseas, but it caused a food shortage at home. Most farmers were shorthanded after the war and now the pandemic hurts them even more.

How could it have gotten so bad, William wondered as Rochester's pandemic grew in intensity. Physicians, whose ranks were thinned by nearly a quarter due to wartime service, were overwhelmed with cases. Nurses worked round-the-clock. By early-October it became clear that the general hospitals soon would be overrun with patients.

Beyond the overcrowding of hospitals, the effect extended to other areas making life even more unbearable. Basic services such as mail delivery and garbage collection were hindered due to flu-stricken workers. That meant no communications passed between families who yearned to know how their loved ones were doing and the stench of decaying garbage left a foul odor lingering in the air.

The business that William had successfully built now faced a decline. But William took it in stride. It was the same for everyone. So William sought ways to become involved and offered his services where needed.

Even in 1918, while William was in the progress of setting up his business and building his home, he wasn't ignorant of what was going on in the world and he felt a need to do something. The real solution to the problems faced by the war became his way of helping when the War Chests organizations were formed.

The first he heard of them was when one was started in Syracuse and Rome, in New York State. and then in the spring of 1918, Rochester. It was determined that a concerted drive on a large scale to raise money for war purposes was the way to go. So when local philanthropic organizations asked to join the Chest, and thirty-six of them decided to accept, William joined. In the speech to gain support for the War Chests it was said, "*It is not necessary that every man fight at the front, nor is it desirable. Everyone knows that. But it is necessary that everyone who does not fight at the front, fights here at home. He must fight by working for victory, by sacrificing every day until victory comes.*"

It wasn't just William and the other men who found a way to help. Georgia and her friends filled their days volunteering for the Red Cross during the war and later during the flu pandemic.

By the end of October, over 10,000 cases of influenza had been reported to the Bureau of Health, and nearly 450 patients had died as a result. It seemed that the latest cases were milder and soon the number of influenza patients in the city's hospitals had decreased. But being cautious, the lifting of the closure orders was not done immediately.

After an additional week of decreasing case reports, on Tuesday, November 5, Election Day, the closure order was removed.

Chapter 10

Rochester slowly recovered from the pandemic. Yet despite the high numbers, Rochester's experience was much less severe than that of many other American cities, including those in New York. It was Rochester's quick reaction to the growing number of influenza cases in the city that appeared to save them. The officials enacted social distancing measures within a matter of days after realizing that the pandemic had begun.

But the women weren't done as they returned to providing for the soldiers. Georgia was among the groups of women who met all the troops coming in on trains and saw to it that the men on their way to camp or overseas were given a welcome and a pleasant interlude on a tiresome journey. Along with the accommodations which the Red Cross provided for the servicemen, many other organizations and individuals took it upon themselves to entertain the soldiers and sailors passing through the city or visiting the area. A recreation room was set up in Exposition Park and the room was open every day.

Georgia worked diligently helping to place barrels and other containers for gifts of cigarettes and candy for the servicemen. And William was proud of how Georgia had stepped up to work with the Red Cross and local institutions, doing whatever was needed to be done.

Rochester was slowly recovering from its effects of the war and pandemic, when the city experienced a slight second peak of influenza in early- to mid-December, but the number of new cases never rose high enough for officials to consider a second closure order. That was seen as a blessing as people were well aware of how much they needed social contact.

It was agonizing for Georgia and William to learn of friends who had lost a family member and they went to console them. When a telegram came announcing a soldier who died in combat, Georgia would make an effort to be at their home when the telegram arrived. It was the least she could do for these people who had given them such a warm welcome to Rochester.

It had been pleasant, their arrival in the area, but now it was time to pay back all that kindness.

The war and the pandemic had stopped progress on the house when one of the workers was stricken with the flu. Then another member of the construction crew got word that his son had been killed overseas.

William had read that the casualties suffered by the participants in World War I dwarfed those of previous wars: some 8,500,000 soldiers died as a result of wounds and/or disease. The greatest number of casualties and wounds were inflicted by artillery, followed by small arms, and then by poison gas. He had seen the results firsthand and felt the pain they felt. Knowing all this the construction on the house was a minor problem indeed.

One evening as they sat at the Glen House huddled around the radio they were appalled to hear the trenches used in the war offered only some protection and were still incredibly dangerous, as soldiers easily became trapped or killed because of direct hits from artillery fire. Even more devastating was at the end of the report they gave instructions to families to get in touch with war officials if they wanted their dead brought home.

Georgia turned to William and said, "Why even ask that?"

"I know it sounds uncaring, but they have to."

At that moment there was a knock at the door. Georgia jumped and William immediately asked, "Who is it?"

"Sir, we have a telegram for Mrs. Bemish?"

Georgia grabbed her husband's hand, holding him back from answering the door. She needed a minute. She had no contact with her parents in quite a while and though she was anxious to hear from them, she knew this couldn't be good news.

The telephone system fell victim to the flu. For all the telephone's theoretical practicality during the pandemic, there was one *gotcha* that proved overwhelming; maybe not everywhere, but in much of the country. Phone-companies depended upon the operators who manually made each connection between the person placing a call and an intended recipient.

Telephone operators were just as vulnerable to the Spanish flu as anyone else; maybe even more so than some, since they sat at banks of switchboards in tight quarters, elbow to elbow with any infected coworkers. And their ranks were depleted by illness at the same time that the flu was increasing call volume.

It had gotten bad and on October 22, The New York Times reported that 2,000 New York Telephone Company operators, making up almost a third of the workforce, were out sick. Unable to keep up with demand for its service, the company-imposed cutbacks, including a 50% reduction in the ability to call from payphones and warned that operators might inquire about the nature of a call to ensure that it was absolutely necessary.

Georgia's parents did have a phone, but that didn't matter now, or much before. Georgia had called the operator and asked, "Can you connect me to 10628?" She had called the number several times and been told each time they couldn't be reached and so she had asked the operator to connect her to her father's business line at '8076'. She had done this several times to no avail, so when there was a knock at the door of their hotel and the bellhop said he had a telegram to deliver, she was anxious to know if it was from them, but afraid at the same time.

Taking a deep breath, Georgia finally released William's arm and nodded. He opened the door, gave the bellhop a tip and thanked him. He closed the door and then turned to Georgia.

William handed her the telegram, and with a shaky hand, Georgia accepted it. She stood peering at it for a long time before she finally had the courage to open it.

William watched his wife and in seconds, he knew. Georgia's face paled and her body began to shake. She let the telegram flutter to the floor and William quickly picked it up and read it. He was at Georgia's side and caught her before she tumbled forward.

William helped her over to the couch and once she was seated, he went to the bathroom to wet a washcloth before going into the small kitchen to get a glass of water.

When he returned to the front room, Georgia was whimpering.

"I know, my dear, I know." He said trying to console her as he handed her the water and placed the washcloth on her forehead.

Georgia dropped the glass of water and grabbed hold of him, sobbing uncontrollably. William just held her tight. She had just learned her mother had died several days earlier and because of the limit of eleven words allowed, not much else was said.

Chapter 11

Georgia felt punished and her heart kept breaking every time she thought of her mother. It was a strange and painful feeling that she felt deep in her soul.

For days since receiving the news She dealt only with herself feeling depressed and as though she was the only person in the world who had suffered such a loss. It was as though her life could not continue because now there was a void that could never be filled, and she didn't want to go on.

It was William that saved her sanity. "Georgia, baby," he said lovingly. "You'll miss her, probably more than you'll ever miss anybody in this entire world. It's a rollercoaster of emotions you are going through, and no one can stop it. One minute you'll be at peace with her death, the next you'll feel the heart-wrenching feeling that she is never coming back."

Georgia knew he was right, and she managed a smile, but days later she was back where she started, and William was there to lift her up, saying. "Hearing her name will pull at your heart; it will leave you feeling unsettled, especially when you know that she is missing extreme milestones in your life. It is dark. It is upsetting. It is miserable. But think of her, as a person rather than a lost loved one, and all of the moments the two of you have shared together, allow each and every lovely memory to flood through your mind."

Georgia looked up at him. William smiled and hugged her closely. "My darling, the love she had for you will always outweigh her death. When you think of your mother, feel happiness; feel content; feel loved."

From that point on, every time she felt sad, she remembered how lucky she was to have her as a mother.

How could so much happen in such a brief period of time, Georgia wondered as she wished she could go home and be with her family. Once she had recovered from the shock of the news of her mother's passing, she had tried to call again, but was unsuccessful so she telegrammed, then waited until finally she heard word. It was as she suspected. She was not to come home, not to jeopardize her health by taking a train and taxiing to their door. It was not safe.

She knew her father was right, and she knew that the burial would not be more than him saying his goodbyes since New York City was still under precautionary instruction, and no one would be attending a funeral.

It hurt deeply, but it also helped too. When she heard of family or friends dying from the flu or at war, she really did understand what they were going through, and William had supplied her with the words needed to console them.

The radio reported on ships returning with fallen Americans being transported home for burial and as the world began to open up, she cried with those who had received the government post card asking if they wanted the body of their brother, their son, or their husband shipped home for burial. Most of the families she had sat with checked, 'yes' on the appropriate line. So the government was kept busy identifying, locating and exhuming bodies and then shipping them home.

Between the sorrow of those around them and the personal one at home. William had a hard time keeping his spirits up. He had once been told that no matter how terrible things appear, there is always a ray of sunshine to follow. But he was finding that to not be true. When, finally able to make a trip to the construction site, he met up with his lead contractor who told him about James, a young, happy-go-lucky sort who was part of the electrical crew. James was twenty-eight and had been married only a month before he shipped out. He left in July and by October he had died, not in battle, but from pneumonia.

"I am so sorry to hear that," William said. "Is there anything I can do?"

His contractor thought for a moment and said, "If it's not asking too much, we are taking up a collection to help his wife with the burial."

"Say no more. I will be glad to add to the collection."

It would be a year after his death that his wife was able to post a memorial notice in the paper. It read, '*He sleeps beside his comrades, in a grave across the foam; But love and memory linger in the hearts of all at home*'. When Georgia and William read those words, they both cried.

Because of the pandemic she had yet to meet the couple Russell and Margaret Hallauer that her friend Alfreda Strehle had told her about. Russell and Margaret were regulars at Seabreeze and Alfreda was anxious for them to meet. When word came that their son had died in the war, she wanted to pay her respects, but the pandemic stopped her. It was one of the first contacts she made as soon as life was getting back to normal and she asked Alfreda to accompany her, and she accepted.

Margaret was not what she expected from the

description Alfreda had shared with her. Standing in the doorway, this woman was dressed as though she had slept in her clothes. Her hair was in disarray, and she looked as though she hadn't eaten in days. Georgia, careful not to show her surprise on her face, gave the woman a hug and introduced herself. She stepped inside and Alfreda followed. The two women exchanged words and then Alfreda went to the kitchen and put on a pot of water. When it boiled, Georgia helped her serve them tea and they sat down together.

"I'm so sorry for your loss," Georgia said.

Margaret looked over at her and replied, "Which one?" and began weeping. It was the first she heard that not only had Margaret loss her son, but her husband had died after catching the flu.

"What can I do...what can we do?" Georgia asked tearfully.

"No one can do anything for me now. My son was so happy when we last heard from him, planning his first furlough ... that I cannot believe he is dead," His body was brought back and the funeral was held and James was buried next to his father, and..." She couldn't finish.

They sat quietly unable to find words to console her except to tell her that there were people who loved her and were there to help her. When they left with heavy hearts, they could only hope that their words had comforted her.

Chapter 12

The day finally arrived when the house was completed, and all the necessary appliances had been delivered and installed. It had been a long troublesome wait, but even though it was over, and they would soon be in their new home, so much sorrow blemished that day.

Near the end, William had been busy getting his museum up and running again and along with that, spending as much time as possible at the construction site. Georgia, on the other hand was too tired to spend any time worrying about the house. She had experienced too much to find any joy in something as trivial as moving into their new home.

When the movers arrived at the Glen House she had everything packed and ready to go. Since William was pulled in many directions, she went to the storage area and supervised the packing of the larger items stored there.

She was happy she had made all the major purchases before the War and the Pandemic hit so now they would be comfortable with all the things they needed. Later she would shop for any missing items, but until then, they would be fine.

Georgia went about thanking the staff at the Glen

House for making them feel welcomed and comfortable during their prolonged stay. It had been a godsend to have found such a wonderful place to launch their life in Rochester and she told them so.

Then it was time to go. With her purse swung over her shoulder she took one last look around to make sure she hadn't forgotten anything and seeing she hadn't, she made her way to the streetcar that would take her to St. Paul Blvd and drop her off right at the corner of her home.

She climbed on board, wishing that William could have joined her, but he had said he would meet her there later.

That was fine, really, she had a lot to do before he arrived home. She wanted to prepare a nice meal for him since she was sure he hadn't had one in a long time.

That was on her mind as she stared out the window viewing the scenery and trying to be happy. Then when the trolley came to a stop, she got out of her seat and went to the doors at the front. She thanked the driver, and he wished her well as she made her way down the steps to the side of the road. In less than five minutes she was at the door of her new home.

It was all she had dreamed it would be as she stood staring at the structure in front of her. It was exactly as she pictured it, with large windows and brick siding on the exterior, sitting on a four-acre lot that gave them lots of privacy now and in the future when more people began moving to Irondequoit.

As she walked between the two brick pillars at either side of the driveway entrance, she surveyed the area. There was no landscaping in place, or a proper driveway, but those she was sure William had discussed with the builder.

William had given her a copy of the key when he

announced they would be moving in that day. He had been so excited and had wanted to see her first reaction when she stepped over the threshold. That would not be, but she would be sure to share with him how impressed she was with the final design.

Georgia put the key in the lock and using both hands, pressed the lever down and pushed the door open. It was spacious, this 3,200 square foot house and she already loved it. From the four-acre lot to the house design, she went through her new home, room by room, going in and out of the four bedrooms and three bathrooms upstairs and then hurrying back down to move through the sitting room, the living room, and the dining room. She saved the best for last, going first into the half bath on this floor and venturing into the kitchen where she paused, admiring the appliances she had chosen. They were state-of-the-art, beautiful and useful at the same time. She ran her hand over the surface of the counter tops, liking the look and feel of them.

Georgia was happy with her new home, and she couldn't wait to let William know. Just then, the doorbell rang, and she hurried into the foyer to answer it. It was the movers delivering their belongings.

She had labeled everything and now she showed them where to place the items in the proper rooms.

The day wore on as she continued guiding the movers until the last of the furnishings were in place. They even hung every curtain for her, which, she believed, hadn't been part of the deal.

Then, with their job completed, Georgia gave them a tip and walked them to the door. She stood there a moment before she closed the door and turned to face the job ahead of her.

All the boxes were in the rooms, but the items inside still needed to be put away. With a sigh she started in the kitchen, unpacking and putting the dishes and silverware in the new dishwasher that got the workout of its young life.

There was no time to think as she began washing and drying the linens, then once she found the broom, the duster and mop, she gave the whole house a good cleaning, moving from one room to the next.

While the laundry washed, she arranged the rest of the items in their places and when the load finished, she went about going into the bathroom to put the towels on the racks and their personal supplies in the cabinet.

Each time she went through the kitchen, she emptied the dishwasher and put the dishes away before starting the next load.

Outside of the kitchen and the bathroom, she had a few decorative items to unpack and put in the other rooms. Then she went upstairs to stock the master bathroom cabinets and counter tops with their personal items, putting off doing the other three bathrooms upstairs. Those she could attend to later. But she still had their bedroom to set up.

She had carried down the linens and now, brought them back upstairs with her. She started with them, making the bed. She unpacked the pillows and the rest of the items for the room before tackling their clothes, which had been with them at the Glen House and washed before being brought to the house.

She moved about putting their clothes in drawers and closets and when she was done, she plopped down on the chair in the room, exhausted.

She sat there a moment looking around and then forced herself to get up and went back downstairs and straight to the kitchen.

In the kitchen she put in the last load and then sat at the counter working on a grocery list. She had to get all the staples since she had nothing in the cupboards at all.

She had just finished her list when she was in for a

surprise. There was a knock on the door, and she paused, wondering just who it could be. She had just moved in. With a sigh she went to the door and opened it.

There stood a delivery man. He handed her a note.

With a puzzled expression on her face, she took the note and opened it.

'*Through all our happiness and sorrow you were there to lend a hand and now we want to show you our appreciation. We thought it best to express our gratitude in this way. This gentleman is delivering all the supplies you will need to stock your kitchen. We love you*'.

Alfreda Strehle, Margaret Hallauer, Beatrice Graffrath, Mrs. Belmont and Laura Thompson signed the note.

Georgia was in tears by the time she finished reading the note, and it took a moment for her to find her voice. "Please, come on in."

The men entered carrying boxes of supplies and Georgia guided them to the kitchen where she stood as they went back several times before they finally had delivered everything.

Georgia went for her purse and took out a tip. "Oh, no Madam, we have already received a tip for this delivery."

"Well," tearfully she said. "Thank you." Then she showed them out the door.

As soon as it was closed she bawled. It was such a wonderful, heartfelt surprise and she needed a moment, before she was finally able to wipe her eyes and begin putting the food away.

There was every single thing she needed and more. They had thought of everything and saved her a trip to the market.

She sat down and wrote a personal thank you to each of them and told them to look forward to an invitation to dinner at their home. And she let them know that with just one gesture, they had turned a joyless day into one of the most wonderful days of her life.

As she was going about getting out the preparations for dinner, she remembered she had forgotten to take the toothbrush holder upstairs after she had taken it out of the dishwasher. So she hurried upstairs with the holder and was on her way back into the bedroom when she felt a small jolt followed by a few stronger shakes.

She hadn't heard him come in, so was surprised to see William behind her. It wasn't the way she had planned to welcome him home, nor had William planned to say what he said when he entered the bedroom and stood at the doorway with a puzzled expression on his face. "What was that?"

Georgia repeated his words, "What was that?"

William shrugged his shoulders.

As soon as it happened, it was over, and just as quickly they put it out of their minds as William smiled at her and she said, "Welcome home darling."

William took her in his arms and kissed her. He moved her back from him and said, "I can't believe you did all of this today."

"It was nothing, really. I had everything organized before the move, so it all went smoothly.

William joined her in the kitchen and watched as she went about putting together their dinner. She was not a cook, but she made pasta and meatballs and used a jarred sauce. It was ready in seconds, and they sat at the island and ate. Between bites she told him how her friends delivered all the food supplies for meals and stocking the pantry.

"You're kidding."

Georgia got up and came back with the note. She

handed it to him to read and she could see he was moved by it as he handed it back to her.

"I've already put thank you notes in the mail and told them we will be inviting them over for dinner."

William nodded and finished his plate.

While they loaded the dishwasher, Georgia said, "You know how they raved about this dishwasher?"

He nodded.

"Well, every word of it is true. It stood up to a marathon of loads with no problem."

That evening as they sat in the living room, exhausted and listening to the radio, suddenly there was static followed by a jolt that was followed several seconds later by a continuous wave of shaking.

William stood up and went over to the window but couldn't see anything. It came again and he realized what was happening.

"Don't worry, dear, I think we are experiencing an earthquake."

"An earthquake?"

"Yes, I think so."

He moved them to the center of the room, making sure they were not near anything that could fall and hurt them. Soon the radio was back in working order and they relaxed a little.

The Geological Survey, agency of the United States government reported that there had been an earthquake in the area. A few minutes later they reported the magnitude of the earthquake was 4.7. The announcer said that that magnitude is often felt, but only causes minor damage. They had nothing to worry about.

They were too tired to worry about anything anyway. That evening when Wiliam and Georgia turned in for the night, William could see from her reflection in the mirror, she was smiling.

"What are you smiling about, my dear?"

"I'm just so happy. From the minute we stepped off that boat, I was happy. It is the only way I can imagine I have been able to accept the loss of my mother and not being able to say goodbye. I know she is going to always be here," she said pointing to her chest. "So I can be happy." With that she climbed into the bed and soon was fast asleep.

They woke to the light shining through the trees in their bedroom window. William was up first and headed to the bathroom, while Georgia propped herself up on the pillows. Suddenly she heard a thunderous sound and she turned to look out the window. She saw the trees that blocked their view of St. Paul, suddenly drop downward and she ran to the window to see what was happening.

William heard it too and came running to join his wife at the window. "Aftershocks, I think. Yes, it must be aftershocks."

The whole side field of trees had disappeared and from their vantage point they could see they had been swallowed up in a massive sinkhole.

Georgia turned to William. "Are we in danger?"

"No, I don't think so. It's not that close to the house to put us in danger."

He was right. There was over an acre between the sinkhole and the side yard of their home.

"What do we do now."

William shook his head. "I don't know. I'll call the contractor and see if he can shed some light on what we should do.

William got dressed but before he left he cautioned Georgia to stay close to the house until he returned. She was good with that.

They had delivered his car and he said a little prayer before going into the garage. It had sat for a long time, and he was afraid it wouldn't start. It did. He backed out of the garage and headed toward St. Paul Blvd, getting a good look at the sinkhole before he made the turn and headed downtown.

There was no one on the streets and as far as he could see, there was not much damage anywhere as he made his way to the contractor's office. Once there, he quickly hurried inside and was happy to see him sitting at his desk. William smiled and watched as he came over to him.

"Good to see you Mr. Bemish. Hope you don't have a problem."

"Well, I do, but I don't think it's on you. I think that earthquake did it. We now have a big sinkhole at the west end of our property."

The contractor rubbed his chin and then looked up and said, "Come on, let's go out and take a look. Do you mind if I have my son come with us? He's into science and may be able to tell us exactly what it is."

"Sure. Thank you."

Soon the three men were on their way back to the house and no sooner had they walked through the doorway, Georgia greeted them with a worried expression. "I think a bit more tumbled into the hole," she said.

"Madam, don't worry, we'll take care of it."

The men went over to the side of the house. As soon as they were near the edge, the son, whose name was John, said, "That's a sinkhole all right."

"Okay. Is the house in danger?"

"Oh, no, it's far enough away. It's probably done. I think what your wife heard, or saw was the trees at the far edge falling in since their roots were gone."

William nodded and John continued. "Sinkholes are

formed when the land surface above collapses or sinks into the cavities or when surface material is carried downward into the voids."

"Son, could the construction have caused this to happen?"

"Well, maybe, but I think it might have been agitated by the earthquake we felt."

"That's what I thought," William said.

The men returned to the house and accepted the iced tea that Georgia had made. While they had been out looking at the hole, Georgia had been thinking and now said, "It looks like a mess, especially from the upstairs bedroom window. I was wondering if...well, I read somewhere about sunken gardens and thought...well, could we make it a sunken garden?"

William looked at the contractor, who turned and looked at his son. His son said, "I think that's a wonderful idea. I can almost guarantee that it won't go any deeper or wider so why not take advantage of it.

And that's how the sunken garden began.

Chapter 13

Work began. Georgia didn't mind the noise as she sat at the upstairs bedroom window watching and planning what the garden should look like. When the ground had been packed firmly and the shape revealed, she was against flattening out, liking the slopes of the ravine. When the crew informed her that an underground pond had been discovered, she went down to the site herself to see it, smiling happily as it could be transformed into the central attraction of the garden. That night she told William and together they went down so he could get a closer look.

"So, what do you think?"
William didn't answer her.
"William?"
After a few minutes William turned and smiled at his wife. "Sorry, did you say something?"
"I asked you what you thought we should do about the pond."
"Well, I see a small bridge over the pond and a trench going from there to a central circular cement pond with maybe some kind of figurine." He paused staring into the sinkhole. I think we need a mason to help us design it, but that's what I envision."
"I like it, William, I really like that idea. I'll talk to the contractor..."
"No!" William said adamantly, scaring Georgia. "Sorry, I didn't mean to yell. It's just that I want this to be special and I will get an architect to design it before anyone

does any digging or planning.""

He paused and Georgia watched as he suddenly went further into the sinkhole, walking around and taking it all in, then returned to her side and said, "Yes, we need a designer who can create a garden that is right for this space.

Georgia didn't say anything. "Honey, do you agree."

Georgia nodded her head.

So from that point on, what she had seen as her project, became William's baby as he hired an architect and they worked together, coming to the site and then creating the drawings of the final design. Not once did William ask her advice and soon, Georgia washed her hands of the project. Instead she spent her days with her friends. They would ride the trolley downtown and shop or gather their gear and spend the day at Sea Breeze. It was fun, but more so, it kept her mind off the garden that was coming to life without her.

William spent every free moment with his architect and was there when the concrete bridge was shaped and built. He watched closely as the deep concrete trench was designed running all the way to the center of the sunken garden that William refused to call the sinkhole. Because of the length of the trench, two walkovers were designed to allow moving across at the front or the back of the garden.

While they waited for the statue, the architect had a crew build stone steps down to a domed structure that stopped four feet from the bridge. At that point, a cement walking path was poured that would go around the perimeter of the sunken garden. Later their vision was to have a matching path running along the lower slope of the garden. That path would circle closely around the bridge and then down either side of the trench before it circled around the cement pond.

While a crew worked on the pathway, stone retaining walls were built along the edge of the garden area and at one point a wall was created in a four-foot circular pattern that spiraled into a small circle. In the center of this circle a star design was outlined in concrete.

Near to the front where the ground level was close to thirty feet above, a covered arch way was designed to match the structure of the home and around it was matching stone and cement. From that covered area above, steps led down halfway and at that point split to either side of a wall of cement and brick that was open at the front. The oval was three feet deep and at the back a brick and stone enclosure was made to hold flowers or shrubbery.

Behind the bridge over the water was the second stone bridge with thick stone and cement columns on either side of a circular arch. With the help of their talented mason who had corroborated on all the significant parts of the garden to make William's vision come true, his next request required additional expertise. His mason contacted a metalworker to create an iron gate with a spider web design, to be placed in what William called the *moon gate* at the northeast corner of the garden under the bridge.

With the base of the area completed, it was a matter of waiting for the statues that Wiliam had commission. The first to arrive was a Griffin that was placed on the bridge over the *moon gate*. When Georgia asked her husband about it, he said, "It's a winged, four-footed animal. It has the body of a lion, but the wings and head of an eagle."

"So, why did you choose that. It's not very…very inviting I guess is the word I'm looking for."

"Griffins are misunderstood because they are said to be the enemy of the horse. They also say a griffin will tear a man to pieces or carry him to its nest to feed its young." He paused staring off in the distance. "The truth is griffins are strong enough to carry away an entire live ox. They are also known for digging gold from mines and I chose it because it will be the protector of the bridge."

"Protector of what?"

"Just a protector is all," William said, finally turning to look at her.

The next item to arrive was the cast iron Garden Sundial Antique Design Weatherproof Garden Ornament. William would share with her that it dated back to the fourth century A.D. and was mentioned in the works of scientists, philosophers, and poets. Then he said, "It adds architectural interest to the garden."

First the griffin to protect the garden and then a sundial to draw in visitors. What next, Georgia wondered.

There were several other statues, but when the final one came, William was so excited, he asked Georgia to join him as they installed the statue in the center of the cement pond. And so she did.

She stood beside him watching as it was lowered into place and positioned. It was huge and she was impatient to see what was in the wrapping that covered it from head to toe. When it was finally visible, she let out a gasp.

It was Poseidon, a grand-scale rendition of Poseidon, the god of the sea. He held his famed trident and stood astride his symbolic triple dolphin.

The size alone took her breath away. This powerful god exuded the power attributed to him in mythology. From its antique stone finish it spoke of grandeur and gave her an eerie feeling.

"So do you like it?" Before she could answer he continued, "It is a statement, a real statement."

Georgia couldn't hold her tongue as she said, "Do you know that of all the Greek gods who lived on Mount Olympus, Poseidon is depicted as being among the most bad-tempered and grumpy. This statue reflects the unpredictable and often dangerous nature of the sea." She paused to catch her breath, realizing she was babbling. "I don't understand. I really don't understand your choices."

"Oh, come on honey, it's just a statue." With that, he put his arm around her and walked her back up the stairs and out of the garden. As they made their way into the house he told her that she could be in charge of the planting of the gardens. "You have a free hand in placing the shrubbery and flowers you wish to adorn the spaces."

"Are you sure?"

"Yes, it will be your own project."

As appalled as she was with the statues, she did want to have a hand in designing the garden, so she put aside her negative thoughts. She planted shrubbery on every level and along each pathway so they would serve as a background to the flowers. And there were a lot of flowers of assorted colors to brighten the area since with all the masonry there was little space for grass. When she was done, she thanked her helpers and couldn't wait to show it to William.

It was beautiful, simply beautiful, taking away from the weirdness of the statues that were everywhere. Maybe that was what blinded her to the reality of the garden. If she had only known that this would be the end of their story.

Chapter 14
1995

It was in February of 1995, a cold, windy day when Neil and Barbara Sanders arrived in Rochester.

Once they had settled in, Neil was ready to call a realtor to take them around and show them the vacant properties, but Barbara had begged off saying that she needed to get busy meeting the locals and establishing herself. She told him to take pictures and they would later look at them together.

That was fine with Neil. Besides, he was happy that Emily Watson had befriended Barbara.

He had met Jack Waters five years prior at an architect convention in New York and had found him to be a remarkably interesting man. Several times during the four-day convention, he had an opportunity to speak with Jack. On the last day of the convention Jack had said, "If you are really serious about moving out of the city, you might want to consider Rochester. Sure, our weather is iffy, but it has the draw of the businesses in the area." Jack smiled, "and you know what big business brings."

Neil laughed. "I do, my friend, clients, clients with a lot of disposable income and big ideas."

They exchanged numbers and had a last drink together before parting ways.

"Neil, I will call you. Maybe we could become partners together...open a firm, Watson and Sanders, Architects, or something."

Time got away from them and with the size of New York City, there wasn't a chance they would bump into each other, but over the years they had kept in touch.

It was during their last conversation when Jack had invited them to his wedding in Rochester.

"Neil, I want you to be my best man."

"You're kidding."

"No, I'm serious." He paused. "Are you still considering a move?"

"Are you reading my mind? I was just talking to my wife Barbara, about it and she thought it was a great idea to get out of the city."

"What does Barbara do?"

"She's an interior designer. We thought it would be profitable to go into business together and offer both services to our clients. But competition is stiff here and as I'm sure you know; you have to be known to get the wealthy clients interested."

"I do. But not here. I think we could do well here. I have already gotten a lot of, shall we say, elite clients and my business is self-sufficient."

"Less than five years? How did you do that."

"Well, I met my fiancé who was born and raised here. Her name is Emily, and she has connections. Her family owns the Sibley department stores here in Rochester.

I did some work for the family, and I met her, fell in love and we're tying the knot."

Needless to say, Neil accepted the offer of being his friend's best man and so, they had come to Rochester, stayed at Emily's family estate and while the newlyweds were on their honeymoon, they had gone back home, gathered their belongings and paid the balance of the rent on their apartment. In a little over a month they were settled in the City of Rochester.

When the Waters returned from their honeymoon, the men worked together on the property her parents had gifted them. Barbara had helped Emily design each room, starting with the first floor. It was like they had been friends forever as they spent a lot of time together.

Everything was moving fast and soon the partnership was official and business was booming. It was time to find a home of their own.

Neil had contacted a realtor that Jack had recommended, and he began the search. At first, Barbara would join him when the realtor called with a place he wanted them to see, but once she decided on the area she wished to live in, she stepped back, and Neil continued on his own.

"So Mr. Sanders…"

"Please call me Neil."

"Okay, Neil, my name is Warren, Warren Pendergast. I was wondering what line of business you are in."

"Ah, the kind that likes to be known. I am an architect." He paused and smiled. "I have to tell you that I am impressed by the architecture of this town."

"I hadn't really looked at the buildings. So you build buildings?"

"No, I design buildings. I leave the building up to skilled construction companies."

"So then the contractor builds from your designs?"

"That's correct."

Warren was thoughtful, then asked, "So, you just design buildings."

"Yes, but that's putting it bluntly. I do much more than that."

"So you supervise as well as design that building."

"Yes, but in that design I have to make sure the project meets safety requirements as well as be visually pleasing to the eye."

"So in other words you have to design buildings that fit in the area as well as consider all the regulation requirements."

Neil nodded. "That is why one of the first things I do when coming to an area is connect with the Architectural Foundation, which here is the AFGR, to get directions. "

Aware that most people knew each other in the city he added, "I met Mason Matsegna and Ashley Aurand who are helping me get my feet wet, so to speak. But like in any business, you have to prove what you can do before you can attract the masses."

Warren nodded thoughtfully. "That I understand. In my business it's not until you make that big money sale do you get recognition. Until then you are just another realtor. But to keep that status you have to continue along that track if you want to stand out from the crowd."

"Exactly." He paused. "So, what can you tell me about the house," Neil asked as the realtor drove them to the site.

"Well, I can tell you that it's what you are looking for…a private lot, with lots of acreage and in need of work."

Neil nodded. "Yes, if I am to have a business here, I need to give my clients a taste of what I can do. You say this property is well known and that people are aware of its history and how long it has been vacant?"

"Yes, they are."

"So, the original owners, the Bemishes...he was an art dealer?"

"Yes, that's right and his wife was heir to the J.K. Post Drug Company."

"I've never heard of it."

"Yes, I hadn't either, it was a long time ago."

Neil had read up on the area they were headed for. He had already decided he wanted to live in Irondequoit, New York so when Warren told him about the property, he was eager to see it.

He liked what he had read about the area, which, in the early years the Winona, St. Paul area was home to many small farms, orchards and wood lots owned by three farmers, Colt, Grant and Leake. He had managed to track down members of the Leake family and get a history of the area. Though John Leake had passed, he had shared history with his son and then his grandson. Now Warren was all too willing to share what he knew.

Warren had lived in Rochester a long time and being a realtor he got around. He started by telling Neil that the farm had been good business back in his dad's time, but as the years passed trolley and rail lines were run through the area making it more appealing to live there and soon the farmland was broken up into tracts of land. "Farming is a segregated business, you know. Large plots of farmland kept neighbors at bay. But open areas brought in new people."

Keeping up a running chat, Warren continued. "As these transportation links between the city and the lake became appealing demand for housing increased and by the late 1900's many areas along St. Paul Boulevard were experiencing a rapid acceleration in development."

Warren paused to reflect. "You can't have a successful farm in the midst of all the construction and later with all the houses, so it was impossible to hold back and keep the land. One by one the farmers and their friends sold off parcels of their farms. They couldn't fight the image the town portrayed of cutting through a field of oats and presenting the area as a picturesque woods to entice city residents to consider life in the suburbs."

Hearing the sarcasm in his voice, Neil had asked, "So what do you think started the change."

"You ask me, I would say that house started it all."

Neil gave him a pensive look. "What house?"

"The house that the Bemishes built."

"What house is that."

"The one at Parcel 076.06 Winona Blvd."

"Mr. Sanders, we're here."

Neil was about to ask what he meant by that, but his next words stopped him from asking the question as he stared out the windshield to take in the estate home they had pulled up in front of. "So this is the house."

"Yes, it is."

Not waiting for the realtor, Neil climbed out of the car and went through the brick posts at the edge of the drive for a better look. The estate home sitting on Winona Boulevard was surrounded by a steep ravine on either side and the cavernous space was heavily wooded, and piled with debris and underbrush, but the house seemed to be well preserved.

Warren came up beside Neil. "Impressive, isn't it?"

Neil nodded as he followed the realtor to the door. He waited while Warren opened the massive door, then stepped back so Neil could enter first.

Neil gasped. The inside was massive as he proceeded to wander about the place, checking it for structural damage or any major projects that might surface. He covered every inch of the downstairs, then went upstairs again to check for signs of structural damage. He saw none.

Smiling, Neil returned to the main level and headed through the kitchen. There he saw what he was looking for, the door to the basement.

"Do you have a flashlight?" He asked.

"Hold on. I think I have one in the car."

Warren left and in minutes he returned. "Here you go."

"Thanks," Neil said and headed back through the kitchen and through the door.

It was more a cellar than a basement with stone walls, but everything seemed dry. He was happy as he went back up the stairs and returned to the front room.

"Having been abandoned for so long, the house seems to be in great shape."

"I agree, but you should get an inspection done."

"Yes, I'll do that."

They wandered about the outside of the property taking in the area. "I have to say this is a mess. The lawn will probably need to be reseeded, but outside of that the land off to the sides does not necessarily need to be manicured, just cleaned up."

Warren nodded, keeping his head down and allowing Neil to make his own decisions. "So, what's next."

Neil paused and placed a finger under his chin. "I think I will speak to Barbara, my wife, and if you can set up a time for us to see it together, that would be great."

"That will be no problem. It is abandoned and I am at your disposal, so just shoot me a date and we'll get together."

Neil climbed into the car feeling an attachment to the property, but he did not want to make it obvious to Warren, though he felt Warren was an honest man. But honest men like money too.

If he had known how anxious Warren was to rid himself of the property, he would have started thinking about getting the property below market value.

All Neil could see was that this was a gem of an estate, and he wanted it. He was quite sure that Barbara would feel the same once she had a chance to see it.

He was ready to sign the deed, but waited until his wife, Barbara, had a chance to look it over. He called Warren and he drove them to the house. Barbara had the same reaction he did when they approached the property. Once inside, she was as excited as he had been checking out the place from top to bottom. He wasn't sure who had said it first, but the words were out from both of them, "We'll take it."

From the minute they arrived in Rochester they felt welcomed. They had done a lot of sightseeing and of all the areas they had visited, they were smitten by what Irondequoit had to offer. The property was right off St. Paul Blvd, so it being the main thoroughfare, made it easy to get to and from their office downtown.

They moved in June of 1995 and from that day on they worked on getting the property back to its grandeur, inside and out. By the time they finished with cleaning up the yard and updating the appliances and fixtures inside, Barbara had decorated it from head to toe,

Barbara stared pensively out the window of their bedroom feeling so wonderfully blessed. They had come to Irondequoit, New York with high hopes for their business and it had paid off. Neil was doing well as an architect and her interior design firm had been welcomed with open arms. Life was good, that is it was until later when it happened.

Chapter 15

Barbara left the bedroom and went downstairs. There were times like this, when the house was so quiet that she felt scared; of what she didn't know. She shook off the feeling and went into the kitchen, got out a cup and put a pod into the Keurig, then stood staring out the window as she waited for her first cup of coffee of the day.

By now they would have been bustling about, getting things ready for a busy day, but that was then, and this was now.

Her cup of coffee ready, Barbara carried it with her into the family room and turned on the television, already knowing what she would hear and wishing that it had never happened.

They had it all, love, success and friends. Life was a dream come true, but like all dreams they must end.

It started out to be the most wonderous discovery. Months after they had completed the updates to the house there had been an earthquake, not a noticeably big one as it only reached a magnitude of 4, but that was enough.

Neil had felt it first and had woken her. "What was that?"

"My dear, I believe it's an earthquake."

"Be serious…"

"I am, I think it is an earthquake."

The vibrations came again.

"So what do we do?"

"Stay away from windows, fireplaces, and heavy furniture or appliances."

"Well, no chance of that," Barbara said as she started to get out of bed.

"And…"

Barbara turned, "And what?"

"If you are in bed when an earthquake starts, do not get out of bed. Instead, lie face down to protect vital organs, and cover your head and neck with a pillow."

"Oh, come on Neil. We can barely feel it. It's rattling about and I bet nothing is disturbed. This is not like California."

Neil had to laugh. "You're right, my dear. You're right."

"Well, I'm awake now, let's get up and have our coffee."

Barbara got out of bed and was on her way around the bed when the house shook violently. She turned to face Neil. "What…?"

He motioned her to the bed, and they sat with their backs against the headboard, staring out the bedroom window.

Barbara reached over and grabbed his hand. "Neil! Look!"

Out the window they watched as the trees and brush separating them from St. Paul Blvd. began to descend downward. "What is going on?"

Neil hurried over to the window and soon felt Barbara at his side.

"It's sinking…"

"Yes, but don't worry, that's still quite a distance from the house."

"What should we do?"

Neil looked down at his wife and seeing how frightened she was, decided a joke was in order. "Well, my dear, we must go down with the ship."

"That's not funny. Not funny at all."

"Well, I'm out of my element here, but since there is no movement in the house, maybe we should go downstairs, get some coffee and turn on the television."

Barbara nodded as she grabbed her robe and put on her slippers. Together they made their way downstairs.

"You go and turn on the television and I'll fix the coffee."

She was glad not to go into the kitchen. She was scared just being downstairs though the earthquake, if that was what it was, seemed to be over. Barbara turned on the television and sat curled up in a corner of the sofa, waiting for Neil to join her.

"Neil, come on, they're talking about it now."

Neil didn't answer. "Neil?" Still no answer. Barbara worriedly got up off the sofa and hurried to the kitchen to find Neil staring out the window, entranced by what he saw, and had not even heard her. She hurried across the kitchen and tapped his shoulder.

Neil jumped, knocking the waiting coffee cup off the counter and on to the floor where it broke into a million pieces. "What the…"

"Sorry Neil. I was calling you and you didn't answer. I got frightened, but obviously not as frightened as you." Barbara started to laugh and make light of the matter saying, "The earthquake didn't need to break things. I have you for that."

Neil didn't say a word but pulled her forward so that

she could see out the window.

"What is that?"

"I don't know, but there is something out there."

Barbara leaned even further and could see that in some areas where the dirt and debris didn't cover, there was obviously some kind of structure peeking up from a hole at the far side of their lot. "It's a sinkhole?"

"That's what I'm considering. It's far enough away from the house that I don't think we need to worry." He paused. "Maybe I should get dress and go out there."

"No…Neil, no. I have a bad feeling about all this. Just stay inside and watch the news and hear what they are saying.

Neil nodded and got out another cup while Barbara cleaned up the broken China. They left the kitchen together and headed back into the living room. They were just in time to hear the announcer say, "Earthquakes can set off avalanches, but much smaller vibrations can trigger them as well." Then jokingly the announcer continued, "Traditionally, giant holes with worlds at the bottom don't really bode well for those who discover them. We can never really know what's down at the end of a drop we can't see. But hopefully, that's only for the movies." Not wanting to be outdone, the co-anchor added, "Only one person told us, at the bottom of a sinkhole in their field there was an area uncovered that looked like a mini forest."

Barbara turned and looked at Neil, finding that discovery interesting and not scary at all. But then the newscaster added, "Some avalanches have uncovered caves and I wouldn't be surprised to know that there are species found in these caves that have never been reported or described by science until now." He turned to his co-anchor and let out a weird laugh.

Feeding off him the co-anchor said, "We just hope

none of those species are monsters like the ones from *The Descent* were a well-preserved forest existed at the bottom of the pit. And in it, there are seemingly prehistoric trees and trees could indicate the presence of other creatures in the giant sinkhole." At that point, the newscasters got serious and presented the news of the day.

Barbara turned to Neil. "So, do you think that the earthquake caused the sinkhole…if that's what it is?"

"Sounds likely, but I don't think we're going to hear anything about it on the tv."

"Why not?"

"Well, I don't think it's been reported…ours or anyone else's…"

"Right. So should we report it?"

"Well, let me go on the internet first and see what I can find out. I want to talk intelligently when I make the call.

With Barbara leaning over his shoulder, he began searching the internet. He read out loud passages as he found them, 'Because a sinkhole can develop suddenly and expand rapidly, the sudden appearance of cracks in the earth should be taken as a serious safety hazard at any location, more so in an area where sinkholes are known to occur."

"Do you think sinkholes are a common occurrence in Irondequoit?"

"I don't know, but I don't think so." He padded Barbara's hand and then continued reading. "A rapid sinkhole caused by well drilling or other sudden alterations to the terrain may not give any warning signs. Otherwise, the collapse process usually occurs gradually enough that a person may leave the affected area safely."

Neil leaned back on the sofa and Barbara sat quietly beside him. Finally he said, "For some reason that must have been a weak area."

"But don't sellers have to share that information with

any new buyers?"

"Maybe, if they knew about it. I think we should get dressed and go into work and I'll call the realtor to see if he has any information on the property, beyond what he told me, or we could see."

With a plan in place, they both felt comfortable as they carried their cups into the kitchen and put them in the dishwasher before going upstairs and preparing for work.

It was a busy day at work as Neil and his partner Jack met with clients to finalize job details or in some cases, meet with clients on finalized jobs. Barbara was just as busy but found time to lunch with Emily. She was anxious to tell someone about their morning and Emily was her go to.

"Emily, something happened this morning?"

"Yes, I know. That was one of the bigger earthquakes to hit our area."

"Do they happen often?"

"Jack says they probably do, but most are not felt at all. Don't worry, you haven't moved to an earthquake area. I should know as I have lived here all my life and I think that is the first time I felt one."

"That's good to hear, but something else happened?"

With a frown on her face, Emily looked at her friend. "What do you mean?"

Barbara took a deep breath and then started. "Well, the left side...the side of our property that borders St. Paul...collapsed."

Emily had been staring at her in disbelief. "What do you mean, collapsed?"

"Just that. It sort of fell into itself...trees and all."

Both women were quiet, thinking until Barbara

asked. "Do you think someone in your family might know something about our property that maybe hadn't been disclosed or just happened so long ago no one remembers?"

"It's possible. Let me ask them. They would know since they have been here for a long time. If they don't, they know who will have answers."

With that settled, the women went back to their lunch, parting ways afterwards and agreeing to be in touch soon.

At the end of the day, Neil sat down with Jack and told him what had happened at the property that morning. Jack had a puzzled expression on his face.

"What is it," Neil asked.

"Well, as I understand it, sinkholes don't just happen. They occur because of some disturbance to the soil in that area. If that's the case, it should have been disclosed when the property was sold to you."

"I know. But maybe it wasn't known. I looked over the deed carefully and I didn't see any reference to any construction at that area."

"Interesting...Do you mind if I come out and take a look?"

"Sure, but we should be cautious and not get too close to the edge near what I am assuming is a sinkhole."

Chapter 16

Several days had passed since the incident of the sinkhole opening up in their yard. Neil had his partner, Jack and his wife, Sandra over for dinner, but the real purpose of the get together was so they could take a look at the sinkhole. By now the authorities had agreed it was indeed a sinkhole and though they felt it was not going to expand any further, for the time being it would be best to stay away from the edge.

That was not a problem for Barbara as she had been frightened by all the scary news reports on sinkholes, but Neil was anxious to take a closer look. So was Jack, so the dinner was more for the women than the men.

It was while they were chatting over dinner that Emily got a call. Not wanting to interrupt the dinner, but seeing who was calling, she excused herself and got up from the table. She had been standing with her back to them when she audibly yelled, "Get out!" Only hearing one side of the conversation, all eyes immediately stared at her back.

"What is it, Jack?" Neil asked.

"I'm not sure. She says that when she's shocked or surprised by what she's hearing but she says it the same way." Jack pauses. "Oh, yes, she says it a lot to express possible disbelief." He smiles. "You guys are from New

York. It's a very casual expression at best and it's used often on the east coast."

"No kidding…that doesn't help much."

Neil, Jack and Barbara stop talking and turn toward Emily, hoping to catch a word or two to explain what is being said on the other end of the conversation. Finally, Emily says. "Well, thanks for finding out. I'll call you back later."

Emily disconnects the call and turns around. She stands there with her head down as she slips her phone back into her pocket. Slowly she lifts her head and puts her hands on either side of her face as she stares at the three questioning expressions in front of her. Her mouth falls open and her eyebrows raise as she finally says, "I just learned something I did not expect." She paused and if talking to herself added, "After much effort on my part, you're not going to believe what I found out."

Emily saw three pairs of raised eyebrows staring at her as she stood there feeling slightly superior, having the news they were all waiting to hear. She allowed herself to savor the moment a little longer before she blurted out, "That was my mother."

"Okay…"

Emily turned to stare at Barbara. "Barbara, I did what you asked. I spoke to my mother, and she contacted her friends, who like herself are offspring's of the original habitants of the area."

Sensing this was big news, Barbara stood and went over to Emily. "And so, what did she say?"

Emily smiled demurely as she looped her arm through Barbara's, then guided her back over to the table. "Tell you what, fill my glass and I'll tell you."

"E-m-i-l-y!" Jack said, the annoyance clear in his voice.

Emily turned toward her husband and quickly replied

with, "Emily, what!"

Jack turned to Neil. "I hate it when she acts like this," he turned to stare at his wife, "it's so frustrating." Seeing Emily's pleased expression he turned back to Neil. "When she has a secret, she likes to drag it out until her listeners are drooling."

Barbara listened as she poured wine into Emily's glass and managed to cover up her anxious feelings with a smile plastered on her face. She was sure that what Emily heard was substantial and she was afraid it would have her packing and force Neil to put the house up for sale. So, in a way, she didn't want to hear what Emily had to say.

"Well, as you know, my mother has been friends with a lot of the descendants of the original families. Her mother before her was close to their parents so she did have inside information to share since they talked often."

She paused and glanced into each of their faces."

"Come on Emily, it's not funny. Get to the point."

Emily took in her husband's look of frustration and gave him a sheepish smile before casting her gaze on Barbara.

"Well, Barbara, as you asked me to do, I told my mother about the sinkhole and after she got over the initial shock of it, she said she would see what she could find out. She called her friends and told them that the side of your property had sunk down and asked them to see if they could find out what could have caused it."

Again she paused for emphasis, then smiling at each of their upturned faces finally said, "And they did!"

Emily could see she had the undivided attention of everyone in that room and she loved it. The spell was broken when Jack said, "Come on Emily. It's probably nothing worth hearing anyway."

"Wait," Neil said, "Let the woman talk. I personally

want to hear what she has to say."

"What did they find out," Barbara asked cautiously.

Emily smiled. "It's not a bad thing, Barbara, not at all." She took a sip of her wine, enjoying her moment in the spotlight a while longer before finally with an elevated level of excitement in their voice said, It's a sunken garden out there...a sunken garden."

"What?" Jack said.

"I know, it sounds preposterous, but it came from several sources. At lunch today, my friends... Cheri Leake, daughter of John Leake the III, who's family had owned the Leake farm just steps away from here. And Jennifer Gleason, daughter of the founder of Gleason works, plus Linda Sibley whose parents owned the Sibley department stores were with me at that luncheon. They have '*the*' family history in these parts and in speaking to their relatives...individually, I might add, all came back with the same story. There used to be a sunken garden in that area of the property."

There was silence at the table as they all tried to take it in. Then after a while, Jack said, "Maybe it's just a rumor. Who would cover up a sunken garden."

"Well, who would indeed?" Emily retorted.

Knowing his wife he continued with, "So what aren't you telling us?"

Emily sucked in air through pursed lips and glanced around the table. She smiled and finally said, "Well, the original owners... the ones who built the house; the Bemishes that is. William and Georgia Bemish to be exact, also built a sunken garden."

"You're kidding?"

"No, it was the theme of discussion around many dinner tables. People had never seen anything like it before."

"So, I don't get it. Why, or who filled it in?"

Emily smiled. "The word is that Georgia Bemish had it filled in after her husband, William Bemish disappeared, and she moved back to New York."

"Wait a minute," Neil said. "Disappeared...you mean, died?"

"Maybe, but no one knows for sure. He just disappeared."

"Come on," Jack replied, that doesn't make sense."

"No, but that is all I could find out." Emily paused and looked over at Barbara. "You said we could go take a look. Right?"

It was Neil who responded to her question, "Why not." He turned to his wife, "Barbara, lets grab some flashlights out of the garage and take this party outdoors." Neil then turned to Jack. "Jack, can you switch on the outside flood lights. The control pad is over by the side entrance that faces what we now know as the sunken garden."

"You don't have to ask me twice," Jack said as he left the living room to go to the side entrance. He flipped the switch and then walked back to the foyer where everyone was waiting. His wife handed him his coat and soon they were on their way out the front door. Once outside they paused to turn on their flashlights. "Is everyone ready."

"Yes. Let's do this."

They walked cautiously over to the ledge above the area. "We had a surveyor out and he said not to stand too close, but he felt it was safe, here."

The flashlights worked around the area and with the help of the spotlights, they could make out structures that appear as rocks, but had a distinct shape to them.

"You sure we can't go any further, maybe move a little dirt?"

"No," Neil said, "the contractor was specific about that. He thought the sinkhole...I mean sunken garden...sides needed to be inspected first."

The light from their flashlights moved about the area as they all tried to make out what was hidden under the dirt. "Well, should we go back in?" Neil asked.

"Sure." Then as Jack and Neil waited for the women to head back, Jack asked, "So what's next."

"Obviously I need to contact someone who knows how to safely remove all the dirt, trees and debris without ruining what's under there."

They turned and were headed back toward the house when Barbara stopped and turned back around.

"What is it?" Neil asked. He wouldn't have to ask if he had been able to see her face. Her eyes were wide open, and her mouth looked as though she was screaming, but the fear paralyzed every muscle in her body. She fought a rising panic as she finally found her voice and said, "It's nothing, nothing at all.

Chapter 17

That evening after their guest had left and they were tucked safely in their bed, Barbara turned to Neil. "Did you hear anything?"

Neil lifted his head and leaned on his raised arm, his head resting on his palm. "Like what?"

"I don't know, just a sound."

"When? Just now?"

"No, when we were at the sinkhole...Oh, never mine, it was probably nothing. It was just so dark it gave me the willies."

"Well, don't worry, sweetie, I'm here and I will protect you from the scary hole."

Barbara punched him lightly on the shoulder.

After a while, Neil said, "I'm calling the excavators tomorrow. I want to get a look at what is under all that dirt."

Barbara was silent.

"What about you sweetie. Just think of all the decorating you can do in there with flowers, bushes and solid surface designs. You will have a field day. If you need help, I have a landscape designer in our office and individuals who can make suggestions...that is if you want them."

Barbara wanted to say that she wanted them all right. She wanted them to go down in that hole and do it all because she was afraid of it. She didn't know why, but something frightened her, and she wanted no part of it. That was what she wanted to say. Instead she said, "We'll see."

That night they made love and not long after, Neil turned on his side and fell instantly to sleep. Not Barbara. No matter how she turned she couldn't get herself to close her eyes. She knew she had heard something. She couldn't describe what she heard, and it might have been just the sound of the earth settling in its new position, but she heard something. And, she might have seen something too, but that was probably the reflections from the flashlights as they swung over the area. The light could have reflected on something and caused it to look like there was something there. In any case, it was a warning that she was going to heed. She was not going down in that hole and she would use all her womanly powers to make sure that Neil didn't either.

She must have slept because she was opening her eyes to light coming through the bedroom window. She slid her body back so that she was leaning against the headboard, then turned to look at Neil, who was still sleeping.

She turned her head again to check the clock on her end table. It was almost eight. She turned around toward Neil again and leaned over so that her lips were close to his ear. "Wake up sleepy head."

Neil reached up to brush away whatever was on his ear, then his hand felt her cheek. He turned around and smiled. "Good morning, beautiful."

"Good morning, sleepy head."

It was Saturday and they had plans. Since arriving in Rochester, they had tried to absorb the history of the area and today they were going on a boat tour.

"Come on, let's get our day going."

One day at work, Neil was talking to his partner about what to do in Rochester and Jack had said, "Man, if you want to learn more about the area, you should take the Harbor Town Belle tour."

"The what?" Neil asked quizzingly.

"The Harbor Town Belle tour. My wife and I took it, and it is not just a great sightseeing tour, but the boat captain tells the story of the area. But what I found interesting was that after returning from WWII Alfred G. Gilbert met his wife Joyce I. Gilbert and they moved to Rochester where they started a family. They began selling boats and eventually built a marina. Just before they both turned 70, they decided to build the Harbor Town Belle right here in Rochester. The boat was launched on bananas and completed in 1998. They ran the boat until their passing and now the boat is currently run by their Daughter and Grandchildren. The boat was launched on bananas and completed in 1998. The boat is currently run by their Daughter and Grandchildren and the boat is also still launched on bananas."

He paused to add, "The boat captain may have dressed up his history, but it was informative."

That night, over dinner, Neil had presented the idea to Barbara, and she was excited. "What a wonderful idea. It beats grabbing bits and pieces from our friends or reading about the area. Let's do it."

So they had made the call and today was the day.

That morning they took turns in the bathroom and then went down to have a breakfast of cheerios, coffee and toast. Because they would be on the boat later, Barbara felt they should eat light so as not to end up with their stomachs upset.

After breakfast while Barbara returned some calls and worked on her calendar for the following week, Neil went out to look at the sinkhole. As he stood staring down into the hole, he felt a pull... It was like it knew he was there, but not in a threatening way. While he stood there, he took out his cell and searched for excavators in the area. He came across several, but the one that caught his eye was the DirtWorx company. So he called them.

He had run across the name in his business before and the company had gotten complimentary reviews as being a top-quality excavating contractor.

He dialed the number and after a few minutes, the call was answered. Since he was familiar with the company and knew their work from jobs that his partner, Jack had been on, he didn't hesitate to make the arrangements. He explained the situation and was put on hold. When the phone was reconnected he heard a male voice. "Hello Mr. Sanders, what can I do for you?"

"Whom am I speaking with?"

"I'm the owner, Nathaniel Parker and I know your house and the surrounding area very well. How can I help you."

Neil told him about the evening they had the earthquake, that the side of his property facing St. Paul Blvd had collapsed into itself. He thought it might be a sinkhole. He was afraid to share the information he had learned, so instead said that the sinkhole was filled with trash along with trees and dirt. He added that he wanted it removed safely because it had been his experience that this wasn't a normal happening unless the ground had been previously disturbed or maybe water had built up in an underground spring.

"I agree. It's always best to be careful in situations like this."

Neil thought he heard an undertone, but it might have been his imagination. He listened as Nathaniel said, "We aim to provide the best quality excavation service and the only way we can do that is by being able to not only excavate, but grade, till, clear the area and till the soil if need be."

Nathaniel paused, "that is if you want all that done as well."

"Yes, that would be great, but I need it to be done with care. I think there might be something of interest under that pile of rubbish and I want to preserve what is there no matter what shape it is in."

"Don't worry. If it's okay with you, I'll come out and survey the area…take pictures, measurements and study the area closely before we decide to take on the job. It's for our safety as well as making sure we know what we are dealing with."

"I like that Nathaniel. My wife and I will be away from the property today, so if we aren't needed, you can even come out today if your schedule permits."

They talked a little longer and Nathaniel agreed to review the job and get back to him before the end of next week.

With that done, Neil went back into the house and started to tell Barbara but stopped. He knew his wife was sensitive about the sunken garden that might or might not be under there. Whether she had seen or heard something was up for debate, but he wasn't ready to tackle that just yet. It could wait. After all this was to be a fun day for the two of them.

When it was time, Neil and Barbara climbed into the car. "So, where are we going?" Barbara asked.

Well, Jack said that we take Pattonwood Dr. and turn onto Marina Dr. at the light. We then veer to the left and we will be facing the river."

"Ah, the Genesee River."

"Correct. Then Jack said we would see a house on the left and we should turn to the right."

With the help of his GPS, Neil had no problem following the directions.

"I see it, Barbara said excitedly, pointing ahead. I see the Marina and the parking lot for the Harbor Town Belle. The Belle is docked right there, pointing in that direction."

Chapter 18

They had arrived a little early so together, they walked the length of the boat, taking it all in and by the script used, it bore its name, 'The Harbor Town Belle' with pride. The upkeep of the exterior was impeccable.

Barbara could feel the excitement building in her as she had not expected such a large boat. It had three levels; the first of which was several feet above the water level and had curtains in the windows so she assumed that must be the dining area. There were seven large windows for excellent viewing and a red door entrance, that matched the big paddle boat wheels, of which there were four at the rear of the boat.

Soon it was time to board. Barbara watched the faces of the other passengers and smiled when she caught their eye. Everyone seemed friendly and as excited as she to be taking this tour. She wondered if they were new to the area, or just liked taking the tour.

Once everyone was on board, the Captain came over the loudspeaker announcing they were about to get underway. He went over the terms for the parts of the boat so that they would know in which direction to look when he began his history on the locations they would pass. He made a joke. "For those of you who can't respond quickly. Don't worry. Just like yourself, the fact of the matter is you will have plenty of time to take in the sights since the paddle boat is not known for speed." Several people tittered.

They were off. The captain introduced himself by making an appearance once they were lake bound. His name was Captain Roger Englert and there were two crew members whom he also introduced and then he began his talk.

"You are about to experience the beautiful Genesee River and Lake Ontario. The Harbor Town Belle harkens back to simpler times when her sister Riverboats plied the greatest American waterway, the Mississippi over a century ago. For your pleasure you will find a full cash bar. The Belle also offers heat and air-conditioned decks and can accommodate up to 128 people." He went over the safety rules and pointed out where they were posted on the vessel.

"The Genesee River is the lifeline of Rochester. From its source atop a hill in Potter County, Pennsylvania to its end at Lake Ontario within the City of Rochester, the Genesee River flows 160 miles north and drops 2,250 feet through a full range of rural, suburban, and urban communities. The Haudenosaunee Indians called the river *Ge-ne-see*, meaning pleasant banks and rightfully so as the banks shift to imposing beautiful waterfalls and gorges in Letchworth State Park, and in the City of Rochester: High Falls, Middle Falls, and Lower Falls. Having three impressive waterfalls within its borders makes Rochester aquatically unique!"

He paused the history and pointed out areas of interest and then continued. "In the early 1800s European explorers infiltrating western New York found the high falls of the Genesee as a wonderful power source. Mills sprang up on the falls and in a remarkably abbreviated time Rochester became a milling and then an industrial powerhouse. People referred to it as: the "Flour City...the grain not those pretty flowers you see all around." In 1825, the Erie Canal was completed, and crossed the Genesee River on a fascinating aqueduct right downtown. This aqueduct remains, with the Broad Street Bridge built over it."

Neil looked at Barbara and saw how interested she was and smiled, not saying a word. Soon the Captain continued. "Here we see the High Falls also known as the Great Seneca Falls. Historically, the river's gorge formed a natural border between the lands of the Five Nations of the Iroquois to the east and the related tribes of the Erie people along the west side of the gorge."

Again the Captain pointed out areas as he talked, "This portion of the City of Rochester contains two Olmsted-designed parks—Maplewood Park (formerly Seneca Park West) and Seneca Park East.. The Lower Falls Park is adjacent to the Lower Falls and offers beautiful views of the sedimentary rocks in the gorge and green spaces for walking and relaxing above the Genesee River. In this park is the famous outdoor sculpture, The Seat of Forgetting and Remembering. It is a sculpture that depicts the faces and hands of the community's youth and was built around 2001. If you get a chance, take a hike and take a moment to reflect."

Captain Englert reached lake Ontario and slowly glided through the lake, close enough to take in all of the historical landmarks that told of the past and the present.

Neil had booked them on a two-hour tour that included lunch and at first Barbara was hesitant to eat on a boat, but now she was glad they would.

The talk ended and the passengers started moving about, finding a table to be seated at and Neil and Barbara were right with them.

Soon they were seated at a table with a couple of gentlemen across from them, men that had been talking with

Neil earlier. They continued their discussion and Barbara wondered where their wives were. Every now and then, Neil would turn and smile at her, then continue eating and talking with the men across the table from them.

When she finished eating, Barbara excused herself and placing a hand on Neil's shoulder said, "I'm going to the upper deck and get some air."

Neil nodded and Barbara turned and headed toward the stairs. She reached the upper deck and started across the floor when she heard someone behind her. Startled, she turned quickly, almost losing her balance.

"Sorry, I didn't mean to frighten you."

Breathing heavily she saw the woman behind her and breathed deeply, calming herself. She had seen the woman off to the side downstairs, standing with a gentleman that she assumed was her husband, but later he had moved over to the men talking with Neil and she had been left alone. "Birds of a feather," Barbara said jokingly. No need to apologize."

Barbara smiled. "I'm on a boat with lots of people, I don't know why I jumped like that."

"I know why. Your mind is a million miles away, right?"

"I guess so."

"So is mine." Then after a slight pause she continued. "By the way, my name is Mindy."

Barbara stuck out her hand. "Barbara."

The woman smiled. "Come on Barbara, let's go to the stern."

Barbara gave her new friend a puzzled look. Mindy laughed and put her arms around her shoulder. "I know. I didn't learn that just now. We have a boat, and I knew the names of the parts of a boat before coming on this tour."

As they made their way to the stern, Mindy said, "The front part is called the bow and the back part is called the stern. Don't ask me why because I don't know."

They were both laughing as they made their way to the stern and paused to look down at the paddle.

They stood there staring down and saying nothing and then Mindy spoke. "Barbara, I have to confess. I know you."

Barbara turned. "You do? I don't remember meeting you."

"You haven't. I know you…because people have been talking about the Sanders that purchased the Bemish house."

Barbara looked at Mindy. "What are they saying."

"Nothing bad. Just that you and your husband purchased that house. It's a remarkably interesting place and tales about that house goes back a long way."

Barbara was interested. "Pray, tell me more."

"Well, I am the granddaughter of the Leake's who…"

"Yes," Barbara said with interest. "Yes. We heard of your family. They are quite famous and go back a long way too."

"That's right," Mindy said as she leaned over the rail to see the paddle better. After a bit, she turned. "Barbara," she said hesitantly without looking up to face her.

"Yes?"

"I want to tell you something, but I don't know if I should."

"What is it about, Mindy?"

"It's about the house…"

At that moment they were interrupted by their husband's joining them on the deck.

"Mindy, what are you up to?"

Mindy turned and smiled at her husband while Neil moved to Barbara's side and gave her a hug.

"Nothing my dear. Barbara and I were just checking out the paddle, is all."

With that, the foursome headed to the bow with the rest of the passengers.

Chapter 19

At the dock they parted ways. As Barbara walked beside Neil to their car she couldn't help thinking that there had been something about Mindy that spoke volumes above any words she said. It was like she had a deep dark secret that she was forbidden to share with anyone. Maybe even her husband didn't know. In any case, Barbara needed to talk to her some more.

"Hon, you seemed to be getting along famously with Warren Worthington."

"Who?"

"The man you were talking to on the boat?"

"What man?"

Barbara stared at him. "The man, Warren who stood with you and the other two men you were talking to."

It was Neil's turn to look puzzled as he shook his head. "I don't remember talking to anyone but the two men you saw me with and who later joined us at lunch."

She started to question him further, mentioning how the four of them had been standing at the stern, but now that she thought back, she didn't remember Neil doing or saying much beyond putting an arm around her. Was it possible he hadn't seen them?

That was ridiculous, she told herself. He had to see

them. They were standing there with her. How could he not see them? But she knew her husband well and at that moment, knew he wasn't kidding. He didn't remember or hadn't been talking to the man Warren. Maybe he was just near the group of men Neil was conversing with. As for later, well she couldn't explain that except maybe he was busy looking at the other passengers getting ready to depart. As they made their way to the car a cold shiver ran down her spine.

Cautiously she paused before getting into the car. "Neil, honey, do you remember hearing anyone talk about the Leakes?"

He opened the car doors and waited until Barbara was seated and belted in. "Yes, they are well known around here. I think the family has been here forever."

"Yes they have." Barbara carefully asked, "Have you ever heard of a Mindy Worthington?"

Neil shook his head. "Not sure. Who is she?"

"She's the granddaughter of John Carroll Leake. She married a Warren Worthington."

A puzzled expression was on Neil's face again. "What are you getting at Barbara. I'm not following."

"Oh, nothing, just making conversation is all. But do you know any of the Leakes at all?"

"No, not that I recall. I've heard of the family though."

Barbara leaned back against her seat trying to understand what had just happened. Was she seeing and hearing things, or had it really happened?

They drove in silence back to the house and as soon as Neil pulled the car into the circular drive, he almost yelled, "Look at that! Can you believe it?"

Barbara followed the direction of his eyes to see a large earthmover and several smaller ones working at the side of the house. In one motion Neil quickly turned off the car and jumped out, heading in that direction.

Barbara climbed out, started to follow him, then changed her mind. Instead she went into the house and made her way to the side entrance. She opened the door and stood on the patio to watch.

The men had made a lot of progress and she could see that in the area close to the road they had uncovered an upper path of concrete and stones that had steps off the side going even lower into the abyss where she could distinguish a couple of statues. She couldn't make out what they were, nor did she care to go closer and find out. Instead she went into the kitchen to make herself a cup of tea.

While the tea kettle was heating, she got out a teabag and sat at the counter to wait for the kettle to whistle.

Who was the woman Mindy and where had she come from. By now, being surprisingly good at reading body language, she had a feeling she was the only one who had seen her because as they disembarked, the two weaved their way through the crowd and no one even glanced their way. That was weird because the people were always smiling or saying, 'hi', to her husband and her, or others on the boat and now that she thought about it, there had only been about thirty people on the boat and not until they sat at the dining tables had she even seen this Mindy.

Another cold shiver ran down her spine just thinking about Mindy Worthington. At that moment, the kettle whistled, causing her to jump, then recognizing the sound, she laughed at herself and got up. One thing for sure, she was determined to do a little checking on her own. She had to figure out what had happened to her, but first, she really needed a cup of tea.

The rest of the day went by with Neil watching as the men worked on uncovering whatever laid beneath the rumble, and she remained inside. She hadn't realized how tired she was until she sat down in the living room. She turned on the television and started watching a PBS special and the next thing she knew, someone was calling her name.

Startled, she opened her eyes to see her husband standing in front of her. "Neil?"

"Who else baby."

She smiled and he lowered his head to give her a kiss. What say we order in tonight? It has been quite a tiring day, I see," he said as he smiled down at his wife.

"Okay, okay, smarty. I just took a short nap. I'm entitled." She stood and put her arms around his neck. "I think ordering in is a good idea. Let's do that and just veg for the rest of the evening." She paused, "I know. I'll find us a movie to watch."

"Okay," Neil said. "But pick something we can both enjoy. Nothing too sappy. Okay?"

"Aye, Aye, captain. Nothing to sappy at all."

While Barbara went to pick out the movie, Neil placed a call to their favorite Chinese restaurant. He knew what Barbara liked so he ordered for them both and when Barbara returned with her movie choice he had to laugh.

"What? You like this movie too."

"Yes, I have to admit I do. 'Just like Heaven' is a classic. It's a perfect choice since it's not sappy and it has humor in it too."

Barbara smiled. "So what did you order?"

"Chinese."

"Perfect."

"So now we should take a shower and put on some comfy clothes."

"I'm with you on that. We have the time. They said it would be close to an hour before they delivered."

Barbara and Neil went upstairs and stripped off their clothes in the bedroom. When Barbara stepped out of her panties, she looked up and gave Neil a look that he read immediately and carried his clothes over to the hamper. She smiled her appreciation and then they went into the master bath to take a shower together.

This was something they often did as a fantastic way to wrap up the day. They would tell each other the highlights, then ease into their personal plans for the coming week. It was their time together with no outside interference. It was like a wall was built around them and they gathered energy from each other.

Barbara climbed in first and Neil was right behind her. They washed each other's body and shampooed each other's hair as they talked. They did this methodically until their bodies heated from more than just hot water. Then it became their foreplay and as they dried each other, it added to the foreplay. By the time their bodies were dry, they were anxious and ready to make love.

They moved as one over to the bed and were instantly in each other's arms. There was no time for talking now as they enjoyed climaxing together. Afterwards, relaxed and clean, they fell asleep.

The doorbell rang and startled them back to consciousness. At first Barbara was disoriented. "What was that?"

"I think it's our food." Neil replied as he grabbed a robe and slid his feet into his slippers. "Hurry down. I'm starving."

"Don't worry, I'm starving too."

Barbara was relaxed as she forgot about everything except spending the evening with her beloved. Once they settled down to eat, she let him do all the talking as she smiled, and half listened until he mentioned the sinkhole.

"Sorry, what did you say?"

"I said, it may have been revealed by the earthquake but it's not a sinkhole."

"It is a sinkhole."

"No, it is a sunken garden."

"Enough talk about that hole. Let's watch our movie and then get some sleep. We have a busy day at work tomorrow. I still have to prepare my boards for the meeting room in the building and you have to go make sure the contractor has the updates for that building we talked about."

"You're right, dear." Barbara got up and put in the movie and then they cuddled together on the sofa. When the movie ended, Barbara was the first to stretch.

Neil could see she was tired and said, "You go up and get ready for bed and I'll join you shortly. I'll clean up this mess and put the DVD back in its jacket."

Barbara laughed as she punched him lightly on the shoulder. "What? Two food containers, and some napkins?"

"And chopsticks. Don't forget the chopsticks."

Chapter 20

Barbara had a dream.

Barbara drifted off to sleep. She was in a deep sleep when she heard the sound of something she couldn't make sense of. She opened her eyes and saw a small hole in the wall. She got up to see what it was and leaned down to stare into it. She jumped backwards and scooted across the floor. She saw the eyes of someone watching her every move.

Her heartbeat fast in her chest and the hole got bigger and bigger until it was large enough for her to walk through.

And there stood Mindy beckoning her to come through. At first she hesitated, then slowly managed to stand. Barbara tilted her head to the side sensing she shouldn't, but Mindy was so nice to her on the boat, and she had something she wanted to tell her. And Barbara wanted to know. So she went through the whole.

They were walking alone in the woods, and it was so dark she couldn't see her hand in front of her face. Barbara tried to talk, but her throat was soundless as they made their way to the sinkhole.

She wanted to stop, but she couldn't. She wanted to scream at Mindy to stop, but she couldn't and so they continued down to the pathway at the top of the sinkhole. It was then she heard the sound of several male voices yelling out for help.

She turned her head, and she could see them, shadowy figures of grown men yelling out for help. Her heart lurched in her chest as she tried desperately to turn and leave this place, but she stood there frozen until finally Mindy turned back toward the house. Over her shoulder she said, "I have more to tell you."

Barbara woke screaming, terrified and uncontrollable as Neil tried desperately to soothe her. He held her in his arms, rocking her back and forth until she finally calmed down. Then he gently laid her on her pillow. And just like that, she fell back to sleep.

She scared him. Neil had never heard such a scream and especially not from Barbara. Should he wake her up? Should he call someone? Something must have hurt her to have her scream like that.

He thought he was too worried to go back to sleep and looked over at the clock. It was only 3 a.m. It was too early to call anyone. He looked over at Barbara. She was sleeping peacefully now so he laid his head down on his pillow and stared up at the ceiling. Soon he fell back asleep.

The alarm went off, shaking them both awake. Neil scooted back against the headboard and Barbara followed. Each tried to catch their breath, and when they did, they turned to face each other. Barbara smiled and Neil smiled back. Barbara smirked and they both started laughing.

Barbara leaned over and kissed Neil and then they both turned to sit up with their feet dangling on their side of the bed. A minute later Barbara said, "We've got to hurry if we want some breakfast before going to the office. We have a busy day ahead of us…a terribly busy day."

Then he remembered. Neil stared after his wife shocked by her composure as she made her way into the bathroom. From her actions, he was quite sure she didn't recall the nightmare that had scared her to death. It was either that or she didn't care to tell him about it.

Neil considered the matter a moment longer. He had seen her during the nightmare and now and he could only surmise that she didn't remember because she wasn't a good actor. He could always tell when something was bothering her, and nothing seemed to be bothering her now. It was as though nothing had happened, and it had him worried because he didn't understand.

He did a half turn and swung his body back into a sitting position and leaned against the headboard and thought about the events of last night. For his own sanity he stressed over the matter asking himself if he should say anything to Barbara and decided against it.

Just then he heard the shower stop and he got out of bed and went into the bathroom. They met at the doorway and Barbara paused to give him a big kiss before moving into the bedroom and he continued into the bathroom.

Later as he stood under the water in the shower, he felt his body relaxing and when he finished all thoughts of that night seemed to flow down the drain. When he stepped out, he felt refreshed and went into the bedroom to dress.

Barbara was putting on the finishing touches of her make up when he finished dressing and after brushing his hair, Neil headed downstairs, going straight to the kitchen to start the coffee. When Barbara joined him he pulled out two bagels, toasted them and sat them on plates with the cream cheese they both liked.

They ate quickly and they each carried their plates over to put in the dishwasher. Barbara went back to the counter and picked up the cream cheese and put it in the fridge before turning around to ask, "Ready?" Neil replied, "Aye, aye, captain." Laughing, they headed out the door together.

Since they were going to the same jobsite later they only needed one car, so Neil drove, and Barbara climbed in the passenger side. Neil started the car and then they both fastened their seatbelts. With one last check to be sure they had everything; they soon were on their way downtown.

Neil opted for the scenic route. He drove the car toward Parkview Ter on St Paul Blvd. and continued on St. Paul to Cooper Rd, then turned right onto Titus Avenue. He drove a short way and then turned left onto Hudson Ave. He continued on to North Street and then to North Chestnut Street before turning right onto Woodbury Blvd. He drove down Woodbury until he reached S. Clinton Avenue where he turned right. Sixteen minutes later they were at 3 City Center.

When they had searched for a place to set up their offices they chose this location, known as the epic center of downtown Rochester, for its modern amenities and value as well as its location at the gateway of Rochester. 3 City Center was a relatively new building located in the Innovation Zone, but it was surrounded by historical and serene Washington Square and Manhattan Square Parks. They could have taken 490 downtown as the office was conveniently accessible to that throughfare, but it was a more interesting drive along this route.

At the office, Barbara gathered her boards and checked to be sure she had all that she needed to show the client. Neil did the same. The sun shone brilliantly in the clear, blue sky. It was a bright and sunny day so they opted to walk the short distance to the client's building where he would meet them.

Neil disappeared, following the noise of the contractors who were already at the project of demolishing walls, while Barbara went to the front office to consult with the wife of the building owner who was, in conjunction with Barbara, charged with decorating the interior of the rooms.

When they first were in contact with this client, the Locksmiths, they had a big laugh over the name, but once they met the couple, who like them were going into business together, they gained a respect that overshadowed the faults of having that last name and being financial advisors. They were in the business of welcoming clients, not locking them out.

Just as efficient as the Sanders, the Locksmiths were good at what they did and doing it together made them easy to approach. Barbara and Neil had learned a long time ago that couples in business gained more respect from their clients than singles. It could be because there is a personal connection made with the business and their clients and having that business represented by both makes the couples comfortable because at some point the customer becomes the businesses prime concern and this could cause friction in a marriage.

Chapter 21

Barbara finished her presentation to Sara Locksmith and leaned back in her chair, feeling good about the design she was presenting. As was her usual strategy, after finishing her presentation she allowed the client time to think about the proposal as she sat quietly by.

Barbara never worried about whether they would like it or not. She knew she had done the best presentation and had designed the best décor for the space. If there were any questions about it, or hesitations over any points, she was always at the ready explaining her choices of style, color and materials so that the client understood the big picture of her design, but it usually didn't come to that.

It was within seconds that Sara smiled, stood and walked over to her. She presented her hand as she said, "Where do I sign?"

Barbara smiled back as she shook Sara's offered hand. She then went over to her briefcase and pulled out the contract. The two women sat down as Barbara explained it to her new client and after she had signed the document, she thanked her. "When can I get a copy of the contract," Sara asked.

"Well, our office is just down the street. If you want, we can walk together over there and you can have a copy today."

"Sounds wonderful."

"Okay," Barbara said. I'll meet you outside. I want to go tell Neil I'm leaving and then I'll join you."

Sara nodded and they parted ways.

Neil was checking out one of the entranceways and Barbara cleared her throat to get his attention. When he turned, she said, "I'm done. I'll meet you back at the office."

Neil nodded and walking gingerly through the construction zone she made her way out of the building to meet up with Sara.

Together they started walking the short distance to the Sanders office building and once there, they entered, and Barbara gave Sara a minute to take it all in.

"Why this is stunning," she said turning toward Barbara, "Absolutely breathtakingly stunning."

"Well thank you, but yours will be too. We didn't have much here to work with except the structure was sound and though not as old as the buildings around it, it seems to fit in."

"It does. Indeed it does."

The two started walking again and soon were in front of her office manager. "Sara Locksmith, I'd like you to meet my office manager, Jennifer Leland."

"Good morning Ms. Leland. Nice to meet you."

"Nice to meet you too, but we aren't that formal. You can call me Jennifer."

"Thank you, Jennifer."

When the introductions concluded, Jennifer turned toward Barbara and in a pleasant voice asked, "Is there something I can do for you?"

"Jennifer, can you follow us to my office. I need you to make a copy of a signed contract."

"Sure, no problem."

What she liked most about Jennifer was that she always had a smile on her face, and she always took the time to congratulate the client. As they made their way to Barbara's office, Jennifer said, "Welcome to the family, Ms. Locksmith."

"Thank you, but please call me Sara?"

"Sara it is."

Once in the office, Barbara pulled the contract out of her briefcase and handed it to Jennifer, who smiled and left the room. When Jennifer was gone, Sara asked, hesitantly, "Ms. Sanders…"

"Please, call me Barbara."

"Okay, Barbara. I have a request."

Barbara tried not to show her surprise as she sat there beside her client. What could it be? Had she done something wrong that Sara didn't like? Sara had signed off on it. Before she got herself into a titter she managed to say, "Sure, Sara. What would you like."

"Well, as I'm sure you know. Irondequoit is a small town and so when things are happening, word gets out."

Barbara nodded. "Yes, I know. It's probably what I love most about the area."

Gaining her confidence, she continued. "Well, my husband. Paul and I would love to come out and see the…ah…the sunken garden."

Barbara felt relieved, then gave Sara a genuine smile. "Of course you can. But we are going to wait until it's done. You know, I'm sure that once it is uncovered, there will be a lot of work needed to make it presentable. They are just now meticulously removing all the dirt and debris from the surface and it's not anywhere near completely uncovered. Then they want to have the ground around the area inspected to make sure it is safe and secure to walk there."

Barbara paused catching the change in expression on Sara's face and immediately added, "You understand that

I'm not putting you off. When it's ready, we would love to have you come see it."

Slowly, Sara nodded her head. "Thank you for explaining." Leaning toward Barbara she asked, "So, what do you know about the garden?"

Barbara shook her head from side to side. "Nothing really. We didn't even know it existed. I plan on doing some research, though, because... she paused as flashes danced behind her eyes. She slowly recovered and couldn't remember what she had just said.

Barbara could see the concern on Sara's face and that of Jennifer who had entered to deliver the copies for Sara. They both said, "Are you all right?"

Barbara rubbed her hands down her face and when she removed them she had a genuine smile. "Yes, I'm fine." Glad to change the subject she said, "Jennifer, thank you." Jennifer walked over and handed Barbara the copies, whispering, "Are you sure you're alright?"

Barbara nodded. She watched Jennifer leave the room and she handed Sara the signed contract.

Sara looked worried and Barbara wasn't sure what had just happened to her. She sensed she needed to assure her client and said, "Really, I'm fine."

"What just happened there. It was like for a moment you were about to faint."

Thinking quickly she replied, "No, it was just that something you said made me remember something I needed to do, and my mind blanked out."

Sara nodded. "I know what you mean. I've had that happen to me. I think when you are in business you are always thinking ahead and if you're like me, you probably need to jot that thought down before you forget it, so I'm going to get out of your hair. I'm sure we will talk later."

Barbara walked Sara to the door and Jennifer stepped

forward to continue with her, saying, "Sara, your husband is waiting for you downstairs."

Barbara went around her desk and sat down. She leaned back in her chair. She didn't need to write anything down. She knew what she was thinking and what she needed to do. She lifted the top of her laptop and sat thinking where to begin.

Barbara was free until one in the afternoon. At that time she had a luncheon meeting with some friends who had started out as clients, but now were more than that and they often tried to get together for lunch. So, before she got too engrossed, she set an alarm on her phone and laid it next to her, then she started looking up old historical files on Rochester and found most referenced several books to read. She jotted down the titles and author names.

She continued her search through the internet pausing to read snatches of Rochester's history and became captivated by how it all began. She was learning about the area and how it got its name when the alarm went off.

Despondent, at first, she wished she had more time, but she knew there would be plenty of time later to continue so she got out of the internet and shut her laptop. Just as she was about to leave, Jennifer arrived at the door. "Barbara, you have a luncheon engagement at one."

She smiled. "Yes, I know. I was just getting ready to leave."

Jennifer left and Barbara came out from behind her desk and hurried to the doorway which she usually kept open allowing her to feel a part of the building and not shut off in a corner of it.

On her way out she said, "Bye," to Jennifer and was almost at the door when she stopped and turned and spoke.

"Jennifer, if you have some time this afternoon, could you do me a favor."

"Sure. What would you like me to do."

"I wonder if you could do a little research on the Irondequoit area."

"Anything special you would like me to research?"

"I'm not sure. Just anything you find interesting about the suburb and jot down where I can find the information." She turned to leave, then turned back around. "Oh, yes, and names…names of people referenced as well."

Jennifer nodded and Barbara was on her way out the door. She got into her car and headed for The Spaghetti Warehouse on Central, where she was meeting her friends. They had wanted her to see it, since they thought the interior design was quite clever and would appeal to her. They also said that since the restaurant was part of a Dallas-based chain, they had a feeling it wouldn't be around long. When she asked, "Why," her friend, Marla Dickerson who worked at the Times-Union said, "It's hard to bring in a '*new flair*' restaurant, but even more so if it is in this location."

One of her first friends in Rochester, Emily Watson had explained saying, "The restaurant is part of the revitalization of downtown Rochester and only opened five years ago. The food is inexpensive, but quite good, but it's mainly the atmosphere of eclectic mixes of antiques and curiosities that I'm sure you will enjoy. Can you believe it," she had said excitedly, "It has a railroad excursion car that was converted into a dining room and a 19th century buggy which it is said, Mary Todd Lincoln is alleged to have ridden in."

At first Barbara had been hesitant as she knew the area was not on the top ten lists of places in Rochester to go, but thinking about it more she realized they were going during the daytime and she had to admit she was interested in seeing it as well and if Marla was right, she might not get another opportunity.

Her first impression as she arrived at her destination was that it was indeed clever to actually use an old warehouse structure and the parking lot was substantial. She parked her car and went inside and while her eyes adjusted she looked around the expansive first floor area, trying to take it all in. Then she saw the railroad excursion car where her friends were meeting her.

She had thought that it would be an extension, outside the building. That as well as the buggy, but they were right inside and part of the dining experience. "How clever she whispered." A waiter came up and asked where she would like to be seated. "Oh, I'm meeting my friends here and we have reservations in the excursion car?" She said questioningly not sure how they referred to it.

"Great," he said as he walked her over in that direction, telling her about the place and what it had to offer. "Is it your first time here?"

"Yes, it is."

"Well, be sure to check us out. There is a lot to see."

When they arrived at the table inside the excursion car, her guide nodded at her friends and then pulled out a chair for Barbara. "Enjoy your meal." Then he was gone.

"So, what do you think?

"I think this is amazing. Even if the food isn't high quality, the atmosphere makes up for it."

"Do you think they will mind if I take some pictures?"

"No, I think they will be flattered."

"Wait," Marla said. "No need. I have pictures of it being constructed. I even have photos of them bringing in the dining car and the buggy…history on both of them too."

"What about…"

"What about the final layout. I've got them from all angles." Remember, I did the article on it coming to our quaint small town. Whatever you need, I've got it in my files, and I'll send it to you."

"Thank you Marla, I appreciate that. There's a lot of ideas here that I might want to consider in future projects."

At that point, the waiter arrived, and they placed their orders. Even though the restaurant was large and almost filled with patrons, their food arrived quickly, and Barbara could tell her friends were as pleasantly surprised as she was. It was very tasty and there was lots of it.

They had each ordered a different item off the menu and shared with each other as they laughed and talked about the food. "Who would have thought something as quaint, serving delicious food like this, would settle in such a questionable area."

"I can answer that," Emily piped in, "It's the warehouse. They always open their restaurants in old warehouses."

When the conversation died down, Barbara raised her question. "Marla, Emily, what do you know about the sunken garden at our house."

She could see the surprise on their faces and knew instantly they were as shocked as she was by the discovery."

"What do you mean? You found a sunken garden on your property?"

"Yes."

"When?" Marla said as she moved to the edge of her seat smiling, smelling a good story about to unfold.

"You know that earthquake we had recently?" The women nodded. "Well, it opened up what we thought was a sinkhole on the east side of our property…"

"Your house!"

"The house is fine, it's a safe distance from the house."

The women let out a sigh of relief.

"Anyway, we thought it was a sinkhole, but we saw some plaster or concrete sticking up from the debris and it was, you know, shaped. Neil has them digging it out…cautiously and the more he uncovered, the more we found it was not just a sinkhole. The ground most likely collapsed because the earth had been disturbed and from what we are seeing, it is a sunken garden." Barbara paused, looking at her friends.

"You've got to be kidding."

At that moment, the busboy came and cleared off the table and the women ordered coffee. Then when they were alone again, Marla gave Barbara a questioning look and Barbara shook her head in reply.

Marla stared at Barbara with interest. "Tell you what, I'll check out the archives at the paper. There must be something about it. There is no way such a secret could be kept in this small city."

"Yes," Emily said. "And I'll ask my family. The Sibley's have been around for ages and I'm sure there is someone who knows something about it." She paused and said, "Barbara, have you checked the attic or the basement. There may be some papers there that give you information."

Barbara was so busy appreciating her friends offering to help, she only half heard the final request as she reached across the table and grabbed their hands. "Thank you so much. I really appreciate anything you can find out about it."

The women were quiet, drinking their coffee, but inside the impact of what Barbara had shared, played in their minds. Too soon they realized it was getting late, so they paid their tab and parted ways. "See you soon." They said to each other before they climbed into their cars and went their separate ways.

Barbara sat a minute longer, thinking. She thought that had gone well. She had been afraid they would ask more questions and if they did, she would probably tell them she had a bad feeling about that garden. Now as she sat pondering it, she sort of wished she had. She had also wanted to ask them about Mindy Worthington. Was she really the granddaughter of John Carroll Leake? But that would come later since at this moment she wasn't sure the woman actually existed. What she planned on doing was researching William and Georgia Bemish. She was sure that Marla would find out a lot about them, but she wanted to see what she could find.

Then she remembered Emily's parting suggestion, Barbara, have you checked the attic or the basement. There may be some papers there that can give you information.

Why hadn't she thought of that?

Chapter 22

Barbara wondered if the person she thought she had met was actually the granddaughter of John Carroll Leake who she herself knew was quite well-known all-around Rochester, but especially in Irondequoit. As she sat pondering the matter, her office manager, Jennifer gave a light tap on her door. Barbara looked up, smiling. "What is it Jennifer."

"Well, I did a little research...I will do more, but for now this is all I could find." She walked over and handed Barbara an envelope that contained several sheets of paper.

"Sit, Jennifer," Barbara said as she turned her attention to the envelope. She opened it and began looking over the three sheets of paper. There was quite a bit of information in the file, but not much more than she already knew.

"Thanks Jennifer."

"You are welcome. I know that you probably have read this information before because it was part of public files on the Net, but can I make a suggestion?

"Sure. What is it."

"Well, from what I found online, no one has lived in that house since the Bemishes. It has been closed up for a long time." Jennifer paused. "I remember you saying there was a lot of old furnishings left in the house?"

"Yes," Barbara said, offhandedly, thinking that she had a feeling that Mindy Worthington had some connection with that house after the Bemishes. She didn't know why she thought that, but she did.

"Well, if that is true, I'm sure there is something in that house worth finding because it wouldn't be easy for anyone to get in there without permission. Say, in the basement, or the attic...I know, there may even be some hidden openings in closets or under floorboards. You know that was where a lot of people hid money and things."

Barbara mulled over the idea in her head. With all the redecorating, the house needed very little in the way of structural changes so not every nook and cranny had been touched. She looked up at "Jennifer. I think that is a brilliant idea, Jennifer. Just brilliant."

Jennifer beamed. Barbara was glad she had said that. It was just what gave Jennifer an ego boost and she deserved it.

"No problem. When I have a free moment I will see what else I can find out." Jennifer started to leave and then turned around and handed her a message. "I almost forgot. This came for you when you were out."

Barbara took the message and nodded then returned to reading through the information Jennifer had given her. Finally she forced herself to turn her attention to the message and resignedly made the call, but happy when she realized they may have another client.

That done she went back to thinking about what Jennifer had told her. It got her wondering. Jennifer was as new to the Rochester area as herself and her family had never lived there at all, but she wondered if, like herself, Jennifer had heard rumors. Beyond their office association, she knew little about Jennifer. Did she have a lot of local friends that may have shared a detail or two? She thought about that a bit longer. Jennifer was young and single. Her friends were probably the same age. They probably had other things on their mind. Barbara smiled. It was not likely history was high on their agenda. Why would it come up in a conversation unless someone had ties to the property or knowledge of what had taken place there?

Barbara went back to working on jobs that needed her attention.

At the end of the day, Barbara was ready to go home and talk with Neil. The minute she drove up to the house she had an odd feeling. She couldn't quite explain it, but something told her to take a look at the sunken garden. It was the last place on the property she wanted to visit, but the 'push' in that direction was overpowering her and she hesitantly climbed out of the car and shut and locked the door. She stood there a moment, then, realizing her hands were empty, she shrugged her shoulders and unlocked the car door again so that she could get her briefcase and purse out. She then gave a reprimanding shake before heading toward the garden.

She didn't have to go far before she saw Neil, standing like one of the statues that were now visible in the garden. They had done a lot of work the last couple of days and now, most of the garden had been excavated and Neil stood staring as if… She couldn't finish that thought.

Instead she wondered how he had gotten home. They had driven in together and she had the car. Then she remembered that his partner, Jack Waters had mentioned something about giving him a ride home.

Barbara went up to Neil and slid her arm through his. Neil jumped, almost sending them down into the garden below. "Sorry, sorry. I didn't mean to startle you."

Neil reached up and wiped his eyes as though something was blinding his sight and he needed to remove it. He turned and smiled at his wife. "It's okay. I didn't expect you so early. So, what's on for the evening?"

She thought that was a strange thing for him to say. It wasn't something he would normally blurt out at a moment like this, but she let it go and said, "Dinner and a little television. I'm actually not very tired." She paused, gave him a kiss and then added, "Let's go inside and you can tell me about your day."

He was staring off in the distance again, but came back to her saying, "In a minute. Tell me, sweetie, what do you think about this?" He asked his arms spreading out to include all of the area in front of them."

Barbara hesitated, trying to find the right words that were true and not what she really thought at all. "Well, I can see that someone had spent a lot of time on this garden and though, the design style is all over the place, it's not bad," She paused and turned her attention to him. "But I think we need to go inside now."

"Wait a second, Barbara. From an architectural design, I think it is well planned. I think that the person or persons who created it were expressing their every thought and idea in this garden, and it wasn't a matter of what worked with what, but what feeling they felt at that moment."

"You may be right about that." They remained standing at the side of the garden that faced the house as they spoke.

"I know I'm right and I can't wait to see what is at the North End and how far back it goes.

"I know, but can we go in now, I'm hungry and I have a favor to ask."

"What's the favor."

"Let's talk about it over dinner."

It was hard, but as they put dinner together, Barbara kept the conversation on the work she had done that day. She also shared that she had picked up another client that was interested not only in decorating their house but adding on an addition. "So, I told them I would check with you, and we could set up a date to discuss it."

"That sounds great. Who is it?

"Well, it's the McBrides."

"Ah, I know them, or I should say I know of them."

They finished making the dinner and carried their plates to the dining room. While Barbara got out the wine glasses, Neil went about selecting a wine and opening it. Soon all thoughts of work dissipated as they ate and enjoyed being alone and together. During their conversation they set up plans for the weekend.

As they carried their plates out to the kitchen and cleared the dining room table, Neil paused and turned. "Yes, I knew I'd heard that name before." Seeing the surprise on Barbara's face he added, "You said you wanted to visit a winery this weekend?"

"Well, not just one, but yes."

"Well, the McBrides own a winery." They continued into the kitchen and Neil began sharing that he had met a Joseph Vinton whose grandfather came to Irondequoit some years back and they have a home on Irondequoit Bay. His father bought seventy acres of land and turned it into a resort called the Newport House and then the third generation, Joseph built a house above the resort. Is that the house you're talking about."

"I'm not sure. I spoke with an Andrea McBride."

"Yes, the McBrides own the property now. The last I

heard, the Vintons owned it up until the mid-1900s, but it was the Vinton's who established the winery." He paused adding, Vinton Road was named after his family."

"Ah, so someone has been doing his history."

Neil smiled. "Yes, in my business it's important to know the history of the home and the area. It helps me get an idea of what the owner is looking for."

"Yes, I know. I do it too." This was going in the direction that Barbara had hoped for, but it wasn't because she had guided it there on purpose, still she was happy it did and decided to indulge him further. "So what else do you know about the McBrides?"

"Well, the first McBride was Asa who visited the Vinton vineyards and was impressed by what he saw so he formed a partnership with a man named Joseph Warren and they purchased the vineyard. They built a stone wine cellar that stood for many years, halfway down the hill, on the Bay front. I hear it was very innovative for the times as it was thirty by forty feet with the cellar part in the side of the hill and the filling and shipping room on the level with the roadway in front."

"Go on," Barbara said as they carried their coffee over to the island and sat, facing each other.

"Well, McBride bought out Mr. Warren and developed a majorly successful wine business and near the end of the 1900s he built a new wine cellar on the level ground at the end of Ridge Rd. above the Bay."

"I think we saw that on our boat tour."

"Yes, I think we did. McBride operated the business until the beginning of 1899 when the Irondequoit Wine Co. was formed. McBride remained active and head of the Company for 55 years. He died in 1922 at the age of 90 years."

Barbara shook her head. "Here I was telling you

about a new client and you end up sharing all the details of the building."

"Okay, I have to be straight with you. Jennifer told me you had received the call and I saw it on your calendar that you were meeting with them. I did a little research ahead to help you out. You know I have the best research team at my fingertips. I would have shared them with you, but it was more fun this way."

Barbara smiled. Now it was her turn. "Okay smarty, if you have so much research help, have you thought about getting more details on this house."

"I did."

"So, what did you find out."

"Come on, let's go into the living room and sit. It's more comfortable there."

Barbara nodded. They refilled their coffee cups and carried them into the living room. Once they were seated, Neil said that he had started with the property deed and knew that the Bemish family had built the house probably in 1910 and Mr. Bemish was an art dealer which would give some credence to why they have this sunken garden on the estate.

Barbara considered it and it did make sense. "So, did you find out anything else?

"Just that his wife, Georgia was heir to the J.K. Post Drug company that was a big deal back then."

"Humm."

"So, do you have anything to add?"

"Not really…at least not yet. I've put out a few feelers, but the best suggestion so far came from my business manager, Jennifer."

"What was that?"

"She said that since the house has been vacant…or so it seems …since the Bemishes died…departed…whatever, no one has lived here. That means that nothing has changed since then. She suggested that we check for secret compartments in closets and under floorboards and that we check the attic and basement. There may be something there…maybe even about that sunken garden."

"I like that idea."

"So they agreed to spend the morning searching the house from top to bottom and then they would clean up and head to the McBride winery that afternoon.

Chapter 23

After a restful night's sleep with no dreams or resulting events, Barbara and Neil wake up the next morning refreshed and ready for their adventure. Barbara can hardly contain herself as just the thought of what they might find excited her.

"Okay, Babe, we will start right after a good breakfast."

Barbara gave him a sad face.

"No, that's not going to work. We are going to do our morning routines and then go down to breakfast...maybe chat a bit," he smiles at her, "then we will begin the hunt."

Barbara could see he wasn't going to be persuaded and gave in. She turned and went into the bathroom to brush her teeth. When she was done gargling, Neil entered the bathroom and began his routine at the sink while she striped off her nightgown and climbed in the shower.

She could feel Neil's eyes on her and any other time she would encourage what he was thinking, but not today. Today she had a mission that had to be done and she would not allow one more delay. So when Neil entered the shower, she quickly slipped by him, kissing his shoulder and said, "Not today old man, not today." Then once she was wrapped in the towel she turned and added, "But if you do a good job...and we find something interesting...who knows."

Neil gave her a look and started washing his body vigorously as she made her way back into the bedroom and opened her closet to pull out a pair of jeans and a top. She put them on the bed and went to her dresser and took out her underwear, bra and socks.

She was in the midst of pulling up her panties when she heard the shower stop so she stepped it up wiggling into her underwear, putting on and fastening her bra, then quickly stepping into her jeans and pulling them up over her bottom. Without fastening them, she picked up her t shirt and pulled it down over her head, her arms up and ready to slide into the sleeves.

When Neil entered the bedroom she was dressed. Barbara was not about to entice him until after they had finished their search. Besides, they had the whole weekend to indulge themselves and she just wanted a few hours to solve the mystery.

Neil was whistling as he entered the room. He smiled at her. "What's that about, calling me an old man."

"Well, we are older my friend, maybe not old, old yet, but we're getting there. Besides if I had said handsome stud, there would have been no stopping you from carrying out your side mission."

Neil pouted as he went into his closet. When he came out, Barbara was already on her way downstairs. She went directly to the kitchen and started breakfast.

It was the weekend and though she wanted to make it quick, she thought it would be wrong to not give him a proper breakfast; especially since they had plans to visit the winery later today even if they didn't finish the search.

By the time Neil joined her in the kitchen, she had

the coffee going and the pancake batter made. She was getting out the pan when she felt him behind her, and she turned. He drew her into his arms for a deep, sexy kiss. She reciprocated before gently pushing him away and going about getting the breakfast ready.

Neil sighed and realizing she was not about to back down, went to get the orange juice out of the fridge. He carried it over to the table and went back to retrieve two juice glasses, while Barbara concentrated on the pancakes, not wanting to burn them.

Neil's urges calmed as he finished getting out the dishes, utensils and pushed the napkin holder in reach of their seats. Then he paused to consider if he had forgotten anything and over her shoulder, Barbara said, "Don't forget the syrup and the butter."

"Yes," he replied, "that was what I was about to do."

By the time Barbara had the pancakes ready and brought them over to the table, Neil was already filling their coffee cups and they sat down together.

The first few minutes were spent putting pancakes on their plates and adding the toppings. The next few minutes involved taking those first bites until finally it was time to broach the subject of the day.

Barbara started. "Neil, I want to begin in the attic."

Neil, his mouth full, nodded in agreement. He took a sip of his coffee and then spoke. "After that we can do the basement and as promised, you will explore the sunken garden with me."

Barbara hesitated, wanting to tell him she was scared to go into the garden but because she didn't understand why she decided to keep that to herself and just nodded instead.

She took another bite of her pancakes and washed them down with her orange juice. Then she remembered, "Oh, yes, it was suggested that we check for loose floorboards and built in cubby holes in rooms...especially the bedrooms."

"Barbara, that is going to take all day."

"It takes what it takes, my friend. Besides, we have the whole weekend. So, less pouting and more eating. As soon as we clean up the kitchen we can begin."

Neil finished his plate first but showed no signs of getting up. Instead he started drinking his coffee and watched as she cleaned up the kitchen. When she was sure she had turned off the stove, she put the dishes in the dishwasher and went back over to the table with a sponge. She handed the sponge to Neil then picked up her coffee and downed the last full mouthfuls as he wiped down the table. Then she stood waiting for Neil.

He continued to sip his coffee, keeping his eyes lowered so she couldn't see his face. There was no sense in rushing him. If she did, it wouldn't be a fun exploration, but instead a pain in the ass search for him. After a bit, he was done and carried his cup over to put in the dishwasher. Then he turned and said, "Ready! Let the search begin."

Even though there were lights in the attic, they each grabbed a flashlight to take with them as they headed up the back staircase that led to the attic. Neil opened the attic door and flipped on the light at the head of the stairs. He stepped over the lip of the entryway and Barbara followed.

They stood in awe. Their eyes going around the area trying to take it all in. It was a huge open space, filled to the brim. There were cobwebs and dust but for the most part it was quite clean and full...very full of all kinds of things.

Barbara turned to Neil and slowly a smile covered both of their faces. "Can you believe it?"

"You didn't come up here during the inspection?"

"No, no reason to. It was dry, the roof was in great shape and there were no leaks or wiring problems observed so I told them I was fine with it. They did check out the basement though and reported what was in there."

"Nothing like this, he said, his arms spreading out to take it all in."

This was a gold mine and they both knew it. It wasn't that they needed money, but it was proof that what they were about to uncover had not been touched in years. The original owners, the Bemishes had left this stuff here and the house had not been lived in since their departure that he was sure had to be sometime in the early part of the 1900s.

Before, Neil hadn't been as excited as his wife, but now he was all in. "Okay, it's a lot so let's divide and conquer and if you find something, call out so we can both check it out."

"Okay. I'll take the left side. You take the right."

They stood in awe at what lay before them. What for Neil started out to be a chore he wasn't really into, now became an exciting venture as he looked at furnishings that must have graced the home when the Bemishes occupied it. "They left these pieces in the attic, I'm sure of it, but why?"

Barbara was getting the same feelings as she headed to the opposite side of the attic weaving through slowly, checking out each piece of furniture by cautiously running her hands along the inside, under pillows and bottoms of chairs and tables, hoping to find something connected. Why would they not take these things with them? They were still in good shape and looked to be expensive pieces. "Neil, I can't believe this."

"I'm asking myself the same question. This is going to be interesting to say the least. The remarkable thing is that no matter how well we know the house, we are about to learn something new and exciting."

Barbara nodded. "It's like a real-life quiz in here and

I have an almost sadistic pleasure in the fun and frustration of trying to work out the answers to questions we have been wondering about as we learned the history of this house."

"I agree. I hope the answers we uncover are straightforward in concept and not complex. I want to be clear about what we find."

"Why do you think they left all this."

"Maybe they died, and the estate was held in probate... I don't know."

"Aren't their laws on abandoned property?"

"Yes, someone would have to initiate a complaint to the zoning or building department, but this property is so separate from those around it, no one probably would."

"So what if they had? What then."

"Well, once a property has been deemed to be vacant and abandoned, the mortgagee must take reasonable steps to ensure that the property is secured and maintained in order to minimize public safety risks."

"So, I think we can assume that someone was paying the mortgage or there wasn't one to be paid. But taxes had to be paid."

"Yes, and I think that would be the realtor's company who had possession of the property. They must have taken it over or been assigned control of the property. I just don't know for sure."

"Well, we know someone cared for it since it is not in disrepair. I think since it sits back from the road and the trees and bushes hide most of it, no one worried about the condition of the yard. It just looked woodsy."

"But what about the trash we saw."

"I think it blew in from the street."

"Or teens used it for privacy."

"Okay, less talking and more working. Those are all questions we can ask about later, but for now, let's get on with our search."

Time passed quickly as they checked every inch of the attic finding many treasures that Barbara thought she could use in her business, but beyond that, there was nothing to give them any more details about the property and the garden.

By the time they met at the back of the attic, they were exhausted and covered with dust. Barbara even had a few cobwebs in her hair. But it didn't matter. Even though they hadn't found any papers of interest or even a map of the area that was original to the property, they were happy with what they did find.

Holding hands, they weaved through the attic until they reached the entrance and then headed downstairs. When they reached the kitchen Neil whistled.

"Is that for me?"

"No, you're a mess but look at the clock."

Until entering the kitchen they had not been aware of the time. It was after eight in the evening. They had spent the full day in the attic.

Neil went over to Barbara. "You're a mess lady."

"So are you." Hesitantly she added, "So what now."

"Now, we call it a day."

"But the winery tour."

Seeing the disappointment on her face he quickly added, "We'll have to do that some other time or when we go to the appointment."

Barbara brightened. "The basement."

"Not now, we'll do the basement tomorrow, but we need to check every nook and cranny down there and it won't be as pleasant as the attic. We have to get some rest though so let's call it a day and have a nice dinner…delivered, of course, and while we wait, you can use our bathroom and I'll use one of the others to shower."

"Sounds good. I'll call in the order. What do you feel like?"

"Oh, I don't care. Just some food that I…we…don't have to prepare." With that he headed to the bathroom.

Barbara thought a moment and then placed a call to 'Two Ton Tony's'. She placed an order for their favorite pizza and a side of wings for delivery. Since the restaurant was just down the street, it would be delivered in less than a half-hour. She thanked them and hung up the phone.

She stopped by the bathroom where Neil was already in the shower. "You've got a half-hour before they come with our food. I'm on my way upstairs now."

With that she hurried up to get clean and changed. Soon she was ready and hurried downstairs to join Neil who had finished showering and at some point had come upstairs to get his change of clothes. She hadn't heard him at all.

He was in the living room, watching television. Hearing her enter he said, "Well, it looks like we both got comfy." Barbara laughed seeing they were both in pajamas and robes.

She went into the kitchen and got them each a bottle of water and called out, "Do you want some coffee or tea?"

"No, just water for me."

She left the kitchen, turned out the lights and went back to the living room to join Neil. She had no sooner entered the room than the doorbell rang. "I'll get it," Neil said, getting up from the sofa and waving the money he had in his hand."

"Love me a man who's prepared."

With his hand on the doorknob, he turned and said, "I'm planning on that."

When he opened the door, Neil was quiet and hearing

footsteps, Barbara turned around. "What is…" She started than seeing her friend Emily said, surprised, "Hi, did I forget something?"

"No, oh no. I'm sorry to be dropping in without calling first," she said surveying them dressed in their pajamas, but it couldn't wait."

"What couldn't wait," Barbara asked.

"Oh, I know, Neil" she said turning her head to look at him, "you had some doubts about what I shared with Barbara, and I know it sounds like one of those made-up stories so…"

Emily was smiling as Neil invited the visitor in and they moved into the living room. Emily continued, "My mother thought you might have trouble believing what I said so she went a step further and found out who the builders of the property were. She contacted Magnolia Warner who has been operating her father's contracting office since he passed. When my mother told her what was up, believe it or not, she was so interested in not only helping, but in coming to meet you. She should be here momentarily. And…" Emily paused for emphasis, "she has the original details of the property."

At that moment, the doorbell rang again. "It's like Grand Central Station." Barbara said as she started to stand.

"Sit. I'll get it," Emily said as she quickly got up from the sofa and hurried to the door. When she opened it, Emily was disappointed and it could be heard in her voice when she said, "Barbara, your food has arrived."

"I'll get it," Neil said as he hurried to the door to take possession of the food and pay the driver. Before he could close the door, he saw someone coming up behind the delivery man and peering out, he turned to look at Emily. Emily nodded, "That's her," and stepped in front of Neil.

Emily greeted the visitor and once she had stepped inside, closed the door, then following behind Neil, Emily showed the caller into the living room where Neil and Barbara stared openly at their new visitor.

The woman was quite breathtaking. She stood close to six feet; her body was lithe, and her face was extraordinarily proportioned like that of a model. She wore a long black skirt with an untucked white shirt under a loose-fitting shawl sweater. Her silver and black hair framed her face in a way that made her seem angelic. "Hello," she said, in a velvety voice. "My name is Magnolia Warner."

Everyone in the room remained standing as though they were in the presence of royalty. They watched as she glided across the floor. Barbara quickly said, "Excuse our clothing. We had a busy day."

Neil nodded and shyly asked, "Would you like to have some pizza and wings?"

Magnolia shook her head and said kindly. "No thank you, but thanks for offering." Then they waited.

Smiling, Magnolia tilted her head toward the side chair in the room and Barbara quickly nodded. They watched as she slowly took a seat. Once seated, she reached into her purse and pulled out a six-by-nine envelope that she laid in her lap. She then said, "In this envelope is what you are looking for." She paused and asked, "Can we go to a table?"

"Yes, oh yes," Barbara said, her anxiety dripping off each word as Neil held out a hand to help Magnolia up and they all went into the dining room. Neil pulled out a chair and Magnolia sat and once she was seated, Neil, Barbara and Emily formed a half circle around her.

Magnolia continued. "It is incredibly old, so I need to have you look at it without touching. It has been in my possession, since my grandfather passed, and I wouldn't want anything to happen to it."

"What is it."

"It's the details of what is in that sinkhole. I never

learned why this document wasn't filed. It could have been taxes, or that it being unheard of, there was no need to make reference to its existence. In any case, it was among the files on the property, and it has always been there."

They watched as she carefully opened the envelope and they all leaned forward. They could see it was old, but they could also see it had been well taken care of. "Why haven't you filed this with the original deed of the property."

Magnolia shrugged her slim shoulders. "I don't know. It never came up. The property deed was in the hands of the realtor, but no one asked about any further documents. Why should they. It was an undeveloped, mini forest for many years. And from what I heard, just littered with debris.

They nodded. "Anyway, let's read this." Magnolia began.

"This sunken garden located in a wooded ravine at the corner of St. Paul Boulevard and Winona was created as part of the estate developed in 1918, by art dealer William Bemish and his wife, Georgia. The garden is a mix of Arts & Crafts and Naturalistic landscape design of terraced gardens. Significant parts of the garden are of concrete and stone construction—as well as an iron gate of 'spider web' design, located in the 'Moon Gate' at the northeast corner of the garden."

Chapter 24

It had been an interesting evening, full of surprises and once Emily and Magnolia left, Neil and Barbara sat for a while, eating the cold pizza and wings. Neither said a word as they finished as much as they could then split up the job of cleaning up after themselves.

Exhausted, Barbara headed up the stairs while Neil went about locking the doors and windows. He turned off the lights and made his way upstairs to join his wife.

Barbara was in the bathroom, just finishing up when Neil entered. He gave her a weak smile as he put toothpaste on his brush. Barbara smiled back and ran her hand across his shoulders as she went into the bedroom.

That night they fell into bed, exhausted from their search and the surprise visitors, but they found the energy to make love before they turned over and fell fast to sleep.

Barbara had a dream. In it she was walking around outside in the dark in her slippers and pajamas. She came to an arch that had steps going down and she moved forward, counting them as she took each step. There were six in total. She paused and looked around her to see stone walls on either side and an oval of steps going around a center wall having the same shape.

She started down one side, counting again as she went until finally she stood on level ground; if you could call it that as it was of cracked stone and cement. She paused. It was so dark she wasn't sure of anything as she stared ahead, blinking until she made out a structure with low walls on either side. Since the ground sloped down, she thought it might be a bridge. And then she heard it...a faint cry that grew louder and louder.

At first she was frozen in place, unable to move her body when the sudden urge to escape or run away took hold of her. Slowly her body recovered and that sudden urge to escape took hold as she turned back around and stumbled up the stairs until she was back on level ground. Breathing heavily more from fright than exhaustion, she started to cry at first whimpering, then it changed to sobs that shook her body, waking her up and jerking her body until she fell out of bed, landing on the floor.

The room was dark and quiet as she sat there trying to orient herself and calm her heart that was beating madly in her chest. As she sat waiting, light coming through the bedroom window fell on her and she saw what looked like mud on the hems of her pajama bottoms. Barbara leaned forward and saw that her slippers were also covered in dirt. She sat up straight and looked around her wondering if she was still dreaming, but she knew she was not as she kicked off her slippers and shimmied out of her pajama bottoms before climbing back in bed.

Rapid breathing, an increased heart rate, and gasping for breath held her concentration as she tried to calm down. Until finally her heartbeat slowed, and her eyelids closed.

"Wake up sleepy head."

Barbara jumped, throwing her head back hard into the pillow as she tried to force her eyes open. When she succeeded she saw Neil's face staring down at her.

"I didn't mean to scare you sweetie."

Barbara attempted a smile as she pushed her body up until she was leaning against the headboard. She lifted her hands and began rubbing her eyes that were barely focusing. When she lowered her hands, she was seeing clearer and said, "I'm sorry."

"For what, silly."

Barbara laughed. "I don't know. I'm not fully awake so don't listen to anything that comes out of this mouth until I get a cup of coffee."

"Well, you don't have to wait long."

Barbara watched as Neil went over to the small table across the room and returned with a tray that held two cups of coffee and two bagels.

"What time is it?" Barbara asked, twisting to see the clock on the end table next to her side of the bed.

"It's after nine."

"You've got to be kidding! I don't sleep in that late."

"You don't, but you did. I got up, brushed my teeth and went downstairs already." He paused, "By the way the mat in front of the door is quite dirty. I think the delivery guy must have had dirt on his shoes. Barbara started, "I…"

"Let's just enjoy our coffee for now. While you shower I'll go down and clean the rug. Maybe I'll just vacuum the whole front room while I'm at it."

She didn't say another word as he climbed in beside her and resting against the headboard, relaxed. Barbara was feeling more like herself as she said, "So, are we going ahead with our plans for today?"

Neil nodded. "Yes, we'll take a tour around the basement. I've been in there, so I don't think we're going to find any treasures, but who knows. Once we get poking around we may come up with something."

Barbara took the last sip of her coffee and Neil got out of bed, taking the tray with him as he headed to the bedroom door. "Get dressed in something crappy and don't bother to shower as I'm sure we will be quite dirty after we're done."

Barbara watched as he left the room. She swung her legs over the side of the bed taking note that she wasn't wearing her pajama bottoms. She went to stand up, but her feet slipped, and she landed on her bottom, hard enough to take her breath away.

She sat for a moment and then looked down to see her pajamas, the cuffs filled with dirt and her slippers. She picked one up to see the bottom was covered with dry mud. It was as if she had been outside… The dream came back as she scooted backwards until she rested against her end table. "It can't be," she whispered. "It was a dream."

She sat there, her mind going a mile a minute until she heard Neil calling up to her to get a move on. She managed to scoot herself up to a standing position and called down. "In a minute."

As she went into the bathroom to brush her teeth she stood in front of the mirror asking herself if she was still in a dream. She had to be, because if she was not, she had gone outside during the night and had been in the sunken garden. But that was impossible.

Could she be sleep walking? She never had before, but she had heard of people doing just that. Maybe she had. She finished brushing her teeth and got out a pair of old jeans and a top. She slipped her feet into a pair of canvas shoes and started toward the door. She paused and turned back and went to her side of the bed to pick up her slippers and pajamas and carried them over to the laundry chute. She then went into the bathroom and got a towel, dampened it with water and carried it over to her side of the bed where she cleaned the floor. Then she made the bed and threw the towel down the chute. Those actions told her she was not going to mention it to Neil until she figured out what had happened.

Barbara straightened her body and put on a smile that she kept on her face as she hurried down to join Neil.

Neil was sitting on the sofa, facing the staircase, and he immediately got up and came over to her. He gave her a kiss and then pushed her gently back. "So, want to get started?"

She knew he was anxious to get that done so that maybe they could go out later to visit the winery, or he wanted to have time to explore the sunken garden. In either case she stood on her tiptoes and moved in to kiss him on his cheek. "Yes, let's have at it."

She started toward the basement door and Neil stopped her. "Wait a minute. It's going to be chilly down there. Grab a sweater or something."

"Your right." She noticed that he was wearing a sweatshirt, so she went to the closet and grabbed out a bulky hooded sweatshirt, then slipping it over her head as she started toward the basement, she called over her shoulder, "Ready there, slowpoke?"

Neil said nothing as he followed behind her, He waited as she turned on the light before heading down the stairs that were secure but had a railing that she was not so sure of, so she just dragged her hand over the top.

Once they were down, the light barely lit the interior,

but Neil walked over and pulled on the light chain that hung from the ceiling. Soon the basement was bathed in light. "It's wide open down here. Do you want to work together or separate?"

"Together." She said without hesitation.

So they started first, just walking around the area taking it all in. There was an outside entrance door and she grabbed Neils arm as she headed over to make sure it was locked and secure. It was. She gave him a sly smile, then released her hold as they started searching around the area.

There were a few interesting items like an old wagon wheel and shelves of tools, some rusty and not worth saving, while others Neil told her could be cleaned and would work just like new.

Along with checking around the room, Barbara told him to see if he saw any of the cinderblocks that might have been loose and could maybe have treasures behind them.

It was a slow, tedious process and just when Barbara thought they were not going to find anything, Neil yelled out, "I think I have something here." When Barbara moved in closer, he turned and said, "Don't get your hopes up, they may have loosened it when they were upgrading the service." Barbara said nothing as she watched him pull out the cinderblock.

As he jiggled it out, dust filled their nostrils and Barbara stepped back as Neil continued to gently move the block out of the wall. When he finally had it out he could see something inside it…something yellowed and stuck inside. He carefully sat the stone down and using both hands, removed the paper. He started to open it when Barbara grabbed his hand. "Stop, Neil, it's too brittle. If you try to open it, it will just fall apart."

"So what do we do?"

"I think we take it to someone who knows how to open it without damaging it."

"Who would that be."

"I'm not sure, but we'll check it out later. Maybe there's more. Let's just keep looking.

They did. They came across another yellowed paper and they sat it beside the other one on a wooden table in the basement that looked as though someone had built it out of a tree trunk and had been in there for a long time.

One thing Neil was sure of was that the house had never been broken into, not only because it sat so far back and had been covered with so much brush, but there were no broken windows or doors. The brush had only been cleared when the realtor offered to show the house to them. Now as they worked their way through the basement he realized that it was more than just overgrowth that kept it safe, it had been built like a fort. The doors upstairs and down were all made of steel, thick and heavy, and the shutters at the side of the windows were also of a heavy metal that closed by a switch on a panel in the kitchen. No, there was no way anyone could break in unless they had some powerful tools.

But he couldn't stop wondering why the realtors hadn't had the place checked out. He would later find out that there was a clause in the title that said unless authorized by the owners, no one should step foot in the house or the property itself. Only, according to the realtor, it wasn't until recently they were informed by the owner, which turned out to be a firm in New York, that the house could be put up for sale. So no one knew much about it or cared to find out until now.

They found several other pieces of paper and Barbara wondered, though they had checked the attic thoroughly could there be some papers in the drawers or crevices of the furniture. She decided to make sure she checked each piece again before selling any of it.

After hours of searching through the basement, they finally felt confident they had found all they were going to fine. Neil had gathered some interesting, old tools that he told Barbara he might display at his office. Barbara found a few that interested her as well. There were surprisingly quite a few old papers in the cellar which seemed strange to Barbara. Wouldn't it be safer to keep papers in the attic than in the basement where it might get damp? Then, looking around she could tell that no way was this basement ever damp. There wasn't even the hint of a damp smell.

Barbara carefully picked up the papers they had found and being extra cautious, handed some to Neil to carry, not wanting to crush them. Then Neil followed behind her, turning out the lights as he went.

Barbara paused at the base of the steps and turned to say, "Neil, I have a question."

"Shoot."

"What's the difference between a basement and a cellar. I refer to it as basement, but you call it a cellar...what's the difference."

Neil rubbed his chin as he thought about the question. "That's hard to say. It's the height of the room which is more than halfway below ground level so that makes it a cellar, but that is also why the ceilings are high. Then cellars will have ventilation issues because they are lower in the ground. You've smelt mustiness in cellars before, haven't you." Barbara nodded, watching as Neil walked over and ran his hand along the cement and stone wall. Cellars generally are dank and have a mildew smell and this one doesn't, but the windows are small which some people would say makes it a cellar. He paused again. Let's just say that this is whatever we care to call it, cellar or basement, it's a space below the house is all."

Soon they were back upstairs, dirty but happy with themselves as they took the paper items over to the far edge of the island. Once they had put them down, they both headed for a bathroom and cleaned up. When they were done, they met in the kitchen and sitting at the island with a laptop in front of each of them, they began searching for what to do with the old documents.

Barbara looked over at Neil smiling. "This is exciting." Neil smiled and nodded. They then returned to searching the internet.

It took several more minutes when finally Barbara said, "Look at this." Neil paused and looked over as Barbara turned her laptop so they could both see the screen. She then read the caption out loud. "Historical letter scanning requires utmost care and quality assurance when handling old, brittle pages. Anderson Archival is prepared to handle these originals with gloves and gentle equipment, ensuring the return of your originals in the same condition they were when first prepared."

"Search down and see if you can find any reviews."

There were several and they read through them, then Neil did a search on the company to bring up unsolicited reviews and he shared his findings with Barbara.

Finally, Barbara looked up at Neil, "What do you think?"

"I think we give them a call."

Barbara scrolled down until she found a phone number. Neil already had the extension in his hand and immediately started dialing the number. He put the phone on the intercom so they could both hear.

The phone was answered immediately, which pleased both Barbara and Neil and the person who answered had a pleasant voice. By the time they had all their questions answered, they were satisfied and made arrangements to ship the papers to them.

They sat there a moment in silence. Barbara was the first to speak. "Do you think we should have found someone local?"

Neil nodded, "But, even if there is anyone local, this firm had the most stars and excellent reviews of satisfied clients. This is something that requires the best and we didn't see or read anything close to what this business has the capability of doing." He paused, "No, I think we did the right thing."

"Okay, what now?"

"I say we go to UPS and have them package the document." Neil paused and reading the details on the company's website he saw information on how to safely pack and ship the documents to them. "Print out that page and we'll take it with us, so we have all the information they need."

"Okay, then what?"

"Then we go to the winery and have some fun."

"What about the closets."

"What about them?"

"Checking to see if there are any secret compartments?"

"Oh, I forgot."

"Okay, lets to that first. If we find anything, I'm sure we'll need to send it as well. May as well do it all at the same time."

So they went into every room, checking to see if there were any hidden compartments to be discovered. Though there weren't any secret compartments, they did find a safe behind an old picture hanging in the library. The only problem was they couldn't find the combination. After a while they gave up the search. They put it on their list of things to do and headed out to the winery.

Chapter 25

They had been at it for five hours and both were more than ready to quit. They had spent one and a half days of their free weekend on a scavenger hunt and knowing that sunny, warm days were not to be wasted, were more than ready for the winery tour.

While Neil wrote down the address of the winery to later plug into his GPS, Barbara searched for the closest UPS store. She was glad to learn that they did the packaging for you and in this situation, she needed an expert. She called the store to verify they were familiar with shipping methods of old documents. "Seriously, I have to ship some very important, old documents and I need your assurance they won't be damaged in any way."

The person on the other end responded and then Barbara said, "I hope you're right because I can't afford to have these papers damaged."

When she hung up the phone, she wrote down the address. Then turned around, she saw Neil was standing behind her, smiling.

"What?"

"Nothing"

"Then why are you smiling?"

She saw Neil's Adam's apple bounce as he swallowed. "Well, you know the saying, don't bite the hand that feeds you." Barbara looked at him puzzled. "Well don't insult the man who's going to be handling your documents."

"What? I wasn't rude."

Again Neil swallowed. "Tell me my dear, how does it feel when you tell someone you are an interior designer, and they question your ability to perform the service."

Aghast, Barbara frowned. "I didn't mean to insult."

"I know, but listening to your end of the conversation it sounded like you didn't trust them."

"So, what do I do, find another UPS store?"

"No, an apology to this one will do."

Barbara was worried as they carried their treasures out to the car. She had the printout of Anderson Archrival's website which she planned to give them, along with the address for the UPS Store. So while Neil put the winery address into the GPS, she thought about what she would say when they dropped off the documents. By the time Neil started the car, she was ready.

"Shall we drop off the documents first?" She asked and seeing Neil nod, she added. "It does take us in the opposite direction though."

"I think we should send them out right away. Who knows, they may disintegrate in the open air. So the sooner the better."

The UPS store was just down on Dewey Avenue in the Greece area and from their house, it was just a slight distance. But then, everywhere in Rochester was a slight distance from the other. When they were told they could get anywhere in 20 minutes, they laughed until they found it was true. With low traffic and alternative methods of getting around, one could go from point A to point B in a limited amount of time.

When they pulled up to the UPS store, they climbed up the stairs and entered the building, which was more a room. As she walked up to the counter with Neil behind her with the box of documents, she said, "Hello, my name is Barbara. I called you earlier." She quickly added, "I want to apologize."

"For what?"

"For being short and disrespectful."

The woman behind the counter paused a moment, then smiled. "Oh, yes, you have the old documents you want packaged and shipped." Barbara nodded. "I don't think you need to apologize for anything. I didn't take offense to anything you said. You were very polite, and I could tell these documents meant something to you." She looked in the box that Neil sat on the counter. "Don't you worry, dear, we will be very careful with them."

"Thank you for being so understanding."

"No problem, you can rest assure your documents will arrive safely at their destination."

After that, Barbara gave the information they requested and finally the address of where to ship the papers. When all the paperwork was completed the clerk asked, "Would you like insurance on the shipment?"

She gave the clerk a confident smile. "What do you suggest?"

She could see the clerk felt she was being complimented and replied, "Yes. It's always best. She rattled off the insurance coverage rates, and Barbara smiled at her, again saying. "What would you suggest?"

By the time they left the store, Barbara had no doubts their package was in the best of hands, and she relaxed.

Neil started up the car, smiling at first, then started laughing. "You did good, my dear. You did good."

Barbara grinned watching as he leaned over to turn on the GPS.

The conversation then turned to their planned visit. "I think the McBrides will appreciate our making the trip out to the vineyards. Most clients prefer a heads-up, but not in this case. I'm sure the McBrides like surprise visits."

Neil smiled at his wife, seeing how excited she was about being given a chance to design a vineyard building. She planned on taking as many pictures as possible. She asked, "Neil, did you hear more about them?"

"Well, tell me what else you heard. I want to be as knowledgeable as you seem to be about my new clients."

"Well, two women run the vineyard now...sisters, to be exact. Robin and Andréa McBride and before they started the business, neither knew the other existed. It seems Andrea grew up in New Zealand, while her sister grew up in Monterey, California. They had different mothers but shared the same father. "Asa McBride?"

"That's the man. Asa McBride, born and raised in Rochester, New York."

"Sisters that didn't know each other...how quaint."

"I don't think that is the right word for it, but as the store goes, their father was quite the character. Robin is nine years older than Andrea and her father had a short-lived relationship with her mother whom he met when he visited New Zealand. Rumor says he didn't know of Robin's birth. Anyway, Asa returned to Rochester and met Andrea's mother who was visiting her family and he left with her when she returned to Monterey. It was there they married and had Andrea. But Asa was a small-town boy, and he didn't feel comfortable there and ultimately he decided after Andrea was born that this wasn't the life for him. They parted on friendly terms, and he returned to his home in Rochester."

"So how did the girls meet?

"Well, Asa was getting older and so were the girls

and one day when Andrea visited him, he had just heard that Robin's mother had passed and that she had a daughter by him. It was the first time he knew of Robin, and he corresponded with her and asked her to come join him at his vineyard. She did. Once she was there he told her about Andrea, and they met and that's the whole story."

Barbara was emotional as she said, "That's a sad and beautiful story."

"Isn't that what you heard?" Neil asked.

"No, I only heard about Asa McBride's winery."

"What did you hear about it."

"Like you, I heard from another client who had referred me to do the job at the winery. I suggested you when I learned they not only needed an interior decorator, but also someone who could build and design an addition."

"In any case, in getting some history I learned that a Joseph Vinton whose grandfather came to Irondequoit some years back had a home on Irondequoit Bay. His father bought seventy acres of land and turned it into a resort called the Newport House and then the third generation, Joseph built a house above the resort. I spoke to Andrea McBride who informed me she and her sister owned the property now."

"Yes, the McBrides own the property now." Neil added. "The last I heard, the Vinton's owned it up until the mid-1900s and they were the ones who planted the grapes."

"It changed hands when Asa McBride visited the Vinton vineyards and was impressed by what he saw so he formed a partnership with a man named Joseph Warren and they purchased the vineyard." He paused and turning slightly to look at Barbara added, "As I mentioned earlier, they built the stone wine cellar that stood for many years halfway down the hill on the Bay front."

"And I now know all there is to know about cellars." Barbara said jokingly.

Neil gave her a look, then said, "Well, McBride bought out Mr. Warren and developed a majorly successful wine business and near the end of the 1900s he built a new wine cellar on the level ground at the end of Ridge Rd. above the Bay."

"I think we saw that on our boat tour."

"Yes, I think we did. McBride operated the business until the beginning of 1899 until his health took a turn. Luckily over the years he had introduced his daughter to the workings of the vineyard and later, when he learned of his other daughter, Robin, he introduced her to the job of running a winery. He died content knowing they planned to keep the vineyard."

Barbara shook her head. "Here I was telling you about a new client and you end up knowing more about them than I do."

"Okay, I have to be straight with you." She could tell Neil was smiling. "I heard you were meeting with this McBride, and I did a little research ahead to help you out. You know I have the best research team at my fingertips. I would have shared them with you, but it was more fun this way."

Barbara smiled. "Okay smarty, if you have so much research assistance, have you thought about getting more details on this house."

"I did."

"So, what did you find out."

They had arrived at the McBride winery. "Ah, we're here."

There were quite a few cars in the parking lot as they drove into the parking area. "This is lovely." Barbara said as all thoughts of unanswered questions about their house left her head as her mind caught up with his. This spot before them was breathtaking.

"I agree. Come on, let's go in.".

Chapter 26

At first they were a little unhappy that the McBride sisters were not directing the tour, but the guide whose name was Anton was extremely knowledgeable and they soon settled back, realizing that Anton was truly knowledgeable as he began his discussion.

"Growing grapes is truly a way of life and a means of income for the McBrides, but they love what they are doing and where they are doing it."

The guide was joined by a woman who introduced herself as Lydia and told a little history of the vineyard, which both Barbara and Neil already knew and only half listened as they took in the beauty of the property.

"You are all here at the proper time. Anyone interested in a wine tour should seriously consider coming in the autumn as you have. The vineyards are the most beautiful and vibrant from September to October."

After a pause, Anton continued, "So, if you're ready, let's begin the tour." Lydia added, "I hope you have comfortable shoes. If not we have some boots we can lend you. The paths are not level that run through the vineyards."

When no one spoke up, Lydia led, and they all began moving forward behind her. Anton followed at the rear so that if anyone missed what she was saying or had a question, one of them would hear and answer.

At the top of the hill Lydia paused. "One of the most romantic parts of visiting a winery is gazing out across the endless rows of vines with grapes just waiting to be brought to maturity. Take a moment to take it all in."

The group dispersed to move along the edge of the lawn. It was breathtaking to see the even, manicured rows of vines that rose upward beyond the level of the ground around them.. Someone next to them said, "It's like a picture I once saw in a magazine."

"When have you looked at a magazine." His partner said kiddingly and pushed her body against his side, before moving back behind Lydia.

Lydia walked them to the path between a row of grapes. She turned and smiled. "This is where the real tour begins." She paused, spreading out her arms to expand the area. "I hope you will find each phase of the tour an educational experience as well as enjoyable." With that they started walking down the rows of the season's harvests and at several points they were invited to pluck a few grapes and sample them straight from the vine. Barbara sampled several and when she stuck out her tongue, it was purple. Neil did the same as he pulled her against him in a bear hug before moving on.

A member of the group asked, "How can you grow grapes in our climate?"

Lydia responded, "That's why there are a few known regions in NY that provide adequate heat for producing grapes. These include the Hudson River region, Long Island, the Finger Lakes, and the Lake Erie region. All four of these regions are near large bodies of water which acts as a heat battery that helps to keep the surrounding area warmer throughout the season. We have Lake Ontario."

They couldn't' have chosen a more perfect day for

their visit. This autumn day had their spirits soaring as brilliant shafts of sunlight caress their bodies keeping them just warm enough to be comfortable during the tour. When the tour ended, they resignedly turned around and Anton led the group back the way they had come.

When they stepped onto the lawn again, he said, "Now, we are headed inside to see the production area of the winery."

Neil was excited to see this production area as he had been commissioned to work not only on the tasting rooms, but this part as well.

The wine-making process area was huge, and he paused in awe before stepping inside the building. As soon as everyone was inside, Anton moved them about explaining harvest, grape selection, fermentation, ageing and bottling.

Someone behind Neil asked, "Is it time to do some wine tasting yet?" Several people laughed as did Anton who replied, "No, not quite yet, but soon. He moved forward and the group followed as he took them down to the cellar.

It was indeed spectacular. They were surrounded by beautiful wooden barrels and endless rows of bottles that they walked through smelling the fermenting grapes and hearing all about the process being done before the wine made it to the final process of bottling for sale. When they emerged they were all anxious to now taste what they had witnessed being processed. And thankfully the last stop was to the tasting rooms.

The experience of tasting was not just yet as the guides talked a little more about the grape varieties and their taste. Inside the first tasting room were plaques telling the family history and the group walked about reading them while Lydia told the story that was detailed, but not as detailed as what Neil and Barbara had learned.

Then came the fun part. They were guided into the

second tasting room that was laid out with tables covered with white tablecloths and a basket of tiny bottles of their wine as a centerpiece. Soon they were each given a *flight* of samples of wine to try.

Along with the wine there were grapes, meats, crackers and cheeses provided to accompany the wine tasting.

Four were seated at each table, but there was little conversation at first as they were all quite hungry. But their eyes met at times as they nodded their approval of the wines they were sampling. Finally the experience was over, and Neil said to Barbara and the couple at the table with them, "I would do this again in a heartbeat."

The room had been filled with chatter, but suddenly it grew quiet. Neil and Barbara who had their backs to the entrance, looked at the couple at the table with them, who said, "Turn around. I think it's our hosts."

Neil and Barbara turned their chairs so that they could see them. "Hello. I am Andrea McBride, and this is my sister, Robin. We are pleased to see you and hope you have enjoyed the tour."

Robin smiled and added, "We welcome you to go into the next room that serves as a store front where you can purchase not only our wines, but the food you have sampled during your wine tasting."

"Again thank you for your patronage."

They then turned and disappeared.

Barbara turned to Neil, "Should we track them down about working on the buildings?"

"No, I think this is the proper way to end the tour and we'll contact them later about doing the work."

Barbara agreed and they left to go to the store where they made several purchases before leaving."

Chapter 27

It had been a full day and they were both ready to call it a night as they headed toward home. They pulled into the drive and just as Barbara was about to get out, she heard something. She frowned, hesitating a moment trying to identify what she heard. She wasn't sure what it was so decided it was probably the wind.

When she joined Neil at the front door, he had his key in the lock, but was not turning it. He seemed frozen on the spot, staring at the door. Barbara leaned forward so that she could see his face and her movement brought him back. He smiled at her and commenced turning the key in the lock. They walked in together.

They spent a quiet evening eating leftovers and talking about the plans for the winery. Barbara's head was spinning as she came up with ideas to make it one of a kind and Neil was on the same track as he got up and went into his office to get a sketch pad.

During the tour, Barbara took a lot of pictures. She knew Neil had too, but while he was gone, she found the photos on her cell phone. She opened the photo app on her cell and then went through the photos she had taken, selecting the first one and then tapping the triple dots in the upper right to scroll to print. She clicked on their printer in the list and clicked on the printer icon. She continued, printing out several before Neil returned. They passed each other in the hallway as Barbara headed to the office to pick up the prints.

Neil stopped her. "No need, I got the photos off the printer for you. He held up his hand that held a sketch pad and the photos. Barbara stood on tip toes to kiss his cheek and they headed back to the kitchen island together.

Once seated, they finished the last of the food on their plates and each gathered and carried it all over to the sink to rinse and put into the dishwasher. Then, Barbara started the coffeemaker while Neil got out two cups. Soon they were back at the island. "Rip me off a couple sheets from your pad, please." Barbara said.

Without a word, Neil handed her a couple of sheets and they both began checking out the photos and picking one to start their sketches. When they reached for the same photo, their hands met and they turned to face each other, smiled and kissed before one of them moved to another choice.

They forgot all about being tired as they worked on the rough sketches while the areas not shown in the photos were fresh in their minds. When they were happy with what they had come up with, they laid down their pencils and stretched in unison.

"Show me what you got," Neil said to Barbara as he handed her his drawings.

They looked at the other's renditions and then made comments that had them crafting minor changes. Then they shared the sketches again.

They loved working together like this and never took offense to either one's suggestion for change. It had been a while since they had worked on the same project, if of course you discounted their property, and both of them enjoyed it immensely. Finally the results of walking outside in the fresh air at the vineyard, and the wine tasting they had done set in. Barbara was the first up as she picked up their coffee cups and put them into the dishwasher while Neil went to get the box of wines they had purchased and carried them over to the wine fridge at the far end of the kitchen. When they were done, Barbara went over to join Neil. He put his arm around her waist and together they walked over to turn off the lights downstairs, double checked to make sure the door was locked and then headed up to bed.

Once in the bedroom, they went directly into the bathroom and while one brushed their teeth, the other climbed into the shower. They later switched places. Then after several minutes, went into the bedroom together.

Neil reached over and pulled Barbara close to him. They were no longer feeling fatigued as he pressed his lips against her and pulled her body close to his. He closed his eyes as they moved gently together, forgetting themselves as they savored the moment of being as one.

When Neil fell on his back, breathing heavily, Barbara reached over and rubbed his shoulder gently. Minutes later they were fast to sleep.

Light streamed through the window and Barbara woke staring up at the ceiling until she got her bearings. She then sat up and reached over to Neil's side of the bed. As usual he was already up. She heard him in the bathroom and climbed out of bed and padded over to the bathroom to join him. By the time she entered, he had stepped out the shower and was drying off. "Ah, sleeping beauty arises," he said as he moved closer and kissed her on the top of her head.

"Ah, prince charming. How did you sleep."

"Well, after that wonderful aphrodisiac, fine, just fine." Barbara nudged him gently and then went over to the sink to brush her teeth while Neil headed out the door. She moved over to the doorway and watched as he dropped the towel from around his waist and started rummaging in drawers for his clothes.

Back in college, Barbara had taken an anatomy course and as she stared at her husband she saw the perfect image of a mesomorph body, a body meant to admire. His build was athletic, muscular and rectangular in shape, and he was strong. She was quite his opposite. Her body classification was that of ectomorphs as she was lean, with a delicate bone structure and fast metabolism that made it hard for her to gain weight or muscle mass and that was fine with her.

Just as she admired his body, she knew he found hers to his liking and that made her happy as she went back to the sink, spit, rinsed and then stepped out of her nightclothes to climb in the shower.

She was lucky to have naturally curly hair that she needn't fuss with to make her presentable. She washed her hair and her body and then turned off the shower and put on a towel turban before stepping out of the shower. She stood on the wooden mat and dried her body thoroughly. Soon she was on her way to the bedroom to put on her clothes for the day. Since it wasn't a workday, she chose knit slacks, and a long comfy top. She made the bed and headed downstairs to join Neil.

She found him in the kitchen, leaning over the island and looking over the drawings they had made the night before.

Without looking up he said, "These are good."

"Good morning to you too, my dear," Barbara replied playfully.

"Sorry, sweetie," Neil said looking up and smiling.

"But these are really good."

Barbara went over to him and with their sides touching surveyed their work. "Yes, we did good. I think we can make the call first thing Monday morning to visit our client."

"Great. They will be surprised how prepared we are." He paused and gently pulled Barbara to him. "We make a wonderful team. I'm sure we are one of the few architects and interior designers that come prepared like this."

Barbara smiled. "That's because we want what we want. This way we guide our clients to our conclusions and not the other way around."

They laughed and Neil hugged her tightly. "Okay, enough. Let's get some breakfast in us. We have a heavy schedule today."

Barbara gave him a puzzled look.

"I know you didn't forget. We're going to walk the perimeters of the sunken garden today." As an afterthought he added, "You can take your camera and I'll bring the sketching pad and we can work our magic."

Neil couldn't see the expression on his wife's face, and she was careful to gently pull out of his embrace before she spoke, "Okay, let's see how breakfast goes before we start getting ahead of ourselves."

Neil took his wife's words jokingly and turned to help her get their breakfast on the table.

Barbara stood at the sink filling a pan with water and Neil went to the cabinet to get the egg boiler. He filled four containers with eggs and screwed on the tops before taking them over to Barbara who placed them in the water. She set the timer on the stove while Neil opened the appliance caddy and pulled out the shelf. He put the toaster on it and plugged it in, then went to get two slices of bread. On his way back to the counter, he turned on the coffeemaker and instead of individual cups, set it for the pot, knowing they would probably want more than one cup.

Working together, they soon had their breakfast of soft-boiled eggs and toast ready, along with orange slices and coffee which they cleared the space and sat on the island.

They were both hungry and ate in silence.

When they had cleaned their plates Barbara, wanting to stall the inevitable, started, "What did you learn about this house."

"Come on, let's go into the living room and sit. It's more comfortable there and from the tone in your voice I have a feeling this is going to be a long conversation."

Barbara nodded. They refilled their coffee cups and carried them into the living room. Once they were seated, Neil said that he had started with the property deed and knew that the Bemish family had built the house in 1918 and Mr. Bemish was an art dealer, which would give some credence to why they have this sunken garden on the estate.

Barbara knew he had told her that before and again considered it and decided it did make sense. "So, did you find out anything else?

"Just what I mentioned earlier that his wife, Georgia was heir to the J.K. Post Drug company that was a big deal back then."

"Humm."

"So, do you have anything to add?" Neil asked Barbara.

"Like I said earlier, not really...at least not yet."

Neil had an odd expression as he added, "You know, when I spoke to the realtor he said something strange."

"What was that?" Barbara said, sitting up straighter and leaning toward her husband, anxiously waiting for his next words.

Neil hesitated as if trying to comprehend what he was about to share. "Well, he said not only had they not entered the premises, but they had also been duly sworn not to."

"Why was that...did he say why?"

"Matter of fact, he didn't."

"Well, didn't you ask?"

"At the time I didn't think anything of it, but I wish I had."

"So what else did he say."

"He said that until recently they were told no one was to go near the property and any maintenance should be only to the front lawn so that it looked lived in."

"What about selling the place."

Neil was thoughtful. "Yes, that was interesting too. They have had the property in their possession but were told not to sell, lease or rent the premises under any circumstances."

"But..."

"Yes, I know. They sold it to us and when I asked Warren Pendergast why, he said he had no idea why. Only that someone, a relative, lawyer, or someone with authority called around the time we came here and said that the property was released for sale."

She could see he was struggling with something. "What, what is it?"

Neil hesitantly added, "I don't know." He shook his head and laughed. "Oh, come on, let's not make a big deal out of it. They decided to sell, and we got the property.

That's it."

"Did you tell Warren about the sinkhole."

"Sunken Garden."

"Sorry, sunken garden. Did you tell him?"

Neil was quiet. "Neil!"

"Huh," he said shaking his head as if trying to clear his brain."

"Did you tell Warren about the garden or did he know about it."

"No, I didn't tell Warren and as far as I could ascertain, no one knew it was there."

Barbara looked closely at her husband. "You're holding something back. I can tell. Come on, tell me everything."

"It's nothing, really, but Warren isn't available."

"What does that mean?"

"When I called the realtor office to speak to him…" He paused and stared off in the distance, "Well, I just haven't been able to reach him. At first I thought he was out showing houses or with a client, but now when I think about it, I haven't seen him since he closed the deal on the house."

"Well, that's normal. People generally don't see their realtors once the deal is finalized."

"Yes, I know, but… Oh, forget it. I'm just being silly."

"No tell me."

"Seriously, you're right. We hadn't struck up a lasting friendship, just did a business deal and that was that." Neil shrugged his shoulders and changed the subject. "So if I remember correctly we had a deal."

Barbara looked up. "What was that?"

"You said that once we finished our, ah, scavenger hunt, you would go in the garden with me."

Barbara sought hard for a reason to renege on the promise, if only temporarily. It so fascinated him, but it gave her the creeps so she said, "Yes, I did, but I can't really get an innovative idea for the area until it is all uncovered. I need to see everything that is there. We might want to save some of it so I will need to design something that will blend in."

"Barbara…"

"Seriously. It's the same for you when you need to add an addition to a home, you have to study the property and not just the house itself if you want to design something that works…am I right?"

Neil nodded. "Okay, you win. But we're talking quite some time. When I spoke to the contractor, Nathaniel, he admitted that it was going to take a while to clear the area. They have to go slowly and at some point have to use shovels so as not to ruin whatever is under there. That plus dragging out the tree trunks and bushes which could also cause more damage."

"I know, but I don't mind waiting. It's a mess and like they said, it is dangerous to be out there." Neil resignedly agreed.

"Besides, we have a lot going on and we still need to check closets for cubby holes and find the combination for the safe."

Chapter 28

Neil had heard that Rochester was one of the snowiest cities in the United States, but he took it with a grain of salt.

It had been a great summer for business as well as for the weather and so far there had been nothing but good coming out of their decision to move to Rochester, settling in an historical Irondequoit mansion and fitting into the quiet lifestyle of the area. They both loved living there and they especially loved the house, which for all intents and purposes was done, except in the eye of a designer. In Barbara's mind there was always something to tweak or a room that required a total overhaul.

The best part for them was the fact that unlike jobs in NY City, the work was always within driving distance, and a pleasant, uncongested drive at that. And they were finding most of the work required the talents of them both, so they worked together on many jobsites.

That first year of 95' was amazing. Going to so many jobsites gave them a chance to not only see but feel the pulse of the city and the suburban areas. Even the weather cooperated with mainly good seasonal weather, but then things changed.

Barbara could look back and know the exact day that it happened because it marked the first day that the contractor had informed them they were finally getting somewhere in unearthing the sunken garden.

When they had purchased the house at Parcel 076.06 Winona, in April of 1995 and after an earthquake of noticeable size she was ecstatic to learn there was what seemed to be a sunken garden on the East side of the property. While she did research to help her get an idea of how to design such a garden since it would be her first attempt, Neil was trying to find out who had built it and when. So, on a day trip with little convincing on either part, they went to see the one sunken garden in their area.

It was a cool autumn day as they made their way to Warner Castle. When Barbara was told about the sunken garden nearby, Neil hadn't mentioned that it was part of a castle, so she was in for two surprises.

Neil took the more scenic route to Highland Park. As they pulled out of their driveway on Winona Blvd Barbara couldn't hide her enthusiasm. She had never seen a sunken garden but had figured that it had to be much like any garden in any location. She was deep in thought as Neil turned right onto St. Paul Blvd. They drove five miles and at that point, St. Paul turned into South Avenue. He stayed in the middle lane on South Avenue as directed by the GPS as the lane turned toward the left. In less than a mile he turned right onto Mt. Hope Avenue and drove a little over a mile to reach Reservoir Avenue. In less than 20 minutes they arrived at their destination.

Neil turned to see his wife was busy writing on her notepad, so he tapped her on the shoulder. "What..." she started as she lifted her head and started to turn her eyes toward Neil. Only she stopped midway in awe as her eyes stared out the windshield. There, majestically stood a castle.

"What is this?" Barbara said breathlessly.

"A surprise. I didn't want to tell you ahead of time that the sunken garden was part of a castle. Can you believe it. A castle just a few minutes from our home."

Barbara was shaking her head in disbelief, while Neil parked the car in the small parking lot for Warner Castle that put them directly in front of the building.

"What a surprise."

"I know, I was taken aback when they told me. Over there," he pointed, "is a reservoir and this area is called Highland Park."

They got out of the car and headed toward the door of the castle with Barbara snapping pictures all the way.

Warner Castle sits atop an elevated site, overlooking Mt. Hope Avenue and they stood a moment to pay homage before walking around to the entrance gates that were near the gate house on Mt. Hope Avenue.

Once inside Barbara had to use her imagination to picture what the interior would have looked like, while Neil read information on a pamphlet he found near the entrance.

"The Castle was built in 1854 by Horatio Gates Warner, bank president, court judge, and newspaper publisher. It was an imposing fortress constructed by architect Merwin Austin and modeled after the ancestral castle of the Scottish Clan Douglas and constructed of locally quarried limestone. After Warner's death, the family continued to occupy the house for another generation."

Barbara walked over to view a display and Neil went with her. She read, "The castle, sits amidst a 50-acre farm, located at the edge of the city, In 1902, the castle was sold to Mr. and Mrs. George Ramsdell and, in 1912, to businessman, Frank Dennis and his wife, Merry. Mrs. Dennis replaced an old barn at the rear of the property with the Sunken Garden, designed by Alling DeForest,

Rochester's most acclaimed landscape architect during the first half of the 20th century."

Barbara paused and looked at her husband. "Do you think that this Alling DeForest built our sunken garden?"

"I don't know."

"Someone had to. I'm sure the Bemishes even with all their talent had to have help from someone."

Barbara turned back to reading. "Among his other projects are the gardens at the George Eastman House and Harbel Manor, the Harvey Firestone estate in Akron, Ohio."

Barbara paused again. "Neil, we need to go see those gardens too. That would be interesting and give us some ideas as well."

"We did see the George Eastman House and the gardens there, but if you want, we will go check out the others, the first chance we get."

Barbara nodded absently as she began reading again, "Mrs. Dennis died in the 1930s and the castle stood empty for several years, While there has been some remodeling over the more than 150 years, the interior retains its high ceilings, tall windows, walnut woodwork, marble and parquet floors, and an impressive entry hall with scenic wallpaper and grand staircase."

Barbara was in awe as they walked by the many flower beds on their way to the sunken garden. "I wonder why my friends never mentioned this?"

"Well, from what I learned not many people know about this. It's hidden in plain sight. Right here in Highland Park."

"That's a real shame. Something so awe-inspiring and grandiose should not be kept a secret. It's so mysterious with its secret-filled, labyrinthine; that it should be in all the travel brochures."

They continued walking around the outside of the

castle where there were bushes and flowers planted all around them. Barbara could tell they had planted the gardens so that there would be something in bloom at all times and she made a note in her pad to take that into consideration.

"So, does it say in your pamphlet who owns Warner Castle now?"

Neil looked through the pamphlet he had and read, "Warner Castle served as a private residence until 1951 when the city of Rochester purchased the castle and its gardens."

They continued walking and came upon a small garden planted in a courtyard. And ventured further into the grounds to see Warner Castle's Sunken Gardens.

At first Barbara was hesitant as she stood admiring the garden that she could see had steps going down and bridges going over the area. It was what she had envisioned their own would look like and it scared her.

But then Neil touched her arm and she felt silly as she allowed herself to admire the garden.

There were stone and concrete stairs going down to the first level that had a wrought iron railing. It went over an area that below had three arched openings with wrought iron gates. As they continued down the slope they came to first, three steps, then a short turn to the last staircase to take them all the way down into the base of the garden.

It was indeed breathtaking with a stone wall, decorative bushes, flowers and a designed concrete area with circular inlays. A stone and brick walk served as the backdrop and there was a lot of greenery. At the far end was a large stone planter suspended above a circular container of wildflowers below the ones growing in the stone planter above.

Even the pathways were a design element of squares and circles containing grassy areas. Then in front of them they saw another exit. The exit at this end had two flights of stairs separated by the central display of flowers.

Barbara turned to Neil, smiling. "It's so simplistic in its design and would be quite easy to maintain. I wonder if it has always been this way?"

Neil tilted his head. "Maybe. They may add flowers or just keep it this way all the time.

"Well, I like it, but I think I want more flowers in ours. Lots of color will be nice."

Neil smiled. "You can do what you want in ours. It's your playground my dear so do as you will."

"I'm hoping there are concrete stone walls in ours. If not, I can add them."

"Let's wait and see. So far we know that there is something of stone…maybe a statue of some kind. At least that's what the contractor thinks. But it will be some time before we really get to see it."

"I can wait." Barbara said, wondering why this garden felt so calming and she didn't get that feeling when she first went to see the area that covered up what had been determined to be a sunken garden. She shrugged her shoulders and put her arm through Neil's as they made their way to the parking lot.

When they reached the car, she started to say something to Neil, but the moment was loss when they both turned to watch a woman who was doing acrobatics on the front lawn.

Chapter 29

As they were driving back, Barbara asked, "So, how deep do you think the sunken garden at the house might be."

Neil was thoughtful "Well, I would be just guessing, but I would think it might be around fifteen to twenty."

"Feet?"

Neil nodded. "It's a guess, but the last time I spoke to the contractor he said that just to the top of that cement structure he thinks might be a statue of some sort, had to be at least five feet down."

Barbara wanted to get excited after seeing the other garden, but something kept bothering her. She remembered her dream, if it was that because seeing the dirt on her feet fought off the belief it was. It seemed to be a warning. At that moment she lost the feeling of planning a design for it.

"What's my wife thinking?"

Barbara gave him a smile. "Oh, nothing, just tired and ready to call it a day."

They drove toward home, deciding to stop and pick up something for dinner. At first they thought it would be fun to cook out, but that idea died quickly. It wasn't that they didn't like a cookout, but that they didn't feel like waiting. When they exited the expressway and were sitting at the light, Neil said, "What about Chinese food. We could stop at

Great Win Chinese Restaurant. Sara and Paul gave it a thumbs up."

Yes, let's do that.

The restaurant wasn't busy when they arrived and having decided what they wanted to eat, they placed their orders, then sat on a bench to wait for their name to be called. One thing about Chinese Restaurants, they have their equipment at the ready at all times so getting out the orders is done quickly and efficiently. When they were signaled to come to the counter, the fragrance of the food had their stomachs growling and they wasted no time getting home.

Once at home, they were barely in the door before heading to the kitchen to put the contents of the bag on the island.

"Should I make us some tea," Barbara asked.

"Sure but make it decaf."

While Barbara put on the teakettle, got out the teabags and napkins, Neil unpacked the food. Soon they were seated at the island and enjoying the meal that they ate ravenously. When the kettle whistled, Barbara fell off her stool.

Neil started to laugh, but when he got up to help her and saw her face, he stopped. Barbara was having a panic attack. Neil quickly went to get her some water to drink, and he dampened a paper towel to wipe off her face, which was covered with Chinese food. When she fell, she managed to send what was left of her food down with her.

He lifted her head so that she could drink, then laid her down and began wiping her face and neck. He used his fingers to try and get the noodles out of her curls, but finally gave up.

"Are you all right? Can you hear me?"

Barbara gave him a weak nod.

Trying to make light of the moment, he added, "That teakettle really scared the bejesus out of you. I'm going to give it a piece of my mind."

Barbara smiled. It wasn't the kettle that had scared her. It was that at that moment, she had felt hands on her shoulders and a voice whispering in her ear. At first she thought it was the sound of the teakettle, but this was clearly the voice of a woman. She thought immediately that it sounded like Mindy Worthington, the woman she had met on the boat tour. The one that she apparently was the only person to be able to see.

But then she knew it wasn't her voice. She had talked to her at length and this voice was different, softer as she whispered, "Don't let him near the sunken garden."

Neil helped her up. "I'm going to the powder room. I'll be right back."

Neil watched her leave and then went about cleaning up the floor, the food and dishes on the island.

Barbara stood in front of the mirror looking at her image. There were traces of what they had eaten on her face, and she turned on the water and began washing her face and neck. She reached over to grab the hand towel, then looking in the mirror, started removing the food from her hair. When she was done, she stood staring in the mirror and, surprised herself when she asked, "Who are you?"

She was more surprised when a voice said, "Georgia...Georgia Bemish."

"What?" she asked, fear apparent in her voice, but there was no response. She stood there waiting a moment and then shaking her head said, "Barbara, you better get a grip." She tried smiling and left the powder room.

The one thing about their marriage that she liked the most was that they were always honest with each other, but for some reason she felt as though she couldn't share this with Neil. She knew he hadn't seen Mindy and her husband on the boat and for sure he would be shocked if she said she had seen another ghost, so she didn't mention it.

Instead she gave her husband a smile. "I'm okay, no damage beyond food in my hair." She then went about getting them each a cup of tea. They continued sitting at the now clean island staring at each other. Finally Neil spoke. "Barbara, are you really all right?"

She could hear the worry in his voice. "Yes, I'm fine, really. I guess I was tired and not expecting the kettle to whistle so it frightened me."

"Okay, let's blame the kettle."

"What do you mean?"

"I don't know, it's just that you looked…Oh," he said as he reached across and grabbed her hand. "Forget it, we're both tired. Why don't we have a little wine and watch tv for a while."

"That sounds wonderful."

So, they did just that. Barbara managed to put aside what she had heard, and Neil tried to believe his wife was okay.

At the end of the show, Neil went around checking the windows and doors while Barbara carried their cups to the kitchen. She washed them and sat them in the strainer to dry, then joined Neil. A few minutes later, together they went up to bed.

Chapter 30

Days turned into months and months into years with the activity on cleaning out the sunken garden going slowly. That was fine with Barbara and had to be for Neil as they had a lot of business coming in and were spending most of their time at jobsites. When there was spare time, Barbra spent it trying to find the illusive piece of paper with the combination to the safe and sometimes Neil would help, if he weren't busy working on drawings for an upcoming job.

To make it interesting though Neil turned it into a game, asking her questions and supplying the answers. From the paint on the home's interior to the creaking floorboards, he supplied amazing facts about their home. Of course she knew that the home's front door served as an entryway, the air conditioning system kept the place cool, and those double-paned windows kept street noise to a peaceful minimum. However, every part of the house had countless features that do things she never even knew about. From the secret benefit of dormer windows to the original reason for picture rails, she began to admire what Neil knew about houses and when he finally called it quits, she was a little disappointed, but so much wiser.

One evening Neil, sure there wasn't one more hidy-hole left to check said, "That's it. I'm calling a locksmith."

Barbara would have suggested it, but she had used it

as an excuse to stay away from the garden at first, but then she became enthused with learning about every square inch of their home in a way she wouldn't have if they hadn't done the search.

But, alas, it was time and she watched as Neil went through a search to find a locksmith. "This one sounds like what we need," he said, then read out loud. "*My Locksmith* was founded in 2010 in Rochester, NY. We have been servicing Monroe County and the surrounding area for years. We pursue professionalism and customer satisfaction to meet our customers' needs. Our work is known for its reliable security and quality services."

"Don't they all say that?"

"Sure, but I picked this one just for you."

"How is that."

"It was founded by Sharon Zah."

Barbara read the screen. "She grew up in a locksmith family business, and not only had the experience but also the knowledge of the diverse types of locks and securities solutions." She continued reading. "I like that it says Sharon kept up to date with the newest technology available in the locksmith industry."

When she finished, she leaned closer to Neil and gave him a kiss. "You are indeed a smart man, my husband. A very smart and understanding man. If given the choice I do tend to favor women owned businesses, so thank you."

She leaned against him with her arms around his waist as he made the call and set up the appointment. The appointment was set for the following week.

In the meantime they received a call from the document restorer. Neil put the phone on speaker, and they listened excitedly as the caller said the documents had been restored successfully.

He went on to explain they had to flatten the hard

creases and reduce the adhesive residue along the edges of the piece. They repaired tears, strengthened the paper and deacidified it to prevent further deterioration.

At that point Neil took the phone off speaker and Barbara listened as he finally gave them his credit card number and made arrangements for the documents to be returned.

When he finished on the phone and turned to Barbara she could tell there was something he wasn't sharing. All he said was, "They're mailing the documents to us."

When the locksmith came, Barbara half expected it to be the owner, but instead it was a Mr. Henderson who worked for *My Locksmith*. He began by saying before he could proceed he needed *proof* they were the owners of the safe, but his boss knew the house and that it hadn't been lived in since sometime in the early 1900s. She had checked and verified they had purchased the home, so he was good to go.

Neil smiled as he led him to the safe that was built into the wall. "That's why I couldn't get the model number," he said.

M. Henderson checked it over and finally said, "This is an expensive safe, even by today's standards so, I want to save it if possible."

Neil stepped back and gave the locksmith some room as he went about determining what to do. He came prepared with manuals and shuffled to the one he knew was the brand, then he took his cell phone and dialed a number.

They stood watching his face, trying to piece together the conversation as he gave his company name, his name and some numbers that they didn't have a clue what they meant. When he disconnected the call, he was smiling. "I think we've got it." He moved to the safe and over his shoulder said, "They have an override code for this model." He proceeded to enter it and soon the door of the safe opened.

Still smiling he said, "Okay, I think what you can do is one of two things now. Using the same lock, change it to either a key lock or combination lock."

Barbara and Neil looked at each other and said at the same time, "Key lock please."

Surprised the locksmith said, "Are you sure. The combination lock is saver."

Neil smiled. "Yes, we know that, but I think having the key is best for something permanent like this. If we sold…I'm not saying we will, but if we did, the new owners won't have to search for the combination like we did. A key would be simpler. A key we can hand over easily."

Mr. Henderson tried to keep a straight face, but when the homeowners started laughing, he joined in.

So he reset the safe for '*key entry only*' and on the spot he made two keys. Now they could use the safe and they each had a key.

The restored documents did not arrive due to the worst blizzard in history. It was February 28th when it started and the snow fell for 63 hours straight, making this the worst snowstorm and deepest snowpack ever seen in Rochester. The monster storm halted businesses and disrupted lives through the Great Lakes region, with cities from Cleveland to Buffalo to Montreal reporting blizzard conditions. This storm came on the heels of another storm two days earlier. Parts of the New York State Thruway closed, as did local malls and every other place of business. The storm forced cancellation of most train services, blocked roads, closed schools, and had the electric and gas company doing their best to restore service to those who had lost it, but not much could be done until the storm ended on March 2.

It was like a winter wonderland with snow piled in 10-foot drifts and in other places, hip high making passage impossible. A good portion of this mammoth snowfall was lake-effect from Lake Ontario, so Irondequoit faced major snow removal problems.

Transportation networks grinded to a halt, and schools were closed for two days straight while snow removal services worked on clearing the main areas first. It was several weeks before roads were opened and airplanes able to take off, but passenger trains resumed service much quicker. For most the restoration of heat that was followed by cable, made the waiting more bearable.

During this period, the Sanders stayed huddled up around their fireplace, glad they had the intuition to cut up and store the wood taken out of the sunken garden on the side porch. Since food storage was a problem, they ate a lot of dry cereal and opened cans of soup to heat in the fireplace. It was like they were camping and since the house was well insulated and neither doors nor windows leaked, the heat held in the house.

When mail service resumed, there were several deliveries made each day so once they managed to clear a path, they checked the mailbox often. And finally the restored documents arrived and that gave Neil and Barbara something to do while they waited since the safe hadn't presented anything of interest to them.

It was indeed amazing work that the restoration company had done. At first they just admired each piece of paper before finally looking closely at what they contained.

Neil tried to get Barbara out of the room, but she

wasn't going anywhere and sat on the sofa beside him as they opened each document for a closer look.

Then, just by his actions she was sure she knew what had upset Neil during his conversation with the restorer and what had him wanting her to leave the room, because Neil's face changed as he uncovered the letter.

It was a letter written by Georgia Bemish, the wife of William Bemish. These were the original owners of the house. They were the ones who had it built and Neil was hoping this would tell more about the sunken garden.

Barbara reached over to pick it up. "No, now wait, let's go over the house plans first. Wouldn't you like to go over them with me?"

She could tell he not only wanted her to wait, but he also wanted to wait. So, Barbara removed her hand and nodded.

He leafed through to the large, oversized package of the house plans and they looked them over together. They checked out every inch of the construction of the property, but there was no mention of a sunken garden on any of the sheets. Disappointed, they sat back. "I'm sorry, sweetie. I really thought there would be something about the garden."

"Me too."

"I was hoping to at least find out how deep and how wide it was so I could share that with the contractor. That would help out a lot."

"Oh, well, we'll just have to wait it out."

Neil turned to her. "Wouldn't you like to know the layout beforehand so you could design a plan around what was originally there."

Barbara stared straight ahead, thinking before she spoke. "That would be helpful, but until it is revealed, we haven't a clue what still exists down there." She paused and rubbed her hands together. "And, who knows what can be repaired."

"You're right. Why get our hopes up. I understand."

There were several other documents that laid out the costs and then there was the paper that had been written by Georgia, as well as Georgia's diary. Those interested her the most. She had actually been able to read a few lines before they sent the diary out for restoration and what she read was interesting, even exciting. Georgia had written about her ideas for decorating the house and about people she met, but none of the areas of the book could she read more than a few words. Now as she picked it up and opened the first page, she could see it was legible again. As she checked though it, there were only a few areas they weren't able to restore the full contents, but that was fine. She was sure she would get the gist of the writings.

But most interesting was that document written by Georgia. The restorer had obviously shared the contents with Neil when he talked to them privately on the phone. That was her main interest now as she again reached for it.

"Barbara, I think you should wait on this."

"Why."

"I think it's a little weird and it might…"

"What Neil…shock me?"

"Yes."

"Okay, we will look at it together, but right now. I don't want to wait."

Resigned, Neil gave in and lifted the letter. With Barbara leaning in, they read the document together.

Chapter 31

My name is Georgia Bemish, and I am not crazy so if you have this letter in your possession, I ask that you stay away from IT!

Barbara looked up at Neil. "What do you think she means by 'IT'?

"I'm not sure." He started reading again.

Let me tell you my story.

In 1918 my husband, William Bemish, a successful art dealer, and I came to live in Rochester, New York. I was a young bride then and eager to start our new life together. I had always been happy with my life, but I wanted my future to be with William.

We built a house in the area known as Irondequoit and I'm sure it is quite different from the way it was back then. We loved it almost as much as we loved each other.

We came to Rochester because William had heard great things about Rochester's art culture and that, plus the need to have more space boosted his confidence in settling in the area.

I admit that, born into a wealthy family, I was a little standoffish about coming but I loved him so and William having foresight about many things, assured me that the city was growing and how fun it would be, to be a part of its growth.

So, unsure of being able to fit into a society made up mostly of farmers I was pleasantly surprised to find I loved everything about the area and the people. Of course it behooved us to meet the high-born of the area and I found them to be just wonderful and not snobby or offish to the farmers, but genuinely seeing everyone as equals. I liked that.

Later I would learn it was more than just the business that drew him to Rochester. It was the openness of the area, unlike New York City maybe, but mostly because William had heard of the flu virus and wanted to get away.

In any case, we got a feel of the place on the boat ride to the Glen House where we would be staying. I can tell you the scenery was breathtaking, and the people were extremely approachable.

One person we met and would see often was John Carroll Leake whose farm was on St. Paul Blvd. near where we would settle. I mention this so that if it is still there, he has the most knowledge about the area and about us.

Neil paused. "What is it," Barbara asked.
"I know a John Leake, but it can't be the same one."
"No, but it could be a relative."
Neil nodded and continued.

It was wonderful to be introduced to so many interesting and friendly people even before we were officially a part of the community. I remember one of our acquaintances saying, everything in Irondequoit is fun and it was until...

Barbara pressed her chin into Neil's shoulder. "Ow. What was that for?"

"Sorry, I was wondering why she stopped so abruptly. Please go on."

Neil cleared his throat and began again.

Even hearing about the snow didn't faze me though I had heard rumors that the whole area shuts down during the winter.

Forgive me. I seem to be rattling on. Suffice it to say that the people were wonderful and our destination, the Glen House was indeed not only neat and clean, but its structure; a four-story building that was halfway between being a log cabin and a royal resort home, took my breath away. William felt the same as he asked about the builder. His name was A. J. Warner.

While working on getting the museum up and running, William hired J. Foster Warner, who worked with a McKim Mead White to build our home. From their meetings he learned that it would take a year to complete our home, but it didn't matter as we enjoyed staying at the Glen House.

If I could express what I liked most about William and me, it would be how well we worked together.

Barbara smiled, running her cheek against Neil's. He turned, understanding what she was thinking and then went back to reading.

I was excited about decorating the interior as much as William was excited about the structure. William knew what he wanted and that was the outside to be of brick and have clean lines, which J. Foster Warner was most famous for.

Need it to suffice, our heart and soul went into every nook and cranny of the inside and out.

When World War I came, William had been willing to serve his country as a soldier, but though he met the 5'7-inch height and was below 24 years in age, his weight was below 144 pounds. How he would have loved to brag to his future children that he had played a major part in the Great War, the largest war that the world had seen up to that time. To him it would have been interesting to see Europe and even go to the Middle East; places he never dreamed he would see in his lifetime.

On November 11, 1918, the fighting ended, and life returned to normal, that is until the Spanish flu pandemic came. It was the deadliest pandemic in world history, and it was said to be spread by the troops. When the threat of the flu ended in early 1920, most were afraid to get too excited as they waited for the next shoe to drop.

The War and the Spanish Flu made for a dramatic entrance to our new life in Rochester, New York and every person and business did their part, trying to keep the public safe during the pandemic.

Of course the war and the pandemic had stopped progress on the house, but the worse thing for me and those under unfortunates was learning that my mother had died, and I could not go to be with my family. How could so much happen I wondered, all at the same time.

When we moved into the house I was happy, but I

recalled later what had happened. I was putting the last few things away when I felt a small sharp jolt followed by a few stronger sharp shakes that passed quickly. Later there was static on the radio before we felt a gentle bump followed several seconds later by stronger waves of shaking.

It was William who realized first that we were having an earthquake.

The next morning there was a thunderous sound and I watched as the trees that blocked our view of St. Paul Blvd., being swallowed up in a massive sinkhole.

It was later that I came up with the idea of a sunken garden.

When they came to look at the sink hole, I had given it a lot of thought and broached the idea of turning it into a sunken garden; something I had read about some time ago.

William looked at the contractor, who turned and looked at his son and the son thought it a wonderful idea; especially since the ground was settled and it would not go any deeper or wider. He found the garden idea much more intriguing than just filling it in.

Neil paused. "What is it, dear?"

"Ah, it's just that our contractor asked his son the same thing when they started the project."

"What do you mean."

"Oh, just that our contractor asked his son, too."

Barbara thought that was a little odd, but she wanted to hear more so instead she asked Neil to continue.

And that's how I came up with the idea of a sunken garden.

Yes, it was me who thought of it, but it was William…William who began to change, spending every moment with the contractor and taking over the project. So from that point on, what I had seen as my project, became William's baby as he hired an architect and they worked together, coming to the site and then creating the drawings of the final design. Not once did William ask my advice and so I washed my hands with the project.

When he finally showed me what he had created, I was appalled. There was a concrete bridge over a deep concrete trench running all the way to the center of the sunken garden that William refused to call the sinkhole. Because of the length of the trench, two walkovers were designed.

There was a statue at the center of the cement structure where the water overflow would collect.

Stone steps went down to a domed structure that stopped four feet from the bridge. At that point, a cement walking path was poured that went around the perimeter of the sunken garden and a matching path running along the lower slope of the garden. Stone retaining walls ran along the edge of the garden area and at one point the wall was created in a four-foot circular pattern that wound into a small circle. In the center, a 'star' design was outlined in concrete.

Near the front where the ground level was close to 30 feet high, was a covered archway designed to match the structure of the home and around it was a matching stone and cement fence. From that covered area above, steps led down halfway and at that point split to either side of a wall of cement and brick. The oval was three feet deep and at the back a brick and stone enclosure was made to hold flowers or shrubbery.

Behind the bridge over the water was another stone bridge with thick stone and cement columns on either side of a circular arch. With the help of his talented mason who had worked in all the significant parts of the garden to make William's vision come true in concrete and stone construction, his next request required additional expertise.

So his mason contacted a metalworker to craft the iron gate of 'spider web' design, to be located in the 'Moon Gate' at the northeast corner of the garden under the bridge. The mason's name was Worthington.

"Stop," Barbara said.
"What is it?"
"The name. I know that name."
"Well, it is quite common."
Barbara gave Neil a weak smile, then said, "Go on."

With the base of the area completed, it was a matter of waiting for the statues that William had commissioned. The first to arrive was a Griffin that was sitting on the bridge over the spider web.

The next item to arrive was an antique cast iron garden sundial.

There were several other statues, but not any excited William more than the one he had installed in the center of the cement pond. It was Poseidon, holding his trident.

When he took me to see the finished product and asked what I thought, all I could say was that it was indeed a statement and I left it at that.

It was then that he turned the rest of the project over to me to add shrubbery and flowers. I was glad to do it since it needed some brightening up.

It wasn't until I was done did I realize there was something down there.

Barbara had a puzzled expression on her face as she turned to stare at Neil. "What? She stops there?"

All Neil could do was nod.

Chapter 32

They had a restless night, each keeping to their side of the bed, their intrusive thoughts making them feel uncomfortable. She wanted to ask Neil what he thought Georgia meant, but something in his eyes that evening, said he wasn't ready to discuss it. After tossing and turning for hours, sleep finally came.

Barbara woke the next morning to see that Neil was still sleeping. She started to shake him, but decided he had to be really exhausted to sleep through the alarm she had set. They had been up late, reading that letter and then to clear their heads had taken a stroll around their neighborhood. She had always felt safe in the area, but now, not so much. When they finally headed home they were both tired and not up for any conversation.

Now Barbara got out of bed and padded across the floor into the bathroom. She stood there stretching her body every which way then opened her eyes and began her morning ritual.

In the shower it felt good to feel the hot water flowing over her body and she spent more time than usual enjoying it before stepping out and drying herself off.

Once out of the shower, she stood listening, but there wasn't a sound coming from the bedroom. Barbara could feel herself starting to worry as she made her way into the room.

Neil was as she left him. He hadn't moved an inch and suddenly she wasn't just worried, she was afraid. Maybe reading that letter was like opening pandora's box. What if reading that letter had cursed them.

Barbara rushed over to Neil's side of the bed and shook him, at first gently, then vigorously. When he stirred and flopped back, he stared up at her with a puzzled expression on his face and it was at that moment she knew Neil had forgotten the letter. And she decided, enough was enough, she would not read the diary or speak of the letter again. Pulling herself together she managed to smile and said, "Get up sleepy head. You're going to be late for work."

And so it was. Neither one of them mentioned the letter again, but Barbara had a feeling she was the only one who remembered that evening in its clarity. She not only didn't mention the letter, she soon found that her mind seemed to close up around that memory until it was all but gone.

That day they got ready for work and said their goodbyes quickly as they were running late. They worked together but had separate offices in various parts of the building.

Neil and Barbara were going to start a big project and they decided to meet up after lunch to drive out together. He had worked hard on the drawings for the addition to the winery and Barbara had worked just as hard on laying out her plans for the interior. They were hoping to take it to the next level, but when any changes are made to a building that has served the owners well, it takes some convincing to help them see the advantages because that was their baby.

When the tasting rooms had been added, was when it was the style to separate the workings of the vineyard away from the clients, like walking into the grocery store you know that the food was shipped in, but the trucks always park out back, and unloading is not something the customers ever see.

But today, the mind of the consumer has changed. They want to feel the pulse of the business and not just the results. That especially held true for a vineyard.

Like the outside greenery growing on the rolling hills in viewing distance of the vineyard's rows and rows of grapes they had designed a plan to have the tasting and store front become as one. Back when the vineyard was first built, these areas took over the first floor of the owner's home as it was a part of the vineyard that had come later. Now, the sisters wanted more space since their clientele kept increasing and that was what the Sanders was giving them, only as a separate establishment.

This would be their first face-to-face with the sisters and though Barbara was nervous, she could tell that Neil was just excited to reveal his plans. The meeting was set for one o'clock and they planned to meet in the current winetasting space.

They had no sooner turned into the driveway when the front door opened, and the women stood waiting. Behind them was a gentleman whom they assumed was their lawyer.

Neil and Barbara parked their car and walked up the slope to the house. "Hello, my name is Neil, and this is my wife, Barbara. We are the Sanders."

"Come in." they said almost in unison as they moved to the side to allow their guest to enter. Once they were inside the sisters introduced themselves. "My name is

Andrea McBride," She turned toward her sister who said, "I'm Robin McBride."

Andrea spoke again. We have been waiting to meet you personally as we thought it best not to interrupt your tour the other day. She said it with a smile.

"You saw us?" Neil paused, "How did you know it was us?"

"Oh, come on, you must know how popular you are. People are buzzing all over town about the married couple who work miracles. Your work proceeds you."

"But how did you know what we looked like," Barbara asked curiously.

Robin smiled, "Come on you two. The papers. When you purchased that house out in Irondequoit that had been vacant for so long, pictures were taken of you and published in the Irondequoit flyer."

"What?"

"Oh, there's a little local group that was formed long ago, a neighborhood group if you will, and they publish news on the area where you live. Most people don't know about it, and they keep it amongst themselves. My sister and I learned about it from a client, who has since made sure we receive a copy. It's quite quaint. I'm surprised they haven't included you yet, but..." She quickly added when she saw Neil starting to say something, "But it's probably because they're freelance, and no one makes money on it. It's like a hobby so I'm sure they will ask if you would like to receive a copy."

"But they got around to taking a picture of us?"

"Sure. That was easy. Robin turned and walked away. When she returned she was holding a copy of what they assumed was the paper. It was no more than a couple sheets of paper stapled together. She handed it to Barbara.

Neil leaned in close to his wife and they stared down at a picture of them leaning on the pillars that were at the end of their drive. Barbara remembered that moment. They had barely settled in and came out to the sidewalk to take a break. She had her back against one pillar and Neil was across the drive leaning on the other. At one point he had pointed at the house across the street and her eyes turned with his so that they were both facing front.

Neil smiled knowingly. "I remember, there was a couple walking their dog just before that house. I wondered what they were doing but shrugged it off. Now I know, they were taking our picture."

Both Robin and Andrea nodded and led them inside the tasting room and once they were seated said, "Shall we get started. I'm anxious to see what you envision."

It was a long, but interesting meeting with the sisters asking questions as Neil presented his drawings for the new building and Barbara showed them her designs for the interior. It was easy to see they were excited and that was verified when Robin said, "It's exquisite. We never thought of a whole new building."

Andrea smiled. "No, we hadn't. We were just so used to having it on the lower floor of the house. It was inconvenient, but it worked."

"Well, it probably worked well when the vineyard was not receiving so many people coming and going. Life before was sticking close to home because of the mode of travel and the fact that people were used to having their needs met where they lived. But life is changing now, and it will change even more. The world is not a big mysterious place anymore. We move about as if everyone is our neighbor and it will only get better."

"You're right. We have people coming from all over

the country, and some from other parts of the world."

The group continued talking and finally started signing the contracts for the work to be done. Andrea pointed out that it would work out great since they would still be able to host clients in the old space while the new one was being built. "You two are not only good at what you do, but foresighted in how you take the client into consideration. When we had the lower floor converted I can tell you it wasn't the case. They didn't care how they were disrupting our lives."

Barbara smiled. "So, I take it you will close the other store and tasting rooms when this is finished?"

"Yes. We can't wait," Robin said.

"The house is big but when two women live together, it seems small so we will be able to have a whole floor to ourselves; like private quarters, separate but together."

"I like that," Barbara added. "It was what I was thinking and would love to plan the building for you."

As she spoke she pulled out another set of drawings, not seeing how the women were smiling. She talked through what her plans were for the area, for both the upstairs and down, explaining how, if they wanted to do this, they might want to consider making the interior on both floors suitable to their own individual style. Separately, that would work.

"How did you know what the upstairs looked like?" Barbara laughed. "Sort of how you knew what we looked like, only I used Zillow online to view the interior of the floors above. They have some good pictures."

Everyone was laughing. "No one has any secrets these days," Neil said.

Neither Barbara nor Neil caught the look on their new clients faces as Robin replied, "No. No one does."

Chapter 33

A year, then two, passed without any incident. Barbara never had another dream that carried into her waking hours and Neil's obsession with the sunken garden seemed to lessen as their businesses kept their minds and bodies active. If anyone had asked what job their favorite had been, there was no doubt that both would say, '*the winery*'.

Andrea and Robin McBride were more than pleased with the job they had done. It had taken much longer than anticipated but in the end, it was a work of art. From the layout of the areas to the décor throughout, it became the talk of the town.

Even the D&C as the Democrat & Chronicle was now often called, placed their article on the front page, giving it as much attention as the big year 2000 problem, also known as the Y2K glitch. Many had read about the potential of computer errors due to the formatting and storage of calendar data for dates in and after the year 2000 since many programs represented four-digit years with only the final two digits changeable. That made the year 2000 indistinguishable from 1900. That being such a big '*to do*', having their business gaining as much attention was wonderful indeed.

As for the Sanders, it went beyond anything they could imagine because like Y2K, the story was picked up and carried in first all New York State papers and magazines with pictures. It turns out that the man with the women was a journalist, not a lawyer as they had thought. He documented and took pictures of the project from start to finish.

The story spread like a virus into other states, and they were famous. The Sanders had a good deal of responsibility laid in their lap and they carried it out beyond their wildest dreams. But Robin and Andrea McBride did not stop there. Shortly after the winery was completed, they gave their first tour of the premises and on a private tour that followed, they asked Barbara and Neil to join them. Without hesitation they accepted, cleared their calendars for the day and searched their closets for the most casual, formal looking attire, since they had been informed this was a private tour for particularly important people.

Turns out the private tour was for Time Magazine, and the results would mimic the great French, California wine competition. They were thorough as they took the tour of the vineyard, visited the cellars and tasted the wine. But that was not all. They toured the buildings and heard the story of how they had hired the Sanders and giving them free rein, they had built and designed the most efficient and beautiful building.

It would become a story that rivaled the one published so long ago on how America kicked France in the pants and changed the world of wine forever. No one at the D&C thought the story would go this far and the McBride's hadn't dreamed that their Winery would be listed as one of the world's greatest places to visit. But that was what happened.

The McBride winery was being called the next Napa and praise was not limited to the exceptional wine they were producing, but also carried several paragraphs on how efficient the winery was laid out. They spoke of the building that housed the wine tasting and the store area, calling it the most impressive, innovative layout they had ever witnessed.

As a pleasant result, the McBrides became busier than ever, having to add on more staff to meet their orders and visitors who came from around the world. And the Sanders were being asked to build and design not only other wineries but other businesses that felt they needed a fresh eye to design their environments.

The McBrides and the Sanders were now world-renowned and busier than they could have ever imagined.

Just like the McBrides, the Sanders had to add on more staff and find the time and location where their enlarged staff would be comfortably housed. They finally made the move from the city to build on land in Irondequoit. They built and designed every inch of the building and kept both businesses under one roof.

People would say they would drive down the street and stop to gawk at the 'one of a kind' structure and when they entered the premises, they had to constantly tell themselves to pick up their jaw before it dropped to the floor.

Another year passed and outside of the occasional call from the contractor Neil had to pull back from overlooking the job of uncovering the sunken garden. Most times their day didn't end at five or six in the evening because they had to be available for clients who were in a different time zone. Their staff was wonderful, but they couldn't and wouldn't wear them out on handling after hour business.

So the two spent long hours sometimes together, but other times on different jobsites. Then, to make up for the time they were separated, they usually met for dinner at a local restaurant and the rule was, 'no shop talk'.

On several occasions they met up with friends. Since Barbara was now a close friend of Emily Watson, she wanted Neil to meet her husband. Jack Waters.

Neil had looked at her. "Emily Watson and Jack Waters are married?"

"Yes, she kept her family name which goes back to the Sibley's, who played a major part in Rochester. It was a joint decision...but are you saying you already know Jack?"

Neil nodded. "I met him some time ago. He did mention his wife's name was Emily, but..."

Barbara smiled. "So, do you like Jack?"

"Yes, he's a nice guy."

"Well, Emily wants to go on that fast ferry."

Seeing the puzzled expression on his face, Barbara said, "Come on you of all people must have heard of it."

"Oh I heard of it. The Breeze had daily service between Toronto and Rochester, but in September of 2004 it stopped running. When the Canadian American Transportation Systems owed hundreds of thousands of dollars in fuel fees and did not have the funds to pay it."

Barbara gave him a funny look. "Well did you read that the city of Rochester, bought the ferry from its other investors during a foreclosure auction, I believe in February 2005."

"I guess I missed that."

Barbara nodded. "Anyway the ferry resumed service on June 30, 2005, as The Cat, and it's managed by Bay Ferries Great Lakes Limited."

Neil had been searching the internet and finally looked up at his wife, reading an article he found. "It says here that Rochester Ferry Company is a subsidiary of the City of Rochester, New York and in February 2005 purchased the high-speed catamaran ferry, but it was called the Spirit of Ontario."

"So.."

"Well, what is it called now?"

"I don't know, I just know that Emily said we needed to go on it before this one stops running. She said it's a hoot."

"So what does it say about the ferry itself."

"Well, look here," he replied, as he scrolled down. "It says the ferry features two movie theater rooms, a restaurant, two bars, wireless internet access, duty free shopping, and a children's play area. Fares start at $29 for an off-peak one-way walk-on ticket, plus a $5 passenger annoyance fee. A summer walk-on round trip is $74 per person."

Without looking up, Neil added, "We'll need to check with Emily and Jack to see what they're thinking."

"It looks like it leaves Rochester at 8am and 3:30pm, and leaves Toronto at 11:30am and 7pm, six days a week. On Tuesdays, the ferry makes one round trip, leaving Rochester at 8am and Toronto at 7pm."

"I'll ask Emily which time they want to leave."

"Wow," Neil said.

"What is it?"

"Look at this. The boat…ferry…whatever is massive. It's 284 ft long, seventy-eight feet wide, and as tall as a five-story building. It can hold 750 passengers, 220 cars, and ten buses or trucks and has a top speed of fifty-five miles per hour. It's said to be the fastest vessel of its kind in the world and the port-to-port travel time is about 2 hours and 15 minutes."

Neil looked over at his wife, smiling. "I think we're going to have a wonderful time with Emily and Jack. What fun."

"So, you're on board, so to speak?"

"I am. We can both use a break for some fun time, so we'll just have to adjust our schedules."

"Look and see if you can eat on the ferry."

"It doesn't matter. The Rochester ferry terminal is located at the Port of Rochester, which is easily accessible and has an assortment of quick-service restaurants such as Quizno's, California Rollin', the Nutty Bavarian, a coffee shop and Abbott's."

Barbara looked thoughtful. "Yes, I remember that building."

"Yes, it's a two-story brick and glass structure with a clock tower in the front entrance. It says here the boarding area is called the "Greenhouse" with custom facilities, which I guess refers to restrooms."

"What about Toronto?"

Neil scrolled down and read, "The Toronto ferry terminal is at the south end of Cherry Street." Neil looked up smiling, "I don't know where that is, but since it doesn't say as much, I think there isn't a fancy terminal on that end. Anyway, google says there's a Loblaw's grocery store nearby where we can get water, food, or coffee for the ferry trip to Rochester."

Barbara was laughing. "You're kidding! Right?"

"No, that's what it says."

"Toronto, Toronto...oh, here's more. It's called the Marine Terminal, and it is a two-story steel and glass structure built by the Toronto Port Authority for the ferry service at the foot of Cherry Street. The terminal has a lounge, custom facilities and some retail space." She looked at her husband frowning. "So, it must have something in that terminal, I would think."

Barbara grimaced. "It doesn't matter. I'll make the arrangements with Emily tomorrow."

The boat was white with a blue base and a red stripe

running in the middle. Above the lower level was a thin red and blue stripe. It was immaculate on the outside.

That was a special day as they climbed the stairs to go up to the entrance, then over a short gangplank. Since they had left their car at the parking area, they went down to see what it was like in the cargo hold area.

There was ample space to walk on either side of the cars and yellow pipes easy to see so as not to run into them.

Upstairs was just as pristine. The seats were navy blue along the large viewing windows and in the center were light blue chairs around red pedestal tables. And there were windows everywhere, on either side and skylights above.

The best part of the trip going across Lake Ontario was when they took the stairs to the second floor and witnessed the fantastic view of Toronto as you enter the port. They saw the dome shape to the left of the CN tower that was the Rogers Center. But the star attraction was the view of the sky-piercing CN Tower, the one-time tallest building in the world.

The trip quickly, it seemed, ended. Barbara and Neil and Emily and Jack decided to take the trip again and the men came up with coinciding it with a Toronto Blue Jay baseball game. The one coming up on August 7 was with the Yankees.

Before parting, they made the arrangements, agreeing they should plan on taking one car on the ferry.

"I'm glad we did this," Neil said smiling.

"Yes, it was fun. And I'm glad we took the later trip, so we were able to view the lights in the Port of Rochester. They were reflecting off the water and it was a beautiful welcome home."

Chapter 34

After spending time in the cellar checking for any more information about the house, Neil had been impressed by how dry the cellar was. Later he presented Barbara with the idea of putting a wine cellar in the basement.

She didn't mind the cellar, which is what she saw it as, and since there was a lot of usable space, she agreed. She saw it as his project since she didn't have any interest in building one.

Yes at first she could see the value of having a wine cellar but that was where her interest ended. That was until Neil begged her to help on the wine cellar project, and her business sense took over and she got excited. It was something neither one had done before, making it that more interesting. It started with Neil doing research and then together they prepared sketches. Finally they began creating their '*baby*' and for the most part did it alone.

They chose the cellar because it was well insulated and already cool most of the year. Neil wanted it to be a show piece, not just a bunch of shelves with bottles, so Barbara considered that as she planned the design. The one thing she had noticed about the cellar was that it was always several degrees cooler than the rest of the house which made it perfect for a wine cellar, they just had to decide which area of the cellar to use, which ended up being the space on the right of the stairs as it received no direct exposure to sunlight throughout the day and it had adequate ventilation.

They had worked side by side wrapping the entire area with a vapor barrier to repel moisture. The cellar had lofty ceilings so that part of the job was tediously slow, but they managed.

Neil couldn't hide his enthusiasm. Being able to design and do all the work himself was no longer possible on the jobsites, but here he was able to get his hands dirty. He framed the room with wooden joists. He positioned the boards vertically around the perimeter of the room on the inside of the vapor barrier, leaving sixteen inches of space between each. Then with Barbara helping they secured the joists with 2-3 nails at both the top and bottom ends. Again, when it came to the ceiling the job became tedious. Neil's shoulders ached from reaching over his head for lengths of time and Barbara's ached from steadying the ladder that had to be continuously moved across the room.

Every evening and weekend when they had time, they worked together on the wine cellar and though it was challenging work, they would end the day happy and anxious to see the end product.

When it came time to fill the gaps in the frame with high-efficiency insulation materials, Barbara wanted to just blow it in, but Neil frowned. "No way. We're putting in foam batts between the joists."

Laughing, Barbara said, "Okay, okay, don't bite my head off." She just didn't like touching the stuff, but he had her equipped with a mask, gloves and what looked like a cellophane raincoat that went all the way down to the ground. She just hoped she didn't trip and fall. They put up five and a half thick insulation between the joists on the wall and 10-inch insulation on the ceiling.

Barbara knew he had done the wine cellars at the

McBrides, but this was different. It was not just making the drawings and supervising the work, it was all hands on. She thought about those short deadline jobs they had done, when she felt he was using up the bulk of the time, but now she knew he wasn't just slapping up walls, there was a lot more to it than that.

Unlike working on the McBrides wine cellar, theirs took several months to complete and it was a much smaller area to work with. By the time they were ready to cover the insulated frame with drywall, Barbara was getting over her initial excitement of building the room and having to tape over the seams between the sheets of drywall could not be more boring. But then came the part she could really dig her teeth into. They painted the walls with waterproof paint, putting on three even coats in her choice of color which was a pale lilac.

They then lined the wine cellar with wooden racks that Neil built himself to not only store but show off their collection and together they arranged the racks along the outer walls to maximize walking space.

Barbara was unable to contain her joy when after installing the showroom-style lighting fixtures on the ceiling Neil turned them on. She made Neil wait while she got a bottle of champagne. Neil grabbed the cleanest towel he could find in his work box and popped the cork, then they sat on the cool cellar floor and toasted themselves and the room.

Just as he had done for the McBrides, Neil had the showroom lights on the sides of the walls pointed at areas where they planned to put their most precious bottles of wine. There were quite a few outlets, but they had low voltage bulbs in all of them.

Even though they didn't plan on entertaining in the

cellar, Barbara created a sitting area with a few comfortable chairs and a nice table for times when they would just come down, sit and enjoy the fruit of their labor, but that only happened in the beginning.

Later it was Neil who would run down and bring up a bottle or two when they needed it.

Barbara would admit it had been an enjoyable time she spent with Neil working on the wine cellar and once Neil had done his thing, she had really gotten into helping him create her design for the area.

But all of that had been done together and not once had she been alone down there. That is until now when Neil asked her to get a bottle of wine from the cellar. She started to ask him to go, but feeling silly, she ignored the sudden feeling that came over her and just nodded.

Sure this was the first time she would be going into the cellar alone. She had searched for treasures down there and spent months working on the wine cellar, but that was always with Neil and now going down alone...well that hadn't happened before.

She told herself she was being silly. There was nothing down there to hurt her. But she didn't believe it. That feeling was overpowering as she stepped down on shaky legs, holding on to the wall and hoping the light would turn on when she finally reached the bottom. She ordered herself to stop it, and finally said out loud, "You get a hold of yourself, Barbara."

Somehow she managed to make it all the way down and reached over to turn on the light. That's when something grabbed hold of her hand and she quickly pulled her hand back and ran upstairs.

Fear paralyzed her as her terror mounted she fought a rising panic Breathing heavy and unable to catch her breath, she closed the cellar door and leaned against it, telling herself it was her imagination. There was nothing down there. She had let her imagination take hold of her was all.

Neil came into the kitchen, "Barbara, I was..." he started, but seeing his wife's face he stopped. "What's wrong?"

At first Barbara was going to tell him, but then she couldn't. It was stupid and she said, "I don't know. I guess my day caught up with me and I needed to pause for a second."

"It's been more than a second."

"What, are you the time patrol!" She snapped, "I drank some water and sat down and was just about ready to go get the wine when you interrupted me."

Neil looked as though she had slapped him in the face. He lowered his head in shame as though he had done something wrong. "Sorry." Neil said apologetically. "Look, you go take a shower and I'll go down and pick us out a nice wine and meet you in the sunroom."

Ashamed, but unable to tell him the truth, Barbara nodded and when he walked over to her, she initiated a hug and a kiss before going upstairs.

As she slowly trudged upstairs, she tried to believe it had been her imagination, but when she looked down at her hand on the stair railing, the proof of it happening was visible. There were scratches on the top of her hand. Scratches that had not been there before. And she remembered how cold the hand felt as it covered hers, forcing her to try to draw her hand back as the other hand held tightly, then felt the drag of the nails as she managed to free herself.

It was too upsetting to try and figure it out, so she went upstairs, quickly undressed and climbed into the shower. She felt better when she climbed out and put on her nightclothes before heading back downstairs.

When she returned she saw that Neil was in his pajama bottoms and had on a Buffalo Bills tee shirt. It made her smile as she walked into the sunroom to join him. They sat side by side on the wicker sofa enjoying the rest of the evening.

Chapter 35

After what had happened in the cellar, Barbara recalled, it had been an enjoyable day, spent with the Waters, but it wasn't until they had returned home that she remembered the main reason they had wanted to get with Emily and Jack. It had been to see if Emily had found out more about the sunken garden.

"Don't worry, dear, you can ask her when you see her again. I asked Jack, but he didn't know much more than we did. If either had more to share I think they would have told us."

Neil was right and Barbara put the matter aside.

Barbara was surprised at how well she had been sleeping since the hand incident in the cellar. She had been afraid she was about to have a lot of sleepless nights, but she didn't. Maybe it was because she had made up her mind to bring up the matter with her friends who always seemed to know the right thing to say and do.

She loved Neil, but when it came to something as sensitive as what she was going through, his advice of facing it head on was in no way going to happen.

What she was ready to do was call Cheri, Jennifer, Linda and of course Emily. Emily hadn't been to that first luncheon they had together at the Spaghetti Factory, but she had been told everything that had been shared then.

It would have been nice to go back to the old restaurant, but alas, it was no more so Barbara asked her assistant, Jennifer, if she had any suggestions.

Jennifer thought for a moment. "Are we talking historical type? I only say that because that's what you like."

"Yes, got anything?"

"Uhm, let me think. What about the Genesee Brew House?"

"That's not old."

"No, the brew house opened in 2012, but the Genesee Brewery is historical."

"Ah, I get what you're saying. The brewery and that spot dates back to the 1850's. The restaurant is newer, but it is a part of old history."

"Right, but I suggest it because…just wait until you see the décor inside. That and the excellent views since it sits on a bluff above the Genesee River."

"I knew you would come up with something. Thanks Jennifer.

"You're welcome. I'll call and make reservations. How many should I say are coming?"

Barbara gave her the number and went back to what she was doing. It seemed only minutes when Jennifer was at her door telling her it was time for her luncheon. Barbara thanked her and grabbed her things. On the way out, she saw Neil and told him she was meeting up with the girls for lunch. He gave her a quick kiss. "Good. They usually boost your spirits."

Barbara frowned, then caught herself and quickly changed her expression to a smile. She hadn't thought he had noticed.

Barbara arrived first and waited for the others before going to their assigned table. When they arrived, she could tell they were excited about not only getting together, but her choice in locations and she was glad she had taken Jennifer's suggestion. Her friends, just like herself loved history; especially of Rochester and this was as Jennifer Leland had said a historical location that took advantage of history.

Emily was the first to show and they found a bench in the store area to wait for the others before going upstairs to the restaurant.

While they waited, Emily asked, "So, do you have something to tell us?"

"Why do you ask that. I've just missed all of you and wanted to see you." She paused, "And maybe share a little something." She paused again. "I'm hoping you might have something to share too."

Emily smiled and nodded. She turned her head and saw Cheri Leake, in the doorway. Emily Watson and Cheri went way back. Jennifer followed, apologizing for being late. Jennifer Gleason had also known Emily Watson for a long time as well, as did Linda Sibley who was right behind her. Finally Marla Dickerson arrived. She still worked at the Times Union and had already told Barbara she had some interesting information to share.

It was Emily who had introduced her to these women and made her a part of this group and she couldn't thank her enough. Whenever she needed her spirits lifted or her instincts explored, this was her go to group.

They were all there and together they went upstairs, and Barbara went to the desk and told them they had reservations. Soon they were taken to their table. Barbara was pleased, thanks to her office assistant, they had the best view in a restricted area. The hostess asked what they would like to drink and trying to be traditional, they each ordered a flight of beer.

When the host left they laughed. "So, my friends, when was the last time you ordered a beer out." Chris smiled and said, "When in Rome…"

"I guess we all follow that rule."

Once the beer arrived at the table, they shared their choices with each other and decided it wasn't bad; not bad at all.

"This is nice, Barbara, you made a good choice."

"Thank you, but all thanks go to Jennifer. Seeing the puzzled expression on Jennifer's face she added, Jennifer Leland, my office assistant."

The women nodded in unison; they all knew Jennifer.

"So, I found out something interesting in my research." All heads turned toward Cheri. "Not about the you know what, but interesting just the same.

"What is it."

"Well, I ran across the Glen House in my reading, and it was the place to be. It was where the Bemishes…the people that owned your home…well, who had the house built, stayed."

"Yes, we know they were the first owners, but what does the Glen House have to do with anything."

"Well if you let me I'll tell you."

Cheri gave them a stern look and she heard a few sighs in reply. "Go ahead, then."

"Any way it became the Glen Edith. The place was known for its spectacular vistas and quality food served by the Orlen family. They had this annual thing, a duck dinner."

Seeing she got the expressions she had wanted, she paused and then said, "It was a day that marked the end of the seasonal restaurant's year and attracted hundreds of patrons for more than 60 years."

The waiter came to take their orders and all

conversation stopped. Once their orders were placed all eyes were back on Cheri. "What? That's it. I just wanted to share that with you."

They stared at Cheri until they broke out in laughter, then when they calmed, Marla turned to Barbara. "Well, I said I had pictures and I sent them to Barbara..." She then added, "But I have copies here so we can look at them."

"I have a question," Barbara ventured. "In the pictures you sent I didn't see any on the inside of the house."

"That's because there are none. Once the house was completed, no one was able to get in to take pictures. Sorry about that."

"That's strange, isn't it?"

"No. Did someone come and take pictures of the house when you were done with your changes? I think it's something you request if you want to share every detail."

They could hear the sarcasm in her voice now. "Okay, calm down. You're right. I just thought..."

After what had happened in the cellar, Barbara was disappointed, but remained quiet.

Marla turned to Barbara. "So, what did you find in the attic?"

"Well, we not only searched the attic where there were a lot of antiques, but though there weren't any secret compartments, we did find a safe behind an old picture hanging in the library. Only problem was we couldn't find the combination."

"Ah," Emily said.

"But When the locksmith came, he was able to open the safe for us." Everyone at the table leaned forward. "Sorry, there was nothing of interest in the safe, but we did find some old papers and..."

Barbara took a sip of her beer.

"And, what," Jennifer asked anxiously.

Barbara leaned over to the side of her chair where her

briefcase sat. She opened it and as she pulled out the papers, "We had them restored. They were in bad shape, but they did an excellent job on most of them. The worse is the diary."

Heads popped up around the table. "You found a diary?" Barbara nodded as she handed the papers to Emily who handed each one a sheet and kept the rest in front of her.

They began reading. When the food arrived, they paused briefly, looking upset at the space the dishes took up, then moving their chairs back, commence reading again.

Barbara knew what they said so she started eating.

When Barbara was putting the last bite into her mouth, she saw Marla staring at her. "What is it."

"You found a lot, but I feel bad since I am a newspaper woman I should have been able to uncover a lot of this."

"You can't uncover something that was not shared with anybody. I believe just like that map and details about the sunken garden that Emily's mother's friend, Magnolia Warner shared with us, this couldn't be publicized without proof it's real. Ms. Warner had that map and that diagram only because her father had left it behind. He operated the contracting company that built the house, but these documents are just papers about a place that never were filed with the deed."

That made Marla feel better as she tackled her food. When she had cleaned her plate she lifted her head and they saw a sly smile on her face. "Do you want to know what I found out about William and Georgia Bemish."

By now the women had scanned most of the documents and were attentive as they worked on their food.

"Well, it is rumored that Georgia Bemish, who would be over a hundred now, spent her last years in the home for the mentally ill."

"You're kidding."

"Yes, I checked it out and she was there."

"So, what happened?"

"Now that's the good part of my story. It seems that her husband vanished."

She could see the surprised expressions and slowly she continued. "Yes, they of course think she murdered him though there is no proof and they didn't have all the tools of the trade back them to help find out the truth. In any case, she was so far gone when they found her. She couldn't speak so they decided she was in shock. She was taken to the hospital for a time, but then found to be mentally ill so they transferred her to the criminally mentally ill unit where she died, never revealing what really happened."

"They never found him?"

Marla shook her head. "No, never, but there were a few people in the area that said in the end, that is before he disappeared, he was spending a lot of time in that sunken garden."

"What about his wife."

"His wife told many of her friends that she wouldn't step foot in it. She said there was something about it that scared her...scared her immensely."

Everyone was quiet, thinking about it and Barbara figured it was the perfect time to share. "I have something I need to tell all of you."

All eyes turned to Barbara. "First, I haven't gone near the garden either. I sensed something, heard something. Dreamt something, I don't know, but it gives me the willies."

"But before I get into that, I also want to tell you that we built a wine cellar in the cellar...I refuse to call it a basement. One day Neil had me go down to get a bottle of wine. I had no fear at first, but because the switch to light the bottom was at the base of the stairs, that gave me a little dismay, but I made it down and when I reached over to flip the switch, something...someone touched my hand."

"What was it?"

"You think I stayed to find out! I ran back up the stairs as fast as I could and Neil found me leaning against the cellar door, breathing heavily. I didn't tell him what happened, and seeing I hadn't gotten the wine, he went down and got it."

"Did anything happen to him?"

"If it did, he didn't tell me or look like he had seen anything."

"Wow, Barbara," Emily said as she padded her hand. "I envied you having that lovely house, but now…"

"Me too, several of the women piped in.

"Thanks, but that's not all of it."

"What else."

"Well, back when we went on that boat ride when we first came to town, I met a Mindy Worthington and I thought Neil met her husband, Warren."

"Thought he had?"

"Yes because I thought I saw him talking to Warren, her husband while I was talking to Mindy, only when I asked him, he said he hadn't met any Warren Worthington. When I told him I had been talking to a Mindy Worthington and went to take him to meet her, he acted or really didn't see her. She was standing right there, and he didn't' see her."

"You are just sharing this now?"

"I guess it sounded so crazy I had to wait until I was sure you were my friends and wouldn't judge me. Maybe if Georgia had told her friends, she wouldn't have ended up like she did." Barbara paused. "Do you think I'm going crazy?"

"No," everyone said at the same time. "If you're crazy, so are we because we believe you. We need to do more checking. We need to find out who this Mindy Worthington is or was and anything else we can about her.

Maybe she came to warn you."

"There is one more thing…" Barbara told them about the dream she had and how when she woke her feet were all muddied as if she had been outside walking in that garden. When she finished she took a deep breath and leaned back against her chair. After a few minutes, Emily said pointedly, "I'm scared for you."

The others piped in and then Marla, who had the diary now, looked up with concern. "Ah, Barbara?"

"What is it?"

"Well, what was the name again."

"What name?"

"That woman you saw on the boat."

"Mindy Worthington."

"Well, I can't read all of it, but in Georgia Bemish's diary here it says something about meeting a Mindy Worthington and her husband, which it's a little blurred but I think it's Warren. Anyway she says she met Mindy on the boat tour, but William Bemish didn't or couldn't see them."

A hush settled over the table.

Chapter 36

While Barbara was out lunching with her friends, Neil took the opportunity to make a trip to the library. The Rundel Library was close to the office so Neil decided to walk. The weather forecast said they were in for a beautiful autumn day of sunshine and warmth. They were right. It was indeed a beautiful day.

Neil put on his sunglasses and headed down the street. He was halfway there before he realized he hadn't told his secretary where he was going. But it didn't matter. He had his cell phone so if she needed to reach him, she could call.

When he arrived at the library he stood admiring the building. As many times as he had passed it, he still couldn't help but have a high regard for the architect and since it was a nationally registered historic building he wasn't alone in appreciating the structure.

The library was surrounded by terraces on all sides and sat at the end of South Avenue, directly adjacent to the Genesee River in the City's Central Business District. He had done some research on the structure and learned it was built in the 1930s and was supported by a steel and concrete framing system. The building was faced in smooth Indiana limestone, representing a mixture of Beaux-Arts style with Art Deco detailing and stylizing. As for the name, Rundel, that was attached in honor of Morton W. Rundel whose estate helped finance the venture.

Neil had visited the library on many occasions. There was a lot of information to be found on the internet, but more, in this library. It was an important part of his job as an architect to not only take in the style of buildings in the area, but to learn about them, since its history plays a major part in its overall design. And there was just some history that he found fascinating.

The idea of a centralized public library had been supported and frequently requested by Rochester's citizens throughout the beginning of the 20th century. Due to an ongoing war and budgetary concerns, however, construction of the project was continuously postponed. Then, in 1911, Morton Rundel, a wealthy art collector and cousin of George Eastman died, it was surprising to find that he had bequeathed $400,000 to the City of Rochester for the construction of a central library and public arts center. That along with monies from the City of Rochester, the financial situation was solved. Neil smiled thinking that in today's market, that would hardly be sufficient money to build some houses, but back then, that would translate to roughly $1.3 million.

Someone brushed him and whispered a quick, "Sorry". It was just enough to get him moving, though, as he went up the steps and into the mezzanine area that had been known for its spacious and ornate design. There were intricate carvings on the limestone façade and murals on the floors. As he stared up at the lofty ceilings he remembered going through each location to get a feel for it. There were three main floors, a mezzanine, two underground levels, a catwalk level above the river, and a penthouse area for equipment. He thought it innovative for the Rundel Memorial Library to have a "Secret Room" down a hallway on its second floor that contained a local doll collection and an abundance of children's literature. Neil was headed to the second floor, but not to that area.

As he made his way up the staircases, admiring the architect of concrete and stone, he tried to focus on his objective, which was to find out all he could about the house he had purchased and the sunken garden on the property.

On the second floor, he made his way down the hallway, pass the reference room that contained digital equipment, microfilm readers and vital records, which he may later peruse, but that wasn't his objective today. He continued, pausing to turn and walk down the local history hallway and exhibit area which he always found fascinating. Finally he continued and went pass the city historian's office and into where he had planned to begin his research, the Local History and Genealogy section.

Once inside, he was all business. This Division had the largest collection of source materials on the history of Rochester and the Genesee Valley, as well as a vast assemblage of resources to help research family history. He had to do all the research in this room as the materials not only could not be checked out, but they could also not be removed from the room.

Neil got to work. First he went through the materials, identifying what would help him to find out more about the people who built his house and the sunken garden. If there was more information to find, it would be in this room.

Neil was busy working away, happy that he could spread out since he was the only person occupying this space. When his cell vibrated, he didn't feel it, but after answering it the second time it vibrated, he realized that his wife had called earlier.

"Sorry, I was…how do the kids say it…'in the zone'.

Barbara laughed, then told him she was on her way

back to the office.

"Oh, what time is it?"

Neil had been putting notes into his notepad and for the first time looked down at his watch to see it was after six. "I didn't realize it was that late. Listen. I'm at the library but I'll pack up and meet you at the office."

"I'll be there. Love you."

"Love you too."

This was one of those days when they had driven in together, so Barbara had taken the car to meet up with friends for lunch. Now as he hurried, putting things back, ignoring the rolling shelf that had a sign saying, 'put all reference material used here' since he knew where he had removed the items he had used.

Finally he was ready to leave and went down the hallway and again chose to use the stairs. He was at the head of the stairs when his briefcase flew open.

Neil stood there at the top of this stone staircase watching his papers flying every which way and his notepad go tumbling down to land at the bottom. He knew there was no chance of survival, but it didn't matter since he had the cloud turned on so all his notes were recoverable, not so lucky would be the notepad.

He worked his way down, gathering his materials when a man started joining him, picking up papers and handing them to Neil. They worked their way down, not saying a word until the gentleman picked up the notepad. He looked over at Neil with a frown on his face that at first seemed to suggest he didn't know what he was looking at.

Neil brushed that thought out of his head as he extended his hand, and the stranger handed him the notepad. Leaning the briefcase on the step, Neil bent over, placed the notepad inside and pressed the latches, twice, making sure they caught. He then stood and said, "Thank you, ah...?"

"Oh, my name is Warren, Warren Worthington."

"Well thank you Warren Worthington. My name is Neil Sanders. I appreciate your help."

Warren nodded, "You're welcome." Then added, "You should be more careful with your things."

Neil was stunned, unable to speak as he watched the man hurry down the stairs in front of him. He stepped up his pace, watching his feet as he went.

Suddenly Neil stopped dead as his mind worked on the name, 'Warren Worthington, Warren Worthington. Where had he heard that before.'

Unable to remember he shrugged his shoulders and began hurrying across the floor and to the exit doors, but when he stepped out, the man was nowhere to be seen. A little perturbed, he grunted. He gave another look around and not seeing the man, headed back to the office.

Barbara was waiting for him at the entrance. "Do you need to go up?"

"Only to shut down my system and turn out the lights."

"Already done, my friend."

"What say we grab a bite to eat downtown and then when we get home we can just chill."

"Sounds great," Neil shifted his briefcase to his other hand and reached over and put his arm around his wife's waist. "What do you feel like?"

"I had a sensible lunch so I'm going to say, pizza."

"I had no lunch and I say, pizza it is."

It was one of those wonderful autumn evenings that happens off and on when the temperature remains in the seventies, so they walked to the pizza place and ate their pizza outside. When they finished, they headed back to the office and climbed into the car.

They had eaten in silence and now as they drove, the comfortable reticence lingered. Once they arrived home, Barbara parked the car in the garage, and they entered through the side door of their home.

"What say we have a nightcap?"

"Sounds good. We still have the wine from the night before. It's in the fridge, on the door."

While Barbara went to the cabinet to get glasses, Neil retrieved the wine. As was their custom they carried everything into the sunroom. They were almost there when Barbara paused. "We need a snack." She handed Neil the glasses and went back to the kitchen for crackers and cheese.

They settled down and Neil asked, "How was the luncheon?"

"It was great. We talked a lot, but I'll tell you about that in the morning since it was basically what we already knew. But tell me, did you find anything interesting at the library?"

"I found some things, but nothing that solved our questions about the sunken garden." He paused, but then said, "But, as I was leaving my briefcase spilled out on the steps at the library and this kind gentleman helped me. But when he left, he said something that made me think he wasn't so kind after all."

"Why, what did he say."

"He said I should be more careful with my things. Do you believe that? I was about to give him a piece of my mind, but he was gone before I could say anything."

Barbara had a smile on her face as she looked at her husband. "Well, he's right in a way." She paused. "Did you thank him for helping…oh, did you get his name?"

"Yes to both your questions. I wasn't rude at all."

"So, what was his name?"

"Warren Worthington."

Chapter 37

No matter how busy Barbara was, her mind kept going back to that night she woke from a bad dream and found dirt on her feet. This was one of those many times she stood in the kitchen preparing breakfast. She looked at the clock and saw it wasn't yet five in the morning. They had no plans for the day except to go out and do more digging.

As she stood there watching the coffee drip into her cup she couldn't help thinking it wasn't a dream at all, that she had been out...maybe sleepwalking. As for what she dreamt, it was fading and she could only remember bits and pieces now for the most part, but she did remember Mindy Worthington was in it.

When Neil had mentioned the man on the staircase at the Library for some reason she didn't acknowledge that she knew that name. She didn't know why, probably because he didn't remember her mentioning that name before.

Since the day they met they had been open and honest with each other and basically knew everything that the other knew. But since moving into this house she had kept so many secrets and among them was the Worthingtons.

Barbara tried to shake the thought, but it wouldn't go away. She knew that when she was on that boat trip when she first met Mindy, Neil was talking with Warren. Hell, she saw him turn his head toward the man as they stood in a group, but when she mentioned it and he said he hadn't spoken to this man Warren, she believed him, and she believed he hadn't seen Mindy when she tried to introduce him to her.

She knew that for sure. Barbara shook her head violently. She had to get out of her head before she went too deep, because she knew somehow Mindy, and Warren now had something to do with that sunken garden. She paused in thought and then looked down at the floor in the kitchen, in her mind seeing the cellar below where that hand had touched her hand. It was all crazy and she laughed out loud. "Sure Barbara, ghost...obviously ghosts are part of it all right." Even though she laughed, she didn't think it funny.

When Nathaniel Parker, who owned the DirtWorx company had suddenly called to say he wasn't able to work on the garden for a while, they had been polite enough to accept that without asking for a reason. They liked his work, so they hadn't called in another contractor to replace him either. Instead they decided to work on it themselves.

They had been digging out that garden for a long time now and it was coming alive. 'No silly', she reprimanded herself silently, 'not alive, its being revealed'. What had originally been their idea to do while they waited for the contractor to return, became their regimen and any spare moment they were out there.

Neil had told their friends what they were up to, and they joined them when they could. At least that was the case in the beginning as they worked the Winona part of the sunken garden down to the base and had gone through layer after layer of dirt and removal of the back end and the area started coming into view.

It was comical really, Barbara thought at first when

the women stopped coming to help and when they met up for lunch or talked on the phone and she asked why, they were evasive, but Barbara knew because she wouldn't want to announce she thought there was something down there, something dark and evil. She hadn't had the heart to share that yet with anybody.

Alone in the kitchen Barbara laughed again. "Whatever it was made Georgia bat ass crazy." Quickly, as if she were heard she said, "Sorry…sorry."

What she did know at the present time was the fact that the women were afraid, yes afraid to stick around and see the final unveiling. But not the men. At first they would laugh and joke while they shoveled dirt, then when they started uncovering something they would shout out like they were on a scavenger hunt. Then they would all work together, digging carefully until the figure was revealed. They didn't talk about what they uncovered, none of them did. Instead they continued to dig like it was their job and they had to get it down to the bottom. The only way that Barbara could explain it was it was if they were driven.

Barbara's friends told her they had to threaten their husbands to spend time with them and get out of that 'hole', so they were glad to have winter come and fill it up with snow and ice.

When that happened, or when it was so cold the ground was hard to move, life went back to normal. It was work and parties above ground and no mention of that sunken garden that Barbara wished another earthquake would come and cover up again. "Now that would be funny". She could laugh about that all right but somehow she knew that whatever was down there would not allow it. The snow would melt, and the job would begin again.

By now Neil knew they were all feeling some push that kept them in that sunken garden, desperate to uncover what lay beneath. He couldn't put it into words any more than the others could, but it was something.

When winter's cold and snow set in, the men seemed lost, and it was more of an order than a request that Neil not cut them out of the job. They wanted to help until the garden was uncovered fully.

So unable to dig, life for everyone seemed to go back to normal. There were parties, birthdays and family visits and the times when they would get together with one or more couples for a concert, dinner, or lunch.

Those were the good days, but even then they were overshadowed with searching for information about that garden and the couple who had lived there before them. Every moment she had free, Barbara would turn the pages of that diary and when she wasn't sure what it said, she would ask one of her friends to see if they could read it, so to speak, between the blurred lines.

During one of those winters, Barbara managed to find a family member of a nurse who had worked at the psychiatric center where Georgia had spent her last days. Once she had the name, she began calling around, hoping to find this person.

The one beneficial use of telephone books back in the day was that you could trace down a name and get the phone number without a problem since everyone had a land line back then. Now it was the internet she had to depend on, but she was persistent in finding someone who could help her.

She started with the name Bemish on the internet since she wasn't sure of Georgia's maiden name. Over weeks and then months she managed to find out that there were very few people with that last name. She was careful in her search since there were a lot of *Beamishes* showing up.

Finally she found a Colonel Brad A. Bemish. She read he was a career USAF intelligence professional and member of the National Security Studies Department faculty at the Eisenhower School. She was able to get in contact with him through the school and was disappointed to find he was not related to anyone, named William, who had lived in the Rochester, New York area. When she asked about an older relative, like his parents or grandparents, he said no one had ever mentioned a William married to a woman named Georgia. Finally she accepted this was a dead end.

She kept searching and eventually came up with another prospect, a Karl A. Bemish. This one was disturbing to say the least. Clicking on the name she saw an article of a Lakewood, Colorado man who pleaded guilty to first-degree murder after murdering his girlfriend. Hilary Engel. Whether or not he was a relative, she didn't pursue it any further and went on to the next.

She tired of the search eventually and had to put it off for several days, then weeks as her work required her attention. When she got back to it her hopes went up. She clicked on a website called 'Ancient Faces'. It had appeared in the listing for her Bemish search, and she was excited as she went to the link. Her hope vanished as she read, 'Bemish Last Name History & Origin. *We don't have any information on the history of the Bemish name.*'

Another dead end. It was days before she got back to her search and more for kicks she went to a site that had the meanings of names and found that Bemish name meaning is hesitate, travel lover, good understanding. She paused, her mind reading into it more than the words she read. Finally she came out of it and continued her search.

She was sure she had hit paydirt when she came across a Sarah Bemish. Sarah was a nurse practitioner in Manchester, NH. She didn't let the location sway her since nurses traveled a lot and maybe she could be a sister of Williams. So she called, several times before making contact and when she reached her they talked for a long time. At first she thought it was possible as she had heard there was an artist in the family, but once they shared details, she realized this was not her relative. But she offered to check further and if she came up with anything she would give her a call. So Barbara gave her the number.

Even as she continued searching, she kept telling herself this was not the way a successful woman operated. This fascination with finding a needle in a haystack was useless. She was forty years old now; just in her twenties when she moved to Rochester, and was this how she wanted to spend those last working years before retirement?

She tried desperately to stop and work again took precedence over her search and forced her to set it aside. But several weeks later she was back at it and that was when she came across Jeffery A. Bemish, 64, of Kittanning, passed away Thursday, Jan. 7, 2021, at ACMH Hospital, after fighting a hard-fought battle against COVID-19.

"Ah, Jeffrey," she found herself saying. She sat back in her chair as if about to cry or say a prayer, but as she leaned back her eyes fell on a paragraph below. 'He is survived by his wife of 20 years, Rebecca (Bowser) Bemish."

Her forehead furrowed as she thought, this could be a lead. She read through the obituary and found a phone number and was about to dial when Jennifer entered her office.

"Yes," Barbara looked up with a smile that probably looked like she had just been caught with her hand in the cookie job.

"Looks like I disturbed you, but you didn't answer the phone."

"What?"

Jennifer could tell that Barbara hadn't heard it. "Uh-oh, either you didn't hear it or there's something wrong with the line. I'll try it again."

Jennifer left the room and Barbara, who was sitting with a surprised expression on her face, knew that she had been in some kind of trance, focused so deeply on her finding she closed herself out of the real world. She tried to tell herself this was a warning and she had to stop. It was then that the phone on her desk rang. It rang loud and clear. She picked it up.

She started to say something stupid like it hadn't rung before or she had been in the bathroom, but she decided to just be quiet. She had been caught up with what she was doing, and she really hadn't heard it ring.

"Sorry, Jennifer. It seems to be working now."

When Jennifer returned to Barbara's office, she tried to hide her face as she lifted her eyes. "So, what is it."

Jennifer swallowed whatever she might have wanted to say and instead said, "Sara wanted to speak with you. I told her you would give her a call back."

"Sara? Sara, who."

"Sara Locksmith. She is one of our clients..." Jennifer trailed off her response.

Barbara frowned while her mind went around searching for the name and finally she focused on it. "Ah, yes, I remember the Locksmiths. That was some time ago, wasn't it." She looked up at Jennifer. "What did she say?"

"All she said was she wanted to talk with you."

Barbara nodded her head. "Thank you Jennifer."

As Jennifer left, she was already locating the number in her cell and when she found it, she made the call.

As she waited, she refreshed her mind and by the time the phone was answered she recalled the job they had done for the Locksmiths.

When they first were in contact with this client, the Locksmiths, they had a big laugh over the name, but once they met the couple, who like them were going into business together, they gained a respect that overshadowed the faults of the name. They were financial advisors and were very successful.

She heard Sara's voice on the line. "Hello, Sara. Sorry I missed your call."

Sara told her not to worry about it and seemed to be dancing around as if all she wanted was to have small talk. Barbara listened, actually enjoying the interruption and having her mind on more pleasant things. Finally Sara asked, "How did you like the Great Win Chinese Restaurant."

Stunned, Barbara quickly tried to ascertain what she meant and then it came to her. Sara and Paul her husband had suggested they try the restaurant.

"Oh, it was fantastic. We've gone back several times since you told us about it. Maybe we can all go together some time."

She could tell that she had just given Sara the opening she needed. "We would like that. Maybe we can also take you up on your offer to let us come see the garden."

At first Barbara didn't understand, but slowly she remembered that she had offered to show them the sunken garden when it was done. "Oh, I wish we could, but it isn't completed yet." Barbara explained how the contractor had been unable to work on it for some time and then the weather kept interfering. She told Sara they, with the help of some of their friends, had been digging it out.

"You're kidding."

"I wish I were, but no, we have been at it for some time."

There was a pause. "Well, we want to help."

"I'm sorry, what do you mean."

"Come on, you did a fantastic job on our house, and we want to show you how much we love what you did."

"I can't ask you to help dig out our garden."

"You aren't asking, we are offering. I know Paul will be happy to help and we have some equipment that might be useful…"

"Ah, that's great, but because of the statues and such, we are down far enough that using equipment might not be feasible."

"Tell you what, I will ask Paul and he can talk with you or Neil. He can explain the equipment better than I can." She paused. "So, can we set a date for dinner. We could go with you to the Great Win Chinese Restaurant and then, check out the sunken garden?"

Barbara was smiling. She could tell that Sara was interested in seeing the garden as were most of their friends, so she gave in. Barbara checked her calendar and together they set up a dinner date.

Later that evening while they were eating a dinner of leftovers from the day before, Neil said, "Remember the Locksmiths…the real Locksmiths, not the one who opened our safe."

Barbara grinned. "Yes, I do, and I know you got a call."

Puzzled, but remembering that women talk, he said, "Paul thinks he can help with digging out the sunken garden.

He has a Kubota."

Laughing now, Barbara said, "What's a Kubota."

"Thought you would never ask. It's the perfect equipment for the job. It's a stand-on track loader that has wide tracks, narrow body. I've seen them. Landscape contractors generally use them since they have a 9.8-inch track on a narrow, 36-inch machine. It's low impact and minimizes damage to grass and landscaping."

"Ooh, I love it when you talk dirty," Barbara said as she moved closer to her husband and gave him a kiss that he eagerly reciprocated.

"Wait, let's clean up first. And, oh yes, she turned as she began carrying the dishes over to the sink, we're going out with them."

Neil walked over beside her. "I know. To the Great Win Chinese Restaurant, the one that Sara and Paul gave us a thumbs up, when we did that work for them."

Barbara gave her husband a grim expression. She could see how proud he was to be the one to tell her he also knew what they were going to do."

They finished in the kitchen and turned out the lights as they made their way to the living room and Neil picked up the remote. Soon they were watching the Big Bang sitcom.

Chapter 38

"Look at this," Barbara said pointing to her laptop screen. Neil, who had been making toast, came up behind her. "What is it."

Leaning over his wife's shoulder he read, "The Rochester Police Department has launched its cold case website that investigators hope will generate new leads in old cases. The original idea was simply to add unsolved murder victims' photos to a website, indicating that there are people who care, and their stories will never be forgotten. That quickly expanded to offering insight to survivor families and law enforcement."

Barbara paused. Neil who couldn't see the full screen as her head blocked it, said, "Don't stop. Read on."

"There are more than 550 open cold cases currently in the city of Rochester the Rochester Police Department Capt. Frank Kingsley said. The cold case website is an effort that has been a work in progress for some time, but gained momentum when Diane Tanner stepped into the role as interim chief of the Rochester Police Department."

Barbara stopped reading. "So, how does that concern us?" Neil asked.

"Come on Neil. Look, it says, Experience has shown that cold case programs can solve a substantial number of violent crime cold cases, including homicides and sexual assaults." Barbara turned and stared up at Neil, "Cold cases go back...way back. Maybe that's where we will find out more about the Bemishes."

"Yes, it might, but we know what there is to know about them. I'm sure a sunken garden is not part of a cold case..."

"Yes it is. Remember we know that the last time Georgia saw her husband was in the sunken garden. We know that from her diary."

"Okay, but I don't remember it saying she called the police, or anyone in authority and told them that; unless you know something I don't."

Barbara was pensive. "Well, maybe not, but it's worth a shot."

Neil looked down and then, pointing at the screen read, "The website is designed to bring awareness to unsolved cold cases by providing all of the public information about the case in one location,"

Barbara read with him and then added, "It says here the site is interactive, and people in the community can share anonymous tips."

"So it does my dear. Are you saying that you want to send a tip on the disappearance of one, William Bemish? If so what are you planning on saying; something like in or around 1918 a man named William Bemish disappeared..."

"Neil!"

"Don't interrupt me Barbara, I'm not finished. "That you think he disappeared in the sunken garden he created next to his house?" He looked at the expression on his wife's face and continued. "You can give him all the documents we have and tell them that and, oh yes, don't forget his wife Georgia who penned it all, died in a mentally ill asylum..."

"Stop. You're not being fair."

"I am Barbara. It won't make sense no matter how

you express it and besides, nowhere does it say he was murdered. They are trying to solve murder cases, not the *magically he suddenly disappeared in thin air* cases."

"Okay, okay you made your point."

Barbara was grinning as she said it, but inside she was already planning on going to the precinct at the first chance she got. Maybe there was something in their files they would share with her.

Steps away from their office, at police headquarters downtown, the detectives were being assigned to the newly formed cold case department. It was to be on a volunteer basis, and they could work on any of the cases in the files that suited them. The captain went over the details with the twelve officers picked to attend the meeting.

The captain began telling the squad, "Some cold case squads are formed because the volume of new cases or police initiatives prevents any work from being done on old cases." He smiled, "That's not the case here." The twelve officers in the room laugh, then grow silent as the captain continues. "Then some squads are formed out of convenience when a decline in new murder cases provides departments with the personnel and other resources necessary to begin investigating old cases." Again he pauses and looks out into the group. "Definitely not the case here. But it's what other squads are doing and so we are too."

The captain looked at the men before him. "This is not a cushy job." His face is serious as he says, "Cold case investigators have to be experienced and highly skilled individuals, to investigate unsolved homicides, missing persons cases, police-related shootings, and unidentified persons cases. When you look through the folders you will see that cold cases are defined as cases that are unsolved after a specific period of time; usually a year, as well as those with no identifiable leads."

Again he pauses and takes a sip of water. "Gentlemen if you decide to be part of this cold case division you will need to review a case to determine if new technology or new evidence exists that may help solve the case, so you may find in a cold cases file recent information has been added since we generally review them every time additional information about the case becomes available. But that doesn't mean they will be the easier to solve."

"As part of the squad you will be detectives in cold case investigations and utilizing the newest technologies and employ community policing partnerships when working cases. For example, recent advancements in DNA technology and other forensic techniques have allowed cold case investigators to reopen latent cases."

He pauses, then adds, "These detectives often spend their time inventorying evidence, seeking information from the investigators who were previously assigned to the case, re-interviewing witnesses or suspects, and working closely with forensic scientists. This systematic review of cold cases allows you to assemble and deploy resources and increase your chances of success. So are you interested?"

All twelve officers nod.

"You will break up into pairs and each pair should take a different case from the file. When you are sure of the one you want to start with, inform the other members of the squad. Is that understood?"

"Of course, if in your findings you come up to help on another case, immediately turn it over."

He scans the group. "The twelve of you meet that criterion, but only two of you can work full time. The rest of you will assist when you can, or work on a case of your choosing.. Do you have any questions, detectives?"

Several raised their hands. When all the questions had been answered or the detective given directions on how to find the answer, the Captain asked for two volunteers to head the group.

Both Detective Pagnelli and Greenberg raised their hands.

"Okay, then to start or head the cold case unit it will be Detective Pagnelli and Detective Greenberg. They will review and continue the investigation of unsolved homicides or suspected homicides in which the lead detective initially assigned may have retired, transferred, or otherwise left the case.

"Remember, all of you in this room have been considered because you have the right mix of investigative and supervisory talent but because of our work load we can only assign two full-time, but the rest of you can assist when needed. Outside of the squad here in this room, the two chosen can with discretion use the services of agencies such as the Federal Bureau of Investigation, coroner's office, or internal and external specialists."

"We'll start small and it if goes well, we will add on more men later. A smile, a nod of the head and the group dispersed.

It wasn't that the squad never worked on cold cases, but there had never been anyone specifically assigned to a cold case division, dedicated to the real cold cases that went way back. Detective Pagnelli and Greenberg had worked on cold cases before and knew that these older cases were the hardest to solve since the people concerned were dead and the evidence was scarce. It presented a challenge, and they were up to it, so they made arrangements to have the files from storage sent to the office the Captain had assigned to them. It wasn't until the next morning that they saw what had been delivered.

"What the?"

"I know."

"I thought."

"I know."

Catching their breath as they stared at the boxes surrounding the room, Detective Pagnelli said, "So, okay, let's just start a sheet summarizing each case in as few words as possible. You know like name, age of case, location maybe, and then what happened."

"Then what?" Detective Greenberg asked.

"Let's just start there."

Chapter 39

It was time for their dinner with Sara and Paul and Barbara and Neil met them at the restaurant. Unlike them, they got a slow start that night after a full day at work and when they arrived, Sara and Paul were already seated at a table.

"Can you forgive us," Barbara said, "we are so sorry to be so late. It's way beyond being sociably late and we apologize for keeping you waiting."

"Come on guys. We know how busy it can get in your line of business."

Barbara smiled and reached over to take hold of Sara's hand. "Thank you. Thank you for understanding."

That out of the way, the couple started catching up on what had been happening in their lives. When Barbara asked, "Should we order?" Sara gave her a sly smile and replied, "We, knowing what you like, already placed an order. I think you'll like our choices."

They had chosen a sampling of the most popular Chinese dishes and as they were placed, one by one on the table it was an array of color, aroma, and tastes.

It turned out they did. There was Beijing Roasted Duck, savored for its thin and crispy skin to be eaten with pancakes, sweet bean sauce, or soy sauce with mashed garlic.

Next to it was the Kung Pao Chicken. The major ingredients being diced chicken, dried chili, cucumber, and fried peanuts.

There was also Sweet and Sour Pork with its bright orange-red color, and a delicious sweet and sour taste.

And it didn't' stop there. The dish next to it was a surprise for Neil and Barbara. It was Hot Pot one of the most popular dishes in China. It was cooked in and eaten from a simmering pot of soup stock on a gas hob in the middle of the dining table with foodstuffs and condiments around the pot. They could add and cook whatever they desired in the hot broth.

There was not much talking as they tried everything and wanted to eat it while it was still steaming hot. When they had finished with only a few scraps left, the table was quickly cleared and replaced with a steaming pot of black tea and a bowl of fortune cookies. And that's when it got interesting.

They took turns reading their fortunes out loud. Paul went first. " A good way to keep healthy is to eat more Chinese food." He looked up with a smirk on his face and they laughed.

Neil followed. "A new voyage will fill your life with untold memories." He paused frowning. "I wonder what that means?"

"It means you are in for a surprise. That would be my guess," Paul replied, and Neil gave a hesitant nod.

"Okay, let me read mine," Sara said, quieting them down as she began. "A journey of a thousand miles begins with a single step." A frown appeared on her face as she stared at her message, then looked over at Neil. "I guess we're going to take a journey together pal. Shall we bring them along?"

"Funny." her husband said, and everyone laughed

again.

"Okay, it's your turn Barbara."

Barbara had been listening as they read theirs and now she unfolded hers and started, "Right now is the best you're ever going to feel. Give up."

No one said a word for several minutes and then finally, trying to ease the tension at the table, Neil said, "These fortune cookie messages are a hoot, aren't they.

They could visibly see the tension being released in their faces, and then their shoulders as everyone began breathing normally again. At that moment, the waiter came with the bill. Neil and Paul settled up while Barbara and Sara went to the lady's room. Once inside, Barbara turned to Sara and started to speak.

"Don't say a word, I know what you're thinking Barbara. That was a cruel message, but it's not real. It's a fortune cookie for god's sake. Don't let it get to you."

Barbara stared at herself in the mirror then turned to Sara. "I'm going to be honest with you Sara. I have been worried ever since we uncovered that sunken garden and the closer we get to revealing it, the worse my *Spidey* sense goes off. On the chance of sounding crazy, I'm telling you there is something down there and I don't want to find out what it is; especially in the dark, so I'm asking that we don't go to look at the garden tonight." She paused and reached over to take Sara's hand. "Between that and now the fortune cookie I hope you will understand and beg off tonight and we'll set up something during the day tomorrow…anytime you wish. Just please not at night."

Sara could see how frightened her friend was and immediately agreed. "Sure. Don't worry about it. It's late and I'm tired too." As they started to leave, Sara gave her a hug. "Always believe your senses, they usually prove true."

Barbara managed a smile. "Now that's a great fortune cookie message."

Laughing, they left the ladies room and joined their husband who had moved over to the bar and were enjoying a cup of Saki.

"So, where's ours," the women said in unison. Neil called over to the bartender and soon there was a cup in front of them. They sipped it and chatted for a while longer before they went out to the parking lot. It was then that Sara said, "Listen, I don't know how you are all feeling, but I for one would like to call it a night."

"But, honey, we are going to see the sunken garden. Did you forget?"

"No, but all that food and the Saki has me begging to differ. I think the right choice is to call it a night and set up something later."

Barbara nodded. "I'm with Sara. Why not have a luncheon at our place tomorrow around noon and we can then go see the garden."

"Oh, yes, and we can put on our digging clothes. Right?"

"I agree with that," Neil replied.

Chapter 40

It wasn't a lie; they were all tired and quite full after the meal they had consumed. Barbara was proud of how Sara had managed to end the evening and equally proud of how she had come up with an alternative. It didn't sound planned. Now as she got ready for bed, she felt relaxed and ready for a good night's sleep. Barbara was tired and as soon as her head hit the pillow she fell into a deep sleep that soon after closing her eyes draws her into a hellish nightmare.

It is dark, cold and raining but she is in her nightgown wandering in the yard and making her way down the steps into the sunken garden. She tilts her head wondering how she got there and feels a hand pushing her forward and she doesn't resist until she is suddenly pushed face down and feels a weight on her back. She struggles to no avail and tries desperately to breathe, but it's hard with the weight holding her down. She stiffens and her muscles are rigid as a cold dread hits her.

Finally it ends and she waits a moment to be sure no one is there before she pushes herself up and wipes the mud from her hands on her nightgown and then reaches to the back of her nightgown and pulls it forward to wipe her eyes.

She senses someone near and at first keeps her eyes shut, but finally opens them to see a woman standing in front of her. She looks like a shadow and Barbara has the feeling that if she reaches to touch her, her hand will disappear inside her body.

The woman's features appear sorrowful, and Barbara doesn't hesitate when she beckons her to follow. She takes her out of the garden. They walk across the lawn to the far side of the house and then suddenly they are in the basement. and no matter how hard she struggles; she can't pull away. It is like her body is no longer in her control.

Afraid, she keeps her eyes squeezed tightly closed, praying that it will end and when it does she manages to open her eyes and sees a woman with wings standing in front of her, beckoning her to follow her and this time she does without fear.

At first they are gliding across the lawn and then suddenly they are back in the basement. Barbara no longer feels safe and lets out a small gasp. Her skin tingles and a heavy sensation is in her stomach. She feels threatened and she no longer trusts this woman, when suddenly the woman has her faces inches from her, and she senses they are sharing the same vision as the letter written by Georgia comes to life.

Barbara tries to wake up. She can feel her heart pumping madly in her chest and her body jumps backwards as she tries to get away.

Again, she forces her eyes open and this time she sees Neil leaning over her. It is easy to read his feelings as she stares into his face, his eyebrows pulled up and together, his mouth stretched and drawn back, exposing teeth. She realizes he is sensing her fear.

Slowly she manages to pull herself out of her nightmare and reaches up to grasp Neil's neck and bring him down beside her. He pulls her into his arms, and she feels his strength flow into her.

Neil finally releases his grip and pulls back, and she

sees he has a distraught expression on his face as he asks. "Sweetie, why are you covered in mud…and your dripping wet."

She wants to tell him, but is afraid he won't believe her, so she just laughs it off and says, "Why do you think?" Before making her way into the bathroom..

She stays in there a long time trying to make sense of what happened and knowing it was more than a nightmare but how much was true. She climbed in the shower and scrubbed her body hard and when she finally felt clean, she got out and dried herself. When she entered the bedroom she saw that the sheets had been changed and Neil was sound asleep again. Barbara went over to her side of the bed and laid down. She surprised herself. It wasn't until she opened her eyes did she realized she must have slept because the light of day was coming through the window.

Barbara rubbed her eyes and stretched her arms above her head. She turned and saw that Neil was already up, so she hurried to get ready. She brushed her teeth and hair and seeing the nightgown on the floor in the bathroom, she picked it up and put it in the laundry. The movement was quick, and she didn't take a moment to study it. She had stepped out of it, showered and gone to bed naked. Now as she stared down at the floor she saw not a speck of dirt. "How can this be."

She then went back into the bedroom and checked the floor around it and the bed itself. Strange, she thought as everything seemed clean. There was no mud anywhere.

Shaken, she hurried and put on her clothes and rushed downstairs where she found Neil in the kitchen making breakfast as if nothing had happened. She went up behind him and put her arms around his waist. "Good morning sunshine."

"Good morning." Cautiously she asked, "How did you sleep?"

"I slept like a log. I was exhausted."

At that moment she knew he either didn't remember the night or she had dreamt it all, right up to waking this morning. Somehow she wasn't sure that was true.

Neil had prepared a big breakfast for them of eggs, sausage, toast, hash browns, orange juice and coffee. She set the kitchen table and helped him bring the food over. When she finally sat down, she realized she was ravishingly hungry. From the way Neil was forking it in, he was too.

They ate in silence and when they finished, Neil got up and bought the coffeepot over to refill their cups. On his way back he turned on the television.

The anchor is giving the news summary. "These are our top stories. More flooding is possible for the storm weary Northeast. Wildfire smoke affects air quality in over a dozen states, Phoenix experiencing a heat record, and the weather is looking good."

Neil smiled at Barbara over the top of his cup as he took a sip of coffee. She smiled back. Slowly they got up and carried the remains of their breakfast over to the sink. Barbara rinsed the dishes and handed them to Neil who put them in the dishwasher. When they heard the news anchor say, "Here's the weather report for today." They stopped what they were doing and went back to the table.

The weatherman made a slight joke and then began.

"After record breaking rain and thunderstorms yesterday evening that lasted into the night, the sky looks clear and bright today. Expect temperatures in the high sixties with no rain in sight. The temperature will reach an overnight low of 40s so get out and enjoy this great autumn day."

"Well, it should be okay to work in the garden today."

Barbara didn't answer right away.

"Barbara, what do you think."

"Sure, oh sure. Sara and Paul are looking forward to it. Do you want me to call or you."

"I'll call them, Neil said as he picked up his cell."

"Don't you think it is too early to call them now?"

Barbara had barely gotten the words out when her phone rang. She picked it up and then looked over at Neil. "Apparently it's not too early," she said as she connected the call. After a lot of head bobbing and yeses, she disconnected the call to see the anxious look on her husband's face.

"It's all set. They will be coming over for lunch at noon and after that we will spend the day digging in the garden. I told them to dress appropriately as it was going to be wet and muddy."

"You think?" Neil said getting up and checking out the window. "It looks pretty dry out now and it should be fine by then."

Barbara followed and looked outside, not surprised it wasn't like she thought it would be. "Yes, it should be fine."

They finished cleaning up the kitchen and while Barbara started the dishwasher and put in a load of laundry, Neil went out to mow the lawn.

While she waited, she planned the lunch. She checked the pantry and the fridge to see what they had and wrote down some items they needed to purchase. When Neil came in after mowing the lawn, she sent him upstairs to shower and change. "You stink my friend."

"But we're going to be digging in the garden."

"So. You don't have to smell beforehand. Take a shower and I'll go to the grocery. I need to get a few things for lunch."

While Neil showered, Barbara went to Wegmans to make her purchases. Of all the people not to run into when she was in a hurry, it would definitely be Ashley Aurand, whom she had met only twice but had found her annoyingly obnoxious. The woman was an architect and so was her husband. But Ashley lived and breathed her work which was obvious since she, along with her husband Mason Matsegna were serious members of The Architectural Foundation of Greater Rochester. They weren't just members, they recruited, and helped fund the foundation.

Under different circumstances Barbara could admire a woman like Ashley, but she had a feeling it wasn't the same for Ashley. Of course she worked basically in the same field, but she just couldn't measure up to architects in Ashley's eyes. She also felt her distaste for women who took on their husband's names. She had actually said, "That's so quaint, wouldn't you say," Barbara had wanted to respond to that, but she felt Neil putting pressure on her arm and she knew not to say anything. Besides, if you were a member of the Architectural Foundation, you were up for the best jobs.

Now as the woman came towards her she put a smile on her face, glad she was a successful woman because if not, Ashley was also the type to make you feel small…exceedingly small.

"Hello Ashley."

"Hello, um, I'm at a loss."

"It's Barbara, Neil's…"

"Ah Neil Sanders." She tossed her head as she moved toward Barbara. "I'm sorry. I didn't recognize you. It's been a long time."

The two women started chatting about the business, the jobs they had worked, and once Barbara felt comfortable, she said, "Well, I'm glad we ran into each other, but I have to scoot."

Ashley raised her eyebrows. "You have to scoot."

"I mean, I have people coming over this afternoon and I have to get back to the house."

Again Ashley's eyebrows raised. "Anybody I know?"

"I'm sure you do. It's Sara and Paul Locksmith. We're just having them over for a little lunch."

Ashley moved her cart in front of Barbara's and leaned across it. "Just a little lunch."

At that moment, her husband Mason joined them. "Oh, hello Barbara. Good to see you."

"Hon," Ashley said, "Barbara saying they are having the Locksmith's over for a little lunch."

The way she said it made Barbara feel as though she was a little kid trying to pull something over on her mother and before she knew it she was smiling and saying, "If you are not busy this afternoon, would you like to join us?"

Ashley gave Mason a coy smile and he nodded his head. "That would be wonderful Barbara. What time should we be there?"

"Around one is fine. It's a casual thing so you don't need to dress…"

"I know," Mason said. "Neil told me that you ran into some problems with the contractor that was supposed to dig out your sunken garden. It seems he just disappeared or something."

Barbara interrupted him. "He didn't just disappear. I think he was worried about using his equipment and destroying the structures in the garden so he's working on an alternative plan."

Mason's expression changed as he said, "You don't

know?"

"Don't know what?"

It was Ashley's turn to let Barbara know she was aware of what was going on at their house. "Yes, we know Nathaniel Parker who owns DirtWorx. We've used him on several occasions. He's an honest man and doesn't usually just quit a job."

Now Barbara was interested and didn't mind that it probably showed on her face. "So, why did he stop coming. I think Neil had trouble trying to even reach him."

Mason nodded. "I know. He mentioned to us he was available but didn't give us the whole story; just that he wasn't able to complete the job for you. When I asked him why, he said that it was delicate work, and he didn't have the right equipment."

"So, that's it, then."

"Yes, but I know Nathaniel well. If he didn't have the equipment he would have gotten it to complete the job. He's not one who takes his work lightly." He paused staring off in the distance. "I think it was something else."

Barbara was worried. "Did he take offense to Neil. Did Neil or I offend him in some way? Because if we did, we would go over to his office and apologize in person."

Not her usual way, Ashley surprised Barbara. "No, no, honey, you did nothing, nor did Neil do or say something. The man was scared."

Barbara relaxed. "Ah, I see. He was afraid he'd ruin something. I can understand that."

"No, not exactly. He was afraid of the sunken garden."

Barbara didn't know what to say and she remained quiet. Finally Ashley said, "We also know that you need help digging and many of our friends have been helping. They say, in your own words, it's a hoot, getting their hands dirty and anxiously awaiting the conclusion. It's the talk amongst our group that there is something down there. It's also the rumor…"

"Ashley. Enough already" Mason said, then turned to Barbara. "Barbara, if you don't mind, we would love to join you not only for lunch but going out and helping with the dig. Watching excavators is thrilling, but in this case it's like a prize at the end of the tunnel and we want to join in."

Barbara smiled at both of them. "Why not. We'll see you around one this afternoon."

"Great. We'll bring a special bottle of wine we have…" Ashley leaned toward Barbara, "Yes, we know about the wine cellar. I tell you, there's no secrets in this town."

Barbara finalized the details and then went about doubling her order of groceries, all the time thinking to herself, 'Yes, there are secrets in this town, Ashley. Yes there are.'

Chapter 41

At the checkout Barbara placed a call to Neil.

"What's up, sweetie."

"Well, there will be two more for lunch."

"Oh, who else is coming?"

"Well, I happen to run into Mason Matsegna and Ashley Aurand; the architects."

"You don't have to explain who they are. They are the reason I've been so successful."

"No, you are the reason you are so successful."

"Right, right. Okay it sounds good to me."

"Aren't you going to ask me if they plan on digging this afternoon."

"Don't need to. I know they will join us. They're our kind of people. They love being a part of an adventure."

"Call it that if you want," Barbara whispered silently.

"What was that?"

"Oh, nothing. Say, do you think it will be all right with Sara and Paul? I mean, they were expecting us four."

"Are you kidding. They will be excited to have them join in. To be honest, I can't wait to begin. I'm sure that Mason can answer any questions I have."

"What kind of questions do you have."

"Just about the statues we've uncovered and the layout of the concrete paths…. and."

"I get it. See you soon."

As Barbara made her way home, she drove pass the Irondequoit United Church of Christ building on Titus Avenue and wanted to stop, but she was running late. So she kept going. Then on St. Paul Blvd she glanced over at the Presbyterian church and again felt the need to stop but didn't. The urge was there, but the words were not. Telling a stranger what she was feeling about a sunken garden was not something anyone could easily explain. Besides that, how did she expect to explain something that she herself didn't understand.

Soon she was pulling into the garage and before she could turn off the engine, Neil was at the side door of the house. She pressed the garage door button, planning to act as excited as he did about the upcoming festivities.

Neil went to the back of her car and grabbed several bags of groceries while Barbara turned off the car and got out. She then joined Neil, taking the last bag out of the trunk of the car. She carefully arranged her face before looking up at Neil who was still smiling. He gave her a quick kiss, then he headed for the door with Barbara at his heels.

What was going to be a simple lunch, while shopping she had decided on a more sophisticated meal of Spring Salad with Berries, Crispy Chicken Thighs With Roasted Radishes and Lemon-Orange Chiffon Cake

As Neil helped her put the groceries away, Barbara supervised announcing what she needed left out in preparation of the meal. When she was ready to start, Neil worriedly asked, "Barbara. Do you think you can get everything ready in time?"

"Yes, it sounds involved, but it's quite simple." She went over to the computer in the kitchen and pulled up the recipes, sending them to the printer and without being asked,

Neil went to retrieve them. He was reading out loud and walking as he returned to the kitchen. "Okay, I'm your sous chef. Tell me what to do."

They got right at it, laughing and talking a mile a minute about nothing as they put the meal together and Barbara's uneasiness vanished as they prepared the food. They sliced, diced and measured to perfection and since they didn't need to dress for the occasion, it was all they had to do before the guest arrived.

The first to arrive were Sara and Paul. They were no sooner inside the door than Neil announced, "There will be another couple joining us."

"That's great. The more the merrier. Who is it?"

"It's Mason Matsegna and Ashley Aurand."

Paul smiled. "We know them. Ashley and Mason are our clients. They've made a lot of money through investments we have sent their way." Paul paused. "By the way when are you two going to hire us as your financial advisors?"

Neil laughed. "Funny you should ask. I mentioned that just the other day to Barbara. We've been so busy we haven't thought about it, but we know we need your help in that area."

"Good," Paul said as he walked with Neil into the kitchen. "Now, tell me, what can I do to help."

Barbara turned to Sara and gave her a hug then walked over to Paul and hugged him. "Welcome you two and," turning toward Sara added, "thank you for being so understanding."

"Of course. Us women have to stick together, but I can't lie. I am anxious to get out in that garden."

"Well, lunch first and then we dig." The two were laughing as Sara started helping in the kitchen. They were in the midst of putting the salad together when the doorbell rang again. "That will be Ashley and Mason," she giggled. "Can't introduce them any other way since she kept her last name. It's Mason Matsegna and Ashley Aurand or just Ashley and Mason."

Barbara and Sara were giggling, then managed to get serious so they could finish preparing the lunch.

With Sara's help and Neil taking care of the rest of their visitors, the luncheon was a success. Barbara could see they appreciated the effort she had put into the meal and her spirits were lifted, keeping her mind off the second half of the afternoon. Everyone helped with cleaning up the dishes and putting the food away. Then, once that was done, Mason turned around and picked up the bottle of wine he had brought. "My friends, this is Armand de Brignac Ace of Spades Brut Gold (750 ml). They say it is rich with the old-world traditions of champagne blending, it is a trio of vintages from some of the most lauded terroirs in the region, resulting in a prestige cuvée that expresses vibrant fresh fruit character, and layers of complexity."

Mason was comically dancing around with the bottle of wine and when he completed his repertoire he paused in front of Neil. "This is for you, my friend. You can put it in your wine cellar, which I hope we will get a chance to see, and later, once the garden is revealed, we can all get together," he added with a flourish, "And toast the sunken garden."

Everyone was laughing at his joviality and when Neil had caught his breath he said, "Okay, my friends, first of all, I thank you for this exquisite bottle of wine." Then surprising Barbara, added, "Now, if the kitchen is cleared, we will all go down and put it in the wine cellar so if anything happens to any of us..."

"Neil," Barbara said, no longer laughing.

"I'm just kidding Barbara. Nothing is going to happen, but all of us will know where the bottle is stored on that special day when the sunken garden is complete."

Barbara felt Sara rub her back lightly and turned to smile at her. They all headed down to the cellar with Barbara and Sara following behind everyone. "It's going to be fine," Sara said, sensing her friend was nervous about all of this. "Just fine."

Barbara managed to smile and gave Sara's hand a squeeze. "That's twice you saved me."

Not sure exactly what Barbara meant by that, she knew not to question her, and they made their way to the wine cellar where the others had already gathered. They stood near the back and watched as Neil with a comical flourish of his hands and a bow of his head, placed the bottle in one of the open slots on the front wine rack. He turned to his observers and said, "Today we vow together that when the sunken garden is completed…"

Barbara cautiously added, "That means that not only is it revealed in total, but all the plants added and whatever needs repairs has been done."

"In other words," Neil said, smiling. When the project in its entirety is complete…" he looked over the heads, smiling at his wife and she nodded.

"Then, and only then will we return to this wine cellar and get this bottle." Neil's face went serious as he added, "That includes Sara Locksmith, Paul Locksmith, Mason Matsegna, Ashley Mat…Ashley Aurand, Barbara Sanders and me, Neil Sanders."

"Okay, enough with the dramatics, let's get out there." Mason said. We've been waiting long enough. I would have snuck by here if I didn't respect people's property and taken a serious look, but, alas, my mother taught me well. So without further ado, can we get started?"

It was like someone pulled the cork out of a bottle of

champagne as they all bubbled over with laughter. "Oh, Mason, you are such a card," Ashley said as she put her arm through his. Neil moved through the group and did the same with Barbara. "Come on then, times a wasting. Follow me and get your choice of weapons."

The rest followed them to the other side of the cellar where they kept the tools for digging. They picked up shovels, rakes, pruning shears, hatchets, axes and mauls. As they made their way upstairs, Paul asked, "So, where's the Kubota?"

"What," Mason asked and Paul, over his shoulder said, "A Kubota is a stand-on track loader that has wide tracks, narrow body. Landscape contractors generally use them since they are low impact and minimize damage to grass and landscaping."

"Yes, then," Mason added. "Let's use that."

"We will," Neil said, but it's in the back of the garage, along with the wheelbarrow." He is thoughtful then adds. "We will put all of these tools in the wheelbarrow…" He turns to Barbara, "Sweetie, can you move your car over to the side of the driveway so we can get them out?"

"No problem." Barbara said as she hurried through the house, grabbed her keys and when into the garage. She was just parking the car off to the side when the rest of the party joined her.

It was all business at that point. Paul got on the Kubota and Mason who left with Neil put the ramp in place that Paul would drive down, then they both stood guard as Paul expertly drove the Kubota down the ramp.

Barbara, Sara, and Ashley came with the rest of the equipment, some of their equipment fit in the wheelbarrow, while the other pieces the women carried.

Neil guided the entourage to where they could enter

the garden safely. Paul turned to Neil and spoke. "I have a waterproof cover for the Kubota. I'll bring it so you can keep it down here. Once it is dug out completely, it will be impossible to get it back down here."

"Sounds like an excellent idea." Neil said smiling.

That was the last part of the conversation as everyone grabbed a tool and they started clearing the area. Barbara and Sara stayed near the front carefully removing the dirt which was only a light layer above what seemed to be the base of the garden. Off to their left was Ashley, picking up debris and putting it into the wheelbarrow while Mason moved it over to the far side. Since it was down low and there where stairs almost completely revealed, he used them, walking up the contents of the wheelbarrow. After several trips he turned and said, "Did you ever think of putting in a ramp."

At first they were laughing, but then Neil said, "That's not a bad idea. Come on Mason."

The two left the garden and the rest continued digging and clearing out areas until they returned. Paul yelled down, "Guys, get over here. We are going to lower several planks. They are quite sturdy so we can wheel the barrow up and maybe even the Kubota when we're done. That ramp we used before was quite unsteady and we could make something sturdier."

They all went over to the side where Mason and Neil stood above. They began gently lowering the first plank and supervised the placement so that it was on a cleared area and at a slope that was possible to come up with the wheelbarrow. That meant that it practically ran the full width of the garden, but it worked. They did the same with the next three. When they finished they had a ramp that was at least wide enough for the Kubota to attempt being driven up. They knew it was sturdy enough.

That done, they all went back to clearing the area.

Hours passed by without anyone showing signs of quitting. Barbara pulled out her cell. It was close to eight. Soon it would be dark so she said, "I think we should stop now." We'll get cleaned up and order some food." She paused. "And Neil can get us a couple bottles of wine to drink with our meal."

Ashley stretched. "As much as I hate to stop, it sounds great." She gave them a weak smile and added, "I'm ready to call it quits."

"Yes, me too," Mason added and the rest nodded.

They started putting the equipment into the wheelbarrow and Neil carefully pushed it up the ramp. The others took the stairs that were visible now on either side of the front of the garden. When they were all up top they stood looking down, that is all except Barbara. Barbara stared at the entourage. There were faces smudged with dirt, dirt in their hair and all over their clothing. They were lucky that it wasn't muddy like it had been the last time and there were just some spots that left mud caked to their shoes and their gloves.

It had been an arduous task, but worth it as they admired their accomplishment together. "Can you believe it?" Sara said. "Look at it. Look what we've done."

Over three quarters of the garden was revealed now, and the last section was no longer grade level with dirt and debris. There were only several feet still covering that area now.

They started toward the house. Once they were in the garage Barbara said, "Did everyone remember to bring a change of clothes? If not, we have some clothes you can change into."

She saw them nodding, moving slightly slower than they had on their way out. "Let's get inside. Don't worry about the dirt. I'll go in and get some towels so you can clean up before you change."

Several minutes later, they had retrieved their clothes and were in the house. Barbara guided the couples to bathrooms where they could shower and change. Mason and Ashley took the bathroom downstairs and Paul and Sara took the one in the hallway upstairs. Neil and Barbara used the one in their bedroom.

Almost an hour later everyone was clean and in the kitchen where they stood at the island deciding what they wanted to eat. It was first suggested that they eat leftovers, but the final consensus was to order a pizza from Two Ton Tony's. They placed their order over the internet and while they waited, Neil and Paul went down into the cellar to retrieve a couple bottles of wine. Mason checked out the labels and smiled. "Yes, you guys have a very good collection going on, a very good collection indeed."

Chapter 42

The next few weeks Barbara and Neil were so busy at work there was no time spent in the garden. That suited Barbara fine though she had to admit she didn't get that strange feeling she had when they were all down there digging. One evening as they sat outlining the next day, the phone rang.

"Stay. I'll get it," Barbara said as she rushed to the extension in the kitchen. When they had worked on updating the house, Neil wanted to get rid of the wall phone. He actually wanted to get rid of the land line, but Barbara couldn't. Sure the cell was convenient and portable, but there was something about that landline that made her smile every time it rang.

Now as she took it off the receiver she was smiling as she said, "Hello."

At first there was silence and then slowly the person on the line spoke.

"Is this Barbara? Is that you Barbara?"

"Yes, who am I speaking to?"

Again a pause on the other end of the line before finally the voice said, "This is Andrea McBride."

"Ah, Andrea. How are you?"

Neil turned at the mention of the McBride sister and

watched his wife as she moved across the kitchen, uncoiling the phone.

"I'm fine, Barbara. And how are you?"

Barbara could hear someone in the background whispering, "Get on with it Andrea."

"Is that Robin I hear in the background?"

"Yes, it is." There was a brief pause. "Barbara, can you come out to the winery?"

Barbara looked over at Neil and covering the mouthpiece whispered, "They want us to come out to the winery?"

Neil nodded. He knew Barbara was aware of all their appointments so there was no need to discuss it further.

At that moment Neil had a flashback.

He had been on a job, one that Barbara wasn't working with him on, and he and the customer were going over the details for the build, when a man came up to them, "Hi Neil. Long time no see." Neil paused what he was doing and looked up to see a gentleman he couldn't place.

"Sorry, do I know you?"

"See how long it's been. I worked with Warren, Warren Pendergast, the realtor who sold you the house at Parcel 076.06 Winona."

Neil looked up, not even trying to hide the surprise on his face. "That's funny. I tried to reach Warren some time back and no one knew him in town. I checked and he didn't work in any of the real estate offices in Rochester."

"Oh, was there a problem," The man said with a sarcastic tone to his voice.

Neil didn't want to get into anything; especially not on the site of his client so he excused himself and went over to stand next to the man. "Sir...by the way, what is your name?"

"My name doesn't matter. What does matter is that you shouldn't have bought that house. No one should buy that house."

"What is that supposed to mean."

"It means what I said, because you are now in danger."

"How so?"

Neil saw the angry scowl and I realized that it would not be wise to carry on. "Just heed my words and stop that digging. Just fill it all back in and then get out of that house."

Neil was about to ask why, but the man turned and walked away. He stood there in shock, then started to go after him. He made it to the door of his client's store, glanced around, but couldn't see the man anywhere so he took a deep breath to calm himself and went back to his client.

"What was that all about?"

Neil shook his head. "Tell you the truth. I don't know." With that, the two went back to what they were doing.

Now as he sat there looking at Barbara, his mind was going over that strange encounter. He had forgotten all about it until now. He was still thinking about it when Barbara hung up the phone and came back to join him.

Taking a deep breath he managed to clear his mind and asked, "What was that about?"

"Well, I'm not sure. It was Andrea McBride on the phone, and she wants to see me tomorrow morning. She asked if I could come over around nine o'clock tomorrow and I told her I could."

"Am I to come with you?"

"I don't think so. She said she just wanted to see me."
Barbara paused. "It was a funny conversation. Maybe she
wants something changed in the design…I'll find out."

Neil gave her a nod and they returned to what they
were doing.

They had been sipping wine while they worked and
now Barbara stood up, holding the empty bottle in her hand.
"I think we should call it a night my friend. What do you
say?"

"I say, yes. Just let me lock up and I'll join you
upstairs."

Neil went about checking doors and windows. He put
on the alarm they had added to the house a while back. Even
though he thought no one knew about the wine cellar beyond
his friends, he heeded their suggestion that those were
expensive bottles, and he should have some protection.

"You know how people talk, trying to show that they
know more than the next, especially when they are drinking.
Or someone could overhear a conversation about the wine
cellar. In any case, it wouldn't hurt to put in a security
system."

So Neil had done just that. Once he had checked all
the doors and windows, he turned on the security before
heading up to bed.

He had reached the top landing when he thought
again about that mysterious man, and he recalled a
conversation he had previous to that encounter. He had put in
a call to Warren Pendergast, their realtor to ask him some
questions about the property. When he made that call he now
remembered them saying. "There's no Mr. Pendergast

working here or any record of a realtor with that name."

As he stood there, a frown covered his face recalling both conversations now. Both times he hadn't given much thought to the encounter or the phone call since he had been busy and had put them aside, planning to consider the matter later. Only it had slipped his mind.

Thinking of them both now, he wondered what it meant. Then, Neil smiled and said to himself, "Too much wine my friend. Too much wine." He then hurried up the stairs and went about getting ready for bed.

When he entered the bedroom he saw his wife was already asleep, so he turned out the light and climbed in beside her. He kissed the fingers of his hand and gently placed them against her cheek, then turned over and soon was asleep.

They overslept. Barbara woke first and gave him a big shake as she padded across the floor to the bathroom. "Get up" she said anxiously. "We're running late...actually, I'm running late. I'm supposed to go out to meet Andrea this morning at nine o'clock, remember, and it's already eight."

Startled out of deep sleep, Neil glanced around the room, trying to get his bearings. Sensing movement, he stares across the room and watches as his wife disappears into the bathroom. Slowly he stretches his arms above his head and that movement clears the fog from his brain. He swings his feet over the edge of the bed and continues staring at the bathroom door.

From the bathroom comes the sound of Barbara brushing her teeth and then he hears her spitting in the sink before she says. "I'll take my sketches with me, and you need to take your drawings with you. I won't be long, and I'll meet you at the office and we can go to the client's together. That appointment is at eleven o'clock, so we have plenty of time, but if I'm late, you have a backup copy of my sketches in the pile with yours."

Catching up, he considers what his wife is saying and soon translates her words. She is going to the McBrides and will have the sketches for their eleven o'clock appointment with her. She plans on making that appointment, but if she is late, she has given him a copy of the sketches for their client.

It makes him smile to know his wife so well he doesn't need an explanation. And he needs to get moving too. Today is a two-car day for them since they are going in opposite directions.

There is no further conversation as Barbara climbs into the shower. She doesn't wash her hair, but instead quickly washes her body. When she climbs out, she dries herself and then taking her hands, starts fluffing her hair as she moves over to the sink to put on a little makeup and her deodorant before hurrying back into the bedroom.

Barbara starts to say something, but in anticipation of her words, Neil is up and walking toward her. He gives her a kiss before going into the bathroom. In the doorway he pauses and thoughtfully says, "Don't worry, it'll all work out. It always does."

Barbara couldn't remember ever dressing that fast, but she was out the door in record time and on her way to the McBride winery. It was, unlike most places in Rochester, a little more than 20 minutes away, but she forced herself to remain calm, driving the speed limit. Luckily, she managed to make it, only catching two stop lights on the way.

When she climbed out of the car, she grabbed her briefcase. As requested, she went directly to the house. She was about to knock when the door was opened, and Andrea stood there with a funny smile on her face. She hugged Barbara and then moved aside to let her in.

Andrea guided her to the kitchen where her sister Robin was in the midst of laying out a breakfast spread for them. Barbara hadn't realized she was hungry until the aromas hit her.

"This is nice. Thank you, but I really don't have much time for breakfast."

"There's always time for breakfast." They sat at the kitchen table that was up against the window in the kitchen. Barbara sat in a chair facing the window and watched as Robin and Andrea slid into the banquette built under the bay window.

Once they were all seated, Robin, with a flourish of her hand, said, "There's coffee, or if you prefer, tea." Help yourself."

Barbara reached over and picked up the carafe of coffee and filled her cup. She then watched as the sisters did the same.

In the center of the table was a plate of scones. "Try these. Robin made them," Andrea said. Robin added, "I'm known for my scones." She leaned over and pointed to the scones. "Blueberry, Classic Pumpkin and Lemon Blueberry Scones. You have to try them. They melt in your mouth."

Barbara was already reaching for a Lemon Blueberry scone which she placed on the plate in front of her. She then smiling, picked up her coffee. The room was quiet as they drank their coffee and enjoyed Robin's scones. When she thought it was proper, she asked, "So, why did you want to see me this morning."

Barbara saw the look pass between the sisters, before

Andrea spoke. "It's about your house."

Surprised, she said, "Okay, what about it."

"We don't know exactly, but back when you first came to the winery...before it was truly a winery, we both felt something," Robin explained.

"Yes, we did, but we didn't say anything and maybe we should have."

"What did you feel, exactly?"

"Actually we weren't sure until after you left and then we talked. It was a presence attached to you." Andrea frowned and added, "I know that sounds weird, but we felt it...both of us."

"Do you sense it now?"

The women nodded.

Barbara was confused. She took a sip of her coffee questioning if she should tell them and then looking over her cup she said. "I believe you. I think I've seen it. It's a woman named Mindy Worthington. At first I thought she was real, but I know she isn't."

Andrea nodded her head. "It could be, but I only know it is something. We didn't want to tell you because we thought it would upset you."

"No," Robin added, "Not upset you, but you would think we were crazy."

Barbara gave them a half smile. "So what made you tell me now."

"Andrea had a dream."

There was silence as they drank their coffee. Barbara was wondering if she really wanted to know more, but she was intrigued and glad she could honestly talk about what she had been feeling. Finally Andrea spoke.

"I dreamt that this presence...this woman was trying

to warn you about something in the sunken garden. I think it was a dream, but it seemed so real. It felt like I was walking with her as she told me you needed to stay away from the garden, something about going crazy if you let it take him."

Barbara was on the edge of her chair now. "Take who?"

Andrea was shaking her head. "I don't know. I started to ask, but I woke up. It scared me so bad I was shaking for hours and when I told Robin she said, "We have to tell her."

Barbara was quiet, trying to understand what Robin had said. She finally told them everything that had happened to her. She started with Mindy Worthington, about how she had been talking to this woman on the boat, and she thought that she saw Neil talking to her husband, only he said he didn't talk with any man named Warren that day. She told them she had then looked up the name.

Before she could tell them her findings, Robin interrupted her and looking more at her sister than Barbara said, "Mindy Worthington did exist. She is the granddaughter of John Leake."

"Yes, and rumor has it that Georgia Bemish...she's the woman who lived in that house before you, had also met a Mindy Worthington when they took a boat tour and her husband, William Bemish didn't see them either."

"That's impossible...it can't be the same Mindy." Barbara was confused as she stared across the table at the sisters. "So, what do you think that means?" Before the sisters can answer she adds. "This Mindy must have died a long time ago and if Georgia saw her...a really, really long time ago."

The two women shook their heads and Andrea said, "We don't know."

Getting it off her chest, Barbara goes even further and tells them of the hand touching her in the cellar. "Could that have been Mindy?"

Robin raised her brows as she said, "To my knowledge, grant you it is limited, but to my knowledge a spirit lives in one place and can't follow you around. If you met her on the boat, you wouldn't meet her anywhere else." She paused and seeing Barbara's expression added, "That's what I think, but I could be wrong."

Barbara considered it, but then said, "I had a dream and Mindy came to me and she took me into the sunken garden, and I think I saw something...heard something, but I can't remember what. I do know that I woke up screaming and later must have fallen back to sleep. When I woke in the morning there was mud on my feet. I saw it, but I don't think Neil did."

"You must be feeling as though you are going out of your mind. I would."

"I have been, but thankfully I am a strong person. She trailed off...if this is not Mindy I'm seeing now..."

"Oh Barbara. I'm sorry we didn't tell you sooner."

"I don't think it would have changed anything if you did."

They were quiet for a while and then Andrea said, "What do you know about the Bemishes."

Barbara knew what they were asking and said, "Georgia Bemish was mentally ill."

They nodded their heads and finished drinking their coffee. They insisted that Barbara take the remaining scones with her and walked with her to the door. "Listen Barbara, Andrea said, "If something bothers you, or you just need to talk, don't hesitate to call us. We'll help in any way we can."

Barbara gave them each a kiss on the cheek. Thanked them and drove to the office. Before she arrived, she had already made up her mind not to share their conversation with Neil.

Luckily by the time she entered his office they had to leave for the client's jobsite, and he didn't' have time to ask her. After presenting their sketches and talking in depth to the clients, they got the job. It was adding an upper floor to an existing old building, and they wanted it to be like…as they explained it…a crown on the top of the building. Somehow they had worked with that, and the customer was happy with what they came up with.

Neil was thorough. "I have to tell you outright this will be expensive. When building a second story addition it is a big project. We will call the zoning department and get authorization to add another floor as there might be height restrictions. That along with adding another bathroom on this addition may lead to increasing the old septic system capacity."

He paused. The homeowners were nodding their heads and the husband said, "We checked into that all ready." Seeing Neil's expression, he added, "We know you will have to verify it too, but I don't think that will be a problem."

"Great," Neil said as he explained that they were going to remove the roof, frame the new second floor over the existing footprint, and build a new roof. Sometimes the roof can be lifted off intact with a crane and then brought back when the new walls are framed, which may save money. But considering the age of the building, he explained that might not be possible."

Neil turned to Barbara. She smiled and said, "No matter what option I will make sure you have the right style for the addition. This is where the designer earns her keep." She saw the smiles on the customers' faces and continued. "It's one thing to recognize your spatial needs...two bedrooms and a full bath, and quite another to integrate the exterior shell of those spaces into the scale and style of your existing house. That's where I come in. Then later I work on the interior design."

Neil picked up from there saying, "The next step is to have our structural engineer evaluate your foundation and get the appropriate permits." He paused and asked, "Do you have any questions."

"Yes. I know you can't give us a firm quote just yet, but can you give us an idea?"

"Sure. I think you already know the addition will be expensive. Even without running into any problems, it will cost over $100 per square foot, and most likely cost somewhere between $200 and $300 per square foot, but no more than that. The one thing that should ease your conscience is to think of your second-story addition as an investment in your home. Adding a second story will not only increase your home's space, but it may also increase its resale value."

Seeing their faces Barbara asked, "Does that shock you?"

The owners shook their heads. "No, that's what we've heard. You have the job if you want it. Your reputation precedes you and we want it done right. When can you start."

They gave them a tentative date. They stood and shook hands before being shown out.

Barbara and Neil walked back to their cars. Before leaving Neil smiling said, "I don't know about you, but I am excited. It's been a while since we've done an addition to a home."

Barbara laughed. "Yes it has, and I am as excited as you." She meant it and was still smiling as she drove back to the office, following Neil.

Chapter 43

It seemed that Neil was no longer interested in the documents they had found or finding out anything that was written in the diary of Georgia Bemish. Each time that she talked about it, he would hush her saying they had a lot more important things to think about and they should let it rest for now.

But Barbara didn't let it rest. She continued her search and questions whenever she could. By now she was close with the McBride women who she met up with often and when she wasn't working, she was searching the internet.

One day she ran across the name R. Hills Bemish. She sat in her office with a fresh cup of coffee reading it aloud, just above a whisper. Thankfully the cover of her laptop hid her face so that no one passing by didn't think she was talking to herself.

"R. Hills Bemish," she read aloud, "was an American 20th Century artist...he primarily painted landscapes, sheep and wooded scenes, he worked around Utica, New York in the late 19th Century."

That piqued her interest. She knew that William Bemish was an art dealer. If this wasn't a relative, it might be someone he had a chance to meet. And so she went to another google search item.

"R. Hills Bemish (19/20th century) was active/lived in New York. R Bemish is known for Landscape painting. Primarily a painter of landscapes, sheep and wooded scenes, he worked around Utica, New York in the late 19th Century."

"Okay," she said to herself. "Give me more, please."

There was one labeled R. Hills Bemish Original Signed Watercolor Painting, Dated 1946 of Magical Forest and Stream, followed by a more hopeful listing of R. Hills Bemish/Biography. She clicked on it and read, "Biography R. Hills Bemish is an American artist who was born in the 20th Century. R. Hills Bemish's work has been offered at auction multiple times, with realized prices ranging from 30 USD to 200 USD, depending on the size and medium of the artwork."

Disappointed and anxious she reprimanded herself, "Patience, Barbara, patience." She could feel herself being irritated by the search but continued. Another site offered up the same information.

Again she clicked on another site and found more of the same. She was biting her lip as she clicked on another link and read, "R. Hills Bemish, (XIX-XX)." She paused. That meant no actual birth date or death date. After that it was more of the same.

There was one more link remaining, and she clicked on it. She scrolled through the list of artists and came to R. Hills Bemish, only to find the following words after his listed name with no picture of the man. *There is no personal data. Check Wikipedia.* She did and came up blank.

Jennifer stood at Barbara's office door, calling her name. It wasn't until the third time that Barbara stretched her neck up and cleared her mind as she focused on her.

"Oh, Jennifer. What can I do for you."

"Are you all right?"

"Yes, of course. Just reviewing the plans for our next job," she lied. "It's been a while since we did an addition and I'm a little anxious is all."

"Well, you'll do fine."

"Did you want something?"

"Oh, yes, you have a phone call from Andrea McBride."

"Thank you Jennifer."

She watched as Jennifer left the office and she picked up the phone. "Hello Andrea."

A conversation began with Andrea listening to what Barbara had come across and then Andrea said she had learned nothing more after talking with people she knew.

Going back to her finding Barbara asked, "Andrea, do you think this might be a relative of William Bemish. He was a successful art dealer, and he came to live in Rochester, New York. His wife was from the New York City area. Maybe he was from Utica or thereabouts?"

"It's possible." Andrea paused. "Did you check the encyclopedia?"

"Yes, I went to Wikipedia and found nothing."

"No, not Wikipedia, the old books…encyclopedia."

"No. Where can I…Yes, the library."

Barbara hung up feeling hopeful as she put the matter aside and really did do some work on their upcoming project.

Chapter 44

It was days before Barbara could find time to go to the library. She made some leeway on her designs but as they had expected their most recent project turned out to be problematic. They ran into zoning and permit problems that would take a while to resolve, before finally they were able to begin.

Once the permits were in place, the next step was removing the roof. Getting the equipment in the tight space around the home was not the only problem. They also had to make sure that the debris from the roof did not crush a fence or land on the neighbors' property. It was slow and tedious, but somehow they got that done and it was onto framing.

Barbara was wise in convincing the owners they had to stay elsewhere though they kept insisting they wanted to stay and watch the progress. Not trying to scare them, she had nicely explained that there would be no power, and no water coming to the house during the startup and that was enough to send them packing. They rented an apartment not far from the construction site, so that every day one or both would be out there watching.

For Barbara she had concerns in the design. Once the house was inspected and the *do's* and *don't do's* were laid out, they had to change the design of the roof line to meet code. Next there was the problem of the staircase that the owners wanted in one spot and she another. Finally she convinced them to go with her design.

Though she had to battle for her design, it was much harder for Neil. It was an old house and the supplies used differed greatly. He knew that going into the job, but he didn't realize that because of the pandemic, the back orders he would be facing. At each point in the project a delay set back the next step until he was worried they wouldn't get the roof back on before the snow fell. That was the deadline at this point. It had to be enclosed before the snow fell.

So, on this job, it wasn't surprising to see Barbara working side by side with her husband long after the crew stopped for the day. There was so much to do, and they could tell by the sky, their deadline was approaching so they filled in and worked long into the night.

When they finally felt comfortable that they were going to make it, Barbara was able to have some spare time until the details for the walls and room and bathroom layout were up for discussion. She took that time to go to the library.

Neil and Barbara walked to the job, so Barbara walked from there to the library. It was just before lunch hour and the streets were empty of people and only a few cars passed by as she went on her way.

The worse part was the cold. The temperature had dropped dramatically during the last few days and now, even in a heavy winter coat she was chilled. They had been in Rochester long enough to know that there was no depending on the weather. The best times to do any major project that would leave the building open to the environment were spring and autumn, in order to avoid both the winter cold and the summer heat, and in particular, the month of May and from mid-September to mid-October. June was often a good month as well, but sometimes it could be too hot working in close quarters without power.

In autumn, usually around late October the beauty of the trees changing made her realize why they had chosen to live in this city. Only now, it was well past that point and when she looked up at the bare trees lining the sidewalk, she found herself feeling a little depressed. It was chilly and the sky was gray, but when she reached her destination her spirits lifted.

She walked through the doors and looked around, trying to get her bearings, then finally went to the reception desk and asked, "Can you tell me where I would find information on local individuals?"

"You can take the stairs or the elevators and once you are on the second floor you go left and pass the City Historian's Office you will find the Local History Databases."

"What can I find there?"

The Librarian smiled as she leaned down and retrieved a pamphlet from behind the desk. She handed it to Barbara.

Barbara thanked her and headed for the stairs, looking over the information in the pamphlet that outlined the areas on the second floor. Along with the Local History Database section, there was the Local History & Genealogy, and the NYS Vital Records in the Reference area. She should be able to find what she needed in one of these sections, so hurrying to the location, she stopped first at the Database section.

It was not like surfing the internet, but once she got the hang of it, it wasn't half bad. It was sectioned off into American Ancestors, Ancestry, Fire Insurance Maps, a database called Find My Past, Heritage Quest, which was a partner of Ancestry that provides access to genealogical and historical resources for more than sixty countries, with coverage dating back to the 1700s. There was Life Records that included birth, marriage and death notices published in Rochester, NY, newspapers ca. 1960- 2016 and one called ProQuest Newspapers: New York, New Jersey, and Pennsylvania.

That caught her interest. It was like walking down the sidewalk and finding a bag of money. This was all the information that you could find online, but you had to pay for it. Here it was free, and it covered the areas that most interested her. Unfortunately when it came to the name 'Bemish' she couldn't find anything more than she already knew. She noticed the reference to Georgia being the Wife of William heir to the J.K. Post Drug company and did a search on the name, Georgia Post. She found nothing. Next she did a search on J. K. Post and again came up with zilch.

Barbara pulled out her cell and saw that she had been at the library for over an hour. Whether or not she had anything new, it was time to go back to the office, so she gathered her purse and as noted on the wall, she made sure she closed out all her searches. She then made her way back down the stairs, her mind going a mile a minute until she reached the bottom of the stairs. There she paused, leaned her head back and then forward and hummed a tune, something she had learned a long time ago would calm her thoughts. By the time she reached the front door, her head was clear.

Since she was a little girl, she had hummed when she got too into her head, and it still worked for her. She kept humming as she made her way back to the office, barely noticing the cold. When she entered the office, she smiled at Jennifer. "Any messages?"

Jennifer returned her smile and came from behind her desk to hand her the messages and Barbara stood there looking through them. Finally she came to one from Andrea McBride and put it on the top as she turned and went to her office.

Barbara didn't bother to sit as she pulled out her cell and returned the call to Andrea, who surprised her by answering at the first ring.

"Andrea."

"Barbara."

"Yes, you called?"

There was silence for a while and then trying to sound casual, Andrea asked, "Did you find out anything at the library?"

"No, it was a dead end, to start, but there's more places to check out and as soon as I get the time, I'm going back."

"Well..." Andrea started.

"Come on, Andrea, it sounds like you had a bit of success. Spill."

"I don't think you want to hear this, and it doesn't directly concern the house or the Bemishes...that is directly."

"Come on Andrea, tell me. I want to know everything. I'm sure it ties in, whatever it is, but since we don't have a wealth of information...yet...it might not seem plausible."

"Okay. I see your calling me back on your cell and not the landline so I guess I can share it with you now." Andrea was silent, then said, "Sit down. Are you sitting."

Barbara went behind her desk and sat. "I am now."

"Okay, here goes. I talked with some of the off springs of friends of my father, Asa McBride, and at first came up with nothing. That is until later. First I need to ask you a question. Did you happen to see what time it was when you had your, shall we say, dreams?"

"Barbara thought back, but could barely remember the dreams, let alone the time. "No, not exactly. It was after I'd turned in for the night, so it was late."

"Or, early morning," Andrea said.

"So what is it."

"Have you ever heard about the witching hour?"

Barbara thought for a moment. "Yes, the poem by Keats."

Andrea smiled. "Yes, there's that, but I mean about the time of the witching hour. In any case, it is said that three a.m. stands for everything unholy and what's more, it's when the veil to the other world is at its weakest, making contact between the living and the dead fairly easy."

While Andrea spoke, Barbara was getting out her laptop and soon started a search on 'witching hour'. When Andrea finished, she read to her, "The Devil's Hour, which has also been referred to as the witching hour, was given this eerie title because of the belief that at this point of the night demons, ghosts, witches, and the Devil himself are at their most powerful."

"Yes, it is also quite common for supernatural events to take place at three a.m."

Barbara felt a chill and quickly looked around her office. Seeing nothing, she leaned back with the cell phone in her hand. "You think that's when I was having those dreams?"

"Yes, I think so. In any case, I mentioned this to a woman I know, and I found out she also knew you."

"Who?" Barbara was sitting up straight in her chair now as she waited for Andrea to tell her.

"Magnolia Warner."

Barbara's mind flashed back, and she remembered. Her friend Emily Watson had introduced her to Magnolia Warner whose family had been in Rochester a very long time. She remembered Magnolia's father had owned the contracting company that her father had started.

"I can tell by your silence, you remember her. She had an envelope with her that night that her grandfather had given her, and it contained the details on the sunken garden."

"Yes," Barbara interrupted. "I remember. It had never been filed with the property deed for some reason."

"That's right."

"Magnolia was going to send you a copy of the document."

Barbara thought a moment. "Yes, but she never did." As she said it she started to write on a pad in front of her.

"Well, she can't send it because she died."

Barbara's hand paused. "What did you say?"

"She died."

"What happened?"

"Don't know. She was an old woman, but she always seemed healthy to me."

"I know this sounds awful, but what about the map of the garden."

"It was a while back when she passed so I did ask if anyone knew where the envelope was. I explained what it contained, and they said if they find it they will get it to you or your husband."

Barbara was thoughtful. "That's awful...not about the envelope, but..."

"I know. But I wanted to share that with you first. She was elderly, but her family said she had been in good health. It happens all the time so it's not that unusual, only..."

"Only you think it has to do with the contents of that envelope."

"Yes, I do." Andrea paused and then asked, "What do you remember about the description of the sunken garden she had in that envelope."

"Well, let me think." Barbara jotted down points as they came into her head. It was probably made in 1918, maybe by the Bemishes. There are terraced gardens, concrete statues and an iron gate." Her voice went up as she said those words.

"What about the gate, Barbara."

"Spider web design in what was referenced as the Moon Gate at the rear of the garden."

"Yes, and I think that is where…"

"Where what, Andrea?"

Andrea took a deep breath. "That's where my story begins. It seems that the idea of that gate did not come from William Bemish or anyone around here. It seems that it was something that J. K. Post dreamt up."

"J. K. Post?"

"Yes, that was Georgia Bemishes father. A very wealthy and powerful man. He owned the J. K. Post Drug store and had several chains. He was building an empire until the FDA suspended licenses of his medical stores and pharmacies."

"What happened."

"All I could find out was that during an inspection of the stores it was found that they were violating the provisions of some Act and were shut down. J. K. Post was so embarrassed by the act that he moved in or shall we say, hid out in Rochester. He then or maybe earlier had been told about the garden and had the gate designed and built and presented it to his daughter and her husband as a gift. He actually over saw its installation in the garden and then…"

"Don't stop now, Andrea. And then, what?"

"It was said...no one knows for sure, that he went into that garden one night...late at night and he never came back."

Barbara's brow wrinkled. "Never came back? What does that mean."

"It means he went into the garden and never came back."

"Did he die or something."

"Don't know." Trying to offer her some peace of mind she added, "He was depressed, and he had ruined the family name."

"What are you saying."

"I'm saying he might have killed himself and they...meaning Georgia and William...hid the body behind that moon gate."

"Come on, Andrea. That is farfetched."

"Is it. Not when you think about it. William disappeared also and it may have been in the garden as well and Georgia went stark raving mad. Now why is that?"

"Whew." Barbara said. "That's a lot to think about."

"I know, but I thought I should tell you everything that I knew."

Barbara nodded her head. "Thanks Andrea. I'll be in touch. And..."

"I know. If I find out anything more I'll let you now."

With that they ended the conversation.

Barbara leaned back in her chair startled by all that she had heard. It was too much to take in right now and again she hummed to clear her mind. She told herself she would share all of it with Neil and see what he thought.

Chapter 45

Barbara managed to get back to work and when Neil arrived at her office door, she was sitting with a pencil in her mouth, her eyes down. Neil knew that pose well. It was the pose of her awareness of the smallness of her perspective which meant she felt she couldn't possibly draw any meaningful conclusions.

"Barbara it's time to go."

Barbara looked up startled from her melancholic trance. She had been completely absorbed in the vivid sensory details of the design and it took a moment for her to come back to earth.

She lifted up her arms and stretched as she smiled at her husband. "I'm ready," she said, as she closed her laptop and leaned down to pick up her briefcase. She tilted her head left and right as she put the laptop in the briefcase and then gazed around the room making sure she had everything. Then she stepped out from behind the desk and walked over to her husband.

Neil was ready for her, his arms outstretched as she walked toward him, and they embraced. He kissed the top of her head and then slowly she moved out of his arms, turned out the light and with one last gaze, she shut the door.

In the hallway, Neil paused and turned to face her. "Listen. I think we are both tired so why not stop at the Pasta

Villa on the way home? We can eat, have a glass of wine and relax before going home. I think we need some space away from both chapters of our life for a few hours." He paused with a comical expression on his face, waiting.

"You read my mind, dearest. That's exactly what I know I need."

Laughing now as they walked out of the building, making sure the door was locked and the security turned on before getting into the car. They sat for a moment enveloped in the desire to care less and loosen their grip on life. Then Neil started the car, and they were on their way.

Both were silent, as they drove through downtown and onto the expressway, getting off on East Ridge Road where they finally turned into the parking area of the Pasta Villa.

Outside of the sign on the front and the businesses on either side, the villa was just that; a small cozy house with large picture windows a well-manicured lawn and lots of flowers. It couldn't look more out of place, which was part of its charm.

Barbara and Neil walked gingerly up to the back door entrance from the parking lot and stepped into another world. The interior was warm and cozy and the minute they entered they could see the place was packed. So when the hostess asked if they would like to wait at the bar, they nodded and headed to the area which was but a few steps from the dining area in this ranch style house.

Once seated at the bar and placing their orders they sat listening to the couple beside them. They were saying that they grew up in the neighborhood and had been coming here for years just like Barbara and Neil had. It was a familiar conversation that you often heard here and what followed was no surprise either. "I know what good Italian food is all about and, hands down, this place is the best."

Barbara leaned forward and looked up at Neil, smiling. He smiled back. While they waited for their drinks, they looked around and their eyes went to the picture at the bar of Frank "Frankie" Guido his brother Jesse Guido and their late father Frank J. "Chic" Guido. Barbara pointed up at them. "It's nice when family display their relatives. It makes me feel warm and cozy." Neil nodded.

Their drinks arrived and soon after that they were told their table was ready. The waitress carried their drinks for them as she showed them to their table. They were given a few minutes to decide on what they wished to eat and then their order was taken. Like everyone there, they knew the menu and what they wanted. Barbara ordered the Seafood Fra Diavalo and Neil ordered the Artichoke French.

It was a pleasant end to the day, but like most of the regulars, they were courteous to not linger at the table since there were always others waiting to be seated.

Once outside they felt full and refreshed and Neil headed the car toward home. They were barely out of the parking lot when Neil's phone rang.

Neil handed the phone to Barbara, and she asked, "Hello, this is Barbara. Neil's wife."

Silence followed as Barbara listened to the caller. Finally she disconnected and turned toward Neil. "There's been a break-in at the office."

"What? That's impossible. That place is like Fort Knox. No one can get in there."

"I agree, but the police say different. Someone saw a light in the window and a figure moving, so they called the police."

Neil turned into the nearest driveway and swerved the car around. Soon they were headed downtown. When they arrived, the police were still there, checking around the building.

Neil practically jumped out of the car before it had stopped and hurried over to the police. "What's happening gentlemen?"

He stood there as several other officers joined them and he remained quiet listening to what they had to say.

Barbara sat nervously in the car waiting.

She watched as Neil unlocked the door and quickly turned off the alarm. The police joined him, disappearing into the building.

Barbara realized she was biting her nails and she forced herself to stop. Then, finally she saw Neil and the police exit the building. She sat forward on her seat watching as Neil shook hands and then headed towards her. She was patient, allowing him to climb into the car before asking, "Well?"

It took him a moment and then he said, "Nothing. Nothing at all. There are no broken windows, no unlocked or damaged door locks...nothing." He paused and looking directly at Barbara said, "The alarm was set and hadn't gone off."

"But what about someone seeing someone in the window."

Neil shrugged his shoulders. It must have been a mistake.

"So, now what?"

"We go home."

They drove in silence and when they finally reached their home, they were tired, but Neil went about checking windows and doors and turning on the alarm. They didn't linger downstairs, but went straight up to their bedroom, where Barbara headed into the bathroom, while Neil turned on the television waiting his turn, which wasn't a long wait. Soon they were both ready for bed and Neil turned off the television. It was almost two a.m. when they fell asleep.

The next morning they met up in the kitchen. Neil was preparing toast. "I'll have a slice," Barbara said as she made her way to the fridge to take out a yogurt, then thoughtfully asked, "Want one?"

"Sure."

They took turns at the Keurig making their coffee and carried it over to the table where they sat silently eating their breakfast. It was Neil who broke the silence first. "Guess what I learned yesterday."

Barbara looked up; her eyebrows raised.

"You remember Nathaniel Parker." He could tell by her expression she wasn't sure, so he added, "DirtWorx company?"

Barbara nodded.

"Well, I heard that he died."

Her face structure changed as she began soaking in the reality of what he said and she turned, glancing behind as if afraid that someone was about to snatch her from the chair. Finally she found her voice. "What happened."

"I don't know. I heard it from one of the workers onsite who had heard about it from Nathaniel's son, but he didn't go into any details."

Barbara nodded. She remembered once, while Neil was out in the sunken garden watching Nathaniel as he had skimmed off at least three feet of debris and soil across the top area, Neil had said Nathaniel had paused on his way back to start the next past. At first Neil thought he saw something he had uncovered, but when he looked closer, he could see Nathaniel's face. He looked as though he were having a stroke or something.

"Remember when I told you about that day before he

quit coming. Nathaniel had told me he felt a sudden numbness in his face and arms and when he walked over to me he felt it in his leg as well. When he talked, I could tell he was having trouble speaking. I should have told someone, but I didn't."

"Come on Neil, you didn't know. Hey," she said, "Look at me." Neil turned his head to stare at his wife. "You are not a doctor. You couldn't know what was going on. He had been working in the heat, maneuvering heavy equipment tediously so as not to ruin anything as he made each pass. That's strenuous work and if I had been there I would have thought the man had exhausted himself."

Neil was quiet, then finally said, "You're right. But, I still wish I had told someone."

Barbara went around to his side of the table and hugged his head to her chest. They stayed in that pose for some time until the musical clock on the wall started playing a Beetles tune, marking the start of another hour. They had to get a move on.

"Are you feeling better, my friend."

Neil lifted his head and nodded. "I am, but I won't take life for granted. The man wasn't much older than you and me and he had a life in front of him that now…"

"I know, but we have a life too and we need to get back to it. We're running late. We can talk more in the car."

With that they put the dishes in the sink, turned off the lights and headed out the door.

Once they were on their way, Neil said softly, "We need to check everything…make sure nothing is missing at the office."

"I agree."

As they drove to work, Barbara thought about what had happened so far. Nathaniel, Magnolia, the break-in...were they warnings? Should they think about covering up that garden. Should they move? All that swam through her head as they made their way downtown.

It was then that Barbara remembered she hadn't told Neil what she had learned that day. But, considering what had taken place that evening, and along with how hard Neil had taken the news of Nathaniel, she thought it best to wait.

Chapter 46

The project that became known as the *'roof raising'* was going better than expected. Neil had been prepared for problems and laid them out for the homeowners before they made their choice to build up instead of out. So they weren't surprised by the delays.

Of course, he had outlined the advantages as well and as luck would have it, the foundation that he thought would support a second floor was not up to code so work had to be done, but it was far less than expected. The structural engineer reported that the foundation was built to support a single story, and now we were asking it to support potentially twice that mass, so he did have to reinforce the foundation.

This was a house in the city and if you were driving down the street you would miss it since it sat back and amiss much larger structures, but that played in their favor where zoning and structure codes were concerned since they were below the height restrictions to start. As for square footage, that was not a problem either.

For every win, they faced a loss. It wasn't all fun and games when it came to the septic system. It was small and antiquated and needed to be replaced whether or not there were bathrooms involved. They not only had plans that included two bathrooms on this second floor, but both would have large showers as well.

This was a desirable part of the city with many unique and well kept up properties, so he was sure that the clients were well aware they would have to pay to add a second story, but it was going to increase the market value of the home as long as it was done right. Neil had no doubt about the skill of his workers. He had employed experienced contractors that had done this before and he had read through the building codes to satisfy himself it was going as planned.

When the second-floor structure was completed it was time to add on the roof and for once, delivery of the redesigned roof had been delivered and ready for installation. When the first snow fell, the roof was on, and windows were in place.

The homeowners had been on site at least once a week taking in the progress and talking with Barbara on some changes they wanted to incorporate. So, in the end the style for the addition was met with satisfaction.

On that day when the exterior was complete, no one could deny that it blended in well with the neighborhood. They had done all they could to achieve that, as well as making sure the inside worked for the client.

It was at this point when all the construction was completed on the outside and in, the family moved back home, and Barbara started bringing in the furnishings to finish off the project. This never went smoothly; especially after the pandemic when supplies were delayed constantly. But there was so much to do Barbara was busy on other projects that needed her attention, and their clients were satisfied as they were now back home.

The fact that Neil wasn't done with the structural work kept the clients from recognizing any delay on Barbara's part. Neil was busy putting in pot lights and fans and when the glass shower doors arrived, installing them before he was on to hanging doors and blinds.

Finally the stain for the woodwork arrived and Barbara joined him working side by side preparing the floors and staining them. Then they had to wait for them to dry.

During that time Barbara worked with the clients who were now living downstairs. She went over with them on the wall colors and was glad when they decided to do it all one shade of white with a dark accent wall in each bedroom. Barbara showed them paint swatches and had diagrammed out how it would look in a different light. They were happy with it. So as soon as the floors dried, Neil started painting and Barbara took the clients out to pick out the bedroom furniture, and curtains to soften the effect of the blinds. By the time Neil finished painting, the furniture was being delivered and they were about to see the finished product.

It took several days to complete, but when they did, the faces on their clients said it all. The wife started crying while her husband stood in awe, trying to take it all in and not shed tears. Even Barbara and Neil had impressed themselves enough to get a little weepy. This had been the first time they had worked on a project like this, and it had been worth the effort. What was more important, they had met the budget and finished close to their deadline.

They walked away feeling proud of what they had done and by the time they arrived at the office, there were messages from several homeowners wanting them to do additions to their homes. That was the thing about a small town, word traveled fast.

Barbara and Neil went to their offices to pack up for the day and were surprised to see a bottle of champagne and some finger food waiting for them. They started laughing as

Neil did one of his animated numbers putting the gifts on the table in her office. She joined him and watched as he continued his antics, opening one of the bottles of champagne while Barbara read the card.

"To the best building team in New York. A thank you with words is not enough. Enjoy." It was signed. Lena and Paul Murphy.

"How?"

Barbara looked up at Neil. "They had to call it in early, or they talked with Jennifer, and she handled it."

Neil nodded and together they said, "Jennifer!"

They sat relaxed and worn out by the day they had put in so though Barbara hadn't forgotten, she again thought this was not the time to share her news.

Barbara stepped outside so that Neil could turn on the alarm and lock up. They left the office that night feeling good about their life and once they arrived home with their treasures, they finished off the champagne and the snacks. Soon they were on their way upstairs where they took turns getting ready and climbing into the bed.

They slept soundly, their minds and bodies exhausted.

Chapter 47

The next morning they woke up together. Barbara stretched out her body feeling good after such a sound sleep. Neil did the same. Neither one budged beyond that for quite some time then Neil moved over to her side of the bed. She didn't need more than that to know he wanted to make love. She did too.

It had been some time since they had felt so relaxed and unhurried so they took their time, enjoying every inch of their bodies until they couldn't hold out any longer. Then eagerly they joined together.

When they were satiated and breathing hard, they flopped down on their pillows in complete silence as they slowly fell back to sleep.

It was the light streaming through the window that woke Barbara, and she stretched her arms above her head. Neil, who had been cuddling up against her, felt her movement and looked up and smiled at her. She smiled back.

As she slowly begins waking fully, she frowned and said, "What day is it?"

Those words hit Neil like stones as he hopped out of the bed and headed into the bathroom. It's Friday. It's Friday and we were sleeping in like it was Saturday.

No, Barbara thought, it couldn't be. She looked at the

bedside clock that told the date, day of the week and the time and it confirmed Niel's words. It was indeed Friday, and it was after ten in the morning. "How could this happen," Barbara said, checking to see if the alarm had been set. It hadn't. She must have forgotten to set it. She got out of the bed and quickly made her side, tossing the pillows every which way before going over to Neil's side and doing the same. When she was done she checked his clock. That alarm wasn't set either.

"Oh well," she said, hurrying about getting out her clothes for the day and then joining Neil in the bathroom. She started right in, brushing her teeth and when she was done, she reached under the sink for a shower cap. There was no time to wash her hair this morning. She put the cap on and checked to make sure every strand was covered. Then she gingerly stepped into the shower.

Barbara's mind went in many directions, and she thought back to when they had remodeled this house and Neil had pooh-poohed her idea of installing two showerheads. After all it was a big shower in an oversized bathroom. On the original blueprints it was added to be a baby room off the master bedroom so there was more than enough room to accommodate a free-standing tub, double sink vanity, an enclosed toilet area and this oversized shower.

Neil compromised by adding another shower at the other end of the room and added double showerheads in the main one. He told her she would thank him later and she found him to be right. A shower was most of the time a private thing, especially when you were running late and moving your body every which way.

When Barbara finished, she stepped out to find Neil had already left the bathroom, so she carefully removed the shower cap and dried herself off before going to the mirror and putting on her skin cream and a light layer of foundation.

She added a little eye makeup, and she was done.

When she entered the bedroom Neil was gone again, moving quickly like a road runner and she smiled as she tried to do the same. When she stepped into her slacks using one hand and the other reaching up to get her blouse off the hanger, she fell backwards, landing on her butt and she couldn't help laughing at herself. She sat there a moment and then concentrated on doing one thing at a time until she was finally ready to go downstairs.

As she set off down the stairs she started laughing again and was still laughing when she entered the kitchen. Neil turned with a puzzled expression on his face that made her laugh all the more. Finally she settled down and he handed her a travel mug of coffee. Soon they were out the door and on their way to work.

Today day they were on different job sites, but only one of them had to leave downtown so the one car was fine. That was the nice part about the job. Being in the same office together, they decided to hire one office manager, so they shared Jennifer who was efficient in keeping their schedules so that they didn't end up double booked. She had proven herself several times when the business picked up and Barbara would make appointments on the phone and write them down instead of putting them on the electronic calendar. So Jennifer came up with an idea. One day when they entered their offices they found a second monitor on their desk.

Puzzled at first, Jennifer called them together to Barbara's office and demonstrated what it was for. Each time they entered their office they turned the monitor on. It was connected directly to the mainframe so that they both could view it and it always showed their calendar. It worked like a charm.

Admittedly at first it took a little getting used to but soon every time she reached for a pad to write down an appointment, she reached over and turned on the monitor. The keyboard was neatly tucked under the desk in a pull-out drawer, so it was as easy as grabbing a pad. Later, Jennifer added an app to their cells so that they could see the calendar when they were away from the office. Needless to say, after that brainstorm Jennifer was given a raise.

Now as Neil drove, Barbara pulled up the calendar and saw why Neil was in a rush. His appointment was at 9:30 a.m. in Pittsford, while hers was in walking distance from the office. Barbara pulled up his appointment information and dialed the number. As soon as it connected, she said, "Good morning Mr. Anderson, this is Barbara Sanders. I wanted to let you know that Neil will be a little late this morning."

"Oh, don't worry about it darling," Mr. Anderson said, "to tell the truth I was going to call him and tell him to hold off until noon. We can meet and talk over lunch."

"Oh, meet at noon and talk over the project?" Barbara said out loud so that Neil could hear her. He nodded and Barbara said, "That will work out just fine. He'll see you at noon."

"Whew, that was a piece of luck."

"Yes it was."

"So what happened this morning. Why didn't our alarms go off?"

Barbara reached over and touched his arm. "Well, my dear, they didn't because neither one of us set an alarm last night. I guess we were too busy thinking and doing other things."

Barbara smiled and could tell from his cheek; he was smiling too.

Calmer now that they had time, Barbara thought about his upcoming job. "Do they need me for anything?"

"No, it's for storage and nothing fancy." Besides, I saw on the calendar you were busy, so I didn't even suggest it."

Barbara smiled as Neil pulled into their parking space. He checked his watch and saw he had almost an hour to plan for the meeting and she mentally watched his usual habit of relaxing before starting the day.

First he would take a deep breath and his shoulders would drop down, then he would turn off the car engine, take another deep breath, open the door and step out of the car. He did this routine every day and she doubted he knew he did it.

They walked in together and then parted to go to their separate offices. Barbara checked in with Jennifer before going to her office. She had a light day. There were several calls she had to make and one job she needed to quote; otherwise she was basically free as a bird, so she placed a call to her friends, planning to meet them for lunch. She chose the Founders Café. It was a trendy cafe, tea and coffeehouse located in The Academy Building in downtown Rochester. They had an outdoor patio, but the weather had taken on a chill so they would meet inside.

Barbara sat texting them. They all texted back they would be there. She then checked off the jobs that needed her attention before putting on her coat, hat and gloves and grabbing her purse. On the way out she let Jennifer know where she would be and headed out the door.

There was no denying the fact that winter was on the way as she shivered inside her coat, wishing she had picked a heavier one instead of pretending it was still autumn and opting for a light knit coat sweater. She snuggled into the coat and hurried to her destination, warmed by the thought of seeing her friends.

They hadn't had lunch together since they all met at the Brewery and before then, the Spaghetti Warehouse, which was now closed. She had read about it closing in not only Rochester, but in Syracuse as well. Barbara was sorry to see it go, but there were many other interesting restaurants to choose from. Besides, Marla had warned them, saying that it was a Dallas-based chain, and it wouldn't last long.

Barbara arrived first, followed by Marla Dickerson and on her heels came Emily Watson.

"This is a wonderful place, Barbara. Glad you picked it."

"Yes, it's definitely our kind of place."

"What are you saying, it's old and has been given a great face lift?"

Barbara laughed. "No, I'm saying it's got character...we like places with character."

Soon they were seated and placed their orders. Barbara ordered a Founders Chicken Salad; Marla ordered a Ham and Swiss and Emily the Chicken Spinach Pesto Wrap.

They didn't wait long before their food was in front of them, and they were quiet, enjoying every bite and taking in their surroundings. The area was cozy, and they did a little people watching as well. When they finished eating, they ordered coffee and by the time the coffee came, the place was emptying as people returned to work. It was now time to catch up. Barbara started.

"Well," she began, turning to look at Emily, "Magnolia died."

"Magnolia?" Marla piped up.

"Yes, you remember. Emily told us about Magnolia." Marla had a puzzled expression on her face, so Barbara filled her in. "Magnolia Warner who was operating her father's contracting office after he passed. She came to our house, and she had the original details of the property and the only existing document of the design of the sunken garden."

Marla had her elbows on the table leaning in as if she were afraid she would miss something being said.

"So, we know what the garden looks like."

"But you don't have the map. Did they find it and send it to you?"

"Nope, but I have the pictures on my phone from that night. I had forgotten that I had taken pictures until recently."

Again Marla had that expression on her face. Barbara reached into her purse and took out her cell. She went to the picture gallery and opened it and Marla read out loud.

"This sunken garden is located in a wooded ravine at the corner of St. Paul Boulevard and Winona and created as part of the estate developed in 1918, by art dealer William Bemish and his wife, Georgia. The garden is a mix of Arts & Crafts and Naturalistic landscape design of terraced gardens. Significant parts of the garden are of concrete and stone construction—as well as an iron gate with a 'spider web' design, located in the 'Moon Gate' at the northeast corner of the garden."

"Wow…is it…."

"No, it isn't done yet. There is still a lot to do, but it's coming along."

"Say the word and we'll help."

"That's the reason…that is besides the weather, that it isn't completed. The contractor, Nathaniel Parker of DirtWorx company quit, and just the other day, Neil found out he died."

There was silence as they all stared in shock at this news. "So, you're saying that Magnolia who had the map of the sunken garden and then Nathaniel who was digging it out, both died?"

"Yes, but I'm not saying one thing had anything to do with the other. It could be just a coincidence."

"Come on Barbara. You don't believe that."

Barbara was silent but her next bit of news showed she didn't.

"Well, since all this I spoke with Andrea; Andrea McBride."

"Yes," we know her," Emily said as she looked at Marla, who nodded.

"Well," Barbara continued. "When we met Magnolia she had an envelope with her that night that her grandfather had given her, and it contained the details on the sunken garden. She didn't know why, but it had never been filed with the property deed "

Barbara took a sip of her coffee and heard them voice their dismay. "Come on, don't stop now."

"Well, Andrea wanted to know what I remembered about the sunken garden, and I shared the gist of it and Andrea quickly honed in on the gate. I told her it was called the Moon Gate and was located at the rear of the sunken garden. I started telling her about the rest of the layout, but she was like a dog with a bone asking what about the gate. I told her that it had a spider web design and that's when Andrea said, '*that was where her story begins*."

"What did she mean her story."

"Well, if you will give me a chance, I'll tell you." Emily had a puppy dog expression on her face as she leaned back a little. She took her hand and ran it across her lips as if zipping it shut.

Barbara explained that Andrea shared that it seems that the idea of that gate did not come from William Bemish or anyone around here. It seems that it was something that J. K. Post dreamt up.

"J. K. Post?"

"Yes, that was Georgia Bemish's father. He was a very wealthy and powerful man. He owned the J. K. Post Drug store and had several chains. He was building an empire until the FDA suspended licenses of his medical stores and pharmacies."

"What happened."

"Well, Andrea wasn't sure, but all she could find out was that during an inspection of the stores it was found that they were violating the provisions of some Act and were shut down. J. K. Post was so embarrassed by the publicity. So he packed up and moved to Rochester. At some point his daughter probably told him about the garden and he had the gate designed and built and presented it to his daughter and her husband as a gift. He actually over saw its installation in the garden."

She could feel the eyes staring at her and she quickly added, "Andrea said that late one night after the gate was installed, Mr. Post went into the garden and never came back."

She heard the same questions she had asked coming at her. "Never came back? What does that mean."

"It means he went into the garden and never came back."

"Did he die or something."

"Don't know." They said he was depressed and felt he had ruined the family name so he might have killed himself and since no one ever found the body, maybe Georgia and William hid the body behind that moon gate."

"That's really reaching."

"I know, but it was a long time ago, before all the forensics and stuff and cases didn't get solved."

"Plus reputations were always protected."

"Maybe, but anyway, William also disappeared, and it may have been in the garden as well and Georgia went stark raving mad, so they weren't getting any answers out of her."

There was silence around the table until Emily asked, "So, what did Neil think?"

Sheepishly, Barbara replied. "I haven't told him yet."

"You've got to tell him Barbara."

"I know and I will."

Chapter 48

That afternoon as the women parted ways, Emily touched Barbara's arm to slow her down. Once the others were on their way to the parking lot, she turned to Barbara and said, "Seriously, you have to tell Neil."

Barbara turned and looked at her friend, then gave her a hug. "Don't worry, I will."

"Promise me you'll tell him tonight."

Barbara nodded her head, kissed Emily on the cheek, then stood and watched as she went to the parking lot.

Feeling the chill in the air, Barbara turned and quickly headed back to the office.

By the time she reached the office door, she was ready to stop kidding herself. She needed to put on her winter coat, lickety-split. No more putting on a heavy sweater and pretending. It was definitely too cold. As for telling Neil, she meant to but didn't get the chance that night.

Neil was happy and he couldn't wait to tell Barbara all about the project. She was surprised when he said, "Instead of going right home, I thought we could take the

Erie Canal Boat Tour."

Barbara gave him an inquisitive look. "Are you crazy. It's freezing out there...I mean are you kidding? Tell me you're kidding."

"I know, I know. But it's the last cruise before winter and they say that it's heated and enclosed. You can go out, but you can stay inside where it's warm."

Barbara could see how anxious he was, so she nodded. "Okay, you win." Then giving it some thought added "Are you sure it's the last one?"

"Yes, they start May 12th and end October 29th...and today is..."

"October 29."

"Great. So, the boat is called the Colonial Belle and has been providing boat tours on the Erie Canal since 1989. We get on the boat in Fairport which is..."

"I know," Barbara said, mimicking what has become the local slogan. "It's just 20 minutes away."

Neil chuckled. "I signed us up for a 2-hour tour." He glanced at Barbara smiling. "Get it."

"Yes, but we aren't on Gilligan's Island, or lost, or stranded...that is if you didn't ask to have that included in the tour."

"My funny wife. I love you. We can eat and have drinks on the boat."

"Now that's the best thing you said so far."

They drove in a comfortable silence with Barbara recalling when they first took a boat tour and having seen Mindy for the first time. She quickly shook that thought out of her head. That was best forgotten. Instead she concentrated on how happy her husband was as they pulled into the parking area and were soon on board.

There were several other people taking this ride, so they were either all crazy or it was the thing to do. So

Barbara relaxed and decided to forget the cold and just enjoy the ride.

Once everyone was onboard, the boat slowly left the dock and she followed Neil up to the top viewing area, along with all the other passengers. With them all grouped in the bow of the boat it didn't seem as cold and once she took in the view, she forgot all about the cold. It was indeed beautiful, beautiful in a unique way than the time they went during the summer.

Barbara happened to be standing near two officers and was wondering what they were doing on the boat. She decided to eavesdrop on their conversation.

"This has been a bust. You know that Pagnelli, don't you."

"So, far, yes, Greenberg, but I think that if we trace the steps from the beginning on each case we are going to find the answers."

Detective Pagnelli shook his head from side to side. "When they opened the cold case division I was truly excited. We were going to work on cold cases that went back a long way. Being that most of the witnesses and family were deceased, it was working without interference or deadlines to meet so I was all in."

"Yes, don't forget the glory if we were able to solve just one case."

"I saw your face when we walked into that room, Detective."

"It was a wall of boxes."

"Yeah, but we managed to go through them. It took several months, but we are now standing here with but eighteen cases that we found in our jurisdiction or lacked

enough information to forward to the proper authorities..
Once we forwarded those files to the proper authorities, we
only had to summarize the details of eighteen cases."

"And how long did that take."

"So, like you said, we don't have a time schedule to
follow. Let's just enjoy it and go through the list."

"So you think," Detective Greenberg said, "That
being on a boat will help clear our minds?"

"Yes, it will. Boats are peaceful and there's water to
calm our minds so that we think clearly. So, let's begin."

Detective Pagnelli pulled out a folder and the two
men moved back from the group. Barbara moved with them,
trying not to look suspicious.

"Okay, of these eighteen cases we need to decide
from what we've gathered so far, whether it was a murder,
just a disappearance or suicide" He paused. "So let's review
what we've done so far on each of these cases. The
information we've gathered further will eliminate some of
them too."

Detective Greenberg had a similar folder. "The 1995
suicide in Brewster was an unidentified adult male we now
know, discovered in a wooded area in the Village of
Brewster, NY."

Detective Pagnelli nodded. That's Putnam County so
out of our jurisdiction it goes."

"Next we have the disappearance of Suzanne Lyall in
1998 who we learned was last seen getting off at SUNY
Albany campus in 1998."

"Out of our jurisdiction?"

Detective Pagnelli nodded as he stared at the form.
"Okay, I see that those two we called and have turned over to
the proper authorities."

"Yes, on most of them we did, but it's a good idea to check and make sure."

"Okay, so we next have the 1970 murder of Carol A. Fitzmaurice, 23, who was found by her husband..." Pagnelli stopped and looked at Detective Greenberg. "It's in Albany and turned over to the proper authorities." He added, "This one would be easy if it had happened nowadays."

"Why do you say that?"

"Well, her husband reported her missing and she had been stabbed multiple times in the abdomen and neck..."

"I know where you're going, but we've been told to not assume the obvious."

"You're right, you're right. So let's go on. This one is 1964. The murder of Lucy Dade Forrester who was sixty-nine found murdered in her store located on South Litchfield Street in..." He paused. "Herkimer County. Not in our jurisdiction."

Looking up from the folder Detective Greenberg smiled at his partner. "See, it's not really that many. Let's continue."

"Next is the 1973 slaying of Wanda Lee Walkowicz, 11, of Avenue D, Rochester, who never made it home on April 2, 1973. She was sent to the corner store that evening and the next morning, police found her body at a rest area off of Route 104 in Webster, New York."

"That's a well-known case and there were a lot of man hours trying to solve it then and now. The police determined that she had been raped and strangled, but even though they had suspects, it still isn't solved. It's our jurisdiction. Want to pursue this one?"

"Well," Detective Pagnelli said, "Maybe. I'll put a check in the corner and put it on top, but let's continue."

"Let's see,, Next we have the 2003 homicide of Megan McDonald whose body was found in a field off

Bowser Road in Wallkill."

"Looked it up. Not our jurisdiction and the proper authority has been notified."

"Okay, on to the 1980 disappearance of Jeanne Scrima who was reported missing by her attorney after failing to appear at divorce proceedings with her husband. She was last seen at 7:00 a.m. on March 19, 1980, driving to her residence to meet her husband. Her car was found in Fultonville, NY, several weeks later, but eventually turned up abandoned in Michigan."

Detective Pagnelli stared at the report and then looked at his partner. "So, Detective Greenberg what's your take?"

"I think it can't be turned away as not in our jurisdiction because it's not clear where it started or ends so we need to keep that a while longer."

"Good. I agree." Detective Pagnelli put it under the one on the Walkowicz case and continued. "So now we have the 1985 unidentified male, body discovered in a wooded area off Route 301, in the town of Philipstown, Putnam County."

"Not ours and has been passed on to the right jurisdiction."

"Good." Detective Pagnelli paused as he silently read the details of the next case, then he read out loud. "It's the discovery of skeletal remains in a ravine in1991. Found by teens picking berries in the Town of Lewiston. The body had been bound and gagged, and investigators determined he was an African American male between the ages of 30 and 45."

"I remember that one," Detective Greenberg said thoughtfully. "I know it's not one of ours and I contacted the proper authorities, but I made mention of the importance of solving the case. There was another one similar to that and it had been determined to be racial. I suggested they start there."

"Good idea, Detective," Pagnelli said as he put that in the back of the file. "Next we have Hakan Karacay who vanished in 1999. He was a 28-year-old Turkish immigrant with depression." He paused, "ah, he's Lewis, New York and it has been turned over to them."

Detective Pagnelli paused and looked out at the water as if searching for some good to wipe out all the evil before continuing. Soon he picked up the next file.

"The 1972 killing of Rudy Allen Rothberg, 52, of Evans Mills, who stopped his truck at a rest stop on I-81. Another trucker discovered Rothberg, who had been shot in the head with a shotgun."

"Okay, that's another one that needs closer scrutiny.

"I agree." That was put on the top of his file. "Okay we have Linda Holgerson's who was a murder victim in 2007. Her body was discovered in an overgrown embankment at 13401 State Route 23A in the town of Prattsville. She was mentally handicapped."

"Again, we need to do more. It's our case until we find out where the murder took place."

The detective let out a breath and it hung in the air. Then he continued, "2008 disappearance of Lutricia Steel who was 27 and last seen by her family leaving her residence in the city of Schenectady on May 1, 2008."

"Sent to the authorities in Schenectady."

"The 1979 disappearance of James Dean Knox who was reported missing by his grandmother on December 21, 1979. Last seen in the village of Warsaw...so not ours and has been forwarded."

"Okay, the 2003 disappearance of Dean M. Lewis who was traveling around the country alone and staying within State parks. Lewis had failed to check in with his family."

"Another iffy. So we should keep it."

"The case of Donald Webster who was 86 years old. He was struck and killed by a passing motorist outside his home on County Route 1, in Westtown, NY."

"That was passed on."

"The 1991 homicide of Edward Croley a 14-year-old who disappeared off the streets of Albany, New York... passed on to the proper authorities the Detective said and put it at the back.

"The 2006 killing of Sonia Centeno, forty-four who was last seen on Main St. in Poughkeepsie and remains found in the Town of LaGrange. She had been partially buried," the detective added, his voice showing his disgust. He looked up and said to Detective Greenberg, "People can be so cruel."

"That's so true, so true."

"I know this is when we were going to pick the one we wanted to consider, but I think I have already made my decision. This last one I am reading is strange, interesting and old. I would like you to agree to start with this one."

"What is it."

"The disappearance of William Bemish."

Barbara's ears perked up, but the announcement came over the loudspeaker that dinner was being served, so the detectives closed their file and headed down to the dining area. Barbara patiently waited for her husband to work his way over to her and they followed suit.

Once downstairs, she surveyed the area and saw where the detectives were seated and guided Neil in that direction. They were at the last table on the right and Barbara sat with her back to them at the next one. This way she could hear their conversation.

They didn't discuss the case for a while as they placed their orders. Then when the food arrived, they talked about trivial matters until they finished eating.

Barbara tried to look interested in what Neil was saying, but she had her ears perked for any conversation taking place behind them.

She wasn't surprised when Neil asked, "Barbara. Are you listening to me."

"Yes, I am."

"So, what did I say?"

"Ah…I'm sorry. I was chewing…"

"What's up. This was to be our anniversary voyage to celebrate our first trip on this exact boat back when we first arrived in Rochester. Didn't you catch on to that?"

"Yes, I did… Okay, let me be honest with you." She leaned over and whispered to Neil, "See those two detectives behind us…" She gave him a stern look. "Don't stare. Anyway, they are about to discuss our case."

Following suit, Neil whispered back. "Our case?"

"Yes, they are about to talk about the case concerning William Bemish; the man who disappeared in our sunken garden."

Chapter 49

From that point on, Neil and Barbara were unaware of what was happening around them as they listened intently to the conversation going on behind them. When their food arrived, they graciously smiled. When asked if they wanted their water glasses filled, they would nod and not say a word.

Barbara had been right to choose this table since neither one of the detectives could see their faces. That was a good thing because one look at them and the detectives would have known they were listening to their conversation. Each time the detectives lowered their voices, Neil and Barbara would lean toward them, trying to not miss a word they said.

It was comical in a way watching them list back and forth when the boat itself was steady as a rock, but they didn't care.

The detectives took a break from their discussion to eat, and Barbara and Neil took that opportunity to gobble what food was left on their plates. Both were afraid they would miss something that could be important, so they tried to keep the noise down, at least at their table.

That was not the case with the tables close to them.

The diners talked and laughed as if they were the only ones on the boat, or that was how Barbara felt. At one point she whispered to Neil, "I have a mind to ask them to keep it down."

"Come on Barbara. They are here to have fun and they are having it. They're not doing anything wrong so let them be."

"I didn't say I would, just that I wanted to, is all," Barbara replied, adamantly.

Soon the detectives were done eating and they resumed their discussion. Barbara and Neil stopped talking and listened again.

It was obvious that one of the detectives was trying, almost desperately, to convince the other that this was the case to take and the other kept putting up stumbling blocks. At one point to get the other off focusing on this one case, he said, "Come on, come on, you know these files were being constantly updated with the latest details; even ones older than this." He paused adding, "Listen, we want a hard one to solve, but this one is not just hard…it's riddled with unsolved details. You would be setting us up for failure with this one."

As they continued arguing, Barbara couldn't' help wondering why the one detective was so fixated on the Bemish case. That's what Barbara wanted to know.

They went back and forth supporting their reasons and the detective against starting with the Bemish case said, "You know, it may be there were no fresh leads because it had been solved and no one had thought to update it." There was a moment pause before the same detective added, "That happens more often than I like to admit."

Then the other detective was nodding his head and since Neil was sitting across from her, he whispered, 'he's agreeing'.

There was paper shuffling and then the detective with his back to Barbara said, "Come on Pagnelli, we wanted to take a deep dive into one of these cases. I know you would prefer a mysterious murder, but I myself lean toward the dead ends and disappearances because they prove the most interesting."

There was silence and Barbara and Neil ate the rest of their food and washed it down with water while keeping alert for any further conversation. Finally the Detective they now knew was Pagnelli, said, "Okay, Detective Greenberg let's do it. So I won't see my family for days on end, maybe it will be worth it."

"That's the spirit."

"No, now wait. You forget we are to actively investigate no more than five cold cases at any one time."

Detective Greenberg is thoughtful. "Yes, but that doesn't mean we do five simultaneously. We can if we want to, but that's not what the Captain was saying. Keep in mind we are the only ones assigned to this unit. You and me."

"Yes, but we can get outside help or assistance if we need it."

Though Barbara couldn't see him, Detective Pagnelli was nodding his head. "Also, you will probably see more of your family since as cold case investigators we won't be assigned to any incoming cases; temporary assignments, or non-cold case projects."

Barbara went back to her food, keeping an ear on their conversation, but not what they were discussing at the moment.

There was a lot of paper rustling as they went through the files. Then, Detective Pagnelli looked over his notes. "We keep the 1973 slaying of Wanda Lee Walkowicz;

The 1980 disappearance of Jeanne Scrima is more a determination first of who should handle it so this one we work directly with the Fultonville squad until we know for sure whose jurisdiction it should be."

"Yes, and don't forget we need to contact Michigan as well since that's where her car was found."

Detective Pagnelli nodded. "Okay, the same is true of the next one; the 1972 killing of Rudy Allen Rothberg, 52, of Evans Mills, shot in the head with a shotgun at a rest stop on I81."

"Same for 2007 murder of Linda Holgerson, body found on State Route 23A in the town of Prattsville. She was mentally handicapped."

"What about the disappearance of Dean M. Lewis who was staying in State parks. "

Pagnelli thought for a moment then said, "Let's just find where he lived permanently or had family or friends and have them start the investigation first and if need be we'll pick up on it later."

"Agreed."

Again, we need to do more. It's our case until we find out where the murder took place."

Detective Pagnelli let out a deep breath. "So there we have it."

At that point, the waiters were delivering dessert and all conversation stopped. Barbara relaxed and took a bite, then nodded at Neil, "This is good." Neil picked up is fork and tried the dessert. "Yes, this is good," he added. But he was now as hooked as Barbara on hearing the conversation between the two Detectives. So, while he ate, all the time he was keeping an eye on the table behind them. Waiting.

When the Detectives ordered a beer, Barbara and Neil did the same. They continued to stay at the table until the detectives finally got up and headed toward the stairs.

Barbara and Neil followed.

Not wanting to look suspicious they allowed the detectives to make a choice of locations above deck and then they stood near, but within a group of other passengers.

Just when it seemed there would be no further discussion on the case, Detective Greenberg threw a zinger.

Barbara and Neil were transfixed, waiting and staring out at the scenery the boat passed, but their attention was on the words of the Detectives. They had listened long enough to know there was something there; a reason why the Detective they now knew was Greenberg, wanted desperately to convince Detective Pagnelli to start with the Bemish case.

Barbara stared at the lights across the way as night descended and people flooded their homes with artificial illumination. But Barbara felt trapped in the darkness which roared outside. Suddenly one of the Detectives spoke and Neil and Barbara's ears perked. If Godzilla had suddenly appeared, they wouldn't have cared because they were involved with hearing what more the Detectives would say.

"Listen, Pagnelli. I'm going to share something with you that is to stay between us and not go beyond that. Can you agree to that?"

Puzzled, Detective Pagnelli said, "It's not something illegal is it?"

"No…well, normally in certain situations it would be but, not really."

It was a while before Pagnelli replied. "The Captain knows you and trusts you, so I do too. I promise to keep what you tell me between us."

Detective Greenberg drew in his breath and then said, "Once we get deeper into the file on the Bemishes you will see the name '*Post*'. I want you to know up front that my mother's maiden name is '*Post*'. So that is why I am so interested in this case. My great-great grandfather was J.K. Post. He owned the J.K. Post Drug company.

Barbara almost fell, but thankfully she could blame it on the boat that had list at that precise moment covering for her surprised reaction to what the Detective had said. Just as shocked, Neil was right there, catching his wife, his mouth open, his brow squeezed tight.

Detective Pagnelli was quiet, as if trying to visualize the file and when he finally had, he said, "Your grandfather is the man who disappeared...the father of Georgia Bemish?"

Detective Greenberg nodded his head. As if planned, at that moment the Captain announced over the loudspeaker that it was time to depart. Barbara turned to look at Neil and could see he was as shocked as she was. He grabbed her elbow and moved them forward, but as the passengers started moving toward the gangplank, it was hard to stay close to the Detectives.

Finally they were on the dock and Neil started looking around, but he couldn't lay eyes on them.

"We need to find them and tell them what we know."

"I agree."

"We know their names so we can call the precinct and get in touch with them. Between what we know, and they have in that file, it might solve the mystery once and for all."

Chapter 50

The one constant in our lives beyond work is taking care of ourselves. No matter what happened, we didn't miss a doctor's or dentist's appointment and this one coming up Barbara was feeling a little anxious about. She hadn't been feeling like herself for several weeks now and knowing all the lifting and shifting she did, Barbara told herself it was to be expected.

One day she was showering, getting ready to have dinner with the Locksmiths, Sara and Paul, who they hadn't gotten together with since they first introduced them to their Kubota and helped in the garden. It moved the digging process along safely and much quicker than if they had done it all with shovels.

Now as she stood in the shower she noticed a change in her breasts. Not worried but following her usual habit, she jotted it down on the list of things to review at her next appointment.

As she wrote it down, she smiled remembering that after reading Georgia Bemish's diary, she had started journaling her thoughts, or just something she needed to remember. It had proved helpful on several occasions, especially when a client asked if she could do their family room the same way she had done someone else's that happened to be a friend of theirs.

Without those journal entries she might have panicked or felt dumbfounded to recall that room out of the many she had done since they started the business. But she would go and look back in that journal and there it would be in words and in pictures.

She was pulled out of her reverie when she heard her husband call out, "Barbara?"

"Oh, sorry, I'm getting ready."

Neil came to her side of the bed and kissed her forehead. Well, get a move on they'll be here any second. They're going to be disappointed enough to see we haven't done much in the garden, so why add to it by being late?

Barbara finished writing and then hurried to get dressed. They had set up to meet Sara and Paul at the Avvino. They had gone there with Emily and her husband Michael Watson and LOVE, LOVE, LOVED it. Since then they had dined at the Avvino as often as time allowed and never had a bad meal there.

They first met the owners when they did some work for them. Jeanine was an angel and since then they had become friends with her. The Avvino was one of the few restaurants that had a seasonal menu, always using the freshest ingredients when they were at their peak.

As they pulled out of their driveway at Parcel 076.06 Winona Blvd heading toward Brighton, Barbara was already thinking about what she would eat.

Neil headed toward St Paul Blvd and turned left. Barbara felt her stomach do a little lurch but ignored it. When Neil turned right onto Cooper Rd she thought she was going to be sick. She tried not to think of food, but instead stuck images in her mind that would soothe her and soon she was feeling better.

But unable to stay in that state for long, her mind

went to deciding what she would order, and waves of nausea rolled over her. She squeezed her eyes shut and leaned back, swallowing hard.

When they reached Titus Avenue and then turned right onto Seabreeze Drive, she was beginning to feel this wasn't a good idea, but she loved Avvino and they hadn't seen their friends in so long it would be terrible to back out now, so she concentrated on the back of her eyelids.

Neil guided the car easily onto RT-590 S. until they reached exit 2A that would take them to Monroe Ave.

Again she felt a wave of nausea, but she was beginning to think luck was on her side. She hadn't eaten anything since breakfast so there wasn't much in her stomach anyway. She had wanted to work up an appetite for this evening and darn if she was going to let a little upset stomach stop her.

"Are you all right? You're awful quiet." Neil said with concern.

She wanted to answer with words but didn't dare so she nodded her head instead.

"Okay, then. We're almost there."

Those were the words she wanted to hear as she was convinced that the ride had something to do with her feeling so queasy. Soon they were pulling into 2541 Monroe Ave and in front of them was the restaurant.

Barbara undid her seatbelt when Neil stopped the car and not waiting for him to get out, she gingerly put her foot on the pavement and slowly stood. When she did, it seemed the nausea had passed and she turned to Neil, smiling. "So, what are you waiting for." Neil took her arm and they walked into the restaurant together.

The hostess asked their names, checked her list and then said, "Please, follow me," as she took them to their favorite table and left them with the menus in front of them. Neil was studying the menu, but Barbara already knew what she wanted and watched the entrance. Soon she saw Sara and Paul at the front desk.

She watched them as the hostess led them to the table and she smiled. They were as punctual as she and Neil and she liked that. As soon as they were at the table, Barbara and Neil stood and greeted them with hugs and handshakes.

They began catching up and paused to give the waiter their drink choices and then went back to their conversation. They talked in low voices so as not to disturb the other patrons and kept two conversations going. Neil and Paul talked together while Sara and Barbara did the same.

When the waiter came to take their orders, it seemed that Barbara wasn't the only one thinking about what to eat as without hesitation one after the other they spoke their choices. Then, when the waiter left, they continued their conversations.

By the time the food arrived, they had come through an entire year of talk about what they had done or seen and were ready to eat their meal.

Once the food arrived, there was no more talking as they enjoyed their meal. Barbara couldn't help thinking this restaurant seemed to take control of the patrons as soon as the food was placed in front of them. It was like the presentation of the meal, the atmosphere of the dining area, and the aroma took hold and there was complete silence.

When they were done and one by one, leaning back, smiling and full, they ordered coffee. While they waited, they finished their drinks. When the coffee came, they decided against trying to fit a dessert into their full bellies and just enjoyed their coffee. That's when the conversation turned to the inevitable.

"We're glad you picked this place. Sara and I have been wanting to come here. We heard the Avvino has…" He turned to Sara who said, "A calm ambiance." Paul nodded, "It's never noisy and it's beautifully lit. We always lean toward small restaurants as they feel…" Again he turned to Sara. "Intimate and elegant."

Barbara and Neil grinned, enjoying the dual conversation of their friends. Barbara hoped that they would be like that some day when they had time to think beyond work.

"I know, I know what you're thinking."

"What," Neil said, "two peas in a pod?"

Paul smiled and nodded his head. "So Neil, tell us about the garden?"

Neil had a sheepish expression as he replied, "It's still not done."

"You mean not decorated yet." Paul turned to Barbara, "You haven't finalized the design?"

Neil answered him. "No, I mean we haven't had time to clear it all out. It's still pretty much the way you last saw it."

"Oh, I was hoping we could stop by and take a look at it after dinner."

"I know, it's just that business has been demanding and we haven't' gotten back to it."

"We could…"

"I know. You will help, but we just don't know when we will be able to do anything out there." Then, seeing the disappointment on their faces, Neil added, "Tell you what. Without looking at our calendar I am going to say that Saturday afternoon you can come over and we'll have at it."

"That is a date." Paul turned to Sara who nodded her head.

They finished their coffee and talked a while longer before finally going their separate ways. Barbara and Neil walked to their car, and she was glad she hadn't changed their mind and cancelled because she felt just fine now, and the food didn't disappoint.

On the way home, Neil discussed the job they would be working on together the following day and that he wanted to get an early start if that was okay with her.

"How early?"

"What say around seven?"

"Okay, seven it is. We better make sure we set both alarms."

They had a little chuckle over that and headed home. When they reached the house, they decided to leave the car outside and went directly into the house where Barbara went to the kitchen to get a glass of water while Neil checked the doors and windows and set the alarm. She started to tell him not to worry about the windows since it had been too cold to open them lately. But she said nothing. Just waited and soon they went up together and got ready for bed.

Barbara had that same sensation of nausea over the next few days and finally, not waiting for her doctor's appointment she called Emily.

Emily answered almost immediately. "What's up?"

"What do you mean, what's up. Can't I just call to talk?"

"No, you always like talking in person over lunch so, I ask again, what's up?"

Barbara took a deep breath and finally said. "I have my doctor's appointment coming up, but I need to ask something."

She could visualize Emily on the other end, grabbing her phone tightly and stress taking over the features of her lovely face. "You aren't sick, are you?"

"No, calm down, I just wanted to talk to someone

about it. I have been feeling nauseous in the morning and my breasts are swollen. I'm going to call my doctor, but I didn't want to ask if I could get an earlier appointment if it was nothing. So, I'm talking to someone who might have a suggestion or two?"

If she could see Emily now she would be shocked because Emily was smiling, not frowning. "Yes, my dear, you asked the right person."

"So, what should I do or take…is it serious?"

"No, it's not serious, but what you should do is go to the drug store and get a pregnancy test."

Barbara is quiet, trying to decipher what she has suggested. Then, she realized what she was saying. "You think I'm pregnant?"

"Yes, that's what I think, but I'm not a doctor so take the test." Emily paused, "And Barbara, as soon as you know, tell Neil and then you better tell me."

Barbara sat at her desk, laughing inside thinking there was no way that she was pregnant.

Chapter 51

Winter was setting in and soon it would be impossible to work in the garden. So with Neil being as anxious as Sara and Paul to unveil the rest of the garden, Barbara joined them, no longer putting obstacles in the way. She had more important things on her mind now.

They surprised themselves as every evening and bright and early on weekends they were out there working diligently. No work crew could have matched their dedication to completing the job, one that had a lot of obstacles to contend with. Barbara found herself enjoying the physical labor and being able to share the moment with her husband and their friends.

As they revealed more, Barbara kind of wished that Mindy would appear and really talk to her, warn her, if there was a warning to be had because she had begun to feel the pull the others had about the garden all along. She wanted to see it in its entirety, and she wanted to plan to start working on her design next spring. She had so many ideas that she had put away for quite some time and now the time was coming to think about initiating those plans.

They had been at it for over a month when Barbara

started to worry. She had been feeling fatigued even after a good night's sleep. She couldn't ignore it, so she mentioned it casually to Neil.

"Ah, honey, I know we've been burning the candle at both ends for some time now and I'm as tired as you are, but we are almost there." Neil paused. "Listen, if you want, we can back off for a while."

"What, you're kidding, Paul and Sara would have a cow if we did that. No, we're close now and we have to keep going."

Neil chuckled and hugged her closely and for him the conversation ended.

But not for Barbara, as she started doing some math in her head. They had been so busy she hadn't kept track of the fact she hadn't had a period in a while; probably, from her calculations she had missed two.

As she lay there beside her husband she made a decision to go to the drugstore the next day and get that pregnancy test. She was beginning to think it wasn't a fairy tale. With the decision made, she slept; only waking up once to pee.

The next morning Barbara rose a little earlier than Neil. "Thank the gods," Barbara said to herself as she hurried into the bathroom and straight to the water closet. When they had revamped the house, Neil wasn't for adding walls around the toilet that sat in the right corner of their bathroom. He thought it was private enough there. Anyone using it was out of sight of the doorway and the bathroom mirrors. But Barbara finally convinced him it was a good idea. Now as she sat in there she felt the comfort of total privacy as her mind was going a mile a minute. She stretched her arms and had to lower them quickly as the stretch hurt the sides of her breast. Cautiously she touched her breasts and found them to be quite tender.

Barbara smiled coyishly, telling herself she finally

was getting her period. She thought back to the previous morning. Her stomach had been cramping and she had belly pains, but that was just another sign of her period coming. Sometimes it came without warning, but there had been times before when it came with a vengeance. This seemed to be one of those times.

As she sat there she couldn't stop thinking about the nausea she had felt, but that seemed to have passed. Now it was the constant need to pee that had replaced it.

So Barbara whispered, "Go to the drugstore and end this dream, already." Finally she got up, flushed the toilet and found Neil at his sink so she paused to give him a hug from the back and whispered, "Love you." before she went to climb in the shower.

Barbara turned around under the water, feeling some of her aches and pains leaving her body until she had to get out and get dressed. As she began the short walk to the bedroom it was like a bomb had gone off inside her and she gasped for breath. She stood there waiting for the sensation to pass and when it did, she cautiously took several deep breaths.

Slowly she moved forward, glad to see Neil wasn't in the bedroom and happy to see he had made the bed. She smiled and went to her closet and got out her clothes and laid them on the bed. She then went to the bureau and pulled out her underwear, her hand hanging above the drawer with her panties and bra dangling. "My journal," she said out loud.

She went to her side of the bed and laid her underwear on top of her clothes and got out her journal. She dated her entry and wrote down her systems quickly, sensing that if she didn't, she would forget what she had experienced. Satisfied, she went about putting herself together, and when she finished, she did a little twirl in front of the mirror before starting downstairs.

When she entered the kitchen, there was Neil with coffee, orange juice eggs and toast. "What is all this?"

"It's called taking time for ourselves. We've been doing nothing but rushing through each day, so we are going to sit down and have a nice breakfast now before we head out to work."

"I like that," Barbara said, her mind working overtime, reminding her that she needed to get out of the office and pick up that pregnancy test at her first opportunity. By the time she was taking her second bite of toast she was debating whether this was something she should be sharing with Neil. Then she convinced herself with their busy life, it was best to have only one of them dealing with waiting to find out, so she didn't say a word.

That day proved ideal. Barbara went with Neil to their second appointment of the day, but why he was at his first one, she slipped out to get the pregnancy test. She was on her way to the bathroom to take it when Jennifer stopped her. "Barbara, someone named Mindy is on the line. Do you have time to talk to her?"

Barbara stopped dead in her tracks, her heel scuffing the tile as if she had been dragged. Her breathing was fast and hollow like a rush of air over a bottle. She tried to calm herself and finally was able to speak. "I'll take it in my office."

Barbara hurried back to her office and went behind her desk. She took a deep breath to calm herself and then picked up the receiver. "Hello, this is Barbara."

There was silence for a while and then a voice said. "Hello Ms. Sanders," you don't know me, but a friend of a friend gave me your name.

Hesitantly Barbara asked, "Is this Mindy, Mindy...Mindy Worthington?"

If she could see the person on the other end of the line she would know that she was shaking her head, but for Barbara all she knew was it was a long scary silence coming over the line. "No, my name is Mindy; short for Mildred, Walker."

Barbara didn't realize until that moment she had been holding her breath.

"Sorry. So sorry. I don't usually do that. I don't like it when someone does that to me, so I apologize for doing it to you."

"Oh, don't worry about it. We all jump the gun sometimes."

"Thank you for that. How can I help you."

Mindy went into detail on a job she had and asked, "If you want, I have some pictures on my cell that are rather good. I took several angles to give you an idea of the space I would like you to design for us."

They talked further and Barbara gave Mindy her cell number before she hung up. Soon her cell alerted her, and she picked it up and opened the text to view the images. Mindy had asked not only if she were interested in the job, but wanted to know when, how long it would take and the cost so Barbara studied the project pictures.

Mindy had included in her text the room size and from the images she could tell how the windows were placed; enough so that she could easily do a pre-design of the job. Since she didn't have anything pending until 2 o'clock, she began diagramming the area, and using the diagram as a center for her design board where she worked through the hour gathering swatches of fabrics and what she thought would work best in furnishings for the room. She added written descriptions on the board below each item and a summary of what she saw for the design itself. From what Mindy had said, her house was beachy, so she had chosen the same style for this room. When done, she quickly worked up a preliminary quote and the amount of time involved to complete the job. She texted all this back to Mindy along with a time she would be available to come meet with her and see the room.

When Barbara finished, she saw she only had a few free minutes left so she went about gathering what she needed and was waiting when Neil stopped by her office to take her to the next appointment.

This was a project they were working on together and were close to finishing. The client was happy but wanted to tweak the design by adding built-ins along a very precarious wall space and because of that, Barbara needed to revisit the furnishings that she had planned for that area.

It took the rest of the day to work it out and at five o'clock they were headed back to the office. On the way, Neil said, "I'll get on the shelving right away so you can change what needs to be done in the décor. I'll call our client who is set for tomorrow and ask if we can reschedule. If I remember correctly, you have a job at four tomorrow, but maybe we will be done by then" He paused and asked, "What do you think?"

Barbara laid her hand on Neil's. "Calm down. It's all doable. My part is not that big a deal. I'll have Jennifer arrange for the sofa and one chair to be moved to my storage area and then I'll place orders for the replacements which will most likely be two side chairs and a table. That will work great in the area."

"You know what?"

"What"

"You amaze me. You really do."

"You amaze me too."

Smiling, they went into the office and started packing up their things. Soon they were on their way home and it was when they pulled into the driveway that Barbara remembered she hadn't taken the pregnancy test yet.

There was little time to change into their work clothes before the doorbell rang and Neil hurried down to let Paul and Sara in. Barbara joined them and they were soon back out in the garden, working diligently until Neil yelled, "Stop everybody. Come look."

Neil had been working on removing the dirt from the back of the garden and had finally uncovered the gate. Paul and Sara, who had been working on the sides of the garden stopped and went over to where Paul stood, staring as if he had uncovered a bag of gold. Barbara was further away but was soon standing at her husband's side.

"Oh, my god," Sara said. "It's stunning."

"Yes, it is." Paul agreed.

"It's better than I ever imagined it would be."

And Barbara, who became unable to move or act due to shock, said nothing.

After a bit, Neil said, "Come on, come on, let's get back to it. He started barking orders to each of them and before the end of the night, the only thing remaining was to see if the gate would open. They could see through the gate that the ceiling above it was held by possibly a roof as there was no dirt or debris to be seen.

While everyone scurried about clearing up the rest of the remaining dirt in their areas, Barbara continued to stand, transfixed. She couldn't move and didn't until Neil came over and asked, "Is something wrong?"

That brought her back and she turned and smiled. "Nothing that a good night's sleep won't cure.

Neil looked at his watch. I think if we keep going for another hour, we will be finished...I mean really finished with all this digging. What's left is a few spaces with only a little left to remove and as you can see, Sara has done wonders with cleaning off the statues and flower containers in the garden; just as you have cleared all the paths. He grabbed his wife's shoulders.

"Can you believe it? We are done and now we can repair and design."

Barbara gave him a weak smile and got back to work. As Neil had surmised, at the end of the hour, they had finally finished the job. The four stood looking around at their handiwork, pleased with what they had accomplished.

"Sara, Paul, this garden is as much yours as ours and you can come anytime you want."

"Thank you," Paul said, "But it is your home, and we'll definitely want to see it again, but with you both."

They hugged and climbed up the stairs, each of them turning to take a last look before they went their separate ways. With his arm around his wife's shoulders, Neil said, "It's up to you now Barbara. It's yours to design and anything you need to add or repair, I'm here to help you. Then as an afterthought he added, "But the gate with the spider web design and whatever is behind it is mine to work on. Promise me you won't change anything back there."

"That was a promise she could make because from that point on she didn't want to go near that gate anyway, let alone inside and she would have to try and convince Neil not to, at least not to go in there alone.

Chapter 52

Barbara was exhausted and though she wanted to talk to Neil about that gate and how it made her feel, she knew she wouldn't be able to express her feelings without a good night's sleep so instead, she decided to get ready for bed. She was on her way into their bathroom when Neil said, "Sweetie, I'm going to use the bathroom in the hall. I'm too tired to wait."

Barbara waggled her head but was sure he was already outside the bedroom door and couldn't see her nod. It didn't matter anyway she reflected as she went into the bathroom and without lingering a moment, climbed into the shower and began tackling all the dirt and sweat from the evening of digging. Once she had washed every inch of her body and her hair, she stepped out and put on her terrycloth head wrap before going to the sink and brushing her teeth.

She could feel the anxiety of the evening being replaced with lethargy as she rushed through the rituals until finally she unwrapped her hair and slipped into a nightgown. When she entered the bedroom she saw that Neil was already in bed and from his even breathing, he was asleep.

Barbara quietly moved around to her side of the bed, turning off the lights as she went. When she snuggled in under the covers every muscle in her body relaxed and she had no problem falling fast asleep.

Only it would be a restless sleep.

She was lost in a maze of tunnels, and she wasn't alone. There were several people with her wandering within this confusing place. As they go further, she hears something.

Barbara senses the fear of the others. There is something behind them, but she doesn't dare turn all the way around. Instead she glances at the faces around her. She doesn't know them. They seem unsettled and she has the sense she is intruding on their territory.

Crazily she starts turning into tunnels twisting through the maze until she has no idea how to get out.

Again she senses that she is not alone. There is something coming toward her, but she can't make out its features. She leans forward trying to see in the dark. She makes out a shape of something...something that causes her heart to stop and her breath to catch in her throat.

It draws nearer and Barbara no longer cares to find out what 'it' is as she stands frozen, her whole body shaking like a leaf in the wind, her breath coming out in short, ragged gasps. With effort, she forces her body to move; first slowly and then she starts running. But she can't seem to get away. This creature spontaneously appears behind her.

A wave of fear washed over her, a fear so raw and powerful that it threatened to consume her whole body. She runs faster than she has ever run before. Her heart races. Sweat trickles down her brow. Her hands shook as she knew she was running out of time. She needed to find a way out.

A dread, slow and cruel, crept up her spine, making every second feel like an eternity." She can feel terror maturing as she realizes that she, she alone is the object of the chase.

She can't outrun it. The air turned frigid around her. Her heart pounded in her ears, and an acrid smell filled her nostrils. She runs as fast as she can, but whatever it is, it is faster.

Barbara is getting tired and not sure she can continue at this pace, but she must. So mustering every ounce of strength she continues to run as she can and then...there in front of her, coming her way is the creature.

Somehow it has outsmarted her choice in tunnels. She can hear it growling as it comes closer, but she can't move. She is frozen in her spot shaking violently as it approaches, but then it changes. It changes and it has a face and a human body, and she reaches out.

That's when she falls out the bed and wakes.

Neil is there calling her name with a worried expression on his face. "Sweetie, can you hear me."

Barbara lay there trying to get her bearings and when she does she manages a weak smile before asking, "What happened."

"You were thrashing about in the bed. You woke me up and the next thing I knew you disappeared over the side of the bed. Are you all right?"

"I am."

"Maybe I should put bars on your side of the bed."

She could hear the humor in his voice now that he saw she was all right.

"Funny, that's funny," she said as she pushed herself up until she was sitting on the edge of the bed. Neil kneeled in front of her, and she tried to give him a serious look, but couldn't. Instead she started laughing. Soon Neil began laughing too.

When she finally was able to speak she said, "This stays between us, okay. We don't tell anyone about this?"

"About what?"

"That's right. Nothing to tell."

That morning Barbara takes the pregnancy test. She grabs her cell off the end table and takes it with her as she heads to the water closet. She sits on the toilet, carefully reading the instructions and when she is done she unwraps the pointer thing and then looks at the time on her cell phone as she points the tip into the stream of urine. Luckily, she had to pee really badly and was able to get a good stream going for almost ten seconds. She then re-capped the device and placed it on the back of the toilet.

She looked at her cell to check the time and then sat waiting. She wiped herself and put the toilet seat down and sat on it, as she continued to wait out the time. It seemed like forever, those five minutes required for the test to finish processing, but finally it was done.

Barbara had to take a few deep breaths to calm herself and then slowly she removed the cap. She picked up the instructions and read it again. She wanted to be sure she was reading it right. "Okay, she said to herself, "There is a red control line and..." she stared at it. There was a faint line that was also red, close to the end of the device. She again looked at the instructions and slowly a smile appeared on her face. If she was reading it right, she was pregnant.

Barbara stood in the water closet taking deep breaths and wondering what to do next. She could rush out and tell Neil and they could both get excited, but what if it was a false positive. She had heard that happened a lot. No, she decided, she'd wait to tell him.

That settled she left the water closet and took her

shower. She was brushing her teeth when her cell dinged. Barbara looked over with toothpaste dripping down her chin and slid her finger across the symbol so she could view the text. It was another one from Emily; this time threatening to come over with a pregnancy test and not leave until she had taken it.

Barbara chuckled as she texted Emily back.

Just did the pregnancy test. Not sure I did it right. I am going to see the doctor. Let you know the results.

Barbara looked at the time on her cell. She saw it wasn't too early to call her gynecologist, so made the call. Briefly she explained her reason for the appointment and was given a date and time. When she disconnected the call she texted Emily.

Guess what. I have an appointment already.

Her appointment had been set for the following week. Barbara went about her work in a daze and on more than one occasion started to tell Neil, only she knew how hard it was for her to wait, she didn't want him to be anxious too, so she tried to act normal. She must have done a good job of it, that is, up till the time he told her they needed to go through that spider gate, which is what they called it now, and see what was in there.

At first Barbara told him jokingly, "Come on, let's let it be a surprise we can look forward to once we've taken care of the rest of the garden."

That bought her a little time, but eventually Neil said he couldn't wait, he had to check it out. That's when Barbara broke down and told him. "Listen to me Neil. You don't want to upset a pregnant woman do you. I think we should wait."

His mouth dropped as he stared at her. "Are you saying what I think you're saying."

Barbara nodded. "But don't get too excited just yet. I have a doctor's appointment tomorrow and I will find out for sure. I took a home pregnancy test, but they aren't one hundred percent accurate; especially when you're not sure you're doing it right. I wanted to make sure before I broke the news, but I had to say something. I had to. There may be a lot more to do once we go behind that gate and I wanted to think only about getting the parts completed that we can see now."

Neil nodded. "That makes sense. Once you get the news...if we are pregnant, you need to concentrate on getting the grounds done while you can. I understand." After a brief pause Neil asked, "Can I go with you tomorrow?"

"Let's see," Barbara said as she went over to the computer and pulled up their calendar. "Yes, you're free when I have the appointment so we can go together."

Barbara could see the effect the news had on Neil. He was no longer thinking about that garden, blessedly, no longer wondering what was behind that gate. It was selfish of her to spring the news on him at that instant, but she needed some ammunition to keep him from opening that gate.

On the day of her appointment, they were up and dressed early. Neil made it to the kitchen first, which was as usual, and breakfast was on the table when she entered. Every time she looked towards him, he was smiling and when he sat down to eat, he was grinning from ear to ear.

"You have to stop looking like the joker or I'm not going to have you come with me to the appointment and have them wondering just what kind of baby I'm carrying."

"I'm sorry, but I'm so happy."

"Well, don't be so happy until we know for sure. Like I said, I could have gotten a false positive."

"Okay." He replied, the smile falling off his face as he pressed his lips tightly together. That looked even weirder, but she made no comment.

"Oh, look at the time, we need to get a move on."

Together they cleared up the dishes and put them in the dishwasher. They checked to make sure the stove was turned off and then headed out the door. They were in the car when Neil said, "I think we forgot something."

Barbara gave him a puzzled expression and then slowly it dawned on her, "Our briefcases. We forgot our briefcases."

Laughing, they climbed out of the car and went into the house to retrieve their briefcases and as they made their way back to the car, Barbara chuckled and said, "What kind of parents will we be, huh!" They laughed again as they made their way to the doctor's office.

When Neil drove into the parking lot of the doctor's office, Barbara took a deep breath and out of the corner of her eyes saw Neil doing the same. Together they climbed out of the car and walked together into the building. In the doctor's office, Neil gave her a squeeze and then went over to hang up his coat before sitting down in the waiting room while Barbara went to the reception desk and announced, "My name is Barbara Sanders."

"Thank you Mrs. Sanders. Please fill out this form and when you're done, bring it to me, then take a seat and we'll call you back shortly.

Barbara went over to hang up her coat and scarf before sitting down beside Neil. "This is finally happening," Neil whispered.

"Let's not put the cart before the horse. Let's be calm

until we know for sure."

Neil nodded his head so fast she was afraid it would roll off his neck and she couldn't help herself as she giggled. Then, getting serious, she filled out the paperwork and returned it to the receptionist. She was headed back to her seat when she heard, "Mrs. Sanders, they're ready for you."

Neil leaned over and kissed her cheek. Barbara stood and went to the entrance to the examination rooms. In her purse was her list and she padded the sides of it to make sure it was there on her shoulder. On that list was the bout of nausea, some chest discomfort, a sense of bloating.

At the instructions of the nurse, she undressed and put on the robe, following the directions to have the ties in the front. She climbed on the table and sat, waiting.

It was a little chilly in the room, but she ignored it as she waited alone, going over what she was going to say to the doctor. She didn't have to wait long before someone entered.

The nurse whose nametag identified her as Genny Winters, entered the room. She introduced herself and then began asking her the normal questions. "Any recent changes in medications? Any new concerns? When was your last period?"

Barbara responded to each question and then when she came to the last one she said, "Well, funny you ask. I was planning to talk to the doctor about that today".

Genny said, "Your last period?"

"Yes, I don't know for sure. I missed several before I realized I had and when I did, I took a home pregnancy test...but I know they aren't always accurate so I setup this appointment to find out for sure."

"Good," Nurse Winters replied, "Well, let's find out, shall we."

Genny walked over to the cabinet in the room and came back and handed Barbara a cup. "First things first,"

Genny said with a smile.

Barbara slid off the table and couldn't stop the nervous laughter that came out her mouth as she said, "okay". She then went down the hall, holding her gown closed with one hand while the other held tightly to the cup. She came to the door marked, '*bathroom*' and went in to do the deed. She peed in the cup. When she was done, she left the cup in the bathroom, per the detailed instructions posted on the wall, and then made her way back to her exam room and shut the door behind her.

There was a magazine entitled *Parenthood* laying on the table in the examination room, so she pulled it out and carried it over to the chair next to the examination table. She sat, leafing through it as she waited.

The door opened and the doctor entered. "Good morning Mrs. Sanders, my name is Dr. Waldorf. Before the doctor could close the door behind her, the nurse quickly poked her head in and excitedly said, "It's Positive! Congratulations!"

"It's... What?!"

Barbara looked at her, absolutely stunned, and said, "Excuse me, What? It's What?!!!!! Are you serious?!", with her voice cracking between words.

"No doubt about it, you're pregnant."

Barbara stood beside the exam table in her gown in complete shock. She stared at the walls, put her face in her hands and cried, totally unsure how to feel. Excited, nervous, ecstatic, anxious, happy, shocked. Terrified? Mostly terrified. It was one thing to think she might be pregnant, but finding out for sure was a whole different experience and her reaction surprised her.

The nurse remained in the room as Dr. Waldorf encouraged her to get up on the examination table.

"We weren't trying to get pregnant, but we weren't NOT trying. That's what they all say, right? We had planned to start trying fairly soon, but this was just totally unexpected." Barbara babbled on, wanting to stop but couldn't.

She continued rambling on as the Doctor performed the exam. She told them about the sunken garden and how they had uncovered it and how it had all been a surprise that it was there. She told them about her business and how lucky she was to be working with her husband, Neil and she finally stopped her mouth after saying we weren't exactly ready JUST yet."

Smiling, Dr. Waldorf said "That's always how it goes. You're never FULLY ready for a baby. So ready or not, here he or she comes. From what I can tell, you are probably five weeks pregnant. She then went over the regimen she needed to follow and scheduled her next appointment.

"You can get dressed now. Congratulations Mrs. Sanders."

Now what, Barbara wondered as she started getting dressed. She had arrived here feeling surprised, confused with a big whopping sense of disbelief. They both wanted children, but with the business, their jobs and especially that sunken garden, how would they manage it all? They hadn't thought about that, about babysitters and daycares. They hadn't given it any thought whatsoever.

So it seemed right to be a little apprehensive about something so life changing as adding a baby to the mixture. But wasn't this a happy change, she asked herself. They were starting their family.

By the time Barbara was dressed and heading for the waiting room area, she couldn't stop grinning and smiling. Since their marriage they were the only family they had; no brothers, no sisters, parents passed, it had been just them.

Now, they were creating a life and a family together.

When she entered the reception area, she grinned at the woman at the window and continued grinning when she felt Neil behind her.

"What is it? Are we pregnant?" Neil whispered shyly. She finished up paying and getting her receipt that showed her next appointment date, then turned and smiled widely. Before they left the building, they were like two giddy kids with the biggest secret ever. They were pregnant.

"So how far along are you now?"

"Well, the doctor seems to think about five weeks and that is about right, judging from how I've been feeling physically."

"What do you mean."

"I've been very fatigued. I even had a bout of morning sickness…you know, vomiting and such."

"I didn't know."

"Of course not. I didn't want you to know, mainly because I wasn't even sure what was going on. I could have been coming down with Covid, for all I knew."

"So…"

"Yes, I took a Covid test, and it was negative. I knew better than to not take that test."

"And what about the pregnancy test?"

"I felt bloated, and my breasts were sore. But I've never been pregnant before. So I thought maybe it was a touch of the flu or something."

"Your breasts were sore! Now, I should have caught on to that," Neil said smiling.

"You would have, except we've been falling in the bed exhausted every night since we forged ahead on that garden." As she said it, she was careful not to sound disgusted. The last thing she wanted was to have him question her about the garden. As far as he was concerned, she liked the garden as much as he did.

As they headed toward the office, Neil asked her question after question, and she tried to answer as best she could. Finally when they pulled into the parking lot she said, "Listen, I know you're excited, but let's keep this to ourselves for a bit. Give us time to adjust to the idea and also to be sure..."

Neil nodded. She didn't have to finish the sentence.

It was easy to keep the news to themselves since she wasn't showing. They did a lot of planning not only on the jobs they had taken on but the sunken garden, which of course was the topic of many evenings. But the big plan was to start preparing for parenthood. This the doctor, on more than one occasion had told her focusing on the exciting side of the experience would get them mentally prepared for having a baby in their life.

That seemed to be the easy part. They got a lot of books on parenting and followed through. They sung to their baby, though they weren't as sure as the doctor that the baby could hear through all that skin and tissue. She rubbed her belly at every opportunity until it became a habit.

She took care of herself by eating well, staying active, resting when she could manage, which at times was a little cat nap in her office chair. She also had Neil to help manage stress since that was one of the unwritten laws in their business.

And stress overtook her more often than not. Before it had been easy to smooth out the ends and not let it get to her, when a client wanted to change something. But maybe it was the hormonal changes in her body that found her needing a go-between when the customer made a change way beyond the point when it was possible to reciprocate. Usually she was right there with an alternative suggestion, but lately she felt herself wanting to chastise them. Thanks to Neil she was held in check.

Barbara felt remorse at not immediately texting Emily, but she knew Emily would eventually question her. She decided to hold off until then.

By her second trimester, she had an obvious bump. She was twenty weeks into her pregnancy when she was in the shower, washing her body and her hand moved outward when she reached her belly. She paused and moved her hands around her tummy surprised that she hadn't noticed it before. It was like her belly grew over night. When she came into the bedroom with just a towel around her, she said, "I am now officially pregnant."

Neil had been searching his closet for his favorite sweater and turned with a surprised look on his face.

"In doctor terms, my uterus has moved outside my pelvis area. I have a noticeable baby bump. See!" Barbara let the towel drop and did a few poses to accentuate the growth of her belly.

"So, let me see, that means we have seventeen weeks to go?"

"Ah, sorry to bust your bubble, but they are now saying 39 to 42 weeks is full term."

"When did that change. I read in one of our books it was 37 to 39 weeks."

"I guess, like everything else, pregnancy changes with the times."

Neil looked at his wife and let out a puff of air, then started laughing. Barbara joined in and went over and gave him a big hug. "Mister, we are soon going to be parents.

What do you think about that?"

"I think it is the best job we've done. That's what I think."

Barbara smiled, turned and moved toward her dresser, allowing Neil to go back to search for his sweater. Barbara started gathering her clothes as well. When she tried to button her slacks, over her shoulder she said, "I think I need to get slacks with larger waists or check out knitted ones."

Neil nodded, not turning around right away until finally he had his sweater. He then looked at her and replied, "I like knitted slacks." Then he pulled his sweater over his head.

They finished getting ready for work and though they were running a little late, Neil insisted they sit and have a proper breakfast. He was getting good at fixing meals and Barbara liked that. With their crazy schedules it was nice to not be the only one doing household duties since they both exerted a lot of energy in that department on each jobsite.

As they cleaned up after themselves, they put on their coats and boots and headed out the door with Neil paying special attention to her. He was always afraid she would slip and fall, though she had been leaving the house in this kind of weather for years.

As they drove toward work, Neil said, "I think we need to start telling our friends."

"I think so too." She paused and then said, we need to do it in an orderly fashion if you know what I mean."

"I do. That means our closest friends first and since we have a lot of close friends, we can have a dinner party and invite them all at the same time. That way no one feels left out because you know, one will tell the other."

"I agree."

When they arrived at the office and parted ways,

Barbara, first thing, pulled up her calendar. She searched for several open dates when they could have people over. She decided to just tell them it had been a while since they had met up and it would be fun to see everyone in a social situation.

That done, she got ready to go out to her first appointment. When she finished, she met up with Neil and they went to the job they were both working on. By noon they had only time for a quick lunch between checking on items that were supposed to have been delivered and those that they still had to place orders for.

Finally they were back at the office and ready to head out when Jennifer stuck her head into Barbara's office.

Barbara looked up. "What is it Jennifer?"

"I think you already know what I want. But just in case you don't, I'll ask. Are you pregnant?"

"W-h-a-t! She said drawing out the letters as she spoke. How did you know."

"Come on Barbara. I know your style and your size. I do like the change, but it is obvious why you've started liking knits."

Barbara started laughing and Jennifer joined in. "Yes, I'm pregnant, but we haven't told anyone yet."

"Don't worry, my lips are sealed." Jennifer smiled and before leaving, said. "Congratulations. You will be wonderful parents." Then she disappeared from the doorway.

Barbara finished sending out her email to her friends and when she had gathered up her things, Neil was already at her door. "Come on, let's get you home."

"I'd like that she said as she went over to join him.

That night after they had dinner and Barbara put her

feet up, she told Neil she had sent out an email and copied him.

"Give me a minute," Neil said as he went to get his laptop. He opened his mail and pulled up the one she had sent. His head nodded as he went through the names. There will be Emily and Jack Watson, Sara and Paul Locksmith, Marla Dickerson, Andrea and Robin McBride. Everyone knows each other in some capacity along with knowing us so it should go nicely." Finally he added, "So, we have seven people...should we get one more to round it out?"

Barbara thought for a moment. "Okay. What about Linda Sibley? She's not married and will round out the table."

"Great."

So Barbara sent out an invite to Linda. That done she looked at Neil and said, "Come on, let's go upstairs, get into our pajamas and watch '*Law and Order*'. Neil smiled. "Go ahead up. I'll lock up and turn out the lights. I'll be up in a jiff."

Chapter 53

The evening of the dinner party was upon them and even though it was Saturday, they had to do a job before finally being able to stop at the grocery store and pick up the things they needed for the dinner. It didn't surprise them that everyone was coming. These people were their friends, but they were also excited about the sunken garden. Barbara knew that in the back of their minds they figured that was what the party was about. Boy were they in for a surprise.

Hosting a sit down, dinner seems to be going out of style, but Barbara enjoyed them. She would spend hours in preparation and even longer in making sure everyone was having an enjoyable time as they worked through cocktails and hors d'oeuvres. Then dinner, followed by Cognac, dessert and espresso. But the conversations were the main event.

Barbara looked over at Neil, "Don't forget. We need to go to the florist after we finish at the grocery store."

"I didn't forget. Just relax and enjoy the calm because it's going to be a crazy night with all of them at once."

"I know," Barbara said smiling. "That's what I'm hoping for."

"You're, crazy, you know that don't you." Barbara

just smiled thinking she must be.

They were at Wegmans and as Neil looked for a spot to park, she got out her list. She wasn't leaving anything to chance. Everything had to be perfect because in her head she thought that if she didn't make a big deal of it, everyone would be putting the garden before her announcement. That was why she gave Neil strict orders not to think about taking anyone near the garden until after they had finished their dinner. She knew that it would then be too dark to see anything and that was what she wanted. As much as she loved her friends and they loved her, that garden stole the thunder on many occasions. She would not let it happen tonight.

With the list in hand, they entered Wegmans and in less than a half hour she had everything she needed. Everything was going smoothly and when they wheeled their groceries out to the car, Neil insisted she climb in and let him load the groceries. She did, smiling. She liked being pampered.

Once Neil was in the car, Barbara said, "We need to stop at the dry cleaners next."

"What for?"

"I need to pick up the tablecloth and napkins. I sent them to the cleaners a few days back…you remember."

"Ah, the famous tablecloth and napkins."

"Come on, Neil, you know they mean the world to me. It's one of the few things I have to remind me of my parents."

"I'm sorry sweetie. I was just kidding."

Demurely she turned on her seat and said, "You know I polished the silverware."

"I know. That silverware is so old, and I don't think sniffing silverware polish can be good for you; especially in your condition."

"Now, silly boy. I was smart about it. I wore a mask and gloves. It was what I wanted to do for you. We will have, in a way, our parents with us when we make our glorious announcement."

One of the first things that Barbara and Neil had in common was the fact they had both lost their parents in car accidents.

She recalled it was when Neil asked her to marry him that he said he would like to meet her parents.

Barbara was sad at first, but managed to share with him that she was a teenager when she had to face life without her parents. Lydia and Jonathan Jones had died in a car accident in New Jersey on a Saturday evening, on their way to see a play she was in at the high school. It was at approximately 6:30 p.m. when a vehicle was traveling on Warren Road and for reasons that remain under investigation the car smashed into her parents and their car left the roadway, striking a pole then catching on fire. They were pronounced dead at the scene. She being an only child, had to face the tragedy alone."

It was then that Neil had told her that he understood. He explained by saying that his parents, Spencer and Mary Sanders had been on their way to lunch when their car toppled off a bridge and into the river in New York City. He added, "Very sadly both of my amazing parents died that Friday." He told her that he too was an only child. He then said something that seemed to ease both of their sadness. "I am glad that neither one of them would ever have to mourn the loss of the other one. Which is a blessing in itself."

It was the perfect thing to say and over the years, she found that Neil seemed to always know the right thing to say. It was one of the reasons she loved him.

Neil turned to look at her, then quickly turned back and said, "Ah, now I understand all the fuss." He paused, clearing his throat before he added, "You're right. They would have been so happy to know they were having a grandchild...so happy."

There was a catch in his voice, and she knew it was because he appreciated what she was doing. She gave him a minute, then changed the subject. "Can you imagine our friends' faces when we share our news?"

"Yes, it will probably be the same stunned expression they had when they first saw the sunken garden."

Barbara immediately withdrew from the conversation. She realized he was right, and it hurt to think it was true. She allowed herself to pout, but slowly came around. She knew they would be happy for them. Besides, when they had seen the sunken garden for the first time they had been ecstatic, and they would be again. This wasn't about her and her feelings. It was about the baby, so she smiled and was still smiling when they went into the dry cleaners.

Over the years the set had yellowed, but only slightly and now as they handed her the hangers with the see-through plastic cover, they were sparkling white again. "Oh, thank you. Thank you so much. They look beautiful."

The dry cleaner smiled and while Neil paid at the counter, he told her it was made of excellent fabric and should be good for another fifty years figuring it was somewhere around then when it had been made.

Neil finished his transaction and came to retrieve the items from Barbara. She could tell he was impressed, though he didn't speak a word.

They had one more stop to make and that was to the florist. She was glad she had decided on nothing but white flowers and when she saw the rose bouquets layered in astilbe and veronica, it took her breath away. There were ten large cut glass vases and twenty smaller versions and with the help of the florist they managed to get them all in the car, safely placed for their ride home.

Barbara was so excited she could hardly breathe and when she mentioned it, Neil said, "It's probably all those flowers." She looked over at him and she had to laugh.

They arrived home. It took several trips between them to get everything inside. Finally on the last trip, they took a slight break before getting up and taking care of their purchases.

There was no guess work here. Barbara had diagrammed the flower placements and outlined the steps to complete the evening so it would run smoothly. She had made two copies of the diagrams for the flower placements so they each had one.

But first they went to the dining room and together, smoothed the tablecloth on the table. Then, when that was done, they went to the cabinet to get out the chargers and their good China. They placed the China on top of a charger and placed a folded napkin on top. Then Neil went into the drawer of the hutch, and they visited each place again with the silverware. Neil was from a prominent family, so he had done this many times and she marveled at his talent, arranging the pieces to perfection with no guidance from her.

When they were done, they stood back and stared at their masterpiece.

"We can't stop yet, my dear, we need to keep moving."

Barbara had a light blue table runner that she now had him help her place down the center of the table, and then after checking the water level took ten of the small bouquets and placed them down the center as well. The final result was exactly what she had hoped for; simple but appealing.

The diagram she had made showed where the remaining arrangements were to go so they moved about placing them in each location, then followed back around with the votive candles.

Finally they were done. "It's perfect," Barbara said, catching her breath as though she had run a race.

Neil looked at his wife's happy face and said, "Yes, it is perfect."

Barbara was sure that this was what she needed to keep her curious guest inside, at least until after the announcement and hopefully for the rest of the evening as well. She was sure it would be dark out when they finished the meal, and once they learned the real reason for the invite, they would become so excited the garden would be the last thing they thought of. At least that was her hope. If not, she had the lateness of the evening in her favor. It would be too dark to see all they had accomplished.

Barbara was proud of herself as she put the last flowers and votives in the powder room and the downstairs bathroom. These were bouquets of color with bright pink tulips.

As they headed to the kitchen, Barbara abruptly stopped.

Neil, with concern asked, "What is it?"

"We forgot the cards."

Barbara had placard cards made and they were to be placed under each dish so when their friends lifted their chargers at the end of the meal they would see them. The top says simply, '*To You*' and because they were in the business, the inside said, "*Nursery Under Construction*".

Neil's shoulders dropped. He had been tensed thinking something was wrong with her. Now he smiled and said, "Well, let's get at it."

Together they went around the table and placed a placard under each charger. When Barbara looked at Neil she was smiling.

"What is it?"

"Of all the clever, perfect ideas you've had, this is the best one yet."

Barbara tearfully replied, "Thank you sweetie. Thank you."

They stood side by side, then Neil pulled her into his arms and held her. She raised her head and kissed him, letting all her thanks and love flow into that intimate moment until the spell was broken when Neil asked, "What time are the caterers due?"

"They'll be here at five to start prepping the food so we can sit down at seven to eat."

"So, what are we having, again?"

"To start we have grilled oysters, followed by a green salad of tomatoes, cucumbers, pecans and strawberries and because we are all into seafood, we're serving salmon fillets cooked on a cedar grilling plank."

"And before dinner?"

"We'll have cocktails and hors d'oeuvres."

"I take it the cocktails will include champagne?"

"No that will come after the Cognac, dessert and espresso. I have told the caterers under no circumstance should they remove the charger plates so that the placards won't be exposed. Then once the dessert and coffee are served, the caterers will have cleaned up the kitchen and left. That's when you will pour the champagne. "I'll casually say something about them handing me their chargers and..."

"They see the placard and the real festivities begin."

"Okay my dear, it's getting late, so we need to get cleaned up and ready. I'll take the downstairs…"

The shock apparent in her voice Barbara practically yelled, "No, use the upstairs hall bathroom. Please."

Neil smiled. "Gotcha," he said as he took the steps two at a time. Barbara took a moment to take it all in again. She was happy with the results of their labor. At times when they were decorating the rooms it felt as exciting as the days she spent designing each room before finally moving in. Just like then she was happy with what they had accomplished.

Barbara headed upstairs to get ready, her mind reviewing every detail, hoping she hadn't forgotten anything and for a moment wished she could tell them if it was a boy or a girl. But she smiled as she reminded herself she was glad they had decided not to know ahead of time, only just for that tiny moment she wouldn't have mind sharing it with their guest.

Taking one last look around, she pulled herself together and went upstairs to start getting ready. Since she was now showing she was careful to pick just the right outfit for the evening and as she looked through her closet she found it. Her St. John maxi dress would be perfect with its tiered A-line silhouette of floral dot fil coupé. It had an adjustable drawstring waistband and tie shoulders. Neil liked the dress, and she did too.

When she had applied her makeup and pulled her hair back into a ponytail, she slipped the dress over her head. She took a moment to survey herself from all angles and pleased with the results, she headed downstairs.

Neil was standing in the living room when she

entered. He was watching the light fade from the sky and probably thinking about, she hoped, the nice evening ahead of them. But she knew that stare. He was thinking about the garden.

That was fine, Barbara told herself as she stared at her husband. He looked dashing in his favorite pullover sweater and slacks and his pose emphasized his handsomeness. The look was casually formal, which was what she wanted. Barbara cleared her throat to get his attention. Slowly he turned around and whistled.

"Thank you my dear."

She walked over to him and stood by his side, staring out the window. "Tell me again why the sky changes like that.

Neil cleared his throat. "Well, my dear once every 24 hours the Earth turns ...or rotates on its axis and when it does it takes all of us with it so that at one point we are on the side facing the Sun. But it doesn't stop there, the Earth continues its rotation and eventually we are moved to the side facing away from our Sun."

Barbara grinned and squeezed his arm. "I love it when you talk so intelligently about things."

Neil smiled. "I told you I have to know those things so that I give the right advice to our clients on how their house faces and what they should do to enhance their home.

Neil's face took on a serious expression as he turned to face her. "I have been looking for the right record to put on the stereo...any suggestions?"

They were vinyl enthusiasts. They liked the sound of a vinyl record playing. It seemed much warmer than coming from any other medium and it was mostly because it has a more natural, organic sound. Now, they both searched for an instrumental, with Barbara stressing that she wanted one with a lot of violins.

Neil gently moved one album after the other over to the right as he gazed at the label on each one. Slowly a smile appeared on his face, and he lifted a record up. He showed her the front and she smiled at him. "The Chaconne from Sonata No. 2 in D minor is the single most famous and celebrated violin piece in the history of solo violin music." Barbara paused. "If not, it should be."

"I agree." Carefully he took it out of the jacket and placed it on the turntable while Barbara tucked the jacket at the front of the pile of records. This was a modern turntable, and it had several features that the old ones never did. There was a switch he could set, and the record would play continuously. Neil flipped the switch and then set the volume to medium-low. They had just finished when the doorbell rang, and Neil went to answer it. The caterers had arrived.

Barbara showed them to the kitchen and stood a moment watching them as they put the food on countertops and in the fridge. They were like a well-oiled machine and at one point looked up at her and she bowed before making her way out of the kitchen that was no longer her domain.

Neil had to go to the cellar for the wine and champagne, so he apologized for interfering as he slipped through the group and went pass them quickly.

He had gone down there many times since she had that experience with the hand, but though he hadn't mentioned anything like that happening to him, she still worried. This time because he was getting several bottles it took a while before finally he returned, carrying the metal wired carrier that they kept near the wine for bringing up several bottles at one time. He placed the carrier on a sideboard in the kitchen, hopefully out of the area that the caterers were using and then he removed several and carried them into the living room to put on the portable bar. He was making his last trip when the doorbell rang again, and their guest started to arrive.

The first to arrive were Emily and Jack Watson. Neil took their coats, and they handed him a bottle of wine. He looked at the label. "Honig Cabernet Sauvignon 2019, a Cabernet Sauvignon from Napa Valley, California…the one I was looking for and couldn't find. Thank you."

"You're welcomed."

They barely got the words out when a voice said, "Are you going to block the doorway all night?"

Jack turned to see Marla Dickerson behind them. He stepped back and gave her a hug. While Neil went about hanging up their coats. "We were just moving my dear," Jack said with a smile as they stepped inside.

Marla was bundled up in her coat, smiling as she handed Neil a bottle. "Come in, Marla," he said as he shut the door behind her. He then asked, "Can I take your coat?"

Marla took off her gloves and put them into the pockets of her coat then helped Neil slide her coat off her shoulders.

Barbara came over to help Neil, taking the bottle while he helped with the coat. Once the coat was hung in the closet Marla gave them a big smile. Barbara looked at the bottle then handed it to Neil. "You remembered," Barbara said. "The Kanonkop Pinotage 2019 from Stellenbosch, South Africa."

"How could I forget. You went on and on about taking a trip to South Africa and when I saw this bottle, I couldn't resist. Tell me when you decide to go. I'd like to join you."

Barbara started to respond when the doorbell rang again. While Neil answered the door, Barbara continued her conversation with Marla.

Barbara was listening to her guest and barely heard the doorbell until Neil said, "Ah, Andrea and Robin McBride. Welcome." He showed them in and as he took their coats he called over to Barbara. "Look whose here."

Barbara excused herself and went over to give the sisters a big hug and retrieve the bottle of wine they bought. "Ah, Hertelendy Ritchie Vineyard Chardonnay 2018." This we haven't had before."

"Yes, we started to bring one of our own, but decided on something we were sure you hadn't had before. We are all about trying different wines even if they aren't our own."

"This is sweet. I'm sure we will love it."

The last of the group to arrive were Sara and Paul Locksmith with a bottle of Rhone Red Blends from Chateauneuf-du-Pape, Rhone, and Linda Sibley with a bottle of Kanonkop Pinotage 2019.

Seeing Linda's bottle, Barbara laughed.

"What's so funny?"

Barbara swallowed and caught her breath. "It's just that this is the same wine that Marla brought."

"Oh, she beat me here. She remembered the conversation we had too." Linda smiled as she moved into the living room and went up to Marla with her bottle in hand. "Look familiar?"

The two started laughing together.

Since they hadn't been together for quite a while, the conversation flowed easily around the room. Neil played bartender as he moved about talking and checking glasses.

Sara stopped Barbara and said, "These hors d'oeuvres are wonderful, Barbara. How did you find the time?"

Barbara had a sly smile on her face as she guided Sara over to the kitchen entrance so she could see the caterers busily at work. Sara grinned. "Aren't you the smart one."

They strolled back to the living room and were no sooner there than the head caterer announced dinner was ready and being served in the dining room.

Barbara had worried someone would notice her not drinking, but Neil had worked that all out ahead of time. Barbara had suggested she drink tonic water and lime, but Neil quickly pooh-poohed that ideal saying, "They know you don't drink hard liquor. If they see you with a glass of clear liquid they would know right away."

"So, smartie, what do you suggest."

"It's easy. I'll give you grape juice in a wine glass. They won't even think to question it and you know what wines we have. If anyone asks you just throw out a name."

Barbara couldn't help laughing. "My brilliant husband," she said lovingly.

Neil had been right and now as she sat at the table regarding their friends she was genuinely pleased. And when Neil stood with his glass in his hand she smiled knowing he was going to give his toast. She knew as did those seated at the table. At any get together, Neil could be counted on to do just that.

"To the power of friendship. Each of you have been devoted friends giving support without judgement and coming through at any crisis. You always know the right thing to say when it matters most. Each of you has become an essential part of our life, so this dinner is to show you the care and attention you deserve. To secrets being revealed and friendships growing."

As Neil raised his glass, she smiled, observing each of their faces, wondering if they had caught that final part of his toast. But no one seemed to be surprised by it. When her eyes met Neils she puckered her lips giving him an air kiss.

The meal began. The caterers placed grilled oysters on a plate in front of each of them. As soon as each had been served they seemed to disappear from the room but obviously continued to observe as they returned once everyone had finished.

They replaced the empty plates with a green salad of tomatoes, cucumbers, pecans and strawberries.

Everyone ate silently. Appreciating the arrangement of the food on the plate that made it even more appealing. The plate engaged their senses and drew them into the experience as much as a painting in a gallery draws in the observer. Barbara made a note that if she ever had another dinner party, they would be the first to call.

While that thought ran through her head, Sara, who finished first asked, "Where did you find those caterers?"

"They're wonderful, aren't they," Barbara replied. She watched as heads around the table were nodding. From their expressions she could tell they were waiting for her to share the caterer's name. She took the last bite of her meal and then smiling broadly she told them that her office manager, Jennifer, told her about them. She didn't hesitate to call since she trusted Jennifer explicitly.

"So..."

"I anticipated you might all want their name so in the basket near the door is a brochure and their card. Think of it as our gift to you."

Barbara finished her grape juice and Neil took her glass. "Can I get anyone a refill?"

He left the room and returned with one of their favorite wines and held it up so everyone could see, then dramatically began filling the glasses. When he went over to the bar, he reached over and retrieved the grape juice and filled Barbara's glass and carried it over to her. He winked at her and sat back in his seat.

On cue, the caterers returned carrying the main course; a salmon fillet cooked on a cedar grilling plank with baby carrots, their green ends still attached. Again silence prevailed until the last bite had been eaten.

Barbara watched as each one leaned back in their chair and when Emily's husband Jack picked up his wine glass, he held it out slightly high and away from him.

Everyone recognized that signal and raised their glasses too.

"To Neil and Barbara for a wonderful meal, only outshined by their friendship."

"To Neil and Barbara," they chimed.

This time the caterers entered and removed the plates and allowed some time to pass before they returned with the dessert. As one server placed a dessert, another caterer was behind them asking if they wanted tea or coffee. They continued around the table until everyone had been served and then again disappeared into the kitchen.

It took a while for the guests to even place their fork next to the picturesque display. On a plate sat a small circular tower with a candied strawberry seated on the top. At the base they could see a disk of a graham cracker crust.

Neil was the first to place his fork in the dessert. He started, just before the strawberry and slowly worked his knife down. When his knife reached the plate he looked up at their guests and grinned. "You're not going to believe it," he said.

With that, everyone did the same, including Barbara. When she finally had the inside revealed she saw what Neil was excited about. Inside this cheesecake tower was a strawberry surrounded by chocolate. The vision was so perfect she wanted to get up and take a picture. She held back but looking down the table she saw Andrea McBride do just that.

They ate in silence and again, once everyone seated had finished, the caterers entered and removed the plates. Now in front of them was just the charger. It was time for Barbara to make her announcement.

This had been planned as perfectly as the meal. They relaxed talking amongst themselves and after a while, Neil excused himself and went into the kitchen to take care of the caterers who were just finishing up. He stood in the kitchen waiting until the head caterer put on her coat and at that point he handed her the check. "It was superb. I think you are going to get a lot of calls for your catering business. Everyone was impressed."

"Thank you. Word of mouth is how we advertise."

Neil walked her to the door, and she stepped out to join the rest of them.

When Neil returned, he paused at Barbara's chair and leaned down to give her a kiss. "You can thank Barbara for this wonderful dining experience."

Their friends clapped and once Neil was seated, Barbara stood and asked, "Can everyone move their chargers up this way, please."

All heads turned to look down and lift their charger, handing it to the person seated next to them, who in turn placed their charger on top and handed it to the person next to them. That continued until all the chargers were beside

Barbara's.

No one said a word and Barbara was wondering what was wrong. Did the placard stick to the chargers? Daintily she picked one up and tried to unsuspiciously look under it. She saw nothing.

Finally, Emily asked, "What is this."

"Open it up, she said."

The others noticed the placard and following suit opened theirs. Barbara waited.

Finally Sara said, tears in her eyes as she stared at Barbara standing at the end of the table. "Nursery Under Construction".

When she spoke the words, it changed the expressions of all their friends as they picked up their forks and gently tapped the sides of their wine glasses. "Bravo, bravo."

Barbara and Neil started laughing. They had planned the evening perfectly, but there was no way they could have planned the reaction to their news any better. Finally Neil excused himself and went into the kitchen where the bottles of champagne were chilling. He placed the glasses on their silver tray and carried them first into the dining room, placing them on the table in front of him. He then went back to the kitchen and returned with the bottles of champagne.

While he was getting ready, their guests were hugging Barbara and asking her questions. They wanted to know how long before she would deliver and if they could help in any way. The McBride sisters quickly said they would throw the baby shower and though others wanted to, they relented.

Neil was ready and expertly popped the cork. Paul helped him pass out the filled glasses and when everyone had been served, including Barbara with her glass of sparkling water, Neil offered his toast. "To our friends and my lovely wife who has made me so happy." There were audible 'ahs' heard around the table, then everyone started talking at once.

Barbara could not remember when she had been so happy. As she looked around at their friends, tears came to her   eyes.

Chapter 54

By nearly every measurement, Buffalo was in the midst of a historic winter season, amplified by what has been a series of historic winter storms. And yet, just over fifty miles down the thruway, Rochester's season feels like it hasn't even started yet.

It was in early November that winter settled in. The days slowly turned colder and shorter, and the ground rather suddenly turned white with fresh-fallen snow. Outdoor construction had stopped, and Neil and Barbara spent more time at home and with friends. The majestic season, winter had arrived.

Only it was a tease. As the four months of winter took their toll with cold, snow, heavy clothes and cars that needed to be warmed before climbing in, it wasn't as bad as expected. The snowplows had little to do that winter and shoveling out their driveway when they had to leave before their service could get to them, wasn't bad at all. Neil thought about cancelling the service that year, but he knew the companies needed the work, so he kept paying his bill.

As the winter rolled on, it may not have snowed a great deal, but it was cold. Barbara didn't mind not having to trudge through piles of snow; especially now that she had to make more trips to the doctors and Neil enjoyed having the time to take her. But always at the back of her mind she was worried that Neil would go out into that sunken garden.

Barbara had long completed her plans for the garden and Neil had enlisted an art restorer to handle returning the artifacts to their original condition. He had also engaged a concrete specialist for restoring the pathways and steps. Barbara had sat with Neil at the meetings and had to admit she found it interesting. The people they sought to contract were first amazed of their discovery and once they got over the existence of such a garden, they had looked at the architectural drawings that Neil had developed from being in the garden and working with the descriptions in the document Magnolia Warner had given them that day.

"I can say I am impressed," were the general words coming from all those he communicated, and it was easy to make the choice. It was agreed that when the ground thawed work would begin on the restorations.

Outside of her expanded waistline, Barbara felt fine, and the doctor had told her as such. She worked each day avoiding any heavy lifting as she went about designing rooms for customers and when Neil wasn't busy laying out plans for a client to prepare their addition or redesigning their current quarters, he was at his wife's disposal.

As they reached the mid-point of March, they were finally seeing signs of spring. Each afternoon they could actually feel heat from the sun and the days were longer, with sunlight persisting even after supper. And, finally, the snow piles at the sides of driveways began to melt under the warmth of the day.

Yes, winter began to draw to a close, and Neil and Barbara were excited for more reasons than normal. According to the doctor, in one month they would soon be parents.

During this time Barbara had also got back to her research and after several weeks of coming up with nothing, she ran across the name Jean Bemish. She is laying to rest her son, Ronald Hills Bemish. She leans back in her chair, wondering if she has really found someone who is related to Georgia and William Bemish. She says a prayer and then reads on.

"R. Hills Bemish is an American artist who was born in the 20th Century. His works have been offered at auction multiple times, with one drawing being of particular interest, a rendition of a sunken garden."

Barbara fell off her chair as she read it repeatedly. Her heart beat fast thinking this could not be a coincidence. She took a few deep breaths to pull herself together and then began to search for the announcement for an address or number to reach this Jean, but all she could find was the number of the funeral home. Then she got a bright idea. She searched through the internet for his paintings and found the number to contact if interested in making a purchase. This, she thought must be his agent. Taking a deep breath, she dialed the number.

The phone rang several times before it was finally picked up and she introduced herself and explained she would like to contact Mrs. Jean Bemish.

"Excuse me?" the man on the other end replied.

"I would like to have a number or address for Jean Bemish. She's the mother of R. Hills Bemish, the artist."

"I know who she is."

"Well, can you give me a number to reach her. I have to talk with her."

"I'm sorry, I didn't catch your name."

"It's Barbara, Barbara Sanders."

"Do you know Mrs. Bemish?"

"Well, not exactly."

"I'm sorry, why are you calling."

"I just need to speak to her. It's important that I speak to her."

"Well, I'm sorry miss, I can't give you that information until I speak to her personally. If you can leave a number for her to call you, I'll be sure she gets it."

There was something in his tone that made Barbara feel he was not about to do anything, but she gave him her number anyway.

After hanging up the phone she sat for a while wondering if there was some other way to get in touch with this lady. This was her last lead. After a bit she figured that it was time to tell all to her friends.

She didn't have a lot of time before the baby came and she knew that once she was in the hospital, with the weather getting better every day, Neil would find time to go into that sunken garden alone. If she could find out what it was about the garden that scared her, she would have something to tell him why he needed to stay out of the garden.

So, between setting up the nursery and taking care of clients, Barbara found time to arrange a luncheon with her friends. She had wanted to have them at the house, but somehow she figured that was not a good idea, so she first called Andrea McBride. She was sure since Andrea had been living at the winery all her life, she knew more about the area, so it was important she be available.

It was Andrea who answered the phone. "Hello, this is the McBride residence. How can we help you."

"Hello, Andrea, it's me, Barbara."

"I know it's you. I recognized your voice. Since you're calling on my private line, and I know you can't drink wine, you must want something that is non-winery related?"

Barbara laughed, "You're right. I have a personal favor."

"What is it."

"I want to get some of the women together that are familiar with the stories around our house and the garden, but I don't want to have us meeting at the house."

"Okay, I know where you're going with it. Yes, we can meet here...assuming I am included because I have something to share."

"You were the first person I thought could help. I think it's time I shared the strange happenings I have experienced with you and my other friends so that I can hopefully feel comfortable about that garden."

There was silence on the line and then finally, Andrea said. "Let me know the time and how many. I'll handle the rest."

Barbara felt better as she ended the conversation. She then started calling the people she wished to be present and established a time according to their availability. In the end, all of her friends could make it. She let them know where and set the time at 1:30 p.m.

That done, she went over the list she had made and then called Andrea back with the details. It was set for Thursday of the following week.

With that handled, Barbara started working on a list of things to share. There were the nightmares she was having for sure. She jotted it down. Then there was the time she felt a hand on hers in the basement. What Neil had witnessed happening to Nathaniel Parker in that garden before he died. She concentrated some more and then came up with the mysterious Warren and Mindy Worthington.

Barbara looked over her list and grinned. Once they heard all she had to say, they would probably think she was fanatical, but she didn't care. She just had to tell all of them everything she had experienced.

She was three weeks away from her delivery date when she had another dream. In this dream she saw Mindy and she was beckoning her to come with her. Barbara tried to resist, but she couldn't. She followed Mindy out of the house and into the garden and before she could abstain, she followed her through the spiderweb gate. She tried to turn back, but it was like a force pushing her forward and soon she was in a dark earthy tunnel.

She tried to see through the obscurity, but it was a blanket of darkness before her, and she whimpered. It was the sound of Mindy's voice that forced her to start moving again.

At first she went forward slowly with her arms extended in front of her, but when Mindy called her again, her voice came from far away and she hurried forward, not worried about running into something, because she was more afraid of not finding Mindy. She knew her body was not her own as she seemed to be forced ahead.

She yelled out in the darkness, "Mindy, wait for me." But Mindy didn't respond to her call. She yelled louder. Mindy didn't answer her.

She sensed something behind her. This time when she tried to turn, nothing stopped her. She thought it was Mindy, but it wasn't Mindy. Barbara screamed.

Barbara's eyes flew open to see Neil's face above her. She started to smile, but the smile faded before it reached her face as a stabbing pain suddenly and intensely took hold of her. She lay there trying to find her voice when it came again. It was all she could do to not scream again.

Neil was saying something, but the pain was so great,

she couldn't grasp what he was saying. Then he lifted her head and held her in his arms as he said, "It's going to be all right."

Barbara tried to take a deep breath, but it hurt too much so instead with what breath she had, she whispered. "Take me to the hospital."

Chapter 55

Barbara couldn't remember what happened after that. She was no longer conscious of time or space as the pain took over her body. When she finally opened her eyes rays of sunlight welcomed her and then it all came rushing back.

Her hand went to her belly, and it was flat. She screamed and let darkness overtake her. When she woke again, she turned her head, allowing her eyes to dart around the room. Then she saw Neil. He stood over her, his tears falling on her hand that lay clutching the sheet. He didn't need to say anything because she knew before asking. She had lost their baby.

While this was happening, Detective Pagnelli and Greenberg were deep into the investigation of the man, William Bemish who had gone missing over forty years ago. They had started out going through all those boxes of missing, murder or suicide cases and broken it down to eighteen cases in their jurisdiction.

Only instead of working back through the cases, Detective Greenberg had told his partner he had made a choice on which one he wanted to consider. He explained that it was strange, interesting and old. That was why it captivated him. His partner wasn't so sure so he explained that the disappearance of William Bemish would be a deep dive into a cold case.

He knew that Detective Pagnelli had wanted them to solve a murder so he had to convince him that to solve one that seemed to be a disappearance might prove the most interesting."

Pagnelli was his partner, and they would be working on the same case together so he felt he had to come clean and told him that once they dug deeper into the case they would come across the name 'Post' and that was his mother's maiden name.

It was then that Detective Pagnelli had to make a decision. He knew that working on a case that involved a family member was against the rules, but he could see how important this was to Detective Greenberg.

Detective Pagnelli agreed with Detective Greenberg, telling himself this was indeed an old, unsolved case and the people...relatives...were now gone so, he wondered, this might be a loophole in the law. At least that was how he would look at it because he could understand his partner's interest in this case.

Not wasting any more time they were on to trying to solve the mysterious disappearance of Detective Greenberg's great-great grandfather; a man who owned the famous J.K. Post Drug company.

Once they got started they were surprised just how many people knew, or knew about the Bemishes, and they had gathered quite a bit of information about the family. In order to not raise hackles they posed as customers at businesses and as newbies in town to the other residents.

Pagnelli had served on the police force in New York City before settling in Rochester, New York. Big cities can be lonely places, whereas the intimacy of a small city fosters connection. Research shows that having a small number of tight, meaningful relationships is one of the highest predictors of happiness and community spirit which translated to everyone knowing, everybody's business.

It proved easy as pie. What they learned might be coming second hand, but other people backed up the details. It wasn't until they did the undercover interview with the McBride sisters that they ran into a snag.

This was to be their last person to interview before going to the house where it had all happened. They had learned from their interviews that the current owners were not relatives of the Bemishes or had any knowledge of them until the townspeople told them. So they figured they would talk with them afterwards.

Only when they arrived at the brewery owned by the McBride sisters, the women were not fooled by them. It seems the town still talked to each other. It was Lydia, one of the guides at the Winery that they had talked to earlier and who mentioned that Anton had been at the winery longer and could shed some light on the Bemishes, maybe. So, by the time they arrived at the winery where the two worked, their cover was blown.

It was Andrea who met with them, and she explained that Robin hadn't lived at the winery back in the day. She had joined her later. Andrea shared with the detectives that she was friends with the Sanders and because of that, she was willing to tell them everything she knew about not only the Bemishes, but that sunken garden.

The detectives tried not to show their surprise at the mention of the sunken garden. Not that others hadn't mentioned it, but it was the way that Andrea spat the words out that drew their attention.

Most of what she shared, they knew already but

didn't say a word as she went on to explain that what she knew had come from her father, Asa, who had been fond of the Bemishes.

Detective Greenberg was sensing something important was about to be shared. In earlier conversations, they had been told that Asa was a key factor in this investigation because he knew the Bemishes well and what Andrea was about to reveal was coming directly from a personal friend of the Bemishes.

Again they heard much of the same as they had from the other towns people, only Andrea added one more point to the discussion. She said that her father had always felt there was something strange about that sunken garden and that was why, when the Sanders had uncovered it, she hadn't mentioned that she knew of its existence. From what her father said, there was something down there behind that gate and he always believed that whatever was down there, had taken William Bemish.

Detectives Greenberg and Pagnelli had been seated at one of the tables when Andrea dropped her bombshell. They had witnessed more than their fair share of iconic performances but were still taken aback by Andrea's nearly four-hour discussion.

They were on the edge of their seats waiting for the other shoe to drop and explain the strange happening. When it didn't happen, anxiously, Detective Greenberg asked, "Ms. McBride, what do you think he meant by that?"

"I don't know what he meant. I know that he was saying that it was bad and to stay away from that garden. But then it had been covered up and forgotten until that earthquake uncovered it again."

"Tell me about the earthquake."

Andrea had been joined by her sister who sat at the table with them and between the two they told of the earthquake and about the Sanders calling in a Nathaniel Parker, the owner of DirtWorx company, to help clean up the area. "It was Nathaniel who realized there was something there, under all that dirt and bushes. He told the Sanders that was why they had a sinkhole open in that area. It wasn't a normal happening unless the ground had been previously disturbed or maybe water had built up in an underground spring, so he had to proceed with caution. And he did, at first."

"What do you mean, at first?"

"I don't know."

"Well, how can I get in touch with this Nathaniel Parker?"

"You can't. He died."

There was silence around the table, then Robin piped up, "He has a son and I think he is now running the business."

The detectives were jotting down notes as fast as they could and asking questions at the same time. They had half expected to hear more of the same, but it had turned out to be information that might just help them solve the mysterious disappearance of William Bemish.

After a while, Detective Greenberg said, "Well, ladies at this point we are off duty. If you don't mind, we would like to taste your wine."

"That's what we're here for detectives." Robin turned to her sister who was about to get up, "Sit. I'll get it," she said. "Tell them about Magnolia Warner."

"I'm sure Emily told them about her." She looked at the detectives who were both shaking their heads.

"Well, this is what I heard from Barbara Sanders who is the homeowner now. She is close to Emily Watson and when Barbara was asking about the garden, she told her that her mother had contacted a woman named Magnolia Warner who is now operating her father's contracting office and has for quite some time. She was in the same situation as I was when Asa died. To keep the business in the family, you just step in and find your way. Only I had Robin to help me."

At that point Robin returned with a bottle of wine and four glasses. She poured the wine in each glass and then sat down.

Andrea thanked her and the detectives said, "Yes, thank you." Then turning to Andrea, she continued.

"So, Magnolia Warner wanted to meet the new owners and with her she brought the original details of the property. She also had a write up on the sunken garden that she shared with them."

"Wait a minute. If she had information on the sunken garden, why was it a surprise to the Sanders?"

"Because that detail hadn't been filed with the original documents on the property?"

"Why was that?"

"Nobody knows. Not even Magnolia Warner, but she knows about the paper and may be someone to talk to."

Detective Greenberg was silent thinking about all they had learned and was ready to talk to the Sanders now.

The next morning Detective Greenberg and Pagnelli arrived at the Sanders' residence at Parcel 076.06 Winona Blvd. They rang the doorbell, but no one answered. They waited and then decided to just take a walk around the property thinking maybe they were outside and didn't hear the doorbell. They took their time taking it all in. "This is a beautiful piece of real-estate."

"Yes it is," Detective Pagnelli agreed. "Beautiful."

Finally they were at the west side of the property and though not quite visible from the house side of the yard, that is unless you were looking for it, they could tell something was there. They moved cautiously in that direction.

There it was in front of them, the sunken garden. Even in its need of repair, it was interesting to look at. Detective Greenberg started toward the stairs and Detective Pagnelli grabbed his arm and stopped him. "No, we can't go down there. We don't have a warrant or the owner's permission. You know that."

Detective Greenberg nodded and they turned and walked back to the front of the property. They rang the bell once more and then turned to leave. That's when a car drove into the driveway.

Chapter 56

Neil had wanted to stay at the hospital with Barbara, but Barbara insisted that he needed to go home. "Look at yourself, sweetie, you're exhausted, and you need to get some sleep; especially if you plan on taking me home tomorrow.

"I don't care if I'm tired, what if you..."

"If I need anything, there are people to help me, but I am fine; really I am."

As Neil prepared to leave, he couldn't stop reliving that evening in his head. He had been terrified and unable to think, let alone move when he realized something serious was happening. Barbara was in such pain and just holding her was not going to make her better.

He wasn't sure how long it had taken for him to react, but he finally called the ambulance.

He had ridden with her in the ambulance and all he could do was sit and watch as the EMT and a paramedic asked him questions and assessed Barbara's injuries. The speed of the ambulance and the sound of the siren did nothing to calm his nerves as he tried his best to remain calm.

The hospital was only a short distance from their house but when they pulled up in front of the emergency, it felt like an eternity. Once the ambulance stopped, the back doors were swung open, and two hospital attendants stood at the ready.

Neil moved over, as close to the walls of the ambulance as he could get to allow the passage of Barbara on the gurney and once she had been lowered to the sidewalk, he jumped out and followed her into the hospital.

He felt like a third wheel as he hurried behind the gurney and it was like a slap in the face when he heard one of the attendants say, "I think she's having a miscarriage."

He stopped dead, his mind stumbling over those words. Why hadn't he thought of it. How could he not have thought of it? He thought she had hit her head or something.

They rolled her into a curtained area and when Neil started to enter, he was held back. "She's in good hands. Why don't you sit here," she said pointing him to the direction of a chair outside the curtained area.

Once he was seated she asked, "Can you tell me what happened this evening."

Neil took a deep breath and told how his wife had fallen out the bed and when she started screaming he woke and found she was in terrible pain, so he called 911.

The words rolled into each other as they flowed quickly out his mouth. He tried to slow down and make sense, but he couldn't as he realized, finally, he could be of help and that moment was the first time since arriving at the hospital that he felt needed.

While Neil supplied the nurse with the information he watched as she wrote down everything he shared. Neil started to get up, when a doctor walked by and entered the curtained room where they were caring for Barbara, but the nurse quickly held him back and said, "Thank you Mr. Sanders, I'll be back shortly. I'll tell you if there is anything to report." She then entered the curtained room.

Neil sat there an image of the grieving husband, seated alone in mourning waiting for word. He wondered how to function, but there was nothing he could do so he leaned his head back against the wall and closed his eyes, trying not to cry and hoping he had done everything right.

Just as he pulled out his cell to check the time, the nurse came out of the room and sat on the chair next to him.

"How's my wife?"

"She's better now. You did the right thing, calling 911 immediately. You saved her life."

Neil took a deep breath then asked, "What happened?"

The nurse patted his hand and said, "The doctor will be out soon and explain it to you. In the meantime sit tight. I'm going to arrange a room for your wife, and I'll be back. But your wife will be fine."

Neil started to ask about the baby, but she was already heading down the hallway, so he resumed his previous position and waited. He tried not to think about anything as he sat there alone.

Finally someone came out of his wife's room and said, "Mr. Sanders, my name is Dr. Rydell. Your wife is resting now, and we'll be taking her to the operating room."

Neil jumped out of his chair, almost falling as the blood rushed to his head. "The operating room? What happened."

"Take it easy, sir. I know it's difficult, but your wife is fine. What happened is her placental abrupted."

"What does that mean exactly."

"Her placenta separated from the wall of her uterus, completely. As a result the baby did not get enough oxygen and nutrients in the womb, and..."

"You're telling me she lost the baby?"

"Yes, I'm afraid so. The baby didn't make it, but your wife will be fine."

"Fine! She won't be fine. I won't be fine...how could we be fine?"

"I know this is hard to take, but it happens and through no one's fault. What you need to do is be patient and understanding with her now." Dr. Rydell turned to see the gurney come through the curtains and turned back to Neil. "I wish I could explain this further, but we need to go to the delivery room now."

Neil didn't comprehend any of what he said except that he had to let the doctor go and help Barbara. So he nodded and tried to calm down as he followed them down the hallway until he was shown to the waiting room and Barbara was pushed further until he could no longer see the troupe.

He could feel his blood boiling in his veins and his breathing was labored. He went over to the water fountain and took a drink, trying to calm down. It wouldn't do for him to pass out or cause a commotion. All the attention had to be on Barbara.

Feeling more in control he found a seat and sat wondering how this could happen. What did they do wrong?

It was over, at least for the doctor as he came to talk to Neil. "I know this has been hard on you, but I'm sure you have questions that need to be answered now, so I won't wait. I'll tell you both later, only now, if you have anything you want to ask, you can ask me now."

Neil was tired and not thinking straight, but he managed to say, "What Is Placental Abruption?"

"Placental abruption is something that can happen suddenly during pregnancy. It can be dangerous for the mother and the baby."

Neil nodded. His head clearer now he said, "I know about the placenta. The placenta develops in her uterus while she's pregnant. It sends nutrients and oxygen from the mother to the baby."

"Yes, that's right. It also helps get rid of waste that builds up in the baby's blood and is attached to the wall of the mother's uterus."

Neil nods, so, the baby..."

"The baby is attached to the uterus by their umbilical cord. If you have placental abruption, the placenta separates from the uterus too soon before your baby is ready to be born."

"So what then?"

"Well, it can occur at any time after 20 weeks of pregnancy, but it's most common in the third trimester." He pauses before adding, "When it happens, it's usually sudden."

"So why did this happen?"

"Most of the time, we don't know the cause." Dr. Rydell leaned forward. "Does your wife drink?"

"Yes, socially, but not at all since she became pregnant."

The doctor nodded. "Now, don't take offense, but I have to ask, does your wife use any drugs, like cocaine?"

"No!" Neil said adamantly. "Never!"

"There was a pause while Dr. Rydell wrote down something on the pad he carried." When he looked up he asked, "Did your wife suffer a placental abruption in any previous pregnancy?"

"No, she's never been pregnant before."

"Well, Mr. Sanders, what about a fall?"

Neil is thoughtful. "Yes. Barbara fell out of the bed. She may have rolled onto her stomach, but I'm not sure.

Anyway, that's where I found her, screaming in pain, laying on the floor on her side of the bed."

"What do you think happened?"

"If I had to guess. She's been having nightmares and maybe she had one and she fell out the bed." He shrugged his shoulders and gave a weak smile.

The doctor is thoughtful as he says, "That sounds like what caused it, but we may not know for sure. Your wife doesn't remember much at all."

"So now what?"

"Well, the placenta can't be reattached, and the abruption was severe, putting the health of your wife and baby at stake, so we did a C-section right away. She lost a lot of blood so we're giving her a blood transfusion."

"So that's it."

"Yes."

Neil hesitated then asked, "Can we have more children?"

"I don't see why not, Mr. Sanders. Is that it?"

Neil nodded.

"I need to check on your wife now. I'll see you both, later in her room."

With that, Neil watched as the doctor walked down the hallway.

Barbara was assigned a private room after they did the C-Section. Later her obstetrician came to her room and talked to her while doing a physical exam. She reported. "You're doing fine Barbara. Just fine."

Barbara had remained silent throughout the ordeal and when Dr. Rydell came to visit, he shared most of what he had already told Neil. Barbara had no reaction.

It was hard, the hardest week of their life.

It amazed Neil how fast her body healed, and she was

able to get up and move about. A therapist came to the room each day and talked with them, helping Barbara and Neil face the inevitable truth.

Her name was Mrs. Anderson. She told them that people around them won't know what to say, so though it is happening to you, you will have to be patient with them. "And you, Neil, need to understand that losing your baby can be a lonely time. You may feel that no one understands, and you'd be right, but it will be your job to help them understand."

By the end of the therapy session they felt better. The doctor told them that they could have more children, but they should take the time now to recover. Mrs. Anderson added, "Painful emotions do pass if you give them the proper time."

Neil returned home feeling anxious to have the day end and the start of the next so that he could bring Barbara home. He had spent each day and each night by her side and felt lost now that she was still there, and he would be sleeping at home.

But he knew she was right. He had to clean their room for one thing. Barbara and he had talked about the nursery and decided to leave it as it was. If they hadn't talked, that would be something he would have attended to, not wanting her to see it and realize their loss all over again.

Finally he was at the house, and pulling into the driveway Neil was surprised to see two men at his door. With a frown on his face, he parked the car and turned off the engine. Then slowly he climbed out and walked toward the men.

"Can I help you?"

"Yes, sir, are you Mr. Sanders?"

"Yes, and you are..?"

"I'm Detective Greenberg and this is Detective Pagnelli."

Puzzled Neil replied, "I don't understand why you're here. My wife had a miscarriage that is all. I took her to the hospital…"

Shocked, the detectives at first are speechless. "No, no, this has nothing to do with that." Then slowly added, "I'm so sorry for your loss." There was another pause. "If you like, we can come back later."

Neil thought for a moment. He had the whole evening ahead of him and lots of time that would be unfilled. "No, that's okay. Please come in."

Once inside, he could see the appreciative gazes as they looked at the room and something made him say, "I'm an architect and my wife is an interior designer."

The detectives nodded, looking uncomfortable so Neil asked, "Can I get you something to drink?"

"Sure. I'll take a glass of water." Detective Greenberg said and Pagnelli added, "I will too."

"Well follow me. It's comfortable in the kitchen. We can sit at the table, and you can tell me what this is about."

Once they were all seated, Detective Greenberg took a sip of his water and then said, "First of all we need to tell you that we are working on a cold case that concerns the people who use to live in your house."

Neil nodded knowingly. "You're here to talk about the disappearance of William Bemish."

"Yes, we are." Detective Greenberg paused and took another sip of water. It dripped down his chin and Neil got up and came back with a napkin and the detective thanked him.

"So, how can I help you."

"Well, we've spoken to several of your friends, and they told us what they knew or heard about the matter, so we wanted to hear what you have to say."

Somehow Neil realized what they were leading toward but he had promised Barbara he would not set foot in the sunken garden, unless she was there with him, so he kept that in mind as he told them.

Detective Greenberg and Pagnelli were hearing all the same things they had heard before, but they let him finish. "Well, that's all we know." He paused and then said, "Oh, yes, there were a lot of items in the attic; furniture and such that we had to move and when we were cleaning it up, we ran across a diary that belonged to Georgia Bemish and some other papers. They were in bad shape, so we had them restored."

Detective Greenberg sat up straight in his chair. "Do you still have them?"

"Yes, we do. Most weren't that interesting, but there was a letter written by Georgia that was remarkably interesting."

"Can we see it?"

"Yes, give me a minute."

Neil went to retrieve the letter and while he was gone, the detectives took a look around. They peeked into the rooms admiringly and then went back to their seats to wait. Soon Neil returned with the papers with the letter on top of the pile.

"Like I said, we had them restored, but nothing changed at all. We keep the originals in the safe. We didn't know what else to do with them."

Neil went to get himself a drink of water and then returned to the table. He watched the detectives' faces as they leaned close together reading the letter.

Neil wasn't surprised when Detective Greenberg paused and asked, "What do you think she means by 'IT'?

"I'm not sure."

Detective Greenberg nodded and continued reading. He read the next part out loud.

"I admit, that, born into a wealthy family, I was a little standoffish about coming but I loved him so and William having foresight about things, assured me that the city was growing and how fun would it be to be a part of its growth."

That sounds familiar, Detective Greenberg said, raising his head to look at Neil.

"What," Neil asked.

"Oh, nothing…it's nothing."

The detectives read on. This time it was Pagnelli who read the lines out loud. "One person we met and would see often was John Carroll Leake whose farm was at 303 St. Paul Blvd. I mention this so that if it is still there, he has the most knowledge about the area and about us."

The detectives turned and nodded at each other.

"What about the Leakes," Neil asked seeing their reaction to the name.

"That name has come up often in our investigation." The detective said, not looking up as he spoke.

A few minutes later, Detective Greenberg said, "Ah, so J. Warner was part of the McKim Mead White building company, and they built this house."

"Yes, they did, or so the letter says."

Detective Greenberg nodded and continued reading.

Neil could tell they weren't asking for an explanation but were more or less talking to each other as Pagnelli responded, "Can you imagine living through the War and then right on top of it, the Spanish Flu. It was bad enough with the Coronavirus, but this must have felt like they were being punished for something."

Their heads went down, and they continued to read and then suddenly both heads rose at the same time. "You're telling me that the sunken garden was unplanned. It started after an earthquake created a sinkhole on the property?"

All eyes were on him now and Neil nodded. "That is what the letter says."

They read a little more. "And it was Georgia's idea to build a sunken garden." Neil could tell they were back in the zone and not looking for an answer as they continued reading.

As if she knew ahead of time what the reader would say, Georgia's next words had them smiling, "Yes, it was me who thought of it." Their smiles changed as they read on, this time Detective Pagnelli read the words out loud. "But William…William began to change, spending every moment with the contractor and taking over. So from that point on, what I had seen as my project, became William's baby as he hired an architect and they worked together, coming to the site and then creating the drawings of the final design. Not once did William ask my advice and so I washed my hands of the project."

At that point there was only the sound of their breathing as they read through the description contained in that letter. That is until they came to the gate. "So his mason contacted a metalworker to create the iron gate of 'spider web' design, to be located in the 'Moon Gate' at the northeast corner of the garden under the bridge. The metalworker's name was Worthington."

"So we don't know who built the garden, but we do know someone named 'Worthington' designed the gate. Did you ever see if you could find out more about this Worthington."

Neil shook his head. No, Barbara did some research on the garden, but she didn't get around to checking out that person.

Detective Greenberg wrote the name down and then continued reading through the descriptions of the other artifacts contained in the garden and at the end of the description Detective Greenberg said, "So, Georgia didn't like what he had created in that garden, but it doesn't say why. She added shrubbery and flowers..." He paused and then looked over at Neil, "And she wrote she knew there was something down there? What did she mean by that?"

"We don't know. We have tried to find time to do research, but so far we haven't the slightest idea what she meant."

"Well, is there anything else you can tell me?"

"No, I think that letter says it all. I'll make you a copy of it if you want."

Both of them nodded. When Neil left the room they looked at each other. "This is more involved than I thought. Something out there she said. I wonder..."

Reading his mind, Detective Pagnelli said, "No, the man is suffering. We can't ask him to take us into the garden. I say we leave now and come back later."

Detective Greenberg resignedly nodded.

Neil reentered the kitchen and handed each of them a copy of the letter. As he placed it in Greenberg's hand he said, "Promise me if you find out anything, you will share it with us?"

"I promise. And if you learn or find anything more, please share it with us."

"You have my word."

With that, Neil showed them to the door.

Chapter 57

Neil was grateful for the interruption as it allowed him to take his mind off of the ordeal of losing their baby. Now that they had left, he cleaned up and was ready to go to bed. He did his usual rituals of checking to make sure the doors and windows were locked, and they headed upstairs. He was halfway up the stairs when he paused, thinking. After all that talk about the garden he had an urge to go take a look at it.

He argued against himself. He had promised Barbara he wouldn't so he shouldn't and to add more to the fire he told himself it was night and very dark out so he wouldn't see much. Best he waits. He laughed as he made the rest of the way upstairs.

Several times as he prepared for bed, a little voice in his head told him to go see his garden, but he ignored it until finally he climbed into the bed. As his body relaxed, all the stress of the day eased, and he fell into a deep sleep.

Something woke him. His eyes flew open with such a start that he had to act quickly to stop himself from falling out of the bed. Wide awake now, he shook the cobwebs from his brain and looked around the room. There was nothing.

Like a child, he peered over the side of the bed, his mind racing, trying to remember if he had indeed locked up before turning in for the night.

He was close to a full-blown panic attack, and when he finally figured it out he started laughing.

He laughed so hard he thought he would pee himself as he jumped out of the bed and turned off the alarm on his phone before heading into the bathroom and directly into the water closet.

At the time he thought it would be hilarious when he downloaded those stupid alarms. He remembered thinking, as he went upstairs last night, that Barbara and he were getting used to the clock radio alarm and he at least was ready for a change, so he purchased the Zedge alarm package. He had set his cell to play the one called, 'Wakeup'…scarry sucker, very scary.

Neil came out of the water closet and went to the sink to wash his hands, then splashed water on his face. As he raised his head he looked at the clock in the bathroom above the sink. It was already eight a.m. He had to get a move on. Today he was going to bring Barbara home.

Blocking everything out of his head except that one thought, he climbed into the shower. He tried, really tried, but first the tears silently fell down his cheeks and then he was sobbing uncontrollably. He couldn't stop and didn't want to as he allowed himself to let the hurt flow from his body.

He scrubbed hard with the washcloth, and it felt good until he got soap in his eyes, making him cry all the louder. Slowly he was back in control and turned off the water. It was then he heard something. He paused, his heart pounding loudly, realizing how defenseless he was, standing there naked in the shower.

Minutes passed before finally he managed to step out of the shower. "Stop it. Not this morning," he said out loud. "No, not this morning at all."

He concentrated on plastering a smile on his face. It

was hard, but he had to do it for Barbara. He told himself, everything would be fine again, once they were both home.

He was still practicing when he stepped out of the shower and dried himself. But as he brought the towel down after wiping his face, his smile was gone. Sure he was finally bringing his wife home from the hospital, but in the back of his mind he couldn't help thinking they should also be bringing home a baby.

He tried desperately to push that thought out of his head as water dripped down his cheeks, only it wasn't water from his shower...it was water from his eyes. He stood there letting his feelings take over again and when he felt ready, went into the bedroom and got dressed.

It hit him again as he began pulling items out of his dresser drawers and closet until he finally had everything he needed lying on the bed. Then he stood staring down as if not knowing how to proceed. He turned to look at the clock by the bed and lifting his shoulders he shook his head as if he had a chill.

That seemed to do the trick. He finished dressing and then went about gathering a change of clothes for Barbara. Neil got down her overnight bag and went into the bathroom to get her personal hygiene items, then he carried the bag into the bedroom and again opening drawers took out her underclothes and grabbed her loose-fitting sweatsuit out of the closet. He was in the midst of putting the sweatsuit into the suitcase when a thought came to him.

They had been out at Charlotte walking on the boardwalk and Barbara had said to him, "See that woman over there in the baggy top and sweatpants, she's dressed like that because she is either depressed or sad; or maybe both. Neil had looked at the woman's face and she did seem out of sorts. Then Barbara had pointed at another woman and said, "Now there goes a woman who's happy with her life."

That woman was wearing a pretty flowery dress with earrings to match."

Neil couldn't help but smile as he put the sweatsuit back on the hanger and got out her pink Dijon Deauville mini dress and then found on the floor of her closet, her favorite gold Emilia pleated knot mules. That done, he headed downstairs. He was hungry, but he was running late so he decided to stop at Ridge Donuts on the way to the hospital.

Neil climbed into his car and focused as he turned on the engine and then checked the camera view of the area behind him. Seeing nothing, he began backing out of their driveway heading east on Winona Blvd toward St Paul Blvd where he turned right onto Cooper Rd. He drove trying to fill his mind with the scenery around him so he wouldn't think about his mission.

When he reached Titus Avenue he turned left and soon was on Portland Ave. Just before the hospital, on his left was the Ridge Donut Café and making a quick decision, he moved into the left lane and turned into the Donut shop.

It was busy this time of the morning. He figured that most of the hospital staff stopped in before going the short distance up the road to Rochester General, but as usual, the staff knew how to handle a line of customers quickly and efficiently. Soon he was on his way again, pulling out on to Portland, which took a bit of effort since there was no light and traffic was picking up, but he made it and soon was pulling into the parking ramp of the hospital. Minus his stopover, the trip was less than 10 minutes and with his donut stop it took 15 minutes in total.

He found a spot to park in the ramp garage. Neil eased the car in and the minute he shut off the engine, reality hit him like a ton of bricks. He could do nothing but sit there behind the wheel and allow his emotions to simmer. When he felt himself coming back, he took several deep breaths and finally climbed out of his car and went into the hospital.

Once out of the car, his attention turned toward finding his way through the maze of signs to certain colored elevators, making sure he took the right one to Barbara's floor. When he found it, he stood alone, waiting until finally the doors opened, and he climbed in.

Still alone in the elevator, he started practicing smiling again. He touched his face to feel it as he stared at his reflection in the metal of the walls of the elevator. When the elevator stopped and the doors opened, there stood several people waiting. He smiled and stepped out.

Neil walked down the hallway still smiling until finally he was in Barbara's room. The smile dropped as he stood outside her door. He began taking deep breaths and when he was ready, he entered.

Once inside, he lifted his head and saw her face and he wanted to cry. She hadn't been able to prepare for his entrance, that was obvious. She sat in the bed with her food tray and the only thing that touched it was the tears falling from her eyes.

His heart hurt, but he had to be strong for her, so he swallowed and said, "Good morning sunshine."

Barbara raised her head, first slowly and then once she was back in control, lifted it the rest of the way and gave him a weak smile. "Good morning my darling husband. What took you so long?"

Neil walked over to her and planted a kiss on the top of her head. "Well, I did as you asked. I got a good night's sleep."

Barbara smiled. "Good. Good for you." He could hear it in her voice, the fog of sadness lifting, and it made him feel virtuous.

"So, what did you bring me?" Barbara asked.

"What, this?" He held out the overnight bag.

"No, silly. What's in the bag in your other hand."

"Ah, it's a Ridge Donut and coffee...both are sharable size. Would you like half of my donut and some of my coffee, milady."

Barbara nodded. Neil took out the oversized donut and using the knife on her tray, he cut it in half and then, went to get a Styrofoam cup off the small nightstand in her room and poured coffee in it. She liked her coffee with a little cream, but he liked his coffee black.

They sipped their coffee in between bites of the donut. Neither one spoke until they finished. Barbara stretched her arms up over her head and turned toward Neil. "Okay, let's get this show on the road," she said, and Neil stood, bowed and helped her get out of the bed.

Neil was patting himself on the back for how well he was handling the moment when Barbara went over to the overnight bag and opened it. The expression on her face made him feel so proud he thought he would burst.

"Wow, I didn't expect you to bring this for a change of clothes. Thank you honey."

He could tell the clothes did exactly what she had told him that day. It brightened her spirits. He watched as she took her underclothes and personal hygiene items with her into the bathroom. In the meantime he pulled up the covers on the bed and smoothed them, then laid her dress on the top and placed the shoes on the floor there. Then, he moved to the chair in the room and turned on the television. The news was on, and he settled back to catch up with the world.

He was still watching the news when the doctor walked in. He looked around and his eyes fell on Neil, "What did you do with my patient," he said kiddingly.

"Oh, good morning doc. She's getting dressed."

"Should I come back, or..."

"No, sit, please. Tell me how you think she's doing."

The doctor sat. "I think she is doing great. The

therapist reports the same. Barbara is coping with the fact she lost the baby and not letting it cause her unnecessary pain or anguish. Don't get me wrong, she misses her baby, but she has learned how to accept the lost and that's what she needs to do."

The doctor paused. "And you, how are you doing?"

"I think the same as Barbara. We know we can have more babies, but there will still be that place in our hearts missing our first child."

"Good. She needs you to be on the same page with her." The bathroom door opened, and Barbara stood in her underwear. "Ah, so we have company. Good morning doctor."

"Good morning Barbara. You look like you're feeling well."

"I am. Nothing hurts," she said as she walked over to pick up her dress.

"Ah, wait a moment before you put that beautiful dress on. I need to examine you before you leave."

"Of course you do," Barbara said as she climbed up on the bed and Neil turned his attention to the television again, listening though to what the doctor was saying as he examined her.

"You are doing fine. I think you are well enough to go home, and I have no cautions to add to that. As I told you we were able to induce labor, and everything is in tack so you can have more babies."

"Yes. I know."

"You need to follow up with your OB-GYN. She has a copy of your file. Do you have any questions for me?"

"No, doctor."

"Well you are doing fine. I think I will sign your walking papers.

Neil turned in time to see his wife smiling as she

said, "Told you." And she got up and went over to pick up her dress. The doctor turned to Neil. "I think you can take her home. I'll go get things moving."

While they chatted, Barbara slipped her dress over her head. She smoothed it in place and then slipped her feet into her shoes.

"That is indeed a stunning dress."

"Yes, it is, and it makes me feel happy."

"I can see why." The doctor paused and said, "Do either of you have any further questions?"

Barbara knew what he meant and looked at Neil, then at the doctor. "No, I think we have accepted what happened." She paused and again looked at Neil, who nodded his head. "We're going to go on from here. Thank you for your help and all the tools you have given us to overcome the loss of our child. We appreciate it."

"You are welcome. Now, I'll say goodbye, good luck and if you need to, don't hesitate to call."

The doctor left the room. Barbara turned to her husband and said, "Shall we?"

Neil jumped up out of the chair and said, "You don't have to ask me twice."

They packed up her few belongings and when an attendant arrived with the wheelchair, Barbara looked at it and started, "I.."

"Hospital policy. Everyone gets a ride out."

Obediently Barbara smiled and climbed in. Neil carried her things and turning, said, "I'll go to the desk and finalize the discharge and meet you there." He leaned down and kissed his wife and then started the long, crazy journey down halls and elevators until he was at the discharge patient area. When he finished taking care of that business, Barbara and her escort arrived and giving the level color and number, he led them to his car. He unlocked the doors and the nurse helped Barbara into the passenger's seat, while he put her bag in the trunk. They said their goodbyes and Neil slowly began the trip back home.

Barbara was silent, taking it all in. It was cold out, but a bright day, with the sun shining through the car windows warming them.

"So, do you need anything before we go home."

"Not that I can think of right now. I just want to go home." There was silence, then, "So, does anyone know?" Barbara asked.

"No. There were several calls on the service, but I didn't return them. I figure we don't need to rush it."

"Yes, we didn't rush the announcement and certainly we don't need to rush this news either."

They continued in silence until pulling up in their driveway. That's when Barbara let out a sigh.

As soon as he parked and turned off the car he turned to Barbara. "Are you sure you're all right?"

She nodded. "Sure. I am." She patted his hand. "This happens and we just need to put it away in our minds…don't forget…but go on from here."

Neil nodded. "I love you Barbara."

"I love you too."

Chapter 58

One thing that is certain is that if you deal with the public your life becomes an open book and so it turned out to be for the Sanders. They had no sooner come home than the phone rang off the hook and it kept on ringing with friends calling to ask if they were okay and if there was anything they could do for them. Being close to their friends and knowing they didn't have family to turn to they tried their best to explain that they were doing just fine and would be in touch.

At first Barbara had planned to talk to their friends separately and not be bombarded all at once, but she knew that wouldn't do.

At dinner that evening she brought it up. "Neil, what are we going to do about our friends."

Neil was thoughtful. "I'm not sure, but I know that we can't pick and choose who to tell, when. It's not like they don't know each other. If we tell one, we have to tell all, just…maybe like we did with the news…"

Barbara tried not to get all weepy and sad as she thought about it. "Okay, we have to tell them all at the same time." Pausing she leans forward on her elbows. "We'll have a dinner and invite all of them."

"Barbara, are you up to it?"

"I don't know, but I can't think of anything else."

Neil thought a moment and then said. "Okay, you can

get the same caterer for the food, but let's not get into all the décor stuff. Keep it simple and light."

"I agree. I'll call Selena Johnson and we'll work out the menu."

That decided, they now had something to say in response to someone calling to find out how they were doing. A dinner get together, she refused to call it a party, would give them the impression they were doing better and at the same time they could work up something to say one time to all of them.

So, Barbara spent her time planning the dinner and resting. She checked in at the office and Jennifer told her things were running smoothly so she was not to worry. So Barbara relaxed and found a good book to occupy her time.

That proved to be good medicine as she read and removed herself from her life into the pages of the book. She picked a good one entitled 'Body of Evidence' and soon was lost in the pages.

Barbara encouraged Neil to go to work and he did, but only when it was necessary since he had most of his jobs under control.

Along with working on the dinner, Barbara, who had been journalizing since finding the diary, now seemed to be at it all the time. That, reading her book and studying Georgia's diary; especially studying the diary, was becoming a job in itself.

There was something there in those pages that she couldn't read all of because of the water damage, but soon she was able to make sense of what was being said. Before when she first started going through it when she stumbled on some nonsense she would remind herself that this was a woman who spent her last days in a mental health facility so who knows if the rambling actually meant anything, anything at all. But now as she became familiar with

Georgia's style of writing and what she was mainly writing about, she knew this was not the ranting of the mentally ill. This was a frightened woman telling the truth of what she knew, felt and saw.

As the ground was still frozen, since returning home, nothing was said or done about the garden and that was fine with Barbara. It meant she had more time to decide what she should do.

When the day of the dinner arrived, she felt ready to face her friends. She had done a lot of preparation of her soul since she had been released and at some point, talked again with the therapist so she felt comfortable with sharing her feelings about losing her baby.

She needn't have worried. These were friends and friends always considered just how much to ask or say. She appreciated the hugs and smiles and then the compliments on the meal. She felt completely comfortable and loved and when the evening ended, she was glad they had done it this way. It didn't matter that she felt they knew what had happened, what mattered was they had the right reaction.

Barbara had braced herself for someone saying things like '*everything happens for a reason*', or the catch all '*not to worrying they could get pregnant again*'. No, she didn't hear that from the mouth of her friends, and she didn't' hear anyone say that there probably was something wrong with the baby. That would have been the most hurtful thing to say.

Barbara knew that it was because they were so close to these people, they would be as devastated by the news as they were, so even if they had said the wrong thing, she was ready to truly forgive them. But she heard instead sympathetic words one of which was they knew their baby was so loved and couldn't imagine the pain they were now feeling. There were offers to help and letting them know they would be thinking of both of them in the days and weeks ahead and checking in to see if there was anything helpful they could do.

Maybe it was the fact that she was able to drink and that mellowed her out and took the sting off the reason for the dinner. In any case after their friends had left and the caterer had finished up, Barbara and Neil sat in the kitchen drinking a cup of tea. "So," Neil said. "What do you think?"

"I think we should win an academy award, is what I think." She smiled. "People will write about us as the couple who survived a miscarriage and were able to announce their loss at a dinner put on for all their friends. That has got to be a first."

Neil started to laugh but turned to see the expression on his wife's face. She looked distraught, far from the way she had demonstrated that evening and her words now had betrayed her. "Barbara. Are you all right."

She took a moment, plastered a smile on her face and then turned to her husband. "Yes, I'm fine."

Neil started to ask more, but the therapist had explained that their sorrow would rear its head, off and on, throughout the coming days and they were not to question it, but let it run its course.

That along with the reality that she must be tired, Neil gently said, "You must be exhausted. I know I am." He tried to smile. "A good night's sleep would do us both good." He reached over and took her hand and kissed the palm. When he looked up he felt better, more confident. "Okay, my dear, you wash the teacups and I'll go about turning out the lights and checking the doors and windows. We'll meet in the bedroom."

Standing up, Barbara rubbed Neil's arm and said, "That sounds like a plan." She then carried the cups over to the sink.

It was hard, but Neil told himself he would not have another pity party. He had a right to, but now he needed to push it down as far as he could until his moment alone arrived. By the time he had checked everything, he was in control and headed upstairs.

When he entered the bedroom, Barbara was nowhere to be seen. He went into the bathroom and saw the light on in the watershed and returned to the bedroom.

When Barbara came out of the bathroom she started to pass by Neil, but he touched her arm and she paused. He pulled her to him and gave her a kiss. She kissed him back and went over to climb in the bed. It was that moment when Barbara knew they had found a way to grieve without falling apart.

Once her head hit the pillow, she realized just how tired she was, but she managed to read a little more of the diary before finally allowing sleep to overtake her. It was the last thing she should have done.

She dreamt that night of the sunken garden and pages of the diary flashed across in front of her, the words clear and legible. Page by page uncovered secrets and her heart beat faster and faster as she read and saw the verbiage on the other statues in the garden.

At first she hadn't been interested in figuring them out, but now, it was being explained to her and she felt the horror tear through her body. Barbara's heart pumps blood through her veins, faster and faster in hot anticipation of something she couldn't imagine.

Barbara desperately tried to take control of her mind, but in those pages, all the devastation of that garden began to come to life as the remaining three statues were reveal to her as being people, real people who had entered through that weblike gate and tried to return. There had been three unknown statues, but no longer. She now knew they were the original contractor, J. Foster Warner, William Bemish and Asa McBride.

Barbara woke suddenly to find tears wetting her cheeks. She pushed back until she felt the headboard behind her and then taking deep breaths, tried to calm her heart.

It didn't make sense. It was just a dream she told herself. That's all it was. But something nagged at her mind. What if it wasn't? What if what happened to William happened to Neil? Barbara slipped out of the bed and went into the bathroom, the diary in tow. She sat there trying to read it and just like in the dream she was able to read most of it; enough to realize it said what she dreamt it said. Men who went through that gate would come out alive and then turned to stone to stand forever in the garden.

Because she had been afraid to enter the garden, Georgia hadn't noticed the additional statues there. But after William was gone, she had. She tried to ignore them, telling herself that William must have added them, but then she knew how heavy those statues were and she would have noticed a crane and the activity of them being placed.

So, one morning she entered the garden and stood before each of them. She stared at them and recognized the face of J. Foster Warner the contractor, whom she had seen day after day working in the garden and she and William had first met after being told he had built the Glen House. Then she went to another and knew, without a doubt, that face. It was the face of their friend, Asa McBride. Finally she went to the last statue and stood in front of it for a long time. Tears began rolling down her cheeks and she moved closer and hugged it. It was William.

Barbara had managed to find newspapers that had covered the story. It was said that Georgia was found crying uncontrollably at the foot of one of the statues in the sunken garden. A neighbor had come by and being unable to find her, had gone into the garden and found her there. She had rushed inside and called for an ambulance and Georgia had been taken away. She never came back home. Later the papers had covered the trial of the missing Mr. Bemish and that Georgia was the prime suspect. Only Georgia wasn't put in jail. After giving her testimony through bouts of hysterical tears, it was decided that she was not sane. Later doctors agreed and she was put in the mentally ill asylum.

In her research, Barbara had looked up where Georgia had been taken and found it was a place called the Terrence Building, It was the former psychiatric hospital in the Azalea neighborhood of Rochester. That building had long since closed, before Neil and she had come to live in Rochester, so the chances of finding any records there were slim.

Now that she was sure there was no more to learn from the diary she decided to put it in the safe. Barbara carefully got out of bed. Neil turned over and she stood quietly for a moment before opening her nightstand where she kept her copy of the key. Pushing the clothes aside, she went to the back of the closet and opened the safe, carefully placing the diary inside.

The more she studied the diary and the old structure of the garden, the more she began to realize certain things about it. First, the other statues…they were of all mythical creatures. The Griffin which was known to tear a man apart. The ancient sundial, whose design dated back to the fourth century A.D., and the Poseidon installed in the center of the cement pond. This statue reflects the unpredictable and often dangerous nature of the sea. These were imposing statues without any logical connections.

Barbara felt a power come over her. It was time to put on her big girl panties and study the other statues in the garden. Really look at them instead of hanging back.

She was coming out of the closet when she was startled by Neil, standing there with a worried expression on his handsome face. She could tell he wasn't totally awake, so she waited for him to say something.

"What's up?" he said rubbing the sleep from his eyes.

"Oh, nothing. I'm sorry. Did I wake you?"

"Sort of, I heard all those hangers moving about in the closet and wondered what was happening. Thought it was a ghost and was going to check it out."

She saw the beginnings of a smile on his face and knew he was kidding. "Very funny."

"So what were you doing in there."

"Oh, I just put the diary back in the safe. I didn't want something to happen to it."

"Oh," Neil said, "Are you done reading it?"

"As done as I can be. So much of it is ruined that you can't get anywhere with one thought after the other. I'm giving up."

"Glad to hear it."

Barbara paused staring at him, "What does that mean?"

"Nothing. I just thought it was making you act weird, so it's good you aren't filling your head with that nonsense."

Neil started walking away. "Wait a minute. What nonsense."

"What? Barbara I didn't mean anything by it, just that since you started reading it you had an obsession with the garden being evil. It's not evil...it's just a garden."

Barbara nodded her head, giving up. At that moment she knew that there was no way he would believe her. She was having a challenging time believing it herself. But now she knew she had to say something to him, only she knew it would be useless,

She stood there feeling powerless until it dawned on her she knew someone who would understand.

Chapter 59

Barbara had enough of babying herself and returned to work full time. When she told Neil she was ready, he didn't argue.

As she sat at work the next morning, she recalled that conversation shortly after she had first met Andrea and Robin McBride. It had taken place when they were asked to help build an addition to their winery.

Barbara leaned back in her chair recalling that the women had told her they didn't know the other one even existed until later in life when their shared father, Asa McBride introduced them.

Barbara smiled thinking Asa was a smart man. He didn't *'play' close to home'*…not at all. He had a daughter in New Zealand and one in Los Angeles and he lived in Rochester. Robin and Andrea were lucky though that he had decided to have them meet. They had the heart of sisters and because they did, they built their empire together.

A sadness came over Barbara. How she would like to have a sister she could talk to now. That desire had grown inside her after that last nightmare about the garden and it led her to the connection that made sense to her now as she took out her cell and made a call to Andrea.

"Hi Barbara."

"Hi Andrea. It used to be we had to announce each

other, but not nowadays. No, today our name pops up and before you answer, you know who's calling."

Andrea was smiling on the other end of the call. "Okay, I'll shock you one more time by saying, 'yes', we can get together. No problem."

Barbara laughed. "How did you know I was going to ask that."

"I can also tell you it's not about business. This is a personal request."

Barbara nodded then knowing Andrea couldn't see her said, "Yes." She took a deep breath then added, "So when can we meet and where?"

"Lunch today at the winery? We just hired a great chef and I'd love to hear what you think of the menu and how it tastes."

"I'm no expert on food, but yes, I'll be there today at noon."

Barbara disconnected the call and sat smiling, recalling her other conversation when Andrea had called to ask her to come to the winery as she needed to talk to her. At first Barbara thought there was something wrong with the design of the winery because she hadn't asked Neil to come. But it had been a conversation meant for her ears only. Now she had the information meant for Andrea's ears and she hoped, desperately hoped, she was doing the right thing.

While Barbara sat in her office making her plans for lunch, Neil was having his own flashback. He had practically forgotten that day when he was with a customer and a man had come to him and said, "Hi Neil. Long time no see."

He remembered turning and seeing a man he couldn't place as knowing until the intruder told him he worked with Warren Pendergast, the man who had been the realtor who sold them the house at Parcel 076.06 Winona. That had been a while back and he had only met the man once; maybe

424

twice. But that wasn't what was bothering him now.

It's funny how something can just pop into your head and have you thinking about it. Now he recalled how he had tried to reach Warren. He had called the man's office and had been told they didn't have a Warren Pendergast working there.

At the time he figured that maybe Warren had been representing the owners of the property, so he had asked around at other realtors. No one seemed to know him.

Now that he thought about it, the man who didn't think it necessary to give his name, had been a bit sarcastic with him and when he asked for his name he had said his name didn't matter. He followed that by telling him that he shouldn't have bought the house and that no one should buy their house.

Now Neil tried hard to remember that conversation. He recalled asking the man what he meant by that, and he'd said because he, Neil, was now in danger. And when he asked how, the man had said that he should just heed his words and stop digging and fill it all back in and then get out of the house.

As astonishing as all of that had been, he also had watched the man leave and then tried to catch him, but he just disappeared.

At that moment, he sat there thinking about that day. He hadn't told Barbara because it had slipped his mind. Until now. "Why now," he asked himself. He hadn't been thinking about the house or the garden. So why did that conversation pop into his head?

When Barbara arrived at the McBrides, they were both waiting for her in front of the wine tasting building.

"Barbara, it's good to see you. We thought it best to go into our house and not talk here. The chef has already prepared lunch for us and is probably putting it on the table as we speak. He's just that efficient."

Barbara followed them into their residence and as Andrea had said, the meal was on the table. They sat down and ate, holding off what was hanging in the air until they finished. Once the coffee was poured and the pot left for their use, Barbara turned to the chef. "That was wonderful. I thoroughly enjoyed it."

The chef nodded and gave her a smile, watching as his two helpers cleared the table. The women waited until they were alone before they began their conversation.

"Okay Barbara, you have the floor."

Barbara swallowed and attempted a smile. "What I am about to tell you may sound like the ravings of a lunatic; that's what I thought at first, but now I'm not so sure."

"Listen, Barbara, we're the ones who told you that there was a presence attached to you and you believed us and didn't think us crazy."

"Well, yes, that's true. But that's because I thought it might be this woman Mindy Worthington. At first I thought she was real, but I know she isn't."

Andrea nodded her head. "It could be her, but I only know it is something. We didn't want to tell you because we thought it would upset you."

Barbara nodded. "I remember, but most of what I want to tell you is part of a dream and I have no proof."

"Did we have proof when I told you I dreamt that this presence was trying to warn you about something in the sunken garden. I thought it was a dream, but it seemed real. Now I think that in my dream it was Georgia Bemish who told me you had to stay away from the garden, and she said something about going crazy if you let it take him."

Barbara laughed. You're right, you're right. If one of

us is crazy, we all are." She took a deep breath and said, "Okay, here goes. But first I must tell you two things. I have been journalizing and I keep the journal under the linens in the master suite bathroom. And, the diary, the one we found that belonged to Georgia, I keep that locked in the safe. The key to that safe is in our side tables in the bedroom. We each have one. I took mine off the key ring and put it there. Someone needs to know this, and I want it to be you two."

Barbara could see their interest grow and she didn't make them wait any longer. She began by telling them she had been trying to figure out the blurred words in the diary and felt she knew, or figured out some of what it said, but she assured them that she understood she was reading the diary of a woman who was mentally ill, and it might be just that she was rambling on.

She looked at Robin and Andrea. It was the faces of two who wanted to hear what she had to say and would listen with open minds. So she began by saying, "I had a dream." She picked up her water glass and took a long drink as she nodded her head.

"It was about the sunken garden only this time pages of the diary flashed across in front of me, the words clear and legible. And it explained the statues in the garden; precisely explained that three of those statues were real people that had entered through that weblike gate and returned, transformed to stone."

Seeing Andrea start to interrupt, Barbara pleaded, "Please, let me finish. I have to say this." She took a deep breath and said, "There had been three...the contractor J. Foster Warner, William Bemish and your father, Asa McBride."

She saw tears whelming up in the women's eyes as they tried to take in all that Barbara had shared. Barbara sat quietly, giving them time to adjust. It was Andrea who broke the silence.

"I think we knew this." She turned to look at her sister who was nodding her head. "We had a feeling that the garden had something to do with Asa and so we believe you."

"Thank you. I had to tell someone, and I knew you wouldn't think I was crazy. But I also think we need to do something. What if what happened to William is going to happen to Neil if I don't do something?"

"After that dream I went back to the diary, and I could read it and it was just like in my dream. Men who went through that gate would come out alive and then turned to stone to stand forever in the garden. Because she had been afraid to enter the garden, Georgia hadn't noticed the additional statues there. But after William was gone, she did."

"Did she think he had added them?" Andrea asked, doubting it was true.

"Yes, at first, but she knew how heavy those statues were and she would have noticed a crane and the activity of them being placed. So, she had entered the garden and stood before each of them. She stared at them and recognized the face of J. Foster Warner the contractor, Asa McBride and William."

"I can't believe it, no, I can believe it. But I don't want to."

"I don't either," Barbara said, coming around the table and motioning to the women to stand. They stood, consoling each other, then Andrea broke the hold and went to get a bottle of wine. She brought it to the table. Robin went and returned with the wine glasses.

They sat quietly drinking wine. "So, I want to tell you Barbara that I still feel that presence is with you and because of what you've told us this afternoon, I think she,

Mindy Worthington, that is, wanted you to tell us. She brought you to us, so we knew our father was there in that garden. Now, we need to figure out what to do because Georgia went through hell after William disappeared. We don't want that to happen to you."

Barbara nodded thoughtfully, adding. "What's worse is there have been several people missing since we started uncovering the garden and I have a feeling we will find more than just three.

Chapter 60

The McBride sisters had helped her come to the conclusion that she was dealing with an inhumane creature. As outrageous as it seemed, it fit all the craziness they had uncovered. So, from there they had gone through all kinds of monsters until finally agreed that it fit more in the category of a Greek god.

Barbara had to assume that whatever was behind that gate and in those tunnels of her dream was not real in the sense of their reality.

Barbara, with the help of the McBrides, went over all their ideas and Barbara started putting what she knew, dreamt or heard together.

Soon she had a thought about where to start her research, and like herself, Andrea and Robin sat at their laptops, each doing their own search, writing down possibilities, and then, talked amongst themselves and came up with the likely choices. They were looking for a creature that drew mainly men, lived in the underground and turned their prey into stone. They were careful not to assume the logical choice until they had covered all of them. It had taken most of the afternoon, but when Barbara finally left, she had the three choices that were the most logical of the primordial Greek gods.

Barbara turned on her computer and started her

research on the Gorgons. She had forgotten that the gorgons were three sisters and once they read about them, it could be any one of the three. They weren't sure which one, so the three of them decided to study them further since Andrea thought only one of the three would have the power to turn into a visible female form and attach itself to a human body. This might mean they were dealing with more than one, possibly two, of these creatures.

That led to a lively discussion of whether it was a friendly spirit, or God who was meant to warn them. Since they didn't have time to figure it out they decided to start with it being one of the sisters warning them about the other. Now it was time to decide what she was dealing with.

Driving from The Vineyards Of The Irondequoit Wine Company on Irondequoit Bay, Barbara gave a contemptuous little laugh. This thing, whatever it was had already started driving her senseless and she had a feeling that was the plan. "Take the male species and turn the..." She started to say wife. Without checking behind her, she put on the brakes, bringing the car to a dangerous stop right in the middle of the lane.

She could hear the horns honking behind her as they managed to swerve into the next lane and pass her. Barbara didn't move and sat like a stalled car in the driving lane for some time before she snapped out of it and managed to start the car and commenced driving again. Soon she was back up to the speed of the traffic.

She took a deep breath and allowed herself to acknowledge the fact that it was all true. Tears filled her eyes and rolled down her cheeks. As she continued driving she had to admit she had done a terrible thing. Only it was too late. She couldn't take it back.

To share her misery she had put Andrea and Robin in danger because she was sure the reason not a living soul knew where the missing men had gone was because it left no one with knowledge of its existent sane or alive. "Am I right Mindy?" She said in the quiet of the car.

Barbara remembered what Andrea had said and it helped a little. "If God brings you to it, He will bring you through it." She had explained that in other words, God doesn't allow us to face suffering and hardship unless He has a plan for us to walk through it and conquer."

She hoped it was true because she now had not only herself and her husband, but her friends to save. At that moment she swore not to tell anyone else. This was her battle and she had to face it without jeopardizing the life of others.

There wasn't much time. Winter was almost over and soon the warmth of spring would thaw the garden so that work could continue so it was imperative that she come up with a plan.

Barbara entered the office and said, "Hi Jennifer, any messages."

"A few." Jennifer looked down and then handed Barbara several message sheets.

"Thank you."

"Are you all right Barbara?"

"I'm fine. Why do you ask?"

"Um you look like you've seen a ghost or are in shock..."

Barbara paused, smiled and walked over to pat Jennifer's hand. "It's nothing. Just getting back into the swing of things."

That seemed to satisfy Jennifer and she smiled back at her.

Her mind in a fog, Barbara went to her office and taking off her coat, she sat down behind her desk, staring in the distance, then began in earnest to try and solve the mystery of what lived behind the iron gate.

Barbara leaned toward the screen and read. '*The Gorgons were three female monsters in Greek mythology who could kill people just by looking at them. The Greek poet Hesiod named them Stheno (the Mighty or Strong), Euryale (the Far Springer) and Medusa (the Queen). He described them as having snakes for hair, wings, claws, tusks, and scales.*'

Barbara pushed further back in her chair. When she saw the words, '*Greek Gorgons vs Roman Gorgons.*' She sighed. "Now what?"

Finally she clicked on the link and read, '*There are slight differences in how Ovid, a roman poet, depicts the Gorgons when compared to earlier Greek poets. Ovid's gorgons were beautiful women instead of being ugly monsters and only Medusa had hair made of snakes. A punishment given to her by Athena for lying with Poseidon*'.

A smile appeared on her face. She now knew the purpose of the statue of Poseidon; or at least she thought she did. Barbara laughed out loud and then covered her mouth, wondering if anyone had heard her. "That slut," she said and then made a decision. "Ovid, my man, you are the winner." That would explain Mindy Worthington if this was what they were dealing with. That made sense. Barbara was sure she was on the right track.

She read on. '*The daughter of Phorcys and Ceto, Stheno was born in the caverns beneath Mount Olympus. She and her sister Euryale were both immortal. Of the three*

Gorgons, she was known to be the most independent and ferocious, having killed more men than both of her sisters combined. In Roman mythology, she was transformed into a Gorgon for her relationship to her sister Medusa, who was raped by the sea god Neptune in Athena's temple Greek Gorgons vs Roman Gorgons'.

Barbara rested her head in her hands, "That would piss me off, too." She considered what she had read so far and said, "Okay Euryale, you must be Mindy". She started searching for information on Euryale and found that Stheno and Euryale were immortal. Perseus couldn't kill them. They also did not petrify everyone who looked at them, so they were not dangerous. They were also not ugly, and therefore not evil.

Barbara was now sure that in that cave it was Stheno. She came to that conclusion because according to all she read, Medusa was killed, but both of the other two were immortal and not able to be killed. So, Stheno being the most ferocious would be the one who had *statued*...Barbara wondered if that was a word or not, but it didn't matter at this point. Stheno was behind that gate and Euryale was trying to warn her; maybe even help her.

And just like that she knew. The sunken garden needed to be filled back in immediately. It was the only way. Stheno couldn't be fought and would live in those dark tunnels forever. As for Euryale, she would go to be with her sister.

Chapter 61

Conventional wisdom suggests that a couple that gets along with each other under any and all circumstances, has a happy marriage. Barbara sees her marriage to Neil to be as such. From the minute they met, they were inseparable. They have a sense of understanding about one another and the ability to overcome hardships together. Mix that with love and affection and you will have a perfect marriage. If she wants all of this to continue, she has to come up with a plan.

Having a plan and then initiating it was not going to be easy. They had spent most of their married life doing things together. They worked together, came home together, went out together. Their best conversations have always been between each other so how long could she hope to keep this secret from the man she loved.

She had to. How many times had he helped her through a scary situation by having her take a moment to open her eyes and mind so she could feel safe and calm. To know what she knew would destroy that ability in him. Of that she was sure.

This wasn't stress she was dealing with. It was a nightmare come to life and worst of all, it was something she couldn't share with him because if she did, he would go into that garden to prove to her nothing was going to happen. He was a reasonable man, and she could have him stare at those statues for hours and not see what she saw. No, this was a nightmare that she had to climb out of alone and to save his life she had to do it soon.

She began that evening working on a plan with Andrea and Robin a phone call away. Barbara knew that in some way she had helped them by letting them know their father hadn't left them but was a statue in their garden. But along with that relief came the horror of what had happened to him. They had also felt comradeship with Barbara since the moment they met her. It was like she was a member of their family too. They had found each other, so why not one more sister?

Barbara knew all of this, and she knew now that familial had to do with the sunken garden. She had to tell someone the full story, not to share the burden, but to help her realize she wasn't crazy...yet. Andrea and Robin were meant to be her sounding board.

She spent the next several days rereading the diary, looking for a message that might be hidden in the smudged words. Nothing came to her to change the idea that the only way to save her husband was to fill in the sunken garden.

She couldn't waste any more time. She had to get started. As it happened, it was Andrea who came up with the answer.

It had been an early morning for Barbara, and she finished her job before noon, giving her the rest of the day to work on her problem. Neil was still out at the jobsite, and she sat in her office mulling over possible scenarios and then the phone rang. It was Andrea.

"Barbara, I've been checking around about the uh, thing and I have a bunch of numbers for you, but first I need to get back to them with the size...do you know the size."

Barbara looked across the office, her mind working and then said into the phone. "I'll call you back. I think Neil has that on his blueprints." She disconnected the call without waiting for a response and headed to Neil's office. As she went down the hall she worked out what she'd say if she got caught and decided that she'd say she had a few minutes and wanted to layout her plantings for the sunken garden. When she entered his office, she went over to his landscape drawing files and to the drawer labeled, 'personal'. She opened it and began working her way through until she had the one that was of the sunken garden. Barbara went to Neil's desk and took a pad, wrote down the dimensions and then smoothed out the drawing and placed it back in the drawer. She made sure to close the drawer and took the sheet off the pad, putting it back on his desk, along with the pencil.

Neil had a way of placing his things, so they were convenient for him and knowing that she was careful to put everything back exactly as she found it.

Barbara went down the hall and back to her office. Once she was seated she called Andrea.

"Andrea, I've got what you wanted."

"Wait a sec." There was silence as Andrea went for a pencil and paper and then said into the phone. "I've got it. What is it."

"Four thousand square feet, which is approximately the size of 7 tennis courts."

"That's great." I'll get back to you.

Barbara tried to keep busy until Andrea called, but her mind wouldn't focus on work or anything else except that sunken garden. Finally her cell rang, and she picked it up.

"The answer to your question is five to seven weeks."

Barbara was silent trying to figure out what would take them away for that long a period when Neil was anxious to get started on that sunken garden as soon as the ground thawed. "A cruise!"

"What, Andrea said.

"We're going on a cruise."

"That would do it. Let me know the details and I'll handle the rest."

"How will I ever thank you Andrea?"

There was a pause and then Andrea said, "Take me in the garden and let me see my father for the last time."

"Andrea, do you think that's a good idea?"

"Yes, I don't think anything will happen to me. You can, if you don't mind, come with me. I promise it'll take just a second."

Barbara was quiet and finally said. "Okay, I'll do it. I'll let you know when." With that the call was disconnected.

Barbara was not happy with the idea, but she owed it to Andrea. She was sure that Robin would be with her, and she would go too, just for good measure. Barbara leaned back in her chair feeling better. They had a plan finalized and she was sure it would work. Their anniversary was coming up and they usually planned something special so she would suggest the cruise before work got too busy. Barbara smiled and was able to relax as she finished up for the day.

They had driven to work together that day as she would be working in the office while he went to the jobsite. Now as they were finally together he started sharing the details of his day. When he finished, she managed to say the right thing before asking, "Can we stop and pick up some

Chinese food for dinner."

"Sounds like a splendid idea to me. Let's do it."

There was a comfortable silence then "Barbara," Neil asked, "We haven't talked about having another baby. Is it too soon?"

Barbara wanted a baby too, but not as long as that garden was there. "Tell you what. Let's talk about it when we get home. We'll eat Chinese food, drink wine and talk about making a baby."

Neil smiled, then laughed and she joined in.

That night was full of surprises. At one point Barbara weakened and was about to tell him her plan, but she knew that as much as he loved her, he would not agree. He would probably say something that would have her giving in and then, what.

But it proved to be out of their hands. While they were finishing up their dinner, Barbara paused, looking around. Neil did the same. "Did you feel that?"

"I did," Barbara answered. "What was it."

Neil shook his head slowly, then got up and looked out the back window. It was dark outside, and he could see nothing. The same was true of the front windows. "Come on. Let's go out on the side porch."

They hurried across the kitchen and through the den until they reached the exit to the porch. Barbara stood back while Neil opened the door and they both stepped outside.

The stars were bright and along with the full moon, and the lights on the porch, they could see the yard that ended at the sunken garden. All was still and then suddenly it came again. "Back inside, Barbara. Let's go back inside. I think it's an earthquake."

Barbara didn't need to be told twice as she hurried

inside with Neil on her heels. They went through the kitchen and as they had planned long ago, down into the cellar. They stood there, holding each other and praying that it wouldn't be a big one and bury them alive.

She didn't know how long they had been down there, barely able to hear or even feel anything. Finally Neil said, "I think it's over. Let me go up and check first. You stay here."

Barbara grabbed his arm. No way would she stay in that cellar alone. Not after what she had experienced down there so she followed right behind him.

She was surprised to see there wasn't much damage. A few things had fallen off the wall but otherwise nothing more had happened. She turned around to say something to Neil, only to find he wasn't beside her. She called out for him, but there was no answer. She began hurrying through the house calling his name, but he still didn't answer. It dawned on her he wasn't anywhere in hearing distance of her voice.

Then she knew. She knew as adrenaline rushed through her veins and she tried desperately to breathe. She knew as she opened the door and made her way across the lawn to where the sunken garden should be.

Without turning she knew that Mindy Worthington was beside her before she whispered in her ear. "It wasn't just Georgia that loss her husband in that garden…I did too."

Barbara stopped, shocked as a reel of scenes flashed through her head. She saw Mindy and her husband arguing and she watched as he slapped her, and Mindy hurried away from him. She continued to watch and slowly it became clear to her that Mindy and their realtor Warren Pendergast, who no one could reach, was Mindy's lover.

Finally she was brough back to the present and she realized it was gone. The earth around the sunken garden had swallowed it up once more and she knew without a doubt it had waited, waited for Neil to come before the last of it collapsed over him.

She didn't have to explain his disappearance because there was no body. She didn't have to say a word because the news had been alerted of the earthquake happening and had flown a helicopter over the area in time to see it disappear under the dirt, brush and trees that had been around it. They had actual footage of the sunken garden vanishing and reported seeing a figure hurrying toward the garden and watching as the ground dropped from under him and he disappeared. Barbara had been too late, and the garden had taken Neil with it.

If it weren't for her friends and especially Andrea and Robin, she would have gone crazy and spent her life in an institution. But they rallied around her and helped her through it. When she felt especially down, she spoke to Andrea and her sister who knew the whole story and they helped her over the hump.

Eventually she put the house on the market and moved to an apartment that she had built on the second floor of their office building. She continued to run her end of the business while Neil's partner Jack Waters stayed on. He called on her when he wanted to hire another person to help out, so she still felt a part of both sides of the business.

Several months later Barbara was visited by Detective Pagnelli and Greenberg who wanted to talk to her about the Bemishes. She was polite as she listened to them tell her they were following up on a cold case and wanted to know what she could tell them. Of course she could tell them more than just about the cold case. She could tell them so much more, but they would never believe her.

Barbara survived, and whether they knew it or not, everyone else survived because of nature and because she would never tell the real story.

Chapter 62

Back at the precinct, Detective Greenberg and Detective Pagnelli sit reviewing the case file.

"So, what now, Greenberg. Do we go to the captain and tell him we have nothing, or do we wait and then go back and see Mrs. Sanders again."

Greenberg doesn't answer right away. "Well, Pagnelli what we have is a stalemate as far as I'm concerned. We had a cold case to start with and there was very little information, but a suspicion that there might have been foul play and it involved a sunken garden."

Pagnelli nodded.

"In the case file are all the interviews, handwritten and not that legible from when it all took place, back in 1918 and we have reviewed every piece of information. And the only actual details are that Mr. William Bemish disappeared and his wife, Georgia Bemish went crazy. So they could never interview them then and we can't now because they are dead. Just like all the witnesses are dead."

Again Pagnelli nodded.

"We talked to the offsprings, not the people who were there when it happened…when William Bemish disappeared and I stress, *disappeared*. We came up empty because what we really had to work on was rumors that led us to the sunken garden. We interviewed the new owner, Neil Sanders first and he told us what he knew which was nothing, but he gave us two leads, a document written by a hysterical woman that had been *restored*, and that being the active word. Who then told us that there was a diary and that it was in the possession of his wife."

"Only, as he said, it was unable to be restored so there are missing words and sentences that one has to use their imagination to fill in the blanks. But we decided to go back and get the diary and talk to Barbara Sanders, only, nature ran its course again and took away the evidence."

Detective Greenberg looked up with a sarcastic smile. "So, the earthquake covered up the sunken garden and any clues that existed there and since there is no record of the garden in any files, we don't know how or why it played a role in the case. Not only that, but we also have a woman and a man with no ties to the family in our case, except they bought the house and uncovered this sunken garden now, almost like before, the husband has disappeared, only this time we know for a fact it was during the collapse of the sunken garden."

Again Greenberg smiled. "So, Detective Pagnelli, what do you want to tell the captain."

Pagnelli pondered the matter, allowing his eyes to look down at the list they had created of cold cases to solve. He looked up and said, "That this one leads to a dead end that all interested parties are deceased and unable to offer any assistance beyond what we have uncovered."

Pagnelli frowned as he admitted. "We have run into a roadblock that can't be penetrated and we should move on?"

Greenberg nodded. "I agree wholeheartedly."

Greenberg was thinking more on his end, but like the case file, he wasn't going to share it. He now had what he wanted. Proof that Georgia was not responsible for the disappearance of her husband William and that there apparently wasn't any foul play involved in his disappearance. And that was all it was, Greenberg was certain, the man disappeared in that sunken garden and whatever was down there, was now under a good pile of dirt. Case closed.

ABOUT THE AUTHOR

Juanita Tischendorf (J. B. Tischendorf) was born in Philadelphia, spent her adolescence in New Jersey and graduated from Fulton High School in upstate New York. She lives with her husband in the suburb of Irondequoit in Rochester New York. Juanita completed a writing course at the University of Washington, has taken James Paterson training courses and she is a member of the Writers Guild of America.

Her achievements and awards include a career profile by Rochester's 'About Time Magazine', and a taped interview by the Syracuse NY cable TV "Successful Women in Upstate New York'' segment. She appeared on the WOKR-TV program entitled "Shades of Gray", received the 2003 Editor's choice award for outstanding achievement in poetry and is listed in the 1991 edition of "2000 Notable American Women".

Website: jitisch.com

If you enjoyed this book, you may want to check out other books written by this author.

A Secret
Recycled!
The Baby Girl Conspiracy
The Bitmores
The Coronavirus Effect Story
Three Little Girls (*Murder In Rochester, New York*)
Circle Of Seven
All The Missing Pieces (*Secrets, Lies, & Alibis*)
Love Will Find A Way
Playground In My Mind
Body Of Evidence
Don't Look Back
The Selfie - Adolescent/Teen Girl Self Development
Who Says I'm Small
An Unfair Advantage
The Madman The Marathoner
Irondequoit United Church Of Christ

www.ingramcontent.com/pod-product-compliance
Lightning Source LLC
Chambersburg PA
CBHW030911050726
47498CB00003BA/693